BARDO

Also by Krandall Kraus
available from Alyson

THE PRESIDENT'S SON

BARDO

KRANDALL KRAUS

alyson books
los angeles | new york

MANUFACTURED IN THE UNITED STATES OF AMERICA.
COVER DESIGN BY BRUCE ZINDA.

THIS TRADE PAPERBACK ORIGINAL IS PUBLISHED BY
ALYSON PUBLICATIONS,
P.O. BOX 4371, LOS ANGELES, CA 90078-4371.
DISTRIBUTION IN THE UNITED KINGDOM BY
TURNAROUND PUBLISHER SERVICES LTD.,
UNIT 3 OLYMPIA TRADING ESTATE, COBURG ROAD, WOOD GREEN,
LONDON N22 6TZ ENGLAND.

FIRST EDITION: OCTOBER 1999

99 00 01 02 03 ▉ 10 9 8 7 6 5 4 3 2 1

ISBN 1-55583-504-X

LIBRARY OF CONGRESS CATALOGING-IN-PUBLICATION DATA
    KRAUS, KRANDALL.
       BARDO / KRANDALL KRAUS.—1ST ED.
       ISBN 1-55583-504-X
       I. TITLE.
    PS3561.R2879B37 1999
    813'.54—DC21   99-40169 CIP

COVER PHOTOGRAPH BY GILES A. HANCOCK/PHOTONICA.

For Paul and me.
And for you if you have the courage
to step into the Shadow.

Acknowledgments

Deep thanks go to Ron Baumhover for showing me what to keep in, what to leave out, and what to rework;

to Marge Poscher, M.D., who kept me alive long enough to write this;

to Carol Yaggy and Mary Twomey for giving me the house at Anchor Bay where this was written;

to Deborah Schmall, for "the property" in Anchor Bay, where much of the inspiration occurred;

and to Kim Storch, psychological guru, who guided me through the uncovering of my dreams, where most of this material presented itself.

Christianity raised a fine Trinitarian structure but had to reckon with Satan or the devil as the neglected element. Civilization has raised high culture, but it now must reckon with its shadow or dark side as the neglected element. It is the addition of the neglected element that brings an individual or a culture to wholeness.

The Place of the Mothers is where consciousness and cultural and spiritual power originate. Going to the Place of the Mothers...and generating or regenerating yourself, is the act of creating consciousness...a psychologically incestuous act.

—ROBERT A. JOHNSON, *TRANSFORMATION*.
HARPER, SAN FRANCISCO, 1991

I find myself, I mate with myself, I generate myself, I gestate myself, I give birth to myself, I am myself.

—OLD ALCHEMICAL SAYING

Foreword

The *Tibetan Book of the Dead* tells us that *bardo* means the in between place. *Bar* means in between, and *do* means island or mark; most often it is thought of as the place between death and rebirth. However it isn't only the island between death and life but also all the little in between places, the bardos, of living; for in life, death happens all the time. One thing ends, another begins. It is the point in between that is the bardo. The most helpful example may be from Hindu meditation practice. Students of meditation are told to concentrate on their breath. Breathe in, breathe out. And while breathing, they are told to concentrate on the exact point where the in-breath stops and the out-breath begins—and again where the out-breath stops and the in-breath begins; they are told to concentrate on the place in between, which is neither the in-breath nor the out-breath but the point that is neither. That place in between, which is so brief it virtually transcends time and space, is a bardo.

There are six major bardo states in Tibetan Buddhism: the Bardo of Birth, the Bardo of Dreams, the Bardo of Samadhi-Meditation, the Bardo of the Moment Before Death, the Bardo of Dharmata, and the Bardo of Becoming.

At the end of one's life a person experiences three bardo states: the Bardo of the Moment Before Death, the Bardo of Dharmata, and the Bardo of Becoming.

Tibetan Buddhists say there is a kind of uncertainty regarding one's sanity or insanity—confusion or enlightenment—in the bardo state. There exist within the bardo, if one is prepared to enter it consciously, the potential for all sorts of visionary discoveries that occur on the way to sanity or insanity. There is definitely a quality of uncertainty, even paranoia in a bardo. It takes courage as well as one-pointed purpose of mind and heart to exist consciously in the bardo state. It takes all the strength one has.

July 2

EG lies in a white bed in a White Room moving through his life, moving closer to the open door.

The bed stands firm on the floor of the White Room, which is turning, turning around the sun.

The bed stands firm and still while EG moves slowly, motionlessly through the beginning of the end: a tiny white skiff in the immense blue Ocean of Time.

The tip of the bow of his fragile bark scrapes gently on the sandy beach of the tiny Isle of Space.

He lies motionless, moving, rocking like a babe in a cradle.

His eyes are crusted shut, his lips too. A young woman comes periodically to dip cotton swabs in water and gently roll them over his lips. She places a hand on his head, her lips on his cheek. She whispers to him softly, words we cannot hear.

The White Room moves imperceptibly around the sun.

And so EG moves on, and this is what he sees through his crusted eyes as he lies motionless in the firm white bed, which sits on the polished white linoleum floor in the empty White Room.

10:19:59:58:29 A.M.

O son of noble family, now what is called death has arrived. Do not think you are alone in leaving this world; it happens to everyone, so do not feel desire and yearning for this life. Even if you feel desire and yearning for this life, you cannot stay; you can only wander in samsara. Do not desire, do not yearn. O son of noble family, whatever terrifying projections appear to you in the Bardo of the Moment Before Death, do not forget these words but go forward remembering their meaning; the essential point is to remember them and recognize everything as projections of your own mind.

Enter now the Bardo of the Moment Before Death and say this prayer as you tread this dangerous path:

> *Now when the Bardo of the Moment Before Death dawns upon me,*
> *I will abandon all grasping, all yearning, and all attachment,*
> *I will enter undistracted into clear awareness,*
> *and eject my consciousness into the space of unborn mind;*
> *as I leave this complex body of flesh and blood*
> *I will know it to be a transitory illusion.*

10:19:59:58:30 A.M.

All morning EG has tried to comfort The Boy but to no avail. The Boy is convinced that everyone is going to leave him. Nothing EG says or does can assuage The Boy's feelings of anxiety, even terror. Finally EG calls The Boy's mother.

Annabel arrives begrudgingly. She isn't in such a great mood either. She wants to go shopping, and she doesn't want to take the time to come over here to solve a problem she considers to be EG's, not hers. "So what do you expect me to do?" she asks, standing in the living room, one hand on her hip, one holding a Pall Mall in the air. Two thin gold bracelets dangle from each wrist.

"Make him feel better," EG urges. "Tell him you're not going to leave him."

"But I am going to leave him. I'm going shopping."

"You know what I mean. Tell him you're coming back."

"Brother!" she says and goes to where The Boy is scrunched up on the sofa, hugging his knees. He is not crying, but he looks like he might at any moment. "Sweetie, Mommy's just going shopping with Aunt Cecilia. I won't be gone long. I'll be back tonight. Now be a good boy and stay with EG and Hari. Maybe you can all go to the beach later. Wouldn't that be fun?"

"Where are you going?" The Boy asks.

"I told you," she says patiently. "Auntie Ceecee and I are going shopping in The City. Mommy needs to get out for a while and have some fun."

"Can I go?" The Boy asks.

"No, honey," she says. "Today it's just me and Auntie Ceecee. We're just going to women's stores. You wouldn't have a good time. You stay here and go to the beach with EG and Hari. You'll have fun, you'll see."

"Where's Daddy?" The Boy asks.

"He's sleeping. You know Daddy has to go to work tonight, so be quiet and don't wake him up. He'll be up later, and you can talk to him then if you want. You can have dinner with him before he leaves for the winery." Annabel kisses The Boy and stands up, smoothing her beige silk skirt and raising her eyebrows at EG. "He'll be all right. Now I really have to go.

Cecilia's waiting for me in the car." She pats EG on the shoulder and glides out the door.

"Do you want to do something with me?" EG asks The Boy. "Want to go play in the garden or get in the hot tub? "

The Boy shakes his head.

"Well, I'm going to get in the hot tub. If you want to join me, you come on down there." EG goes into the laundry room and gets a bath towel, then walks down the path to the hot tub.

The Boy watches as EG disappears around the side of the house, then The Boy slowly, quietly makes his way toward his parents' bedroom. He carefully turns the door handle, opens the door, and slips into the darkened room. He can see his father's form beneath the sheets, his dark hair tousled, his shoulders round against the crisp white bed linens. The Boy silently removes all his clothes except his underpants and, moving like a slow-motion film so as not to make a sound, slides beneath the sheet next to his father. His eyes grow heavy and he drifts off to sleep.

Sometime later The Boy wakes with his arm around his father's neck.

Still later he wakes with his father's arm wrapped around him, hugging him close. His father's hairy chest tickles his back, and he can feel his father's warm breath on the back of his neck. He drifts back to sleep.

A while later he awakens upside down in the bed, his head beneath the covers near his father's waist. He is awakened by the warmth, the lack of oxygen, the musky smell of his father's skin. He sees briefly in the dark, before he turns around and resurfaces on the pillow, that his father is naked beneath the sheet.

He wakes one last time and looks at the Big Ben alarm clock that sits ticking loudly on the pine dresser across the room. It is six minutes to 5. His father will be getting up in less than an hour. He turns on his side and stares at his father's face. The sun is setting somewhere on the other side of the ochre window shade, and a soft, warm light seeps in at the window's edges, casting his father in a pink aura. In the tender light of approaching dusk, his tanned arms seem even darker. The room's edges shimmer and begin to fade. Somewhere outside a bird is singing a lament for the dying light.

His father is facing him, and he seems to be smiling in his sleep. His father's arms are marked by a sharp line where his work shirt sleeve begins and the sun cannot reach. His pale German shoulders sport wisps of soft hair at the collarbones. A pungent, warm smell rises from beneath the sheets, filling The Boy's nostrils. It is a dark, heavy scent that will re-create this moment for him again and again throughout his life when he smells it in the warm recesses of other men's bodies.

His father opens his eyes slowly, sees The Boy, and smiles. "Hi," he says. "When did you come in?"

"Before."

"Did you sleep too? Did you take a nap with me?" his father asks softly.

"Mommy went shopping with Auntie Ceecee. I came in here with you."

"That's nice," his father says, and reaches out, caressing The Boy's shoulder. He tousles The Boy's hair. "How's that cowlick doing?"

The Boy giggles and tries to smooth down the back of his hair. "A cow didn't lick me."

"Oh, yes, it did. I was holding you in my arms out at Aunt Lizzie's and a cow came walking alongside the vineyard fence and saw your pretty brown hair and thought it looked delicious and she took a lick. She thought it was a caramel-covered apple. Now it sticks straight up in the air."

The Boy giggles more and buries his head beneath the sheet. His nostrils fill with his father's scent. Halfway down the bed, The Boy can see his father's penis falling onto the mattress. He marvels at all the hair it lives in, like a bird's nest. He sticks his head out of the sheet just enough to peek at his father, who is still smiling.

"It's time for me to get up. Want to have dinner with me?"

The Boy nods.

"What shall we have?" his father asks.

"Mommy left you dinner in the oven."

"I know, but what would you like to have if you could have anything you want?"

"Watermelon," The Boy answers without having to consider.

"Do we have watermelon?"

"Uh-huh."

"Then watermelon it is," his father proclaims.

"I have to go pee," The Boy says.

"OK, go pee."

"Can we pee together?" The Boy asks. He likes to pee with his father. Together they make lots of bubbles in the toilet, especially his father, whose stream of urine is more forceful than The Boy's.

"Absolutely. I have to pee myself. Pee Patrol coming up. Let's go," his father says, throwing back the sheet and leaping to his feet. The Boy scrambles after him, noticing that his father's penis is now sticking straight out just like his own. They go into the bathroom, raise the toilet seat, and stand side by side, aiming toward the white bowl. The Boy turns toward his father, whose penis is twice the size of The Boy's hand and exactly level with The Boy's face. He looks up at his father, who shifts his sleepy eyes to The Boy and smiles. He knows what his son is about to ask. It is a ritual.

"Will mine look like that someday?"

"Yes, it will. Just like this."

"And will it have a nest like yours to live in?"

"Yep. Just like mine."

The Boy smiles with the satisfying knowledge that someday he will be just like his father. He wants to smell like him too, but he doesn't ask about that.

"Bombs over Tokyo," his father shouts and begins to urinate into the bowl. This makes the boy giggle, and he begins to pee too. Together they make a bowl full of bubbles.

The light is almost completely gone now, and the two of them stand in the faintest amber twilight, side by side, father and son, big dick and little dick, hairy and hairless, tall and short, big and little, actual and potential, what is and what will be.

The Boy turns toward his father, the man he loves more than any other being in the world so far. His father groans and stretches long and hard, reaching his hands toward the ceiling, standing on tiptoe. The Boy spies a single yellow droplet on the tip of his father's penis, and in an act of spontaneous, unadulterated worship, he leans forward and licks it off. It is salty and warm. He smiles up at his father who smiles back at him. "Are you being silly?" his father asks softly.

"I love you, Daddy," The Boy says. "I want to be just like you."

"Oh, no. You're going to be much, much better than I am." His father picks him up and twirls him 'round and 'round, making him giggle giddily. "Because you are the sweetest, smartest, kindest, cutest, handsomest, funniest, bestest, neatest boy in all the world." And the two of them—naked, laughing, twirling—spin themselves into the dusk of that one twilight, whirling faster and faster and faster, Father laughing deeply and softly, The Boy giggling in his high-pitched voice.

Like ecstatic dervishes enraptured with their love for one another, they spin and spin until all light fades and they are left dizzy and giddy and completely in love with one another, aware of no one else, aware of nothing else in the entire world. Not dinner, not the past, not the future. Not even the juicy watermelon, waiting in the kitchen, pink and ripe and sweet as their mutual devotion

10:19:59:58:31 A.M.

She watches EG from a distance, waiting for him to turn in her direction. If he smiles, she raises her eyebrows. If he waves, she turns away. If he approaches, she parts her lips, closes her eyes, and arches her back. His hands caress her shoulders, slide the straps of her black slip down her alabaster arms. He kisses her breasts, buries his head in her bosom, pressing her full, voluptuous body to his. She throws back her head, laughing contentedly, as he is absorbed into her. He gives himself to her but does not surrender everything. He tells her he loves her, says she is the queen of his household.

If he does not see her, or if he smiles and turns, going about his business, she throws dishes at the wall, rips the sheets from the bed, heaves his clothes out the window into the street below. She dumps the kettle of thick red pasta sauce onto the kitchen floor. Then he throws up his arms in surprise, trails her through the house, pleading. He repeats over and over, "I have a wild thing in the house." She cackles like a *strega*, turns, hands on hips, the black silk slip askew across her enormous heaving breasts. "Get on your knees," she commands in her broken English, pointing to the floor. "Swear to the

Blessed Virgin you will never ignore me again. Swear it. Do you swear it? On your knees, I tell you!" If he kneels, she forgives him, but he must cower for days in her presence.

If he picks her up, carries her to the bed, and ravishes her, she laughs raucously throughout their lovemaking. Afterward, she kisses him all over, goes to the kitchen, stays there all day making eggplant parmigiana.

She is Anna. She is the flame of his soul. Sometimes an ember, sometimes a raging inferno. It is she who must be pleased, she who must never be forgotten. Without her, he is nothing. Without her, he is merely consciousness without energy.

10:19:59:58:32 A.M.

He was diagnosed terminal seven years ago. There is no known cure, at least none the general public has been told of. A giant multinational industry of research and health care has arisen around this illness. Hundreds of thousands of people depend on it for their subsistence.

In subterranean board rooms of leviathan pharmaceutical companies, thin men with aquiline noses, wearing brown suits, white shirts, and blue ties decide that the deaths of a few million people are not too great a price to pay to keep research and medicine and political movements and benefit concerts and home health care agencies and hospitals and hospices and T-shirt companies and condom manufacturers and credit card companies and parade organizers and ribbon vendors and music producers and mortuaries thriving far into the 21st century.

One could look at it as progress of a sort.

EG has worked for the government most of his life. He has worked with bureaucracies and large corporations. He has compromised more than once. He fights as best he can in an arena in which one cannot speak the truth without empirical evidence, even when everyone knows the truth—for this is a man's world.

When he leaves civil service EG takes a job writing funding proposals for community-based health care organizations. He laughs and thinks, *Even I have been assimilated. Now I too am part of the multinational corporation. Like the virus itself, my subsistence depends upon my continued deterioration, my failing health, and eventually my death.*

He tells himself he will try to blow it up from the inside.

Meanwhile, The Boy is terrified, fearing he will be left alone in a world mean and confusing. He clings to EG night and day, holding on to EG's pant leg when he tries to leave for work in the morning, sitting in his lap while he works at the computer, his thin white arms clasped around EG's neck, his cheek pressed hard against his chest.

He takes The Boy everywhere with him, but sometimes he becomes distracted, forgets The Boy is there. When that happens The Boy sits by silently, anxiously, waiting for EG to notice him.

When EG has sex The Boy sometimes watches, fascinated, studying him closely, learning what to do. He has strange new feelings stirring within him, body parts that begin to move and dance without being told, like Pinocchio's nose come to life. The Boy's bodily changes, however, are a manifestation of Truth; they have nothing to do with lies.

Occasionally The Boy whispers to EG, reminding him he is present. EG usually likes when this happens, for The Boy carries the sharpest, brightest feelings of all EG's people. EG believes some people have sex with children trying to get close to the unadulterated authenticity and originality of the feelings that spring from them. Coupled with their enthusiasm and their innocence, children's feelings are close to what most people fantasize It is like. But he thinks—like most ideas people have—these notions are projected from within.

10:19:59:58:33 A.M.

EG wakes at 5:05 A.M. He lies in bed for a long while, then gets up, letting Hari have his place beside Paul. The Doberman jumps up, buries himself completely under the covers, and falls asleep immediately. He is most contented when he's allowed in the "big nest" with one or both of his pack.

A light rain is falling outside. EG lumbers down the hall, stretching his sleepy body, when suddenly he realizes why he woke up: His father is dying. He knows this with utter certainty.

His father is dying alone in the veteran's home in Yountville. Should he go to him? Is this his last chance to speak to his father? Is there unfinished business between them that could actually be worked out? He will make some coffee and ponder what this means as he watches the sun rise over the hills across the bay. He will also ponder the meaning of regret. He had no regrets when his partner Andre died. Will he have regrets when his father dies?

He turns from the window to find Cletus standing behind him near the desk, a pleading look in his eyes. EG imagines it is the same look his father wore every winter morning in the freezing Iowa weather as he huddled in a corner of the front porch until 7:30 A.M., when he would set off for Sacred Heart Academy. Cletus's German immigrant mother, EG's grandmother, left for work at the steam laundry each morning at 5:30 and forced her son to wait outside until it was time to leave for school. In Germany children were never allowed to be alone in the house. It would be no different in Iowa.

"I didn't do that to you," EG says to him. "I'm not carrying that for you. And neither is he," EG says, nodding toward The Boy, who is now hiding behind EG, clinging to him.

Clete sighs and smiles his nervous I'm-having-feelings-I-don't-want-you-to-see smile. "Will you come to Yountville?" Clete asks.

"I don't know," EG answers. "I have to think about it. And don't try to influence me. There's no place for you in this deliberation," EG says, heading for the kitchen, The Boy in tow. "I have to make this decision by myself. You created this situation, not me."

EG pours The Boy a glass of fresh-squeezed orange juice thick with chewy pulp, just the way The Boy likes it, and gets him some animal crackers from the pantry. They sit at the kitchen window looking out at the garden. "It's OK," EG tells The Boy. "I won't let him hurt you. But I have to decide about whether to go see him or not."

"Do I have to go?" The Boy asks timidly.

EG smiles and takes his hand. "Probably," he answers. "But maybe you can wait in the car."

The Boy considers this as he bites the head off a buffalo.

They sit looking out at the garden for a long time, the sun rising slowly above them over the roof of the house, pouring golden light into the opening faces of the blue morning glories.

10:19:59:58:34 A.M.

An award has been given to EG for a life's work in the field of entertainment, so he has flown to Hollywood, where the award is presented. The day after the award ceremony he is sitting on the deck of a friend's house in Malibu watching the Pacific Ocean. In front of the house young people are swimming and surfing, waxing their boards, laughing, chasing one another around in the sand.

This is what I was born for, thinks EG. *All my work, all my effort has led me to this point in my life, and now that it has arrived, I don't feel anything.* EG reflects on a life blessed by hypnotic beauty and magnetic sexuality. *It was my blessing and my curse,* he thinks.

There has never been a time when EG wasn't the center of attention, wasn't fawned over or singled out for special treatment. As a baby in his mother's arms, EG is showered with attention, token offerings, and even presents from store clerks and shoppers, bank tellers and waitresses. And, of course, there is the constant verbal and physical attention. Everywhere the chorus is the same: Look at Him. Him. He. The Beautiful One.

In school He is always seated in the front row, where the teacher can look at Him, rest her hand on His shoulder while she stands at the front of the class; He is chosen for hall monitor, the teacher taking Him by the arm, explaining His duties; it is He who is asked to take messages to other teachers or the principal's office, His teacher taking Him by the arm, pulling Him close, whispering the secret into His soft, supple ear, her lips lightly brushing against His plump, sensuous lobe.

It is He who is asked to read special announcements in the auditorium, He who greets visitors, He who heads the student reception committee to greet the pope when he visits a nearby basilica. And, naturally, it is He who is selected to present the key of the city to the president when his motorcade passes through town.

By the time He entered high school, He is the most envied and sought-after boy in town, and He has grown accustomed to it. By this time He has come to expect certain things from people without having to ask. He expects to be invited to every party, expects to win every competition that isn't based on intellectual prowess, has come to expect that He will have His photo in every edition of the school paper. These are His inalienable rights, it would seem.

His mother's friend Shirley, baby-sitting with Him when He is just 9, makes Him walk around the house naked all evening, and then, when it comes time to put Him to bed, shows Him how boys are different from girls by undressing and getting into bed with Him. When He is unable to achieve an erection, she shows Him how to use His fingers to make a girl wet "down there." She makes Him promise it will be their "special secret."

By the time He turns 12, He has come to realize that nearly everyone He meets wants to be physical with Him. It has been that way for as long as He can remember. From His first sexual encounter at the age of 5, with older boys visiting a neighbor, to the clothing salesman at Roos Atkins in San Francisco, where His mother opened His own private account when He turned 13, everyone wants Him for sex.

In high school He is approached by dozens of pals, girls, and several teachers. His drama teacher is obsessed with Him. His flair for theater and a nearly photographic memory—which offsets His inability to think abstractly or remember scientific facts—makes Him perfect for an academic major in dramatic arts, where He not only excels in every production the school mounts but also earns a scholarship to the University of Southern California. The two-year affair with His acting teacher also doesn't hurt.

It doesn't matter who or what gender He is engaging with because sex is about Him, always about Him. Each partner approaches Him in a state of worship. What can she do for Him? How can he satisfy Him? Where can they go to be alone with Him? The sex act is mostly an act of observation on His part. He looks down at whoever is busy between His legs and thinks, *They are always so ravenous for me.* He looks up at whoever is straddling Him and thinks, I *wonder if they practice these acrobatics as soon as they see me, waiting for the day when I will say yes.* He enters or is entered by His partners to the sounds of accolades, litanies of praise, beatitudes crafted on the spot by His adoring worshippers. But always He feels as though His heart is somewhere else. It is always as though He is not present until orgasm is over. It was His body that was the object of devotion. Did they even know who He was?

College is the same. He takes the University of Southern California campus by storm. Word spreads, even in the land of golden boys, that there is a new student so alluring, so electric, He will surely be the new Marlon Brando, the next James Dean. And, as things go in that part of the country, talent scouts and agents come looking for Him, searching out this youthful Adonis they have heard so much about. When they see Him, one after another, they see what they expect to see, what they want to see: God, Devil, Gift, or Challenge. Handsome, muscular, sensuous, seductively withdrawn, provocatively shy. And each one has to have Him, handle Him, and then handle Him.

For initial exposure it is modeling. EG appears first in local papers, then regional magazines. Within six months He is on the covers of GQ, *L'uomo*, and *Men's Vogue*. He makes a half dozen television commercials and signs a contract for a small film role three days before His 19th birthday. That small role launches His film career and His income for the year He turns 20 exceeds $800,000. It is never less from that day to this.

Just before He went for His first movie audition, a friend who was working for the studio gave Him some strong advice. "This first meeting with the producer will determine everything for the rest of your film career—if you're going to have a film career. This is where they decide if you'll work with them on their terms. It's where they see if you're going to be difficult. So no matter what they ask you to do, do it. If you refuse, you'll never work in this town. Believe me, they talk to one another about these things. Remember, do anything they ask, just this once. And it doesn't matter if you think it has nothing to do with acting—if you get my drift."

He understood better than anyone what His friend was saying. He was ready.

The meeting with the producer goes well for the first ten minutes, just a lot of friendly small talk about the work He has done up to that point. Then the producer says, "The part we have in mind for you is what we refer to as a star-maker role. It's small, but it's going to steal the movie for whoever does it. Are you willing to take a small role?"

"Yes, sir. There are no small roles to my way of thinking," He responds.

"Well, it's only one scene," the producer cautions.

"That's all it takes, if you're good at it, though. Isn't that right?"

"Let me tell you about it, son," the producer says, getting up from the huge ebony desk and walking around the room. "You're the lead's friend and business associate. You're buddies, but you're fucking his wife. Heh-heh, like in Hollywood, eh?" the man chuckles, patting EG's shoulder as he passes behind his chair. "Anyway, he doesn't know that. In this scene his wife has come to visit you in your office. She's nuts about you, can't keep her hands off you. The two of you are in a pretzel hold on your desk when your secretary announces that your buddy's on his way in to see you. His wife jumps under the desk. You sit down and pretend to be going through some papers. The guy comes in and sits across from you.

"Now comes the twist. He wants to discuss his marital problems. He decides you're the person he's going to confide in—even though he's your boss. Meanwhile, the wife—under the desk—begins to get frisky. She goes down on you while you're talking to her husband. You have to go through that scene, letting the camera know you're poppin' your nut under the desk, but you also have to act natural for the lead. Think you can do that?"

"Sure, I can do that scene."

"You want to give it a try?"

"Sure."

The producer smiles. His white linen suit is Italian, his multicolored geometric tie is made from feathers of exotic birds. EG recognizes the tie from one of the GQ's he appeared in. He knows it cost the producer $200.

"You want to try it now? I have to cast this thing by Wednesday."

"Now...sure, why not?" EG says and stands, assuming He's going to be shown to the soundstage.

"OK, let's give it a whirl," the producer says, removing his jacket and hanging it on a Plexiglas coat tree near the window. Then the producer crawls under the desk. "Come sit in the chair and pull it up to the desk," the producer directs.

EG is taken off-guard, but, remembering his friend's advice, He sits down in the producer's chair and moves tentatively toward the producer, who is crouching beneath his own desk. "Closer," the producer orders. EG moves closer. "Now read the paper on the desk in front of you like you're selling something and your rent depends on it. Read the one that talks about the new Sony camera."

EG fumbles the papers on the producer's desk and finds a brochure from Sony Corporation describing a new 70 millimeter camera they're pitching to filmmakers. EG begins to read it aloud in his best "announcer" voice while the producer begins undoing EG's trousers. He slips them down to EG's ankles, along with His Calvin Klein briefs, making a slight groaning sound as he sees EG's tanned, hairy thighs and exquisite penis. EG tries to read without a trace of arousal in His voice as the producer begins to caress Him.

"Now press the button on the little speaker box on the right side of the desk," the producer says with his mouth full. "Press it just once."

EG presses the button at the same time he thinks, *No one has ever talked with my dick in his mouth. That felt good; I have to ask someone to do that again sometime.*

Within seconds the door opens and the producer's secretary walks in. She smiles and sits opposite EG. "Tell me about yourself," she says, crossing her legs and smiling at Him, while the producer is trying to work his hand under EG's testicles to reach his ass with his middle finger, which feels greasy to EG.

"Well, I grew up here in California. In the Napa Valley." EG is now confused. Does she know what's going on? Is He just being used, or is this really the make-or-break session everyone has told Him it would be? Does everything depend on faking it out for the secretary and letting the guy under the desk stick his finger up His ass? Is this how Kevin Costner got started?

"Have you acted before?" the blond secretary asks.

"Oh, sure. My first acting job was in a high school play. Then, the summer of my junior year, I tried out for the San

Francisco Repertory for a small part in *Fortune and Men's Eyes* and ended up with the lead."

"Really? You must have something very special then," the secretary says.

EG decides that the blond is in on this after all and that the sooner He reaches orgasm, the sooner this will end. He also decides to call their bluff. He's accustomed to being used this way, so why not make it pay off? So with His utmost concentration He leans forward, scooting up in the chair so that His cock is pounding against the back of the producer's throat, making him gag. The secretary is now the one who is confused, distracted by the retching noises coming from under the ebony desktop. EG's testicles slide forward off the chair and He lifts himself up, putting His weight on His elbows. This allows the producer to slide his middle finger inside EG to work His prostate.

"Well, I don't know if it's very special, but I do have this one asset," EG whispers, winking at the secretary, who now leans closer, allowing EG a better view down her scoop-neck blouse. "See, the director of that play was a woman, and she had the most gorgeous breasts, sort of like yours." EG reaches out and slides His hand into the secretary's blouse, slipping His fingers into her brassiere and rubbing one of her nipples lightly. "And so one night, while we were rehearsing late, just she and I, I left my pants unzipped. When she told me they were undone, I pretended the zipper was stuck and asked for her help. The next thing I knew, 'pop,' I was creaming all over her pretty face," EG says, as He creams all over the producer's not-so-pretty face.

EG removes His hand slowly from the secretary's blouse. "That's how I got that particular job," EG says, a single bead of sweat trickling down the side of His face.

The secretary, almost laughing out loud with what she realizes now is this sharp young actor's getting the upper hand on her boss, reaches out and wipes the perspiration from EG's cheek, then provocatively places the finger in her mouth. "I'll bet that's how you'll get this job too," she says, then gets up and leaves the room.

One of the surfers on the beach is arguing with his girl-friend. She wants to use his surfboard, and he's screaming, "No way, bitch."

EG thinks of how many surfers come and go in the "indus-try." Producers and directors cruise the beaches looking for blond, tanned bodies, take them back to the studio or their Malibu beach houses, have their way with them, maybe let them work as an extra on one or two films, and then refuse their calls, having replaced them with someone better look-ing, more buffed, or bigger breasted.

Here, at the end of His life, looking out over the ocean, lis-tening to these young people argue about having fun, His past seems like a blur, as though it all happened in the length of a two-hour film. Did letting that fat producer have his way with Him that day make it possible for Him to become one of the most successful actors in the history of the movie industry? Did all the other sexual encounters with producers and direc-tors and Hollywood celebrities account for His success? Or did He have some talent as well? Now, on this deck, with the sun moving westward before Him, approaching the end of the Earth, He isn't at all sure.

The sliding-glass door behind Him opens and his hostess joins EG on the deck. "I brought you a drink," the woman says, handing Him a vodka-tonic.

EG met Gloria about five years prior to this visit, while He was filming a public service announcement for the Human Rights Campaign Fund. Gloria was the "go-for," a job she stumbled into through someone she met at an AA meeting. EG liked her immediately because she didn't kowtow to His fame. Gloria is 65, just five years older than EG, and their birthdays are the same day. They talk on the phone at least once a week.

"You feel better this morning?" she asks, plopping down in the rattan chair next to EG.

"Not really," He answers, sipping His drink.

"Are you ready to talk about it?"

"I don't know how. I'm not exactly sure what it is. I'm not sure it's anything specific," EG muses. A huge white freighter with red Japanese characters on the smokestack is gliding southward on the horizon.

"When did this mood start?" she asks.

"Yesterday morning. I woke up feeling…empty, useless."

"Maybe it's midlife crisis," she offers, smiling, but with a compassionate tone. "After all, you really have achieved everything. What's left for you? You're at the top of your profession, everyone loves you…"

"That's just it. No one loves me. No one really understands me. Except perhaps you, which is terribly sad, given that you've only known me for about a month." They both laugh at EG's exaggeration.

"What about Joey?"

EG takes a drink of His vodka-tonic, then reaches down and retrieves His straw Borsolino to keep the sun off His head, remembering that sunlight turns the peroxide green.

"Joey's gone."

"When did that happen?"

"Last week. I didn't want to go into it long-distance. Besides, it's the same old story."

"Which is…?"

"He's young, I'm old. He's energetic, I'm tired. He has a life ahead of him, I have a life behind me. Wouldn't you think I'd have learned by now?"

Gloria reaches over and pats His hand. "Honey, you're never too old not to learn," she says, and laughs her gravel-throated laugh. "Sometimes I think I'm forgetting things I don't even know."

"Why haven't I ever been able to keep a relationship? Why do they always fall apart?" EG asks.

"You want me to talk honestly, or do you need to be comforted with lies and reassurance?" Except for His former lover Paul, Gloria is the only person who has ever spoken to EG like this. He finds it refreshing that she has never been intimidated by His fame. The first day they met on the set, she shook His hand, said, "Hi, I'm Gloria. I'll get you coffee or whiskey if you want, but in the meantime, it's probably best if you just sit over there and try to stay out of the way until they need you."

"Oh, yeah," she added as an afterthought, "I'm supposed to tell you how much everyone appreciates your doing this." Then she winked at Him.

"You might as well be honest. I don't think I can take any more lies."

"Well, for starters, Joey was 29 years younger than you. I think that probably is a slight handicap to longevity. It wouldn't be if he was an old soul or you were really well- developed."

"When you get to be 60, there's very little you can do to stay in shape," EG says defensively. "Do you have any idea how much I've spent on personal trainers in my life? I mean, this used to be all muscle." EG is cupping his sagging pectorals like they were breasts.

"Honey, I meant spiritually developed. Emotionally developed."

"Oh." EG pauses, reflecting on what Gloria said. "You think I'm retarded," EG says in false self-deprecation.

"I think you've spent a lot of energy on being beautiful, glamorous, well-loved by your public, and notoriously successful. That's brought you exactly what you wanted: a beautiful body, an exciting life filled with rich and famous people, and the ability to make any film you want. You have an excellent return on exactly what you invested in: the material world."

"But all I really wanted was to be loved. All I ever wanted was someone to share my life with, who would love and understand me. Was that too much to ask?"

"Not at all. If that's where you had put your effort, that's what you would have gotten back."

"That is where I put my effort. Well, a lot of effort, anyway."

"Oh, please. You put your effort into pursuing gorgeous boys. Remember Ken?"

"How could I forget him?" EG ruminates wistfully.

"A perfect example. You swept him off his feet, moved him into your house, and flew him back and forth to Europe during the entire shooting of whatever the hell that movie was you were making when you met him. Then—and this is one of my favorite Hollywood stories of all time—when you bought that place in the Hamptons and he didn't like the pool, you had the entire thing ripped up and replaced with a black slate one. Just for your boyfriend!"

"He left me two months later."

"Exactly. So you got what you invested in: a black swimming pool."

"What was I supposed to do? He said he was going to leave me if I didn't make changes in that house."

"Sugar, that should have told you all you needed to know about him right then and there."

"I thought he loved me."

"Well, that depends on your definition of love, sweetie. If love is taking everything another person has to offer without giving anything in return, then he loved you something fierce."

"He was a student; he was poor. He didn't have anything to give me. He was just a kid."

EG can tell by the pained expression on Gloria's face that she's trying to decide if it's really worth going on with the conversation. Sometimes they don't communicate very well. EG has noticed that when their conversation turns to His personal life—or hers—she talks in a convoluted manner. Often He can't even understand her. When that happens He either changes the subject or remembers an engagement He's going to be late for.

In a good-natured way she says softly, "How can a man live 60 years without learning the first thing about himself?"

"Well, it's true," EG says. "He had a part-time job in a deli on Bleecker Street."

"EG, that's not the kind of giving I'm talking about. He didn't have anything emotional, intellectual, or spiritual to offer you. He had one thing and one thing only: a gorgeous ass. And he looked good on your arm at parties."

"Please. Give me more credit than…" EG stops midsentence, Gloria's eyebrows raised at Him, her lips pursed. "All right, all right. But…"

"EG, there aren't any 'buts' here. Come on, it's just the two of us, a couple of old has-beens at the end of the trail, trying to get ready to wind up the third act. All your lovers have been show ponies."

EG looks out over the warm sand to where the surfers are now playing volleyball. EG is particularly struck by one boy

He estimates to be about 19. He has sand-colored hair down to his waist. His skin is golden, his body rippling with muscles. EG thinks the boy has maybe 8% body fat at most. He is wearing baggy plaid swim trunks. He jumps up at the net, his golden arms raised high, and he slugs the white volleyball as hard as he can, sending it slamming into the sand on the opposite side of the net. A point for his team. There is much shouting and hand-slapping.

"How did you get to be so smart, Gloria? How come you know so much about life and I know so little?"

"Well, let's see. It could have been the six years trying to make it as a dancer in New York and sleeping with every director in Manhattan. Or four years of heroin and cocaine addiction. Hmm, maybe it was the drying-out period. Or was it the three divorces? The three abortions? Could it be two daughters who stopped speaking to me by the time they were 15 and pregnant? The son who spent two years in Attica? The overdose of sleeping pills? Maybe it was living in an abandoned car under the Triborough Bridge. Selling my body to pay the rent?"

"OK, OK. But lots of people go through stuff like that and don't make it to where you are."

"And where is that?"

"Living in a beautiful home in Malibu, being a successful counselor, a published author. A wise old dame," EG adds.

"A home you made the down payment for, a counselor as a result of a book that was published only because you introduced me to your agent, and I'm not as wise as you think. Maybe you just have a lot to learn." Gloria reaches over and takes EG's hand. "Look, my dear, I'm going to level with you. You have to start getting your act together. You can't go on buying boyfriends, running from plastic surgeon to plastic surgeon, producing the movies you want to star in because no one will cast you in the romantic lead anymore. There really is more to life than movies, New York restaurants, the Italian Riviera, and sex."

"I know that. That's not who I am. That's what people see, but that's not who I really am."

"Who are you? Really?" Gloria leans forward, resting her arms on her knees in rapt attention.

"I'm a loving, honest, caring person. I have a lot to offer someone."

"Yes, I agree. But what is it precisely that you have to offer—that isn't bought with money, I mean?"

"Love. Concern. Loyalty. Devotion."

"How would anyone know that? The first thing you do when you meet someone is buy him a new convertible. How would someone know you have those things to offer?"

"They never stay around long enough to find out," EG says. "It's not my fault."

Gloria decides to go for broke. They have never had this conversation in quite this way before, and she isn't sure the opportunity will come again. "What about Paul?"

EG tenses up at the mention of the name. His eyes fill with tears, and He sets his jaw. The two of them stare long and hard at one another before EG responds. "He left me, remember?"

"I remember him moving out of the house, if that's what you mean. I'm not sure he left you."

EG glares at her but is lost for words. She's getting convoluted.

"I think you left him—a long time before he moved out," she says.

"I don't understand you when you talk like this. Talk straight, not in symbols or semaphores or whatever you call them." EG is trying to get Gloria to lighten up on Him.

"When Paul told you he wanted things to change, when he tried to get you to cut back on your public appearances, when he found that place in the country he wanted to buy..."

"That place in the country! It was three hours north of San Francisco. Ten hours from Los Angeles. There wasn't even an airport within 60 miles."

"I think that was his point," Gloria says, leaning back in her chair. "I believe that was his way of saying something to you."

"And what might that have been? That he wanted me to go broke? To stop working and evaporate? In this business people forget you if you aren't in the public eye at least once a week."

"Not Paul. He wouldn't forget you if you were invisible for the rest of your life. I think he was trying to tell you that you were all he needed or wanted. It didn't matter to him if you ever made another movie. It probably didn't matter to him if you had never been in movies to begin with."

"Well, he certainly had a funny way of showing it."

"I thought he showed it perfectly. He never asked you for anything—except your time and attention."

EG is practically crying now. He is gritting His teeth and refusing to look at Gloria.

"Isn't that all you want from someone? Isn't that what you've been sitting here saying?" Gloria asks, gently stroking EG's hand.

"I can't talk about this now," EG says, standing up and going to the edge of the deck. The volleyball teams are repositioning the net so that the sun isn't in their eyes. The long-haired boy spies the two of them on Gloria's deck and gives a friendly wave. EG manages a half-hearted wave in return. "I don't understand what you're saying. I loved Paul. He wanted too much. He wanted me to give up everything I've worked all my life for. I couldn't do that. I simply couldn't do that. And it wasn't necessary. He could have had everything. Everything. Lots of people would give their eye teeth to have been in his position. Lots of people."

Gloria gets up, puts her arm around her friend, squeezes him. "I just don't like seeing you so unhappy," she says. "I thought perhaps talking about it would help. I thought maybe we could make things better for you."

"I'm just tired," EG says, turning to her, smiling. Gloria recognizes it as his camera smile, a sure sign he's no longer really there. "I'll be fine just as soon as I get caught up on my sleep."

"I'm sure you will," she says, feeling a deep aching in her chest. "You are definitely a survivor, my friend."

"After a couple days here I'll be my old self."

"Excuse me," a voice interrupts from the sand below them. They both look down over the deck railing. The long-haired boy is standing in the sand smiling up at them. His white teeth sparkle in the California sun, his shoulders are freckled from countless days on the beach. "Aren't you...?"

EG smiles back. "He certainly is," Gloria says.

"Wow! Like you're like my favorite. I've seen like every movie you ever made. Well, most of them, anyway."

EG is beaming now, holding in His stomach, reaching for the sunglasses in His pocket. " Why thank you. That's very kind of you."

"No, man, I mean it. I watch *Last Encounter* like about once a month, at least. You were totally awesome in that."

"Thanks," EG says again.

"I know you must get really tired of this kind of thing, and I don't want to like intrude or anything, but if I went back to my car and got something to write on, would you like maybe give me an autograph?" The young man is visibly excited at meeting EG in person. He is dancing back and forth on the hot sand now.

"Tell you what," EG says, "why don't you come around to the gate and step inside for a minute and I'll sign a copy of my autobiography for you. I have an extra one with me."

"Wow! Really? You mean it?"

EG laughs out loud, completely transformed from the mood he's been in these several weeks. "Of course I mean it. Here, come around to the gate," EG says, following the railing around the deck, showing the boy the way.

Gloria watches as EG goes down the half dozen steps to unlock the gate. Then the beautiful young man with the long, flowing hair and 8% body fat at most, follows EG back up the steps, across the deck, and through the sliding-glass doors. As the two of them step inside, Gloria can hear EG saying, "Actually, I think it's up in my room. Follow me. Have you ever thought about auditioning for a film yourself? You certainly have the face for it. And that smile. You wouldn't even have to have your teeth capped.

10:19:59:58:35 A.M.

Somewhere in the White Room a metronome is ticking out the seconds. EG must stop it. If he can stop it, he might be able to buy time. With time he can gain a fuller comprehension of what is happening. He turns his head and through his crusted eyes sees an old scrubwoman in a white uniform on her hands and knees, scrubbing the floor with a wooden brush. She is brown-skinned, her face wrinkled, her hands callused. As she scrubs back and forth on the white linoleum, the brush knocks against the wall of the White Room.

What are you doing? EG asks.

The old woman straightens up, turns her wrinkled face toward EG, and says, *I'm cleaning.*

Please stop, EG pleads. *I must have silence. I need to think.*

The old woman chuckles and rises to her feet. *The rhythm of the brush is meant to keep you from thinking,* she says, coming closer to the bed. *My cleaning is meant to soothe you.*

But it doesn't. It disturbs me.

Why does it disturb you?

It keeps me from concentrating. Go away.

The old woman laughs. *If I don't clean, you won't be able to see the room. You might wake up and not remember where you are.*

I don't want you here.

You want me here. You just don't recognize me. Look closer.

EG wants to be left alone. He tries to recognize the old woman, but it is useless. He has never known this woman or anyone like her. *I don't know you,* EG says. *Who are you?*

As soon as he has asked the question, the cleaning woman stretches out her arms and the room seems to grow even whiter. EG, through his crusted eyes, can barely stand to look at the brightness. The old woman moves toward him, sits next to the bed, and takes his hand into her two hands. She tenderly kisses his hand then speaks in a soft, deep voice:

"Oh, my son, those who realize true wisdom, held rapturous within their clear awareness, see me as the origin of the universe, imperishable. All their words and all their actions issue from the very depths of worship; they are held in my embrace; they know me the way woman knows her lover.

"Creatures come, creatures disappear; I alone am real, EG, looking out, amused, from deep within the eyes of every creature.

"I am the object of all knowledge, mother of the world, its father. I alone am the source of all things, pure and impure, both holiness and horror. I am the goal you seek, sweet man, the font of wisdom, the Witness to life itself; I am both home and refuge, creation and destruction, the treasure of your deepest, most secret heart.

"I am the radiance of the sun, I am abundance and famine, rain and drought, I am immortality and I am death, I am being and I am nonbeing.

"I am the Self, EG, seated in the heart of every creature. I am the origin, the way, and the end that all must come to.

"Those who worship me with sincere hearts, with their minds and with their bodies, giving their entire lives in devotion to me, find in me their heart's fulfillment. Even those who do not know me, if they are honest, just, and loving, honor me with the truest kind of veneration.

"All your thoughts, all your actions, all your fears and disappointments, offer them up to me with an open heart; think of them all as passing visions. In this way you free yourself from bondage, from both your good and your evil actions; remain free of attachment and you will embody me in utter freedom.

"I, EG, am justice: clear, impartial, hating no one, favoring no one. But know that in those devotees who have rid themselves of selfishness, I shine with brilliance. Even murderers and tyrants, the cruelest of despots, ultimately find redemption through my love if they but surrender themselves to my excruciating yet healing graces. Passing through painful transformations, they find their liberation and their hearts know peace within their breasts.

"EG, I am always with all creatures, every sentient being; I abandon no one. And however great your inner darkness may be, you are never separate from me and my healing love. Let all your *thoughts flow through and past you; keep me near in the light as well as the dark; trust me with your very life because I am you, even more than you yourself are."*

10:19:59:58:36 A.M.

The Boy is sitting in the chilly Napa Valley evening on his Uncle Wes's ranch, waiting for the deer to come down from the hills and feed on the fat plums and golden peaches in the orchard. His father sits next to him, his rifle resting on his knee.

First comes a large buck with huge antlers, slowly making his way through the scrub oaks, sniffing the air, cocking his noble head in the fading light, taking one tenuous step after another. When it appears that all is safe, the buck turns, shakes his antlers in some sort of signal and down the hillside, out of the brush, trot his family—a doe and two fawns.

Clete raises the rifle slowly, finds the buck's heart in his site, and gently squeezes the trigger. The Boy watches as his father's finger moves more slowly than a cloud passing in front of the sun.

Below them, in the fading light, the regal deer's head, its brown eyes wide, lifts toward the sagging fruit, seeking out the sweet purple flesh of the Santa Rosa plums, perhaps the only food left for these creatures in the third consecutive summer of drought in northern California, where nearly everything, including Wes's crop, has suffered beneath the scorching sun. A sharp crack erupts in The Boy's right ear and echoes through the evening air. The buck's eyes bulge, his legs skitter and scamper beneath him in an instinctive reaction to run, but it is no use: His legs are already failing him. The deer slumps sideways, his antlers catching in the low branches of the plum tree. He hangs in the tree shuddering, blood gushing crimson from the white diamond shape marking his breast. His family flees in terror, the doe running and not looking back, her fawns scrambling so that their legs splay and will not move, as in a dream.

The Boy screams and rushes past his father's still-poised rifle, scampers down the incline through the tall grass to the fallen animal. Clete shouts after him, calling his name over and over into the dusk. The Boy falls on the deer, weeping, his arms wide around the animal's neck, his tan jacket turning crimson. The deer's body is still warm, the blood hot against The Boy's cheek, and he can hear his own wails rise through the gnarled branches of the fruit trees, into the violet sky, clashing in protest against his father's calling.

It is The Boy's mother who finally comes to him, rushing into the orchard in response to the duet of loss and anger that Clete and The Boy are singing to one another in the fading light.

The Boy has no idea where his father went that evening or what he said, if anything. What he dreams of for weeks after is the slow lift of the rifle into the air, the resounding shot, and the warm blood of the deer on his face.

In the days and weeks that follow, Clete's eyes grow more silent, more distant. The Boy, for the first time, fears his father. He avoids his father's eyes, turns away from the disappointment, the heartache, the fear he finds reflected back when he looks at him. It is the beginning of their journey away from one another. Like a ship setting sail on an ocean voyage, Clete moves farther and farther into the distance. The Boy, like a broken-hearted lover, stands on the pier, his brown-and-white dog sitting beside him. Together they watch as the ship grows smaller and smaller on the horizon, carrying The Boy's hopes, his aspirations, and the map that might have guided him into manhood. Finally it is just The Boy and the dog at the edge of the cold, dark water. The Boy and the dog, alone at the edge of the world.

10:19:59:58:37 A.M.

Cletus, nearly 80, wanders the linoleum corridors of the Yountville Veterans' Home, childless, institutionalized by his second wife, who now lives with her daughter and a bastard grandson in the house he spent the last 20 years of his life building.

Deep in the Napa Valley, perched on a hillside overlooking oceans of vineyards, the Home he now calls home is not so comforting as he once imagined it would be. His ancient comrades in battle lie abandoned by their children and their children's children. They babble and wet themselves, soil the sheets, dodge mortar fire. He alone is lucid, unmercifully cursed with all his faculties.

Daily he makes his rounds, floor to floor, working the maze of white, yellow, and lime-green corridors, pausing briefly at every window except one. The window where he does not stop overlooks the Home's main entrance and the long drive that leads up to it, where no one he knows ever travels. A man of logic and strict economy, he stopped looking out at this station years ago.

He knows he has a son, had one once. He can remember vaguely his face, but it is the face of a 10-year-old boy seen in a rearview mirror. The Boy is seated squarely in the backseat in a starched white shirt, and, although he can't see them, he knows The Boy is wearing gray corduroy trousers and black leather school shoes. It is his uniform from St. Catherine's Academy, which he will soon no longer attend because it doesn't have a football team. His son is going to play for Notre Dame some day, so he must transfer to a school with an athletics program.

He knows he has a son, but he can't remember what that feels like.

He remembers what it feels like to wait two hours on December mornings on the open porch of his home in Iowa, his mayonnaise sandwich freezing in the thin paper bag. He remembers knowing that when Mr. Baumhover across the street opens his door each morning and leaves for the flower shop, it is time to set off for school. He remembers not understanding, when his mother leaves each morning at 5:45 for the steam laundry, why he can't wait in the house.

He remembers his Aunt Gert and her brood of 19 kids and how he worked every summer on her South Dakota farm while his mother sailed the Mississippi until early September, cooking meals for the steamboat crew. He remembers the day he received his certificate of completion of eight years at Sacred Heart School and the bronze medal with a purple ribbon attached that read in gold letters FOR EIGHT YEARS OF PERFECT ATTENDANCE.

He remembers—although he was only 3 years old—the white hospital room and the last time he saw his father's stubbly gray face, cold and rigid in death, even though he can't remember the man when he was alive.

And he can remember that he has a son, can even see his rigid reflection in the rearview mirror. But he can't remember what it feels like.

So he wanders the endless white, yellow, and lime-green corridors. He is waiting for no one. He is hoping for nothing. And he is not trying to remember anything.

10:19:59:58:38 A.M.

EG decides to visit his father in the Old Soldiers' Home against all advice and his own best judgment. It has been 12 years since he has seen him, and he searches the corridors, peering into each room, walking every ward, viewing the beds' occupants the way one searches for a missing relative in a makeshift morgue following a natural disaster.

Finally, just as he is about to give up, there, at the end of the last ward, sitting in a wheelchair on a small veranda overlooking a lush muscatel vineyard, he spies his father. He walks slowly to the door, stands looking through the rusty screen for a moment before opening it and stepping out.

The old man turns slowly, looks up, squinting his eyes. He is much older than EG remembers him, but he is not frail, not feeble. He gives EG a puzzled look, thinking momentarily that this is a new orderly come to announce the afternoon meal. Then, very gradually, a look of recognition passes over his features. His eyes flood with tears and he struggles to his feet, his arms outstretched. "My son, my son," he whimpers softly. "I'm so sorry. I am so sorry."

The old man wraps his arms around EG in a tight embrace and he kisses his boy over and over, struggling for words between kisses, between sobs. "Please forgive me. I didn't know how to be a father. Please, please forgive your old father now. Let me die knowing you have forgiven me. My boy, my boy, my only son."

10:19:59:58:39 A.M.

He has come to think of It the way he thinks of electricity: an invisible force that moves within all things.

He makes the following entry in his journal:

All motion is that which we call It. We have given It the name of God because we need to name things, need to attach a word, an image, an incarnation in order to understand.

In the beginning was the Word. Once we had a word, then Man looked for an image to attach it to. The sun. A cloud. The tallest mountain. Thunder. A jackal. A full-breasted woman. An old man with a beard.

By attaching the idea to a word and the word to an object, Man could establish a relatedness to It. I see the first shamans, the first priests, those venerable ancient theologians with their primitive yet wise ways: "It is there. I am here. Now I can observe and contemplate It. I can know It in relation to me. If It is motion, I will imagine It as a dancing man. I will give Him a name: Nataraj. When It is in the act of creation I will call It Brahma. When It is in the process of sustaining that which It created, I will call It Vishnu. When It is in the act of destruction, I will call It Shiva, or if It is a woman, Kali."

Unfortunately, he thinks, we have confused the images of It for the Thing Itself. In order to try not to confuse It with the images of It, he tries to think of It not as a "thing" but as an invisible force or energy, like electricity. Just as electricity makes a fan blade turn, a lightbulb burn bright or dim— depending on the wattage and current—or lightning flash in the evening sky, so It courses through all things, causing them to exist.

In winter, when he walks across the carpet and touches the metal door handle and receives a small electrical shock, he smiles at The Boy. "It is reminding us that It is everywhere," he says. "In the carpet, in the door handle, in our fingertips, and in the air between."

Even what we consider to be evil is It, he finally decides. It also manifests in a destructive energy. Humans make the judgment as to whether that destruction is good or evil. It makes no such distinctions. It just is.

EG considers that true evil exists only in humans, never in animals, plants, or minerals. It is people who do hurtful things. If only that energy could be turned into something else. If only people would concentrate on lighting cities rather than building bombs.

He makes another entry into his journal:

I cannot control the actions of others. I can sometimes barely control my own. I will focus on being as virtuous as I can, but I must remember that as soon as I conceive of good or virtue, I have, by definition, created, if not its opposite, the definite potential for its opposite. I must be very careful not to be proud. I must be very careful not to judge. Like the elephant walking through the jungle, trampling down a path for the Raj, I must send my ego forth to clear a path for my soul, for the Self.

10:19:59:58:40 A.M.

He has known death since he was a child. Not the slow demise of aging grandparents or sickly aunts but the unexpected collapse of adults around him. He has seen in his dreams men clutching their chests, women coughing up blood, adolescent bodies knotted among shredded tires and twisted metal.

Helen Cohen, into whose care he was delivered each morning when his mother left for work, lost her only child one May morning to what in those days was called "natural causes."

Harry had gone to the town swimming pool to help a friend drain the water, scour the bottom, and give the concrete a fresh coat of aquamarine paint. It would take them three days, and for their efforts they would receive not only enough money to purchase flying lessons at the Calistoga airfield, but, more importantly, for those three days they will be the towns-people's central attraction.

Children linger at the Cyclone fence on their way to Cal-istoga Elementary School, mesmerized by the immense blue canyon revealing itself, as the water mysteriously disappears somewhere into the earth beneath them. The water level drops and drops before their very eyes.

At 3 o'clock The Boy and every child from third to seventh grade who doesn't have to ride the yellow school bus—and even some who do—will stampede through the double doors of the red brick schoolhouse behind the tiny Greek Orthodox church on Fourth Street; they will race past the frozen food lockers of Martin's Meat Company, where The Boy's father's six-point buck hangs from a single icy hook, waiting for the silent boning knife; they will careen around the corner of the Bank of America where, inside the cool steel vault, The Boy's Christmas Club of $12 lies coolly collecting 3% interest.

The panting children clutch their tattered textbooks—used last year and the year before and the year before that by this year's high school cheerleaders and quarterbacks, now too old and too important to talk to them. On they race to the end of Washington Avenue, hand-knit red sweaters, yellow macs, and green jumpers fluttering and rippling like flags in their arms. They run like wild ponies to see the progress made thus far at Patchetaw's Pool by the two shirtless men who only a few short years ago clutched these same textbooks and ran these same streets each autumn to assess the same pool's transformation.

The stampeding herd careens around the basalt wall of the boys' dressing room, slams against the wire mesh of the cy-clone fence, and one after another the anxious children utter an audible gasp, for there before them lies the most amazing sight. The vast concrete pool—where Boy Scouts earn their life-saving badges and Eileen Berlotti teaches 7-year-old girls to perfect the breast stroke—now sits empty, as deep, they imagine, as the Grand Canyon. The aquamarine chasm slopes sharply toward them so that the bottom of The Deep End is not even visible from where they stand.

And sitting on the edge, shirtless, swigging a hard-earned Lucky Lager, King of Beers, Harry Cohen grins at his appreciative admirers. They shout questions at him all at once.

"How deep is it?"

"Where does all the water go?"

"How long did it take?"

"Aren't you scared you'll fall?"

Harry Cohen, who barely finished high school; Harry Cohen, who drinks Lucky Lager beer, smokes Chesterfield cigarettes, rarely unlatches the front door before 2 A.M.; Harry Cohen, who knows the road that winds through the vineyards of neighboring Yountville to Ivy's cathouse better than the lines of a hypotenuse triangle; Harry Cohen, barely 31 years old and deeply loved by his widowed mother, Helen, throws back his head and laughs with abandon, his perfect teeth sparkling in the October sunlight, his blue-black hair shinier than Superman's, the lines of his chest and shoulders the archetypal image of masculinity that the boys looking on at pool's end will take with them into the desert of their lives; Harry Cohen throws back his head, raises his Lucky Lager with one hand, his Chesterfield cigarette with the other in a wide embrace of the startling blue sky above the Napa Valley, and freezes motionless for an indeterminable length of time, while just beneath his muscled, sweaty chest, one inch below the soft brown fur and the tanned skin that knows the touch of every painted finger at Ivy's, a tiny blue vessel sighs and rips away from the pulsing pump that charges the lean, kind, confused, and much-loved body that Calistoga calls Harry Cohen.

At this perfect moment in his not so perfect life, feeling like a matinee idol, the most important, envied youth in all of Calistoga, the man who drained the pool at Patchetaw's, loosens his hold on the Lucky Lager beer in his right hand, drops the Chesterfield cigarette from his left hand, puts both palms to his chest, leans forward, and exacts a full somersault into the now-empty Deep End.

As he tumbles through space, bumping his knee, his shoulder, his head against the aquamarine wall, the black numbers indicating the depth he is achieving float slowly past his failing view—7-8-9-10—and Harry thinks to himself, *This pain is not so bad. Dying is not so hard after all.*

The schoolchildren carry Harry's image with them into their futures, the laughing hero tumbling from view, sailing down into the blue concrete canyon where three days later the season's first lifesaving classes will begin.

Now Cohen turns to The Boy to be her son, and he, at 8, is only too willing. Having watched Harry Cohen tumble laughing into eternity, his idea of death is unencumbered joy: The town's most beautiful man—his rippling furry chest and strong shoulders aglisten with perspiration, his Pepsodent-perfect teeth flashing in sunlight, his superhero hair so black it shines blue—at the happiest moment of his life, dives into the aquamarine chasm of eternity, laughing, joyful, disappearing from sight but etched indelibly in the minds of all who witness and countless others who only hear the tale told and retold up and down the length of the Napa Valley.

This is Death's introduction. This is the beginning of a long, intimate relationship.

<u>10:19:59:58:41</u> A.M.

This is what he knows: The universe is composed mostly of space; the planet is made up mostly of space; all things are composed of particles, which we refer to as atoms; atoms are composed of subatomic particles; between the subatomic particles within the atoms exists a relatively enormous amount of space; the energy that occupies that space is what holds everything in the universe together; this energy "dances" in that space, holding matter—or what we perceive as matter—in certain forms; when the energy dances one step—say, the atomic waltz—the energy is perceived as milk; the same step at a different speed causes us to perceive cream; at yet another speed, we perceive butter; the energy dancing a different step—say, the atomic tango—causes us to perceive the energy as redwood; at yet a different speed, as oak; at a slightly different configuration and speed as rhododendron; and so on.

This energy, which he thinks of as the Energy, is what he believes people are actually referring to when they say the word *God*—or *Allah* or *Buddha* or *Yahweh* or whatever name they have chosen to attach to their concept of the transcendent force in the name of which they worship, fear, idolize, kill, maim, persecute, save, or comfort. It is this Energy he refers to when he refers to It.

It is not, he knows, a person, neither an old bearded man nor a large-breasted woman. It is not a fat, smiling Asian man nor a boy with the head of a jackal.

It is not a thing. It is all things.

It is not a person. It is all persons.

It is not an animal. It is all animals.

It is not a mountain nor a rain cloud nor a lightning bolt. It is all mountains, all rain clouds, the very ionic surge that gives birth to all lightning bolts.

And It—dancing in the space between the subatomic particles of all existence—is all these things at the same time.

It is more complex than any human can comprehend, which is why humans always "picture" or "imagine" It in some concrete form—eagle, grandfatherly man with white beard, infant with halo.

Since It is not just a concrete thing but all concrete things and more, he refers to the Energy as It, with a capital *i*. It transcends gender, species, classification.

He keeps these things mostly to himself. He sees no reason to talk about That which cannot be captured in words.

This is what he knows. He has always known It. Even before he knew.

10:19:59:58:42 A.M.

EG has gone to the Vedanta Temple in San Francisco after requesting a meeting with the swami in charge of the temple, Swami Prabuddhananda. He wants to ask the holy man one question.

EG is kindly ushered into the swami's office by a truly blue-haired woman about 90 years old. Prabuddhananda rises and extends his hand. He is a man of about 60. His head is shaved, and he wears the traditional saffron robes of a Hindu priest. His face is craggy and dark, as though he was born with the scowl of pensiveness and contemplation on his face. When he smiles at EG it is a remarkable transformation. "Sit, please, sir," the swami says in a thick Indian accent, his consonants clicking, the words more sung than spoken. "Tell me about yourself. I have seen you at many of the lectures here at the Temple. Tell me why you have come."

For almost an hour EG tells the swami about his life, about his work, everything he can squeeze into an hour. The swami listens attentively, his hands folded across his saffron-draped belly. Finally EG says, "But, sir, there is a particular question I came to ask you."

"Ask me, then, please. Ask away."

"I see God everywhere. I am aware of God's presence most of the day. But there is one place I cannot find God and that is in suffering and pain. Almost all my friends and acquaintances are dead from this horrible Plague. I watch them die in front of me. I hold their hands, feed them their meals, bathe their bodies, and watch their horrible suffering. It's not that I believe God is not present when suffering and pain exist, but I lose God there. How can I see God in these places? How can I see God in pain and suffering, particularly my own? When I am in pain, how can I see God?"

The swami looks hard at EG, deep into his eyes, deep inside of him, as though he is trying to discern if EG will hear what he is about to say. Then the swami says quite matter-of-factly, "It is not enough to see God everywhere. You must experience God everywhere, in everything. Until you experience your life as God, experience everything as God, then you do not know God."

That is it. The swami stands, looks at EG with compassion, extends his hand, and gestures toward the door. "Come see me anytime. You are always welcome here. And be sure to visit our retreat across the bay. Go there. I tell you, go there."

Later, in Anchor Bay, EG thinks of all this as he walks the drive through the redwoods and madrones, surrounded by manzanitas with their tiny bellflowers hanging in the spring light. He thinks of how his spiritual life has taken on the words of Prabuddhananda, of how often he now experiences every thing, every action, every molecule of existence, and every thought and feeling as the Self, It, the incomprehensible God. He reminds himself, however, that realization is not liberation.

He also thinks now of Jesus, of how difficult it must have been for him to carry on his life with such awareness in his mind, watching the world around him miss the mark. How could Christ hope to contradict the popular notion that God was "up there" somewhere watching, waiting for "his people" to do something wrong so that he could smite them or do something right so that he could reward them, like laboratory rats?

EG thinks of how many people move about thinking that It is "out there" somewhere. How difficult it must have been for Jesus to hang on the cross after only three years of lecturing and know that not only was his message not welcome and not heard by most but also that it was so offensive, so threatening, he was labeled a subversive and put to death.

EG thinks that simply carrying out his own spiritual practice, alone in the woods at Anchor Bay, above the sea, beneath the blue, blue sky, surrounded by the sentient trees, is quite enough for him. Like Jesus' mother, EG thinks it wisest to simply keep these things to himself and ponder them in his heart. He will try to experience even thinking of these things as It. He says aloud, "Even thinking about thinking about It is It." EG laughs at the sensation that comes with the last thought and then laughs harder as he realizes that the awareness of the sensation and the resulting laughter is also It.

10:19:59:58:43 A.M.

He counts the medications he takes: three antiretrovirals, eight antioxidants, one antibiotic, one antibacterial, one psychotropic, one opiate-derivative, three anti-inflammatories, one experimental suspension, and one experimental thymus subcutaneous injection.

Five white pills, three red, two orange, two blue, three pink, three beige. One fizzing drink. One clear serum. And, of course, first and foremost, the banana, without which they all come hurling back up within 15 minutes.

And these are just the morning pills.

10:19:59:58:44 A.M.

It has been three years since Andre's death. EG has had one disastrous love affair after another and has finally come to accept that he has had the one great love of his life and there won't be another. *Don't whine. A lot of people never have even one true love,* he tells himself as he lies on the weight bench at the gym.

"Are you going to use these?" someone asks from the foot of the bench. EG raises his head and looks toward his feet. Standing over him is a handsome brown-skinned man with black hair, large brown eyes, and a mustache.

"Use what?" EG asks, annoyed at having been interrupted.

"These weights here," the fellow says, kicking at two 20-pound dumbbells on the floor.

"I didn't even know they were there. They aren't mine," EG says, and goes back to his exercise.

Just as he is about to lift the barbell over his head, the guy says, "Why do you have on two different-colored shoelaces?"

EG hooks the barbell back in the bench rack and leans up on his elbows. He raises his feet so that he can examine his shoelaces. One lace is bright red and the other is neon blue. "Because," he answers belligerently.

"Because why?" This guy doesn't give in.

"Just because. I like blue and I like red. Why choose if you don't have to? Why not have both?"

"Oh," the man says, rubbing his chin. He picks up the dumbbells, turns, and walks away.

EG watches him. He's wearing baggy sweatpants and a gray tank top. He has a full, well-developed, but not overly developed, body. He's about 5 feet 6 inches tall and his eyes sparkle. EG thinks he could get interested in this guy, but he has two rules he never breaks: Don't date men from the gym where you work out. Don't date people in the office where you work. *Besides, the hair under his arms is too dark*, EG tells himself as he watches the guy doing military presses.

For the next two weeks, every time EG goes to the gym so does the young man, whose name, EG has learned, is Paul. And he continues to engage EG.

"Where'd you get that shirt?" he asks EG in the middle of squats.

"I made it when my late partner died," EG says, thinking that will discourage him from asking any more questions.

"Oh…I'm sorry," he says with sincerity. "What does it mean?"

EG sets down the barbell. "It's a heart floating in the ocean. It's how I feel—a heart adrift. Get it?" EG says all this matter-of-factly and with even a bit of disdain, hoping to discourage the guy from further disturbance of his workout, but Paul is moved. He is staring at the red heart painted on the blue wave, and EG thinks he sees his eyes tearing up.

Paul looks up at him, "I lost my partner too. Last August."

Suddenly all of EG's defenses are shattered. They connect in a place where there are no charades, no games, no lies: the Field of Loss. "I'm sorry," EG says. "I know how tough that is."

"I can tell that by your shirt. I knew there was something about you that was different," Paul says and walks away.

Now Paul brings him things. They are obviously on the same gym schedule, so they see each other three times a week. Paul brings him paperbacks, recorded books, articles from esoteric magazines.

"Have you read *The Tibetan Book of the Dead?*" Paul asks in the locker room as they dress.

EG is more interested in catching a glimpse of Paul's butt than his reading list, but he tries to be discreet. "No, I've never read it," he answers, as he stuffs his sweat shirt into his gym bag.

"Here," Paul says cheerfully, handing him two tape cassettes. "It's read by Richard Gere. I think you'll like it."

"Gee, thanks," EG mutters, adding the tapes to the others that Paul has given him but which have never left the side compartment of his gym bag.

A week later Paul comes up to him on the workout floor and begins a lengthy conversation about Tibetan Buddhism and anger.

"Look," EG interrupts, breaking one of his cardinal rules, "why don't we have dinner some time and talk about this stuff? That way, we can get our workouts done." So they meet for dinner the following Friday at a Chinese restaurant not far from EG's house. The entire meal is spent discussing boyfriend problems Paul is having with someone named Leo.

Leo was an emotional support volunteer for Paul's late partner, Rick, during Rick's illness. After Rick died Leo saw a good thing and began to work the possibilities—at least that's how EG interprets Paul's story. Before long Leo had moved in

with Paul, and Paul was practically supporting him, even flying him back and forth to Oregon to visit his family.

It is clear to EG that Paul is an innocent—despite his obvious intelligence. He can discuss the most esoteric points of
Eastern theology and philosophy, but he hasn't a clue as to
the sophisticated psychological wiles of unscrupulous people.
Having come from Guam, an island community where people
live with greater intimacy, as well as greater dependency, Paul
has come to trust people, to take what they say and do at face
value. He believes that people are basically as honest and virtuous as he is. EG is intrigued and astounded that anyone can
be trusting and open—and so brilliant, a quality he hasn't
found in anyone since Andre.

But here in this restaurant, talking for two hours about Leo
has been a bit much. EG brings the conversation to a close,
and they pay the bill and walk to Paul's car. "So where do you
live?" EG asks, as Paul slips the key in the car door.

"Church and 26th."

"We're practically neighbors," EG says. "I'm at Church
and 19th."

"So will you be at the gym tomorrow?" Paul asks, slipping
in behind the wheel.

"Yeah, it's my regular day."

"Good, I'll see you there. Thanks again for dinner. I had a
really good time." And with that, Paul pulls his car away from
the curb, leaving EG to walk home.

"That's it," EG tells his house mate, Ron, as he pours each
of them a cup of coffee the next morning. "He spent the entire evening talking about his horrible boyfriend and how
badly he gets treated by him, and then he didn't even give me
a ride home. This guy's certifiable."

"Maybe he's shy," Ron offers.

"Maybe monkeys'll fly out of my ass," EG replies, as he goes into the kitchen to answer the phone. It's Paul and he's upset, somewhere between rage and tears.

"Calm down first," EG says, not wanting to talk to him in the first place. "What happened? Start from the beginning."

"I talked to him last night after I got back from our dinner. He's in Portland, remember? Well, he never called at the time he said he would, so when I got home I called him. First, he's drunk when he answers, which really pisses me off. Then, when I confront him about not calling at the appointed time, he starts saying I expect too much of him and that it's just a phone call and what was I so bent out of shape about?"

"So what did you say to that?" EG is rolling his eyes at Ron now.

"He says if I'm so upset maybe I shouldn't move up there after all."

"Move to Portland? I didn't know you were moving to Portland. You never said that." EG is taken aback.

"I didn't mention it because I was beginning to have doubts about it being such a good idea. I've already given notice at work, and I'm supposed to be out of the apartment by the end of the month.

"Whoa. Wait a minute here. You're going to move to Portland to be with someone who treats you like shit? I'm sorry, but this is the point where I have to say some things."

"Like what?"

"Like first of all, how long have you known this guy? About a year and a half?"

"About five months. I know it's not all that long, but I've been reminding myself that I only knew Rick for a few days before we moved in together, and that relationship lasted ten years."

"But I thought you met Leo just before Rick died?" EG asks, puzzled.

"That's right. I met him in June, and Rick died in August," Paul explains.

"August of this year!?"

"Yeah."

EG slaps his head with the palm of his hand. "I thought Rick died a year ago August. Are you telling me he died this August?"

Yeah. August 13th.

"This August. As in August, September, October, November 10th, which is today."

"Right, what'd you think?" Paul asks.

"I thought it was a year ago August. No wonder you're so flaky," EG exclaims and laughs out loud.

Ron has taken a seat at the kitchen table and is reading the morning newspaper.

"What do you mean, 'flaky'?"

"Look, I'll level with you. I thought you were nuts. We meet at the gym, I make it clear I don't want to be bothered, yet you talk to me every chance you get. You're dating some asshole who keeps insulting and ignoring you, yet you keep seeing him. We go to dinner, which I thought was pretty much a date to sniff each other out, and you spend the entire evening talking about this jerk you've been seeing and all the trouble you're having with him. Then to top it all off, you don't even offer me a ride home afterward. I thought you were nuts. Now it all makes sense. You're still in mourning. In fact, you're probably still in shock."

"You think?" Paul says meekly.

"I know. I've seen it dozens of times, and I've been there myself. First of all, dump this asshole. He's broken every professional rule in the book by even dating you after he came to take care of Rick. What the fuck kind of ethics does he have anyway? Answer me a personal question. Did you help him get up to Oregon?

"Well, I paid for his airline ticket if that's what you mean," Paul says.

"Jesus! He's taking you for a major ride. He's seen a meal ticket in you. That's probably why he became a volunteer in the first place. And another thing, it seems perfectly obvious to me that the two of you simply aren't compatible. From what you've told me, he only likes to drink and dance. Does he read philosophy?"

"No."

"Does he go to Mass with you every Sunday?"

"No."

"Does he read things like *The Tibetan Book of the Dead?*"

"No."

"Then what the hell are you doing with him? I'll tell you: You're in shock at Rick's death, so you're acting crazy. Dump this guy. You have nothing in common."

"God, that's it. We're incompatible. I never thought of that. We're incompatible."

"You poor kid. You've got to slow down. Take your time with this. It takes a while."

"You're right. We're incompatible," Paul says.

"Answer me something. Why didn't you give me a ride home last night?"

Paul pauses a moment on the other end of the line. "Because I'm not ready to have sex with you."

"What?"

"Every date I've had in the past two months has ended up with people wanting sex, and whenever I've given in I've felt horrible afterward. I like you and want to keep seeing you, so I don't want to have sex. I was afraid it would just get uncomfortable when we said good night and I didn't invite you to spend the night or something."

"All I wanted was a ride home, for chrissake."

"Sorry. I wasn't taking any chances at fucking this up. You're the first person I've met I can talk to. Do you want to come over? I could put on some coffee?"

There is a moment of silence before EG answers. "Yeah, but only if you'll let me fuck you." There is another moment of silence and EG says, "Just kidding, just kidding. I'll be there in a few minutes."

"You like this guy. I can tell," Ron says when EG hangs up.

"You know, I think I do. I sure didn't at first, but now I think I do."

Ron gets up and shuffles toward his room. "I'll start moving the furniture."

"Why?" EG calls after him.

"Well, I'm sure he's not going to sell his furniture when he moves in."

"Ha, ha," EG shouts. "Very funny."

By Christmas week EG is half-crazy. Paul won't have sex with him, yet they've spent nearly every evening together. They spend the evening cuddling and making out, and just when EG goes to make a move, suddenly Paul has to go home because he has to get up for work or he needs his sleep or some other lame excuse. EG lies awake night after night aching for him.

This is the third night he has been awake at 5 A.M. He gets up and drives to Paul's apartment, without even bothering to change out of his pajamas, and bangs on the door. A light appears in the hallway, and a few moments later the door opens. Paul is gathering a bathrobe around him, running his fingers through his hair, as though that would make him presentable.

"You have to marry me," EG demands, hands on hips. "Or else at least have sex with me. Better yet, do both. I love you."

Paul is trying not to smile too broadly as he takes in the sight of his fiancé, who is standing in the doorway in his blue-and white-striped pajamas. He is wearing slippers that must be ten years old. Paul cannot help but think of Bette Davis in *All About Eve*, saying she's going to get married in something simple, a fur coat over a nightgown.

"OK."

"What?"

"I said OK."

"OK, what?"

"OK, I'll marry you."

"You will?"

"Of course."

"What about the other?"

"What other?"

"The having sex part."

"When it's time."

"God, you're difficult."

"You wouldn't have it any other way."

10:19:59:58:45 A.M.

EG must tell The Boy he is dying. It wouldn't be fair not to prepare him. He must tell everyone. But how? He decides to go to Italy to think about it. He calls his friend Helen. She says, "Come to Rome. Go to the farm in Castelfranco di Sopra. Spend as much time as you like." She is very generous.

In Rome he sees all there is to see. Helen has gone to the United States to visit her mother, so he stays in her apartment in the Campo dei Fiori. He walks the streets of Rome for the first four days without sleeping, eating gelato and pizza *porta via*, surviving on his own body tissue rather than caloric intake. Within four days he has lost ten pounds. He feels terrific, energized, sensual.

He visits the Corso and buys new clothes. Next he books himself into the Hotel Luna on the isle of Capri for a day. It is so luxurious lying by the pool overlooking the Adriatic, he stays for several days. He meets American tourists from Los Angeles, San Francisco, and New York. They party together in the piazza. It is the feast of San Costanzo, the island's patron. There are fireworks everywhere and bands and talent shows in the piazza. People dance in the streets. When the *fèsta* finally winds down in the wee hours, he saunters back to the hotel, down the garden path beneath the pergola. In the shadows on the lawn, a couple make love; near the oak tree two men are kissing; on the hotel porch an old woman shoos her grandson inside, scolding him for being up so late, "*Più tardi*, Angelo, *più tardi.*"

From his balcony he sees the sun begin to rise. Three streets over, winding down the hill toward the boat dock, four men carry a bier covered with black crepe. A widow in black and her family follow behind. One of them is a small boy dressed in a black shirt and black shorts. He is looking around confused. Where is his cat? Why are they carrying his father to the boat dock? Why has he been pulled from his bed so early and dressed in black clothes? Why couldn't he go to the *fèsta* last night for San Costanzo?

EG closes the shutters and takes off his clothes. He looks at his body in the mirror. He wants to make love, to have sex. He wants to live. He does not want to confront The Boy. He falls asleep with the sun glaring off the Adriatic Sea, ricocheting through the slats of his shutters onto the red tile floors.

He opens his eyes. The shutters are dark again. From the balcony he hears the ocean on the cliffs below, sees the stars burning above him. In the garden below a woman in a white gown disappears down one of the paths. He dresses hurriedly and follows her. Down winding paths, through beds of zucchini, tomatoes, lettuce, beneath pergola vines heavy with pungent purple grapes, through arches of trumpet vine and passion flower, he winds his way until he comes to a tiny clearing. On the other side is a cave. He goes toward the cave, trying to see what is inside. He knows whatever it is he must have it. As he approaches the cave's dark open mouth, he looks up. On a ledge above the cave, the woman in the white gown carries a lantern. She is old, and her white hair cascades down her back. EG falls backward a few steps. She passes above the opening of the cave and disappears into the vines that cover the hillside above the cave. He steps toward the cave once more to attempt to retrieve the contents. There is a deep growl from within, but he is not afraid. He knows that eventually what is in there will be his. Whatever the beast is that guards this den of darkness, one day it will allow him to enter, for EG is never afraid of animals.

He opens his eyes. The shutters are still dark. From the balcony he hears the ocean on the cliffs below, sees the stars above. He packs and leaves the island on the first boat back to Naples. He is back in Rome by noon. He goes immediately to bed, closing the shutters, putting in earplugs to drown out the noises of playing children and screaming women in the *vicolo* below.

EG is walking down rickety stairs to an alley along a canal. It is Venice. He turns and looks up. There is an arched bridge above him and his father is standing at the top of it next to the railing. Clete is wearing a pea jacket and smoking a cigarette.

EG looks up once more and then walks on, realizing it is the last time he will ever see his father, because he can never again allow himself to be subjected to this man's hatred and abuse.

When he wakes, it is night. He has now caught up on the sleep that eluded him for a week in the excitement of this new country. Now that he is rested he is also energized again. He dresses—not in any of the clothes of this country, but, he decides, for the purpose in mind he will dress in his American Levi's, T-shirt, and tennis shoes.

He knows as he stands before the mirror brushing his hair that she is sitting on the edge of the tub watching him. Of course she would follow him to Italy. It hadn't occurred to him that she would. He pretends she isn't there, but they both know it is just pretense. He walks out without even glancing at her. He walks down the five flights of stairs rather than taking the elevator. He can tell by the sounds coming from behind the doors of the other apartments and the way people are dressed in the hallway that it is past the dinner hour.

He steps into the courtyard and breathes in the warm Roman night. Sounds of music and laughter, conversation, *vespas* beeping and sputtering rise out of the *campo* and the surrounding streets. He turns the corner and, of course, she is waiting for him near the *gelateria*, the strap of her black slip sliding down her arm. Her raven hair falls to her shoulders unbrushed but not unkempt. Her eyes, like silver roses, reflect the bright lights of the ice-cream parlor. She is laughing. *Buòna nòtte, caro*, she whispers as he passes. Her breasts press against the black lace, full, white, irresistible. *Buòna fortuna, caro mìo*.

He walks the long hike to the Vìa Venèzia, around the monument to Victor Emmanuel, and begins the climb up Mónte Caprino. He wends his way among the huge oak trees, the Italian Stone Pines, up, up to the top, where, among the empty stone buildings used to restore unearthed ancient statuary, he looks out over the city. St. Peter's, across the river, blinks dark as the lights on its dome are extinguished: midnight.

Directly below him, Fiats and Ferarris careen around the base of the hill. Couples, arm in arm, sit on the ancient stone walls surrounding the monument to Italy's unifier. Young toughs shout at tourists and laugh. A thousand *vespas* beep and sputter around the circuses that dot the city, the fumes from their tiny motors visible as they rise into the still night air. All around him, men walk the paths of Mónte Caprino, nervous, quickly glancing this way and that.

He begins to meander through the trees. Soon enough, a young man is following him. He turns right or left depending on which way is darker, which path seems more overgrown. At last he comes to a dead end: a stone wall that rises up to the very top of the hill, where tourists can view the city. He stops, turns around, leans against the wall. The dark stone is cold, even in the warmth of the summer night.

Now the boy is visible. He is young, dressed in running clothes. His dark hair shines in the night. He steps up, leans forward, kisses EG on the lips. He sighs as their lips touch. He presses tightly against EG's chest, taking EG's hands and sliding them around so that they are resting on his buttocks, an invitation. He throws back his head and sighs, lowers himself, takes EG fully into his mouth.

EG rests his head against the wall, keeping his eyes closed. She is there, standing beside him. She kisses him on the cheek, the lips, his closed eyes, rubbing her breasts against him, pushing his face into the cleavage. She laughs as she does this, a low, throaty laugh. "*Ti amo, caro*," she whispers. "*Ti amo.*"

He looks down, watches the boy empty himself onto EG's left shoe as he releases himself into the boy's mouth. The boy smiles, looks up, opens his mouth, revealing his tongue, white with EG's release. EG smiles.

They dress themselves in silence, the boy walking away first. EG, however, isn't ready to go home. Before he can plan his next move, another man takes the boy's place, a large, furry man, taller than EG. The man puts his hands on EG's shoulders and pushes him roughly to his knees, forces himself into EG's mouth. He is huge and uncut, the largest man he has ever seen. The man is heavy, his stomach round and protruding slightly; his thighs seem as large as EG's waist. He smells of rose water, as though he has just bathed. EG comes again, this time spilling himself on the rich Roman soil of Mónte Caprino. Above them a group of tourists has reached the top of the hill and is gathering at the wall's ledge to take in the lights of the Eternal City. They stand less than 20 feet above EG and his anonymous consort. EG can see their heads craning out over the wall's edge. A woman's voice can be heard above everyone else's. She is American. "This is it," she exclaims. "This is what I came to Rome to see. Is that an archangel on the bridge over there?"

"*Vengo, vengo,*" the man moans loudly as he ejaculates into EG's mouth. "*Ai, vengo.*"

"Is there someone down there?" the American woman asks. "Are you all right?" She is leaning over the edge of the wall, shielding her eyes from the bright lights of the surrounding city. The man laughs, pulls up his trousers, and disappears into the brush. EG flattens himself against the wall.

"I thought I heard someone calling," the woman says to the others in her party. Soon a gaggle of other tourists joins the woman, leans over, and peers into the dark.

Now she presses herself against EG, her black silk slip sliding against the bare skin of his chest. She kisses him deeply, relieving him of the contents of his mouth. She turns her head and spits it onto the ground. Kisses him again more tenderly, adjusts the strap on her left arm, slaps his face hard ,and laughs. "*Grazie, caro*," she says. "*L'uomo gentile*."

As he descends Mónte Caprino to the Vìa Venèzia, he finds The Boy stumbling behind, trying to keep up with him. EG smiles, extends his hand. "Are you happy?" he asks, taking The Boy's tiny fingers into his. They both smile. "I didn't forget you, really," he tells The Boy. "I just had to take care of Anna, or she would have been mad at us, and you know what happens when she gets really angry. Do you know what they call Rome?" he asks The Boy.

"What?"

"The Eternal City."

"How come?"

"Because it will always be here. Forever."

"Like you and me," The Boy says.

"Like you and me," EG replies. They walk for a few minutes in silence, then EG looks down at the child. "I have something to tell you," he says.

"I know."

"You know?"

"Uh-huh."

"You know I have something to tell you, or you know what it is?"

"Both."

"Are you scared?"

"Are you?"

"Probably. Are you?"

"Maybe. But it's OK."

"How can it be OK?" EG asks, perplexed by The Boy's calm.

The Boy thinks for a few moments before answering. "Because we're like Rome," he finally says.

"Like Rome? "

"We're forever. You said so yourself."

"You're very brave, you know. And I love you very much."

"I love you too." They walk a little farther along the Vìa Argentina. It is late, but the street is alive with people strolling arm in arm, laughing out of windows, singing in trattorie to the wheezes of concertinas. "I'm glad you came to Italy," The Boy says. "I like it here."

"So do I."

Hand in hand, mòda Italiana, they walk back to the Campo déi Fiori, calm, yet stirred by the warm Roman morning about to break over the hills across the Tiber.

10:19:59:58:46 A.M.

EG has come to Anchor Bay with Hari. Paul is angry and depressed and won't come to the house for reasons he cannot or will not articulate. Although EG and Paul have not had a falling out, something has happened. Paul has begun to drift away and EG feels alone, desolate, as though some wide breach, some irreconcilable difference has isolated him on a lonely island.

As EG turns the truck onto the dirt road that winds to the house, he is acutely aware that Paul is not sitting beside him. He breaks into tears and stops the truck to let it flood forth.

This is what has happened: nothing that can be seen, nothing one could touch; it is like having a demonic cadaver float to the surface of the Sea of Unconscious. It can be smelled, but only by certain animals—cats, dogs, lovers. EG thinks that it is more like an emotional unraveling. It can only be felt in the heart, in nerve endings, on the outermost edges of the soul, where there is a fraying, a ragged edge, like flesh caught in the blade of a saw.

If it were placed beneath an emotional microscope, it would appear like the outer envelope of the virus that floats in their blood streams. Just as the virus is a foreign agent unraveling the fabric of corporeal life as it courses through their bodies, this invisible thing also unravels their emotional and spiritual bodies. Mostly it stays frayed—jagged yet whole. But once in a while, for no readily apparent reason, it unravels slowly, thread by emotional thread, snagged on a gesture, a thought, an oxygen-free radical feeling that has broken loose upstream near the heart and comes tearing through, ramming into whatever is in its path.

Once the unraveling has begun no one can predict when it will stop. Like the dormant virus that may suddenly awaken— frenetically multiplying, infecting other cells, eating nerve endings—this unraveling of the carpet of spiritual and emotional cohesion occurs without warning.

And just as the virus will inexplicably go dormant again for who knows what reason—prayer, rest, the right combination of drugs and supplements—so too will the emotional unraveling respond at various times to equally mysterious appeals: flowers, an outstretched hand, silence, the warm coat of the dog's hide, a kiss on the back of the neck. Sometimes simply silence will heal the wound. Silence and solitude. Going away. Parting when everything inside is shouting to cling fast to one another. Only darkness defines the light.

And so EG is here in the truck on the dirt road leading up to the house at Anchor Bay, weeping, with Hari standing behind the front seat now, poking his long snout into EG's face, softly whining and lapping at the tears, trying to drink up his master's sorrow, trying, perhaps, to take it from him.

Whatever demons are raging inside Paul, EG tells himself, *I cannot battle them from the outside. In fact, more times than not, it only makes things worse, for surely I represent—externally— many of the internal forces lurking in his darkest shadow.*

And so the most peaceful, loving act EG can perform right now is not to act at all. His absence is all that is required.

Alone on the crest of the coastal mountains, overlooking the ocean, EG must be aware of his own shadow figures, of his own inner forms. He must strive in his exile at Anchor Bay to stay calm, stay in the eye of the storm. He must keep The Boy close, must keep The Boy safe.

But, of course, they descend on the house almost before he has unpacked his things. They have heard of the crisis on Church Street and have rushed en masse to EG's side. They can hardly wait to dig in. The Boy immediately goes outside and disappears beneath the deck; the others busy themselves in other parts of the house, waiting their turn to offer their advice to EG.

"What did you do this time?" Clete asks, rifling through the refrigerator.

"There's no beer in there," EG says smugly. "I did nothing."

"Well, that's probably what it was then," Annabel offers, lighting a Pall Mall while she waits for the coffee to percolate. "You need to be more affectionate. Touch more. Little kisses in passing, for no apparent reason. When was the last time you sent flowers?"

"Mush," Clete says, closing the refrigerator door and heading for the pantry. "Flowers—what a bunch of corn!"

EG turns and walks out onto the deck leaving them to argue among themselves in the kitchen. On the deck he finds AD, the 13-year-old, smoking one of Annabel's Pall Malls, staring out at the ocean. He turns and gives EG a pained expression. "Don't look to me for any suggestions," he says to EG. "I'm too fat and geeky for anyone to love me or even to have sex with, so I have absolutely zero experience in the relationship department. No advice here."

"I'm not asking for any," EG says. "In fact, I came here to be alone."

"They'll go away eventually," AD offers. "As soon as they've picked your bones clean." With that he descends the steps and ambles off in the direction of the Bell Path.

EG steps back inside and shouts at the top of his voice. "Out! Get out now!"

"But…" Annabel begins.

EG closes his eyes, clenches his fists, as though to muster all his physical and emotional strength, and screams, "*Get—out—now!*"

When EG opens his eyes, only The Boy is there, sitting in the middle of the long sofa. "Did you like that?" EG asks.

The Boy giggles. "That worked good."

EG goes to the sofa, sits next to The Boy, and holds him close. "Do you know how much I love you?" he asks.

"I think so, but tell me anyway."

"I love you as much as the universe."

"How much is that?"

"A hundred million 44 skyzillion pounds."

The Boy giggles more loudly. EG begins to tickle him, and the two of them wrestle on the sofa until Hari comes bounding up in fit of jealousy. Then the three of them lie in one another's arms, The Boy falling asleep as the sun sets over the Pacific.

Watching The Boy sleep causes EG to miss Paul even more. Is the pain of separation his own pain? Or is it Paul's pain that he is carrying? And if it should be Paul's sorrow and not his own, is it a pain that Paul is aware of and asking EG to carry, or is it a sorrow deeper than that, which EG wrests from him before Paul can feel it himself?

Perhaps it is sorrow in anticipation of the ultimate separation that will befall the survivor when one of them dies. They both have such fears. In that case it might be EG's projection onto Paul of his own fear, which he in turn takes upon himself, lest Paul buckle beneath the anxiety.

EG chuckles at his complex analysis, remembering a proverb his friend Robert likes to cite:

> The simple man comes home in the evening
> wondering what's for dinner;
> the complex man comes home in the evening
> pondering the imponderables of fate;
> the enlightened man comes home in the
> evening wondering what's for dinner.

Try to rest, EG says to himself, curling up next to The Boy. *You really do think too much.* When he wakes, EG will feel no more settled, no less lonely, but he will not be plagued by voices. He and The Boy will wait for Paul to telephone and say it's time to come home. In the meanwhile, he and The Boy have one another.

10:19:59:58:47 A.M.

There are periods when the time is never just right. Fatigue. Conflicting schedules. Moods. Anna paces like a caged panther. EG goes to the beach, walks through the cedars and cypress past the piñons, down the dunes into the thick junipers. A young man appears, lolling near the rocks. He is boyish, slender; his hair is the color of sand. He removes his shirt, leans against a sun-bathed rock. His trousers are cut off at mid thigh. His eyes are closed. He is waiting.

The panther paces faster in her cage, licks her lips, squints her eyes.

EG approaches the boy slowly, diffidently, looking straight ahead as he comes down the hill to stand near the rock. The boy opens his eyes. EG smiles and nods. The boy closes his eyes and rests his head against the rock, taking in the sun.

EG moves closer, stands so close he can see the boy's pulse throbbing in the blue vein that hides just beneath the smooth, translucent olive skin of the boy's neck. EG reaches out, so slowly that a gull flies the length of the visible horizon before EG's fingers come softly to rest on the boy's brown belly.

He gently brushes the golden down between the boy's navel and the elastic band of the white briefs that rise above the waistline of his shorts. The boy arches his back and parts his lips, keeping, the entire time, his green eyes closed against the warm sun, the scorching fingertips.

Without a word EG is commanded to his knees and he obeys. The boy's hands remain at his side, pressed against the rock, one hand holding the white T-shirt he has so innocently, but so deliberately, removed to better take in the sun's warmth and the heat radiating from the rock.

The boy's shorts are unbuttoned, and the zipper slides down so easily, so noiselessly it seems phantom-like. *Perhaps*, EG thinks, *this is not happening at all. Perhaps I am still home in bed, asleep in dream. Perhaps the gull's cries are the whimpers of the dog at the bedroom door, waiting impatiently for his morning walk; the heat of the sun on my neck is actually my lover breathing in his sleep; the crash of the surf below us is only water running in a distant room.*

As the boy sighs, sliding through EG's parted lips, EG gives himself to the moment, in whichever world it exists. The boy releases himself into EG's mouth without warning, groaning and making a laughlike gurgling sound. EG, spent at the same

moment, wakes into the scene as though time had been edit-
ed and spliced back together, minutes removed. There, climbing the hill above him, a young man, shirtless, looking back,
blows him a kiss. Here below he hears the soft sound of a gentle tide ebbing along the shore.

He detects the faint scent of pine wafting on the gentle breeze,
as though the trees were anointing his path with incense. And, although he does not understand it to the point of articulation, he
experiences It in all that has transpired in the dreamlike state. All
time became timeless, the minutes, even hours of the morning all
present in this single moment—all force, all motion, all energy,
pulsating in him, about him, through him in a single beat.

The cry of the birds are like one pulse beat in his ears; the
musky smell of sweat mingles with the light scent of pine
along the trail; the movement of thick, veined flesh along his
tongue is indistinguishable from the warm kiss of the sun on
his cheek; the lingering taste at the back of this throat is no
different from the perspiration trickling down his upper lip;
the glare of the sun off the pyrocanthus appears identical to
the beam from the panther's golden eye.

As he unlocks the door to his car, a woman laughs somewhere behind him. He does not turn to see her, but for a second his hand hesitates, the nape of his neck chills. He must
remember to stop on the way home to buy flowers. Perhaps
that was all she wanted in the first place.

10:19:59:58:48 A.M.

The Boy's life turns into one long nervous wait. He watches his body change and discovers that he too wants to pene-
trate things. He too wants control, even at such a young age.
He knows it is a matter of time only.

While he is waiting for this change to occur, AD simply appears. The Boy rises one morning, goes to the bathroom mirror to wash his face and get ready for school, and he discovers he is no longer himself. The Boy is gone, and AD is there in his place—overweight, pimply, sprouting pubic hair and the beginnings of a beard.

It isn't at all what The Boy had imagined, not anything that he had hoped for. He doesn't look like Sal Mineo or James Dean or Bruce Springsteen. He doesn't have a body like any of the boys in gym class; his Levi's don't bulge in the crotch. His waist curves out instead of in, his arms are straight lines, his chin structureless.

But his sense of aesthetics is already developing, so he knows what he is, he knows what he isn't, and he knows what he wants to be. But he hasn't a clue how to make that happen, and it is what he wants to be that draws him: the biceps he pines for, the 28-inch waist he never had, the rippled abdomen he runs his fingers over in magazine ads. He wants all these for himself, longs to wake one morning to find himself looking out from a long, lean, even lanky body. But that does not happen.

When it is clear that such a miracle will not occur, he finds himself longing to touch what he cannot possess for his own. He falls in love with boys who look the way he wants to look, who possess the self-assurance, the swagger, the raw masculine energy that eludes both his understanding and his experience.

Since beauty is not an available resource, he relies on wit, intelligence and his friends' raging hormones to satisfy his forbidden secret hunger. Much to his surprise, everyone accommodates him, from the captain of the football team to the decathlon champion, from his best friend to the new boy in school. Everyone wants to reach orgasm, and AD—over-achiever that he has become in his adolescence—guiltily, but willingly, assists.

What does it matter that he will burn in hell? What does it matter about his reputation? What does it matter that they might talk about him, call him "queer?" Too grotesque, he thinks, to draw people to him physically, he lures them through talent and cleverness, cunning and charm. He is the most popular teenager in high school. And he's swallowed the semen of nearly every boy in his class.

He always has a girlfriend, and always she is a cheerleader, wins the contest for homecoming queen, or holds a class office. His circle of friends comprises the A-list of the school's athletic teams and social clubs. AD is the kid to know in Benicia High. He even runs for student body president and wins by a landslide. But why? He hasn't a clue. All he knows is that people like him.

The teachers, even when they aren't especially fond of him, find him intriguing. AD is a challenge: superior intellect, creative mind, and a better-than-average vocabulary. Most of his teachers bore him, however, and so does the material they teach. He hungers for creative arts. He excels at drama and writing, barely manages a D-minus in chemistry and biology. He is wittier than the faculty, more precocious than the valedictorian, more melancholy than the homeliest girl in junior year. His teachers engage him, and most of them fear him. He knows which ones "have it" and which ones don't.

The girls flock to him because he treats them with respect. He doesn't try to fuck them or feel them up when they're alone. They assume it's because he has his own steady girlfriend. They confide in him, seek counsel with their love dilemmas, and ask when he'll be studying in the library and if they could discuss something with him—an unreasonable parent, a boy who doesn't take notice, a traitorous girlfriend.

AD is always available, always willing to give of himself to the female sex, alert to everything they say, for they tell him in words and nuance, what the power of the feminine energy really is and how they use it to get what they want. He relates to them emotionally: longing and searching for that elusive sense of completion, seeing the missing parts of himself in the boys around him, feeling even more incomplete after giving in to sex, like having made it to the archery finals and in the last competition missing the target completely. Eros aiming his bow at the genitals, not the heart.

AD understands the boys least of all. He can't figure out what they want. And this puzzlement is at the root of his disorientation. The questions that haunt him are what enlists him psychologically in the army of women: What do these men want from me? How can I make them love me? What will win their approval?

AD rides high on the wave of popularity he enjoys among his male comrades. He double-dates on Fridays to the drive-in movies, where each couple takes turns in the backseat, and on Saturdays drives out to the lake with a buddy to share a case of beer, walk in the moonlight, and talk of the upcoming game and what's wrong with the teachers. Finally, when small talk has wound down to silence, they come—one by one—to the real reason they are there, as AD lays his head in lap after lap, taking into his body the potent elixir of all he feels missing within himself.

He presses his face to the soft white cotton briefs, warm, musky skin, and gentle, downy fur, wherein lies the magic cobra waiting to be aroused by the music of AD's sweet throat. They rise, one after another, from their brown, black, and red nests, ascend amid a warm scent vaguely familiar but new each time all over again. AD makes them dance rhythmically, these one-eyed snakes, bobbing and leaping, plunging and straining, releasing their sweet venom hot and stinging into his worshiping mouth, onto his prayerful tongue. Over and over the seed of manhood is planted within him in ritual after ritual of masculine sowing, but each time it falls on rock or dry soil or is plucked away by the jet black ravens of trickery and despair.

So AD begins his long grail quest for manhood, armed like Parsifal with the armor of his intellect, the sword of wit, the steed of determination, and, alas, the wrong question. He will search for dozens of years until one of these slippery adders, one of these dancing cobras, finds its mark and fills him with the deadly answer to all his problems: the poisonous virus that brings EG to where all paths converge: the tree of nails, the bodhi bush, the throne of the Fisher King. Here, in the arms of Death, watching Cohen's hands peel the reddest and juiciest of apples, he will have one more chance to get it right, one last opportunity to see beneath the shimmering surface of reflective light, and step, however tentatively, into and past the reflection in the cobra's black eyes.

But now, here before the bathroom mirror, staring into the face of a fat, pimply teenager, all he can do is lock the door, open the JC Penney catalogue to the underwear pages, and masturbate into the sink. It may not be the answer, and it may leave him ridden with guilt when it's over, but while he is gushing streams of semen onto the white porcelain, stained red by Annabel's henna rinse, it distracts him from the pain. And at 13 that's all that matters.

10:19:59:58:49 A.M.

The Boy is confused and frightened. AD is self-conscious and anxious. He is bored in self-defense. *This is not where I belong,* he thinks to himself. EG raises his head from the white pillow and rages, "You think I belong here?" The old crone looks up reproachfully from her crocheting. EG lowers his head back onto the stiff white pillow.

<u>10:19:59:58:50 a.m.</u>

Every morning in Anchor Bay, EG does *puja*. *Puja* at the altar to Ganesha, *puja* in the Quan Yin Garden, and *puja* at the shrine to Ahmithaba Buddha near the Bell Path. He doesn't have to explain *puja* to The Boy, this lighting of candles, waving of incense, bowing, and praying out loud. The Boy has always been religious. In fact, The Boy has had his religious conviction tested by fire.

Shortly after The Boy's family moved from Calistoga to Benicia, Annabel and Clete enrolled him in St. Catherine's Academy, a private boarding school run by Dominican nuns. The Boy was accepted as a day student, as were most of the other Catholic children of the town, since the local parish didn't have a parish elementary school.

Once The Boy is enrolled in St. Catherine's, it is discovered that the nuns are far too poor to afford a school bus, so The Boy must walk to school every morning and walk home again each afternoon. On the way home he must pass a certain house where another boy just about his age, named Donny Macgregor, lives.

The Boy understands that Donny Macgregor is different from him in three essential ways: Donny Macgregor goes to public school; Donny Macgregor is a Protestant; Donny Macgregor is beautiful. Hovering over this tense essence of what defines Donny Macgregor is the fact, well-known throughout the town, that Donny Macgregor has an older brother in prison. All these elements combine to make Donny Macgregor "other." He is as different from The Boy as is humanly possible on this planet.

Public school lets out an hour earlier than St. Catherine's, which does not surprise The Boy, because everyone knows that public schools are inferior to Catholic schools. But what this means to The Boy is that either he must walk past Donny Macgregor's house every day on the way home from school, or he must walk around the hill on which Donny Macgregor's house is situ-ated. This adds about half a mile to his trip and is a great incon-venience, especially since, being a Catholic school student, his considerable amount of homework requires him to carry home each afternoon almost every book in his desk plus any he may have checked out of the school library. It wouldn't matter that he has to pass Donny Macgregor's house except for one extremely crucial and dangerous issue: Donny Macgregor hates Catholics. In fact, his entire family hates Catholics, or so The Boy assumes. So, of course, Donny Macgregor persecutes Catholics whenever he can; namely, he throws rocks, rotten fruit, and vegetables at The Boy when The Boy passes his house. The Boy assumes, as well, that while he is a target of Donny Macgregor's demonic pleasure, and while his parents spend every night at the dinner table litaniz-ing—a Catholic practice, if only they knew—the undesirable traits of Roman Catholics, his parents did not openly accost Catholics; they certainly did not throw garbage at them when they passed the Macgregor house. The Boy is not so sure, howev-er, that Mr. And Mrs. Macgregor would actually punish Donny Macgregor if they caught him pelting The Boy with the leftovers from Sunday's dinner since he is, after all, a Catholic.

The Boy happens to know that Mr. Macgregor is a Mason and Mrs. Macgregor belongs to the Order of the Eastern Star and wears gargantuan lime-green ball gowns with countless crinoline slips underneath when she attends their meetings the first Saturday of each month in the Masonic Lodge up-stairs from Leonard's Tot Shop on Main Street.

The Boy now has to make a choice: He either subjects him-self to Donny Macgregor's heathen prejudice and persecution, arriving home bruised from apples and pickle jars and splat-tered with tomatoes and soggy eggplant, or he adds the extra half mile to his two-mile trek home. All through fourth grade

The Boy opts for the extra half mile; however, on the first Friday of November of his fifth-grade year, a major shift occurs.

The first Friday of every month at St. Catherine's Academy is "Movie Friday." And on this particular Movie Friday, The Boy drapes his navy-blue uniform sweater over the back of the metal folding chair in the auditorium, sits back, and for two hours is transfixed by a film that changes, if not his entire life, the direction of his spiritual life for the next several years. It also presents him with the answer to one of his first moral dilemmas. For two hours The Boy is caught up in *The Miracle of Fatima*.

Here, lain out before him, as though it were a message from the Blessed Mother herself, is a real life tragedy as compelling as his own and told only as the historically correct Hollywood researchers could tell such a story. Or, as Cletus wryly explained to The Boy at dinner the same night, "only they had the resources and the motivation to leave every stone unturned in order to crank out the movie before Christmas."

Three children, visited by the Blessed Virgin herself at a most unlikely spot in a field in Portugal, must suffer the humiliation of an entire village, the physical and emotional persecution of the police, and the strictest punishments meted out by their parents. And they do all this in the name of truth, honesty, and religious conviction. If they can do it, why can't he?

So that very day, armed only with his love for the Blessed Virgin Mary and his devotion to the one true religion founded by Christ and passed on to Peter, The Boy walks straight up the hill right past Donny Macgregor's house. He doesn't even cross to the other side of the street. And, lo, Donny Macgregor is nowhere to be found. Either this is truly a Fatima-like miracle, the Blessed Mother protecting The Boy, or Donny Macgregor has stayed late to take part in some violent sport at public school.

The next day The Boy repeats his course home, but this time Donny Macgregor is sitting on his front porch. As soon as he sees The Boy coming over the crest of the hill, his Catholic school uniform a dead giveaway from a hundred feet off, Donny Macgregor rushes to the side of the house, drags the family garbage can to the front lawn and takes off the tin lid. As The Boy arrives at the edge of Donny Macgregor's yard, Donny Macgregor reaches his hand into the shiny metal can, retrieves a large watermelon rind, and raises it above his head, taking aim. The Boy, knowing now that this is the true test of his willingness to die for his religious beliefs, braces himself, holds his book bag tight, and does the only thing he can think of, what he believes the children of Fatima would do if they were forced to pass by Donny Macgregor's house: He breaks into song:

> Hail, holy Queen, enthroned above,
> O Maria.
> Hail, mother of mercy and of love, O Maria.
> Triumph all ye cherubim,
> Sing with us, ye Seraphim,
> Heav'n and earth resound the hymn:
> Salve, salve, salve, Regina!

At first Donny Macgregor is confused. He pauses for the entire first chorus of "Hail Holy Queen"; then, realizing it is simply a Catholic trick taught to all Catholics in case of potential martyrdom and is intended to throw him off-balance, he hurls the watermelon rind and strikes The Boy squarely in the chest. The Boy, concerned that his lamb's wool sweater will be ruined and aware that it is more expensive than his white uniform shirt, stops, sets down his bag, and removes his sweater, singing the entire time. Right there in front of Donny Macgregor's house.

> Our life, our sweetness here below, O Maria.
> Our hope in sorrow and in woe, O Maria.
>
> Triumph all ye cherubim,
> Sing with us, ye Seraphim,
> Heav'n and earth resound the hymn:
> Salve, salve, salve, Regina!

Another watermelon rind, this time with coffee grounds, lands on The Boy's shoulder. The white cotton shirt absorbs it like a sponge.

> To thee we cry, poor sons of Eve, O Maria.
> To thee we sigh, we mourn, we grieve, O Maria.
>
> Triumph all ye cherubim,
> Sing with us, ye Seraphim,
> Heav'n and earth resound the hymn:
> Salve, salve, salve, Regina!

The Boy folds his sweater and places it inside his heavy leather book bag, picks up the bag, and continues on, never even looking at Donny Macgregor. He is thinking only of the beautiful Lady all in white who is hovering, he is sure, just above his head, white pearl rosary dangling from her alabaster hands, her halo golden and brilliant in the midday sun. If only poor heathen Protestant Donny Macgregor could see her, perhaps he would lay down his fruit and repent. Slam! Half a tamale on the side of his face.

> This earth is but a vale of tears, O Maria.
> A place of banishment, of fears, O Maria.
> Triumph all ye cherubim,
> Sing with us, ye Seraphim,
> Heav'n and earth resound the hymn:
> Salve, salve, salve, Regina!

Donny Macgregor is laughing now. He is gathering up more garbage and running to the edge of the lawn near the driveway in order to get a better shot. "Hey, queer. How's the pope?" Donny Macgregor shouts. The Boy stops and turns toward Donny Macgregor just in time to receive square in the chest what feels like a rock but ends up being only a half-eaten Jonathan apple.

> Turn then, most gracious Advocate,
> O Maria.
> Toward us thine eyes compassionate,
> O Maria.
> Triumph all ye cherubim,
> Sing with us, ye Seraphim,
> Heav'n and earth resound the hymn:
> Salve, salve, salve, Regina!

Even as he sings the praises of his heavenly mother, The Boy cannot help but notice now that Donny Macgregor, on this warm October day in sunny California, is shirtless. He is wearing what appears to be navy-blue public school gym shorts, tennis shoes—which Annabel would consider to be

"Okie clothes"—and nothing else. It would appear from the jostling beneath his shorts, that he isn't even wearing underwear, another Protestant practice, The Boy is certain.

Donny Macgregor's black hair shines in the afternoon sun, an almost blue quality to it. His blue eyes sparkle with hatred. His beautiful round shoulders are dark brown from a summer at the public pool, where Annabel has assured The Boy all the children in town are contracting crippling polio and other diseases common among the rabble. Donny Macgregor's chest and dark brown nipples are much more defined than any other 10-year-old The Boy knows. He wonders, as he sings the next verse even louder for Donny Macgregor's religious conversion, if all juvenile delinquents have tight, muscular bodies. He wonders if Donny Macgregor perhaps has spent time in reform school, where he had nothing to do all day but work out in the gangsters' gymnasium, lifting weights and swimming laps.

> When this, our exile, is complete, O Maria.
> Show us thy Son, our Jesus sweet, O Maria.

> Triumph all ye cherubim,
> Sing with us, ye Seraphim,
> Heav'n and earth resound the hymn:
> Salve, salve, salve, Regina!

"You stupid fruit!" Donny Macgregor yells. "You Catholic queer!" Then Donny Macgregor turns back toward the garbage can for more ammunition. The Boy turns too and resumes his journey home, confident that the Blessed Mother is well-pleased. He couldn't have done better had Donny Macgregor been a godless Communist from godless Russia. More garbage goes sailing past, some striking The Boy in the back, some missing him completely. Most of it finds its mark however, as Donny Macgregor is athletically inclined. The Boy remains undaunted.

By now, Donny Macgregor's neighbor, Mrs. Halliburton, has come out to her front porch to see what the ruckus is. The Boy smiles at her through guacamole sauce, which is beginning now to cake just above his right eye. He recognizes Mrs. Halliburton from 11 o'clock Mass every Sunday. A good Catholic woman. He thinks she belongs to the Sodality of Mary because she always sits on the left, way up front near the Blessed Virgin's altar. Now he even has a witness to his religious persecution. If they should someday find his battered, garbage-sodden body in the empty field across from Donny Macgregor's house, Mrs. Halliburton will be able to lead them to the pagan murderer. Mrs. Halliburton turns up her hearing aid for the last verse of The Boy's Marian hymn.

> O clement, gracious, Mother sweet, O Maria.
> Virgin Mary, we entreat, O Maria.
>
> Triumph all ye cherubim,
> Sing with us, ye Seraphim,
> Heav'n and earth resound the hymn:
> Salve, salve, salve, Regina!

All through his freshman year of high school, AD avoids Donny Macgregor. Donny Macgregor is tough and is looked up to for two things: He supposedly has the biggest dick in Benicia High and he drives the choicest, most bitchin' cherry-red '53 Chevy two-door anyone at Benicia High ever laid eyes on. The car is his pride and joy. He has spent hundreds of dollars on chrome tailpipes, glass-pack mufflers, spotlights, and putting it on a "rake" and adding lots of interior details, like a fuzzy dashboard and red lights on the instrument panel.

Donny Macgregor plays every sport in school—even when athletic seasons overlap, rushing from the football field to the gym for basketball practice, then from the gym to the baseball diamond, and from the baseball diamond to the track. He gets his driver's license early, which, AD realizes, must mean that Donny Macgregor has been held back in school at least once, which is a double ignominy since he already attended an inferior grammar school that, rumor has it, doesn't even teach the times tables until fifth grade. But now, since AD has been forced to attend public school by his father, who wants him to "toughen up" and play football to get ready for his college years at Notre Dame, AD must confront Donny Macgregor once again.

For some reason, Donny Macgregor and AD do not acknowledge one another. Each pretends the other doesn't exist. There is no animosity evident, no more anti-Catholic slurs or garbage-heaving on Donny Macgregor's part. Neither does AD let on that he detests Donny Macgregor nor that he even remembers the near-death experiences he had more than once passing by Donny Macgregor's house the year he was in fifth grade. It seems either all is forgotten—on Donny Macgregor's part, that is—or else AD isn't recognized by the antipapist. However, since AD must try out for the football team, he and Donny Macgregor are destined to cross paths.

On the first day of football practice, AD arrives late at the school gym. The other boys are already out on the field running laps. AD dresses quickly and runs out to join them. By the time he gets to the field, laps are over, which relieves him, since running out to the field is itself exhausting for the 195-pound Pall Mall-smoking freshman.

Football practice the first day is nothing more than an hour and a half of grueling calisthenics: laps around the field, sit-ups, jumping jacks, side bends, push-ups, more sit-ups, more laps. AD, sneaking sidelong glances at Donny Macgregor, who is just a row ahead and three spots to AD's left, notices not only that his thick, muscular thighs are hairy but also that these calisthenics don't even seem to faze him. AD is not terribly surprised. He has noticed that except for his friend Gary Harty, who also attended St. Catherine's, Protestants seem to be much more athletically inclined than Catholics.

Back in the locker room, AD faces not only his ongoing nemesis of the locker room—exposing his overweight body to the scrutiny of other boys—but also now, for the first time, he must be naked with his inquisitor, Donny Macgregor. AD covers himself with a towel until the very last second, then throws the towel onto a hook and steps around the corner into the communal shower room. Only two boys are left showering: Victor Lyon, the tallest boy in school, and Donny Macgregor.

AD moves to the nearest shower nozzle and turns it on, barely lathering up his flabby body and rinsing it off in record time. As he reaches to turn off his shower, he glances down to the end of the shower room, and there, engrossed in "sports talk" stands Donny Macgregor, lathering himself up unselfconsciously, his penis bobbing around, half-erect, his body glistening in the bright overhead lights, soap bubbles shimmering an oily mixture of blue-scarlet-green-purple as they form and burst on his back, buttocks, and rock-hard abdomen. And, of course, AD thinks, Donny Macgregor would have, if not the longest, the fattest dick in Benicia High School. It is also the first uncircumcised penis AD has ever seen. AD wonders if most Protestants don't circumcise their children.

Naturally, he can't stop staring at it, and, of course, as AD stands hypnotized by his first "in-the-flesh foreskin," Donny Macgregor, while describing to Victor Lyon what a bunch of queers those St. Vincent's players are and how easy they'll be to beat, turns his head and catches AD ogling his "chick choker," as he notoriously and frequently refers to it. But much to AD's surprise, Donny Macgregor just keeps talking to Victor Lyon. In fact, if AD didn't know better, he would think that Donny Macgregor smiled in his direction. Just a slight smile. And maybe a nod, like he knows this kid from somewhere but can't quite place him.

It isn't until their senior year, when Donny Macgregor begins dating AD's girlfriend's best friend, that AD and Donny Macgregor themselves become friends. They even double-date. They begin to hang out together, drag Main Street, go for Cokes and burgers. But neither of them ever mentions the religious persecution. When AD leaves for college in Texas, it is Donny Macgregor who drives AD and Annabel to the San Francisco airport for the send-off. AD kisses his teary mother good-bye, then turns to shake Donny Macgregor's hand in a formal farewell. But to AD's surprise and delight, Donny Macgregor grabs him, throws his arms around him, and holds him close. "I'm going to miss you," he whispers into AD's ear. "I'm glad we got to be friends. Call me as soon as you get home for summer vacation."

It is early June when AD arrives back in California after his freshman year of college. He has thought about Donny Macgregor off and on while he was away at school in Texas, usually when he was showering in the gym. He would remember Donny Macgregor wet with half a hard-on after football practice, smiling at him, as he told Victor Lyon that everybody who went to St. Vincent's High School was a Catholic queer and the Benicia High Panthers would tromp all over the Saints at homecoming.

AD remembers Donny Macgregor's admonition at the airport to call him when he gets home, and so the very evening of his arrival, he telephones Donny Macgregor who, somewhat to AD's surprise, has been waiting for his call.

"I saw your mom in the Park & Shop last week. She told me you'd be home today. I was wondering if you'd call. I can't wait to hear all about college. Let's party."

So they buy two six-packs of beer, climb into Donny Macgregor's bitchin' cherry-red '53 Chevy two-door and head for the lake. To catch up.

"Man, you got thin. You're almost skinny," Donny Macgregor says, pulling up to the edge of the lake and cutting the engine.

"Yeah. Eighty pounds. Big difference, huh?"

"How much did you weigh when you left?"

"Two-forty, if you can believe it."

"Wow! What brought that on? How come you lost so much weight?" Donny Macgregor is fumbling in the brown paper bag on the seat between them. He's trying to retrieve one of the six-packs.

Outside, AD can see that a family has had a picnic just a few feet from where they are parked. The remains of the day's outing are scattered all along the shore: paper plates, aluminum cans, watermelon rinds.

"Oh, it's a long story," AD says, not wanting to admit he fell in love with his roommate and quickly realized that in order to seduce this guy from South Bend, Ind., who ran track and swam on the swimming team, he was going to have to give him a more aesthetically pleasing body to look at. "Just didn't eat much; kind of lost my appetite for a while. I guess I was homesick or something. You know, scared of being on my own at college, stuff like that. I guess I do look a lot different."

"Man, you sure do. You have a waist! And a butt. And everything." Donny Macgregor is now fishing inside the brown paper bag. He pulls out a couple of Budweisers and hands one to AD.

"So what are you up to these days?" AD asks, popping the top off his beer and dropping the pop-top ring into the brown paper bag.

"Aw, same old shit. Nothin'."

"How's college?"

"Junior college, you mean," Donny Macgregor says, chugging half his beer.

"Hey, it doesn't matter where you are; the first two years of college are all required courses anyway." AD takes a swig of his beer. It burns going down.

"Fuck," is all Donny Macgregor says, and finishes the rest of his beer in one gulp. He reaches into the bag and retrieves another, opening it and chugging half of that one. AD smiles to himself, remembering how he drank in high school—for effect, not flavor. As Donny Macgregor sits with his beer raised, AD takes advantage of the moment to take in Donny Macgregor's bulging Levi's. The moonlight is falling on the front seat of the Chevy, and the mound of denim in Donny Macgregor's lap is considerable.

"Come on," AD encourages Donny Macgregor, "it's not that bad. It could always be worse. You could be out working for a living." AD chuckles, but Donny Macgregor shoots him a look.

"I am out working for a living. My dad got laid off, and I had to go to work for PG&E. So now I'm working and going to school. It's for shit." And now the rest of Beer Number Two goes down the hatch and a third one is opened. "Don't you want another beer yet?" Donny Macgregor asks AD.

"Not yet," AD answers. "I'm still working on this one. Jeez, I'm sorry, man. I had no idea. That's rough."

"Yeah, and besides that, Lois and I broke up."

"No shit." AD is getting into the old high school routine here, verbal expressions and all. He even finishes his beer in three long gulps.

"Yeah, that bitch."

"Wait a minute. I thought you were dating Pat. What happened to her?"

"Oh, fuck that shit. She got all uppity on me, started dating some guy that's going to St. Mary's in Moraga. They don't even have a football team there." Donny Macgregor is now opening Beer Number Three. "Besides, that cunt wouldn't put out any more. I think she was getting it from this guy a long time before we got around to breaking up. What a bitch."

"Oh, well, you're probably better off," AD says, trying to console his old high school buddy.

"Yeah, that's what I think too. Girls. They make my butt ache. I gotta piss," Donny Macgregor says, opening the door, downing the last of Beer Number Three, and pitching the can into the dark.

"Me too," AD says, and also gets out.

They stand at the edge of Lake Herman, peeing into the cold, dark water, the moonlight dancing before them on the lake's surface. As they turn to go back to the car, still buttoning up their Levi's, Donny Macgregor collides with a thorn bush. "Ouch, ouch, shit, shit," he exclaims and begins hopping around.

"What happened?" AD asks, moving toward him.

"I hit this fucking bush, man. It hurts like hell. I think I got a sticker in my pecker. Ouch, it hurts like hell."

AD takes Donny Macgregor by the arm and turns him into the moonlight. Donny Macgregor is holding his dick and moaning. "Move your hand and let me see."

Donny Macgregor is squirming. "It hurts."

"Hold still for a minute," AD says, his own pants still half unfastened. He squats down in front of Donny Macgregor and begins lightly running his fingers over Donny Macgregor's fat, fleshy cock. He finally finds it.

"Ouch, man!" Donny Macgregor shouts as AD's finger collides with the thorn.

"Wait a second," AD says and pulls out the thorn. "There."

"Shit, man. That hurt like hell. Thanks."

The two of them stay where they are, AD looking up at Donny Macgregor, Donny Macgregor looking down at AD while he massages the spot where the thorn was.

"Man," exclaims AD, "you have the fattest dick I've ever seen. Do you know that?"

"Yeah, Pat used to say it was too big."

"I didn't used to like it. I mean the first time I saw you in the shower at football practice."

"Huh."

"Well, it was the first uncircumcised dick I ever saw and I thought it was ugly. Now I kind of like it."

Donny Macgregor looks at AD and gives a sardonic laugh. "Are you really queer?"

The question doesn't throw AD off-balance. A year away from home has built his self-confidence. "Well, I like sex."

"Did you really suck off all those guys in high school?" Donny Macgregor asks, not moving from where his dick is dangling in front of AD's face.

"What guys?" AD asks, beginning to be aroused with "the biggest dick in Benicia High" just an inch or two away. If he stuck his tongue out, he could lick the foreskin.

"All those guys. Ray Holland, Richie King, Frank Miller?"

"Yeah, I guess I did. But they didn't complain. They liked it. We did it lots of times. For years."

"Jimmy Orr?"

"Yeah."

"Phil Reynolds?"

"Yeah."

"Patrick Houlihan?"

"Yeah, everybody I hung out with."

"But what about your girlfriends? What about all those girls you dated? I thought you were fucking all those girls." Donny Macgregor is now weaving a little under the influence of the beers, his dick bobbing and waving in the moonlight on the shore of Lake Herman.

"I did fuck them, so what? Sex is sex. If it feels good, why not do it?"

"Yeah, I suppose so," Donny Macgregor muses.

"Don't tell me no one ever sucked your dick."

"No guy ever did, I'll tell you that."

"Well, that's too bad. That's a real shame."

"Why's that?"

"Because you have to have one to know how to do it right."

"I suppose you want to suck my dick."

"I would if you wanted me to. If I could get the damned thing in my mouth. Look, I can't even get my hand all the way around it," AD says and grips Donny Macgregor's dick, which is half hard.

"I don't know, man. I'm not queer." Donny Macgregor puts his hand on AD's head and pushes him away but leaves his hand on his head, a flirtatious, if not seductive gesture, which keeps AD from moving toward his record-circumference organ but also keeps him from moving away from it.

"Who says you have to be queer to like getting your dick sucked?"

"You don't?"

"Well, girls suck your dick and you like that. Does that make you queer?"

"I never thought about it like that. But you're a guy."

"Think of me as a mouth," AD says, smiling up at Donny Macgregor.

"Hmm," Donny Macgregor says, pulling AD's head closer. "A mouth."

While Donny Macgregor is considering AD's logic, AD takes Donny Macgregor into his mouth. The warm, wet sensation ends Donny Macgregor's deliberations and his "Hmm" turns into a "Mmm," which turns into "Oh, yeah" which turns into "Eat my dick, man," which culminates in "Swallow this, baby."

When it's over they get back into the car, pop open another beer, and drive back into town, talking about how Donny Macgregor has received several offers to buy his bitchin' cherry-red '53 Chevy two-door. But he's holding out for top dollar, and, besides, he doesn't know if he wants to sell it anyway because it's such a pussy magnet.

As AD gets out of the car in front of his house, he says to Donny Macgregor, "I have to ask you something. Something I've been wanting to ask you for a long time."

"Sure, man, what is it?"

"Do you remember throwing garbage at me every day when we were kids?"

"Huh?"

"Every day after school, when I'd walk home past your house, you'd come out and throw garbage and shit at me. Do you remember that?"

"Was that you? I'm sorry. If I'd known it was you, I wouldn't have done it."

"But why did you? Why'd you do that every day?"

"I don't know. I barely remember it. What does it matter now?"

AD sees how drunk Donny Macgregor is, sees that even if he weren't drunk he wouldn't be able to give him any better answer. He decides to drop it. "Well, anyway, thanks, man. That was a great welcome-home party."

"Yeah, well, that stuff's just between you and me, and it'll never happen again."

"Right," AD says sarcastically, but Donny Macgregor, either because he's loaded or because he went to public school all his life, doesn't catch the irony in AD's tone.

"You Catholics sure are weird, man."

"Yeah, well, good thing you're a Protestant. Night." AD watches as Donny Macgregor revs his engine, peels out, and lays rubber halfway up the block. As he watches Donny Macgregor turn the corner and head up the hill toward his house, AD imagines him at home, sitting on the side of his bed, pulling off his tennis shoes, noticing the glob of sticky stuff all over the toe of his right shoe. AD pictures Donny Macgregor sticking his finger in it and trying to smell it but being so drunk he actually sticks his nose in it. *Weird,* he hears Donny Macgregor say to himself, as he wipes his finger on his clean white Protestant sheet and falls back, passed out before his head even hits the pillow.

At 7:30 the following morning AD is awakened by the telephone. It is Donny Macgregor. "Hope I didn't wake you up, man. I'm on my way out the door to work. I get out of class at 9. Wanna get a six-pack and drive out to the lake tonight?"

10:19:59:58:51 A.M.

Alone on the mountaintop in Anchor Bay, all the world looks different. Through the rain, EG can barely make out the ocean. It seems to rise like a foggy gray mist, joining the sky, merging with the rain: water seeking earth seeking water.

Paul has called, apologizing for his "difficult period."

"There's absolutely no need for apologies," EG says, coiling the telephone cord in his right hand, then letting it fall slack to the floor, recoiling it, letting it fall, over and over. "Everyone is entitled to a dark night of the soul. To many dark nights, actually. We both have these emotional unravelings, honey. I do it too, remember?"

"But I was horrible. I projected all of it on you. I came to a basic realization," Paul says. "It's my expectations that are making me so angry, not yours."

EG smiles, remembering the precise moment Paul is referring to. They were backing out of the Church Street driveway and EG had to wait for car after car to pass, even though he was well out into the street. Paul was reading the exasperation on EG's face and in his body language. He reached out and touched his leg to calm him. EG shot him a momentary scowl. "In the 11 years I've been in this house, only two drivers have ever stopped to let me out of this driveway," EG said.

"You know," Paul said, as they backed into Church Street, "for someone who holds the Collective in such disdain, you certainly have high expectations of it."

It had been another reminder for EG about the tar baby of expectation: Stick in a single finger and before long you're up to your shoulder.

"Well, I'm glad you've sorted things out," EG says, carrying the phone into the living room. Outside, the rain begins to fall even harder. The branches of the twin douglas firs in front of the house, which EG has dubbed the Two Sisters, begin to bow at the ends under the downpour.

"Will you remind me of that the next time I'm angry at absolutely everything?" Paul asks.

"Well, I'll remind you of that the next time you're angry at me—I promise you that," EG teases.

"Oh, by the way, thank you for the roses," Paul says softly. "That was completely sweet. I was very surprised. When did you send them?"

"The day I arrived up here, I couldn't think of how to help you in any other way. In fact, the only way I knew how to "be there for you" was to not be there, to go away and let you thrash around in this alone. Then when I got up here, I felt awful. I moped around all day worrying about you, wanting you to work your way through this. Words weren't working: Everything I said just made you angrier. But I wanted you to know I love you. I'll walk through this with you or wait on the edge of it. But I want you always to know—even if you aren't feeling it—that I'll be standing there with you when it's over. I can't always be with you in the shadow of your fears and angers, but I'm always right on the other side, waiting for you to emerge."

Now, with Paul resurfacing into light, EG feels more alone than ever. Isolated in Anchor Bay while Paul was in the dark throes of his dilemma felt safe, if distant. But now, having hung up the phone and being so far away from Paul now that his darkness has lifted, EG feels separated from some deep essential part of himself.

He no sooner has that thought than he knows precisely what to do about it. At least it will begin to help. He turns and calls The Boy. Immediately, he comes running down the stairs, ready for action.

"Where were you?" EG asks.

"Playing in my room," The Boy answers. He is wearing Buster Brown oxfords with blue-and-red argyle socks, navy shorts, and a blue-and red-striped T-shirt. His hair is medium length, but his bangs stop just short of his eyes. He is swiping them off his forehead with his hand.

"Alone again, eh?"

The Boy looks at the floor. He has developed the habit, even at this tender age, of trying to keep the adults from seeing the hurt in his eyes. "You've been busy," The Boy says softly.

"Is that a polite way of saying I've been ignoring you?"

The Boy nods ever so slightly.

"Are you angry with me?"

"No."

"Are you certain?"

"That's someone else. You're thinking of AD. He's the one who gets mad and throws things or slams his bedroom door, not me."

"What about you?"

"I'm just hurt and confused. I feel sad and lonely, and I can't figure out what I've done wrong. I can't understand why you're ignoring me."

"Do you understand it has nothing to do with you—that it's something between me and Paul?"

"No."

"You don't understand that?"

"I'm only 5."

EG and The Boy look at one another in silence. EG is feeling a bit embarrassed, sensing he expects too much of The Boy the way Clete always expected too much of him. Paul's words on the telephone come back to him: It's my expectations...not yours.

"I'm too young to understand anything like that," The Boy goes on, softly but clearly. "I hear what you say, but it doesn't mean anything to me. I'm more like Hari than like you. I live in a world of feelings and instincts. I get by mostly on intuition, things I know in my gut, not in my head. So grownup explanations don't make sense to me."

"But sometimes when I ask you if you understand my explanations, you say you do."

"That's just to get you to stop talking, because most of the time after you stop talking, you hug me and I feel better. Or you'll take me to the beach or for a walk with Hari and we'll laugh and eat candy. That's what I understand. That's 5-year-old language."

"So shall I stop talking now?"

"Uh-huh."

"Want to take Hari to Manchester Beach?"

"It's raining."

"We have rain coats."

"Oh, boy!" The Boy runs off to find his yellow slicker and his galoshes. EG too feels himself rising to the surface of something, floating up toward light, toward air, toward a better view of his life. A view perhaps only possible from Anchor Bay.

10:19:59:58:52 A.M.

EG wakes in the middle of the night now—every night. He wakes precisely one hour and 20 minutes after falling asleep, then again two hours and 15 minutes after that and always— no matter when else he wakes—at 5:25 A.M.

At first he tells himself it is the drugs. The Ultram he takes to ease the peripheral neuropathy makes him speed up, as does the 3TC, one of the antiretrovirals. But on the days when he vacations from those medications, he finds himself awake at the same, established times.

This time—mid January in Anchor Bay—he rises again in the dark of night, pads down the carpeted stairs to the kitchen, where he reheats a cup of cold coffee, lights a cigarette, and stands at the front window. Two giant floodlights aimed outward from the front of the house illuminate two pine trees dubbed the Two Sisters. They tower into the night sky. Thousands of tiny bell-like blossoms on the manzanitas that ripple down the mountainside toward the ocean glow eerily, like miniature lanterns showing the way to the sea.

EG stands in the tall, dark window, seeing himself as he thinks he must be seen by the owls and creatures scurrying in the dark. *How foreign I must look*, he thinks. *How totally incongruous here in the woods, standing in this huge house surrounded by a ring of obscenely bright lights. Like some alien creature setting down his interstellar craft in the middle of a distant planet to observe its terrain. But it actually works out the opposite*, EG observes. *In truth, it is the woods creatures who sit in the dark observing me.*

A few embers from the evening's fire shimmer and glow in the stone fireplace. The two sofas, positioned at right angles to form an *L* shape, sit before the hearth; EG's unattended crocheting lies where he left it on the green love seat.

He moves away from the window to the darker part of the room and sits and watches the embers glow and pulsate before him like a heart hidden in ashes. On the far end of the larger sofa he sees, as his eyes adjust to the darkness, Cohen in her plain white cotton nightgown and her clumsy brown slippers. Her hair is braided into a long gray whip that hangs over her shoulder. It falls to the sofa cushion and coils around three times, its tip resting in the circle's center like a vigilant cobra.

She is peeling an apple with a paring knife and letting the long, unbroken coil of skin ease gently into her lap, a serpent dancing its hypnotic descent to the white field of Cohen's nightgown.

She tosses the apple peel into the fire, cores the fruit, and offers a slice to EG. The room is fragrant with the apple peel baking in the embers, and Cohen begins to sing softly to EG. "On the beautiful isle of Capri, just my baby and me…"

EG moves closer to her. She does not look at him; rather, she slices and hands him, one at a time, thin sections of fruit until the entire apple is gone. EG scoots down in his seat, leans his head back against the soft cushions. He wants to put his feet up on the coffee table, but he knows Cohen would not approve, so he contents himself as he is. He closes his eyes and listens to her sweet soprano lilting through verse after verse, growing softer and softer. He smells her body powder mixed with the scent of baked apple and, comforted by these familiar, succoring associations from his earliest childhood, he falls once more into a gentle, dreamless sleep. He will not wake again until morning, when Hari's warm, wet tongue licks him awake, perplexed by his master's choice of nests.

10:19:59:58:53 A.M.

He doesn't always live in his intellect, but mostly. There are other venues for his being, but in saying that even, just that way—"there are other venues for his being"—he realizes he is in his intellect even now.

10:19:59:58:54 A.M.

Andre and EG have driven out of the Arizona desert from Apache Junction, across Joshua Tree and the Mojave Desert, through the central valley of California to San Francisco. They have brought with them all their belongings, including Axel, the red Doberman puppy, and Dolores, their 12-year-old deaf Dalmatian. They have taken turns driving the 24-foot-long moving truck and the white car, changing vehicles every two hours. The truck is now parked in front of their new home on Church Street, the car tucked safely in the garage.

EG came ahead several weeks before and found this place. It is a huge flat that occupies the entire top floor of an old two-story Edwardian home. Andre is seeing it for the first time. EG leads him through the garage, up the back steps into the garden, and through the apartment: back porch, kitchen, back bedroom overlooking the garden, dining room, lavatory and water closet, hallway, study, living room and a front bedroom.

The flat is enormous, and there are huge sash windows in every room. The living room and study overlook Dolores Park, downtown, and the bay, where, this afternoon, gray tankers, black-and-red freighters, and white cruise ships are coming and going beneath the blue sky. They toot and blast warnings to one another in the choppy green waters.

The last room Andre enters is the front bedroom. EG waits in the doorway as Andre walks into the room, stops in the center, and turns around and around, taking in the walls, the crown molding, and something EG cannot see. As he turns, Andre says, more to himself than to EG, "This is the room I'm going to die in."

EG is horrified by what he has heard and can't quite believe it. "What?" he asks.

Andre stops pivoting, looks at EG, and says again, "This is the room I'm going to die in."

"What a horrible thing to say. Why are you saying that?"

"I don't know. I just have this overwhelming feeling right now that this is where I will die."

"Let's unpack," EG says. And with that, he takes Andre by the hand and leads him down the front steps to the truck.

Years later, when Andre comes home from Health Center One on 17th Street, four blocks away, to tell EG that his HIV test was positive, EG turns his head to look through the open door of the front bedroom. Eighteen months after that, as he covers Andre's body with his prayer shawl and 100 flowers, he will hear Andre say it again. "This is the room I'm going to die in." He will hear it as distinctly as though his lover were right behind him, in the center of this room, turning around and around, looking at the white walls, the crown molding, and something EG cannot see.

10:19:59:58:55 A.M.

EG has decided to travel north to Anchor Bay for a few days. He travels with Hari. Paul will join him at week's end. It is raining all over the northern part of the state. Everywhere spring is pushing at the surface, pressing its tiny fingers through in search of light, opening its pale green eyes on the branches of deciduous trees. Spring's chubby cheeks blush pink in the decorative plum trees that line Church Street.

EG loads Hari into the truck and heads north through the city, around the park, over the Golden Gate Bridge, and up the snakelike coast highway that winds along ocean's edge. He travels deeper and deeper into the forest at the edge of the sea until he comes to Anchor Bay. And there, at hill's crest, overlooking the Pacific, Hawaii, Japan, and all of Asia, the view of his own small life takes on its proper perspective, its relative importance and its immense yet insignificant meaning.

Before EG left, Paul said something to him in passing that has made a deep mark on him. Paul commented that he had begun to look at his waking hours as though they were a dream, interpreting everything and everyone he comes into contact with as a symbol, rather than just what it appears to be.

In Anchor Bay EG tries to practice this, and the consequences are profound. When he looks at a beautiful man with bulging biceps or a stunning woman with full breasts, it is something else he sees, something beyond the body. It is as though they are merely metaphors for masculinity and femininity, attractive surrogates for some deeper archetype: the finger pointing at the moon.

When EG walks along the ocean, listening to the surf, it is not the ocean he responds to, not the rhythmic pounding of the green sea he hears, but something else, something other. What does the ocean mean to him, what does it represent? That other thing is what stirs his soul; that other is what he is really responding to.

As he thinks of making love with Paul, lifting him up to waist level, slipping inside, feeling the warm moistness, clasping his hands around his lover's waist, pulling him closer, he realizes it is not the flesh against flesh that makes his pulse beat faster, his breath quicken; it is the joining, the blurring of the lines between them, the making one out of two that moves him.

When he places a small bunch of violets on his mother's grave, resting them gently against the headstone, it is not the soft green grass or the weathered stone scarred with the letters of her name that opens the floodgates but something more ethereal, something that reverberates around the universal experience of loss and grief and irrevocable abandonment that wails in his chest.

Like dreams, the seemingly incomprehensible images that float around and before him—sailing past on the highway, strolling down the street in the opposite direction, staring out at him from behind bars and cages, sweating for him in furtive ecstasy—all point to something else, all carry other significances beneath their skins. And those significances cry out in inaudible voices to the significance that EG carries beneath his own skin: prisoners sending secret messages to one another on an undetectable frequency. This is how people connect without communicating. This is the principle of *advaita*, he thinks, of nonduality.

If EG holds this in his consciousness constantly, he will go mad. If he forgets it, he will lose his way.

<u>10:19:59:58:56</u> A.M.

EG thinks about his story, the story of his life. He worries about it. Where is the string that runs through it? The string that holds it all together, which, if gathered, reeled in like a ball of yarn, would hold the essence of EG's life in one containable sphere?

Perhaps part of EG's restlessness of late relates to the stringless quality he feels his life possesses—more accurately, to EG's growing awareness that no life has a string running through it from birth to death.

Rather, he thinks, *every life emanates outward in all directions, through all perceptions of time. Like a solar system being born, each life, each action explodes like the aster-shaped pyrotechnics on the Fourth of July, and the sound, the light, the debris, the odor of gases and liquids, the shock of its forceful waves reverberate and resonate, illuminate and inundate everything with which they come into contact. And because it emanates in all directions, nothing is left unaffected.*

Every action EG takes—each breath, every thought, all feelings—takes place simultaneously everywhere throughout the universe, not just here and now. His actions and their consequences do not begin at one time and work their effects at a later time, like a train leaving Boston at noon and arriving in Washington at the dinner hour. A life doesn't live out on a line from one point to another; rather, it unfolds and encompasses like an ethereal dandelion.

Even quantum physics tells us this. Beneath the subatomic microscope, nuclear physicists have discovered that all matter exists only in potential. Only in tendencies, possibilities, probabilities. *Isn't this how we experience our lives?* EG asks himself.

Doesn't every life unfold, one possibility at a time, only to reveal that all possibilities were present all along? Even the language is inept, EG laments. "*Present all along,*" *as though we were tracking possibilities on a graph or a curve, plotting and enumerating events one after another along a straight or curved line. And yet,* EG confesses, *this is the limited fashion in which we perceive our world. It is all we have, the best we can do. This is how we chart our lives—on the graph of Time.*

Where then is his life? Where is his story? What is the beginning, the middle? How does his life end? If there is not a storyline, a lifeline, how will he stand just the other side of the end of his life and take it all in? How can he encompass all of it at once? How shall he ever understand it?

EG decides there is only one way: to sit silently and let his life be within him all at once. To let the ethereal dandelion of his existence unfold within him in a single moment. To sit and concentrate on not concentrating. To simply be aware that he is sitting and that in that moment are all his moments. In that awareness exist no other awarenesses, all other awarenesses. Past and future are mental constructs—concepts we invent in order to comprehend the enormity of the universe, of existence, of It.

It can all be known in a single moment. It can only be known in a single moment, like the woman who steps up to the rim of the Grand Canyon for the first time and is overwhelmed by what she sees. Or the young mathematician who suddenly, for no explicable reason, comprehends the theory of relativity. Or the young father watching his first child being born. All of them, in their individual way, have experienced It in a single moment. Later, they might each describe the event as being "almost a religious experience." And so it was. So it is.

It is early morning at Anchor Bay. EG goes out onto the deck and sits in the green chair facing the pine forest that rolls down the mountain. The ocean shimmers blue in the distance, dissected horizontally by a light blue line at planet's edge more pale than the water.

Next to him, the white wall of the house reflects the intense sun. It is blinding to look at, and EG must turn and close his eyes when he gets up out of the green chair to go in. Suddenly EG feels light-headed. He sits back down and experiences what he can only describe later to Paul as a vision. Sitting there on the deck, trying to regain his equilibrium, he feels as though he is sitting alone in a white room surrounded by invisible people who are also sitting in a white room surrounded by invisible people.

Perhaps, thinks EG, *I am losing my mind*. He thinks of something two professors once told him. One was a professor of literature; the other taught theater and read Tarot cards. Each of them, independently, years apart, said, "The Saint and The Fool: No one can tell them apart merely by watching them."

10:19:59:58:57 A.M.

Paul and EG are aboard the *Tranquillity*, the Neptune Society's 22-passenger boat. It is an extraordinarily sunny day in late June, and they are sailing out beyond the Golden Gate to scatter the ashes of their downstairs neighbor, Don Brown.

Donald Brown died exactly five years to the day and almost to the minute of Andre. Neither EG nor Paul cared much for Don Brown. He was a heavy drinker, loud, abusive to his domestic partner, Jerry Sloan, and, basically, a very mean person. On more than one occasion in the three years he and Jerry lived downstairs, Paul and EG had been awakened in the middle of the night by vicious shouting, crashing furniture, and dishes being smashed against the walls.

Paul and EG aren't sure why they agreed to come to the scattering of the ashes, except that Jerry has been disconsolate since Don's death, living on drugs, crying almost without stopping. They are actually afraid he might harm himself. All he talks about is suicide and how life isn't worth living any longer. They had tried to make excuses for not attending, but Jerry begged them, saying he had no other friends of his own; everyone there would be Don's friends and family. Finally they relented.

Now, bobbing up and down in the rough waters of the Bay as the *Tranquillity* chugs out of the harbor, past Alcatraz and Angel Island, the two of them are appalled as Don's father keeps asking people to move aside so that he can take photos of the city skyline.

"Don't want to miss this opportunity," he says, nudging Paul aside to get to the railing at the back of the boat. "Don't get to see the city from this angle very often."

Meanwhile, in the front of the boat, Don's mother, holding her sixth glass of champagne with one hand and pulling aside the top of her low-cut dress with the other, is showing the captain her left breast for some indeterminable reason. The rest of the passengers, mostly wearing leather, are drinking champagne as fast as they can. No one seems to notice how rough the waters are becoming as they approach the bridge. Jerry is crouched in the bow like a stowaway, hugging the urn of ashes and weeping.

EG and Paul have moved outside the main cabin to the stern of the boat to escape the chaos. They are holding on to the railing with both hands as the boat begins to pitch and yaw dramatically in the rough waters. It feels almost like an amusement park ride but much more dangerous. EG tries to distract himself from his growing nausea by looking up as they pass beneath the Golden Gate Bridge. He has never been out this far in a boat. The bridge is immense and intimidating from this angle, a huge and menacing metal giant.

Scores of happy tourists walk back and forth along the bridge's walkway. *They have come from all over the world to see this*, he thinks. *I wonder how many of them are disappointed that the bridge is more orange than gold?* EG spies someone throwing something off the bridge. It is something large, very large. A bag of garbage perhaps. No, even larger—a knapsack filled with clothes. He nudges Paul with his elbow and points. "Look," he says, "someone has thrown something huge off the bridge."

Paul turns just as EG realizes what it is. A man in a green cotton jacket and brown khakis has leaped from the bridge. He is falling toward them, like some featherless bird, arms outstretched at his sides, falling, falling. He is looking at them. He is smiling. A rebellious angel tossed out of heaven and glad of it. Within a matter of seconds after realizing what they were seeing, there is a splash in the water only a few yards from them and the man is gone, swept away by the undercurrent.

No one else has seen this event. EG turns and puts his hand to the glass that separates him and Paul from the partygoers inside the cabin. Don's father is taking flash snapshots of his wife, who has now pulled both breasts out of her dress for the camera. The men in leather, red ribbons fastened to their vests and motorcycle jackets, are egging her on. Beyond them, Jerry is still rolled into a fetal ball clutching the urn.

A few minutes later, as Jerry is forcing himself to let go of the ashes, while the rest of the party is trying to find something to hold onto as the boat rocks dangerously in the rough waters of the open sea, EG ponders what it means that they have come to this burial at sea only to witness another man's suicide. *How is it that one man struggles fitfully and angrily to his painful death and another can happily and peacefully step out of the world on a bright June afternoon? What, EG wonders, brought this man to such an end? What led him to take that final step?*

EG will see the man falling toward him often for years to come. The image will fill his waking hours but not his dreams.

10:19:59:58:58 A.M.

A white woman with white hair, wearing a white dress, white shoes, and a white hat enters the White Room carrying a large red capsule in a white dish. She smiles as she bends over and extends the red pill to EG. She places one hand behind his head and pulls him toward the red pill.

"Please don't make me take this," EG says.

"It will help," she says.

"It's too difficult," he says.

"Please," she says.

"To you it seems easy to take one pill. But for me it's very hard. I can't explain it. It hurts. Something's not working right. Here," he says, placing a hand in the center of his chest. "In here. I can't."

"For me." It is Paul now, leaning over EG, holding the red pill, an earnest expression on his face. Take this one for me.

"I can't, honey. I love you so much, but I can't take any more pills. I just can't." EG lies back against the white pillow.

The woman in the white dress sighs in resignation; Paul's eyes fill with tears. The people near the walls sigh.

Somewhere in the distance a dog howls. Or a coyote. Or The Boy maybe. Perhaps the entire world is sighing.

10:19:59:58:59 A.M.

The Boy is 9 years old. The Boy is 10. The Boy is 11. His mother works a split shift for the telephone company: 11 A.M. to 1 P.M., then again from 5 P.M. to 10 P.M. His father works a more normal day: 8 to 5.

What this means is that his mother is gone by the time his father comes home from work. So the two of them are alone for the evening. Annabel puts dinner in the oven each afternoon before she leaves for work. Clete doesn't cook. The Boy tries but is too young.

Each evening at 6 P.M. exactly, Clete and The Boy retrieve their dinner from the tepid oven, sit at the dining room table, and eat in total silence. Sometimes they watch the evening news. That way, neither feels any pressure to talk as he hesitantly consumes the dried-out meals: meat loaf, pork chops, scalloped potatoes, ham.

On Mondays, Clete bowls in a league in a nearby town. At 6:30 Clete shouts, "Let's go," from wherever he is in the house. The Boy goes out and gets in the back seat of their pink-and-purple 1956 Dodge Coronet. The car embarrasses The Boy. His friends make fun of it. His father bought it because the dealer offered him $100 off the sticker price if he would take it off his hands. Clete thought it was a bargain. "Why throw away $100?"

He bought a Dodge in the first place because Dodge sponsors *The Lawrence Welk Show* every Saturday night on television. Clete loves Lawrence Welk. He tells people he is related to him. His music reminds him of Dubuque and the Mississippi River and swimming with boys he grew up with and lying in the grass with his best friend, Junior, talking about what they would do if they had $5,000.

Clete and The Boy drive to the bowling alley in Vallejo every Monday evening. They take the back road because Clete hates driving on the highway. He hates driving in traffic altogether. When he was a soldier during the war, he and some buddies on leave in Los Angeles were driving around town in a roadster that belonged to one of the soldiers. There were five of them packed in: the driver, two in the rumble seat, Clete in the passenger seat, and a friend on his lap. A car broadsided them at an intersection, and the man on Clete's lap was killed, although Clete never even lost consciousness and came out with only a broken nose. It took an hour to pry them loose, the dead man caught in Clete's arms.

All the way to Vallejo The Boy lies down in the backseat of the car and watches the eucalyptus trees that line the parkway pass by outside the rear window. Neither speaks during the entire ride.

When they arrive Clete goes immediately to rent his bowling shoes and The Boy goes looking for Patrick Shalen. Pat Shalen is his schoolmate at St. Catherine's Academy. Pat is enormously overweight. He is only 9, 10, 11, but he weighs almost 180, 190, 200 pounds. The Boy doesn't like to look at him and he doesn't like to be seen with him and he doesn't much like to talk to him because Pat seems extremely immature. But there is no one else to talk to for the 2½ hours his father will be bowling. So Patrick Shalen is what he settles for.

Sometimes Patrick isn't there. When that happens The Boy goes upstairs, where there is a kind of balcony gallery to view the bowlers—except from the balcony you can't see the bowlers. All you can see are the ends of the lanes, the pins falling—or not falling—as the black cannonball shoots down the wooden alley. And directly in front of the balcony, suspended from the ceiling by thin metal tubing, are giant screens, one above each lane. Scorecards are projected onto them by some sort of overhead projector near where the bowlers wait their turn, just a list of names with numbers and mysterious bowling symbols next to them suspended in air. His father's name is one of them.

It is the job of one man on each team to enter the bowlers' score each time a man finishes his turn. After each bowler throws his black bowling ball, the shadow of a mysterious hand enters a number and a symbol on the screen hanging just in front of the balcony. Years later, when The Boy reads Plato's theory of the cave and how man sees only the shadows of things, never the things themselves, he will think of this bowling alley, of the projected shadow of this mysterious hand, and of his father's name suspended in air before him.

He spends his time in the balcony alone, looking at the men and older boys who are going in and out of the men's room. He thinks they are probably sneaking in there to smoke cigarettes. One Monday evening, when Patrick Shalen stays home, The Boy, bored in the empty balcony, wanders into the men's room.

He enters, stands just inside the doorway, and watches three men standing at the line of urinals. There is a strong smell of disinfectant, so strong it burns The Boy's nose. The men are looking at one another but are not speaking. The Boy notices that none of them are wearing bowling shoes. He knows they'll get in trouble if they try to bowl without bowling shoes. *They must just be leaving the bowling alley*, he thinks. *Or just coming.*

The man in the middle takes a step backward. The Boy supposes he is seeing how far he can pee. The disinfectant tickles The Boy's nose and he sneezes. All three of the men turn and look at him. The middle man steps back up to the urinal. All three finish peeing at the same time, zip up, and leave. Only one of them, a young blond man with a flattop haircut, smiles and winks at him as he pushes through the door.

No one has flushed the urinal he was using. The Boy has noticed that men never flush urinals. He goes to the urinals and flushes each one, reaching up, wrapping his fingers around the smooth silver handle, pulling gently, listening for the rush of water. Then The Boy washes his hands and goes back to the balcony.

He walks up and down each row, touching the seat of each chair, counting them. There are 101 chairs in the balcony. They are like theater seats, but they are wooden and hard and uncomfortable to sit in. He notices that the screen where his father's name has been projected is now dark. It is time to leave. He rushes downstairs. For some reason that he cannot articulate, he doesn't want his father to come upstairs looking for him.

In the back of the car on the way home from the bowling alley, The Boy lies on the seat looking out the back window at the moon as it flits in and out of the trees that line the parkway. The moon is almost full and casts shadows on The Boy's face. They are the shadows of the eucalyptus trees, shadows of the telephone poles, even the shadows of fat, round telephone wires that droop from pole to pole.

The Boy looks at the back of his father's head, which is in shadow on this dark, lonely road they travel. The Boy realizes that in the year, two years, three years they have been making this trip each Monday evening, they have never spoken to one another. Not a single word. The Boy will wonder why for a long, long time—long into adulthood.

But now, here in the backseat of the car with the moon flashing on and off in his face, the trees flecking his body with the shadows of their heavy limbs, their sturdy, intertwining branches, their thin, long leaves in the shape of witches' fingers, The Boy sinks into the dark silence that fills the family car. He sees the two of them from somewhere above Columbus Parkway, moving slowly along the winding road, encapsulated in a pink-and-purple automobile, working their way silently, darkly away from where men line up at urinals, where men meet to thunderously heave heavy black balls down slick wooden alleys toward white pins with red stripes around their necks, fearfully huddling together near the alley's end. Where men hope to knock each white pin out from under its single foot and send it careening over the precipice behind them into the dark. There, in that pitch-dark place, too dark for the eye to see clearly, another man, a black man, paid 75 cents an hour, will—if he is quick enough, if he is sure enough, if he is fortunate enough—jump out of the way, scramble to pick up the battered pins. Then he will quickly set them back in place and leap back to safety before the crashing thunder warns him that another black ball is hurling toward him.

This, The Boy thinks, *is what my father does for fun*. He does not understand his father or his father's fun. He doesn't understand bowling, the invisible hand, or the men in the men's room. But he does understand one thing. This ride to and from this place where men congregate, this traveling beneath the moon among the eucalyptus branches, this movement in and out of shadow—this he understands. He has no words for it, yet he knows it intimately. It frightens him and it frees him at once.

Here, then, is a knowledge he will take with him into adulthood: As long as he is quiet, as long as he lies down in the dark, or crouches in dim corners, where his father cannot see him, can find neither his reflection in the mirror nor his shadow falling beside him, he will be safe. This is how The Boy travels. This is what The Boy knows.

10:19:59:59:00 A.M.

His sperm shoots high into the air—a twisted white rope; the turbines of the city power plant spin and roar; a lumber truck with redwood trees strapped to its flatbed careens around the hairpin turns of the Pacific Coast Highway; above east Mojave Desert a lone cloud floats, adrift in a sea of sky; a billion blades of grass push through the soil of Golden Gate Park; the flames of the cremation grounds devour an infant's corpse: all at the same moment, all the same Energy, all from the same Source.

Only his perception distinguishes it.

Only his confusion defines it.

Only his mind keeps him from knowing It.

10:19:59:59:01 A.M.

Before he becomes a great Sufi, EG sets out on a pilgrimage to Mecca. On his way he meets a dervish. The dervish, like most dervishes, is in a constant state of ecstasy.

"Where are you going?" the dervish asks.

"To Mecca," EG answers.

"Why?"

"To see God."

"How much money do you have?" the dervish inquires.

"Five hundred gold dinars."

"Hand them over to me," says the dervish. He takes the money and tucks it safely into his breast pocket, then asks EG, "Do you know what you will do in Mecca? You will simply walk around the sacred rock seven times. Instead of doing that, walk around me seven times."

EG hesitates, thinking the dervish quite mad.

"Now hurry!" the dervish commands.

EG does as he is instructed.

"Now, says the dervish, "you have achieved your purpose. But first let me tell you something. Since the day Mecca was built, God has never dwelled there. But since the heart was created, God has never left it. Go home and meditate. Do yourself some real good, for whoever has attained God has attained Him within the human heart. That is the greatest temple of God. Not Mecca."

10:19:59:59:02 A.M.

EG walks down the Bell Path early in the morning. Hari is bounding about, ferreting mice, birds, and squirrels in the woods. The sky is gray, and the redwoods are filled with a dense fog that swirls among the upper branches. The delicate deep green needles are bejeweled with sparkling droplets that fall like a bombardment of diamonds when the wind blows.

At the end of the Bell Path, EG sits on a bench crafted from three madrone logs. He closes his eyes, raises his arms, and calls everyone together. He asks that all of them be present, for he has a question that must be answered now, before he returns to the White Room.

He sees them coming down the path single file. They enter the grotto and, one by one, nod, wave, or smile, then take a seat on a log or stump, lean against trees. The children sit on the ground, cushioned by the thick carpet of leaves and pine needles.

EG looks around this circle of beings, taking inventory to make sure no major players are missing. There is Annabel Laughing, wearing green pedal pushers, a polka-dot blouse open at the neck, and fuzzy pink bunny slippers on her feet; Annabel the Seductress is wearing a red silk moiré evening dress slit up to the hip with high-heeled shoes dyed to match and rhinestone earrings and bracelet; Annabel in Menopause sits on a log in pajamas and slippers, hair disheveled, tapping her left foot and smoking a Pall Mall.

There is Cletus, bedraggled, stubbly faced, with three days' growth of beard. He holds a scratched-and-dented black metal lunch pail in one hand, a Burgermeister beer in the other. The Smiling Mailman stands next to him, bright-eyed, wearing his drab blue uniform, cap tossed back on his head of thick, wavy black hair. He grins broadly as though about to deliver the punch line to a very funny story and explode into raucous laughter. Behind Annabel the Seductress, leaning one shoulder against a redwood tree and smoking a Camel, is Daddy, his white shirt open almost to his waist. His gray pleated slacks are held up by charcoal-gray suspenders, and he smiles as he glances sideways at The Boy.

Then there is Aunt Cecilia, wary, observant. She is sporting black crepe slacks, an olive-green silk blouse, and her good-luck leopard-skin jacket. She is drinking a glass of vermouth on the rocks with a twist. Her auburn hair shows no signs of gray; her face is virtually free of age, for she is ageless, even in old age.

There is Anna, arms folded, glaring, long black hair falling to her bare shoulders. She is wearing only a black slip with a black brassiere beneath it, supporting her voluptuous breasts. Her eyes are like polished coal.

Annabel's older brother, Wes, leans against a tree in his khakis and tan waist-jacket. He is holding a tan cap in one hand, wiping his bald head with a handkerchief with the other. He appears to be very tired. A basket of plums sits at his feet.

Next to them and standing back, almost out of sight behind an old madrone tree is AD. He pulls at his sweater, trying to keep it from clinging to his chest. Although he is only 15 he weighs more than 225 pounds. He wishes he didn't have to be there. He sneaks glances every once in a while to his left at the slender, handsome man who is wearing faded Levi's, a white T-shirt, and tennis shoes. He has a dark mustache and bobs back and forth from foot to foot, as though dancing to an inaudible tune. He is studying a timetable for trains between Rome and Florence.

Sitting cross-legged next to the man is The Boy, nervous, frightened, vulnerable. EG motions for him to come to him. The Boy does, and EG takes him in his arms, hugs and kisses him, then tells him to sit at his feet.

But there is someone missing. EG looks about but finds her nowhere. Then The Boy tugs at EG's pant leg and points over his left shoulder. EG turns and finds, seated next to him, crocheting something of blue lace, Cohen. She is wearing a navy-and-white cotton house dress, heavy black shoes, and an apron with a gold Star of David embroidered on the breast. Around her neck is a silver rope. Attached to it are hundreds of small pewter skulls. Her long gray hair is wrapped in a bun atop her head; wire-rimmed spectacles slide halfway down her nose. She says nothing but tends to her work. Seated on the other side of her, elbows on his knees, leafing through a *Playboy* magazine and smoking a Chesterfield is Harry, her son.

Everyone except Cohen is waiting for EG to speak.

"I've brought you together because I must return to the White Room and before I do I need the answer to a question." He now has their full attention, except for Cletus, who knows he has no answers to anyone's questions, no matter how trivial they might be.

EG asks, "Tell me, who are you and where do you come from?"

Even Cletus smiles. This may be the one question he could actually answer. He grins and says, "What a stupid question. We're..."

"Don't speak!" shouts Anna, holding up her hand toward the Smiling Mailman. "Don't speak. *Non parli, strònz!*" She rolls her eyes and gestures her frustration and contempt to no one in particular.

"I need to understand. How can I let go if I don't understand what is happening?" EG asks.

The group turns in unison and looks down the path, as if hearing something from behind them. Coming down the path are two old men. One wears a gray flannel shirt, baggy brown wool trousers, and boots. He has a hand scythe looped through one of the belt loops in the back of his trousers. He is about 90 years old and has a full head of salt-and pepper-colored hair. On top of his head rests a floppy brown Borsolino, weathered from being worn in the garden for so many years.

Walking next to him is an even older man. The second man looks Chinese. He looks like Paul would look if he were 100 years old. He wears baggy blue silk pajamas with white brocade designs in the shape of weeping cherry trees, pagodas, and arched bridges. Over it he wears a huge quilted gray-and black-striped house jacket exactly like the one Paul made for EG the first Christmas they were together. He carries a bamboo lantern.

Both men are stooped but walk with great dignity. They come and stand before EG. The Chinese man bows; the Caucasian man removes his hat.

"There are others," the Chinese man says. "Do you want to meet them?"

"I'm afraid," The Boy says, looking up at EG.

"That was not the question," replies the man with the hand scythe.

EG turns to look at Cohen. Cohen doesn't look up from her work.

"I want to meet them," EG answers.

"You're afraid to meet them," shouts Cletus, gesticulating with the hand holding the beer.

"Of course I'm afraid," snaps EG. Then, grasping The Boy's shoulders firmly, reassuringly, he says first to The Boy, "Remember Rome. Remember Mònte Caprino." Then to the old men, "Let me meet them."

The two old men step aside, one to EG's left, one to his right. The assembled people cover their eyes with their hands and turn away. There is a rustling in the branches of all the trees and bushes. Leaves on the ground rise and fall. Above where he sits, EG hears what sounds like the wings of a large bird flapping. He wraps his arms tightly around The Boy and squeezes him between his knees. The sky grows dark, and from far up the Bell Path, The Procession of The Dark Ones begins.

10:19:59:59:03 A.M.

O son of noble family, now what is called the Great Luminosity has arrived. You are not alone in leaving this world. It happens to everyone, so do not feel desire and yearning for this life. Even if you feel desire and yearning, you cannot stay. You can only wan-

der in *Samsara*. Do not desire, do not yearn. O son of noble family, whatever terrifying projections appear in the Bardo of Dharmata, do not forget these words but go forward remembering their meaning; the essential point is to remember them and recognize everything as projections of your own mind.

Enter now the Bardo of Dharmata and say this prayer as you tread this dangerous path:

> Now when the Bardo of Dharmata
> dawns upon me,
> I will abandon all thoughts of fear and terror,
> I will recognize whatever appears as my projection
> and know it to be a vision of the bardo;
> now that I have reached this crucial Point
> I will not fear the peaceful and wrathful ones, my
> own projections.

10:19:59:59:04 A.M.

EG is running for elected office. He is living up the coast just across the Mendocino County line in Anchor Bay. Shortly after the Revolution, Anchor Bay became a Lambda Colony, resettled and reclaimed by the members of the GLLM, the Gay and Lesbian Liberation Militia. When the reapportionment of California took place, it was assumed all across the country that California would become home to the "oddballs," those groups considered to be outside the dominant culture. The irony, of course, to the more sophisticated population was that in the midst of a coup d'etat, anyone at all would be considered "oddball." After all, it was the minorities of the country who were rising up to overthrow the government. Where now was the dominant culture? Leaders of the Revolution—all segments of the Revolution—were adamant that there would be no dominant culture. But if there was any subculture or subgroup that still found itself the target of bigotry from all sides, even Revolutionary compatriots, it was the GLLM.

In Mendocino County, where people had tended to fall all along the political spectrum, a few of the wealthy who had purchased or built huge, expensive weekend or summer houses on the ocean, now found themselves needing permanent refuge away from the cities, which were under siege from all sides. Corporations were seized, huge companies and banks and utilities were occupied by Revolutionary appointees. Those hoping to escape the vengeance of the GLLM had long since packed up what belongings and cash they could get their hands on and moved far into the country or even to other remote states, where they were less likely to be bothered. The dominant culture, in other words, had fled to the hills.

Anchor Bay found itself home to many of northern California's wealthiest and most reactionary refugees. The sheer numbers of such political refugees in enclaves such as Sea Ranch, the multibillion-dollar planned community that rolled along 12 miles and 100,000 acres of prime beachfront real estate, gave them some power.

One of the reasons for this was that more outlying areas had not abandoned a democratic form of government. They had, for the most part, been taken over by educated, albeit ruthless, groups that also were able to amass large amounts of capital and rally huge numbers of brave soldiers dedicated to their cause. Thus, Palm Springs was governed by Mexican-Americans, Los Angeles by African-Americans. Most of the towns of northern California were taken over by Native American, gay and lesbian, Japanese, or Vietnamese groups. Seattle and Puget Sound had fallen to Hong Kong Chinese in the first months of the Revolution, and dominant culture hordes fled in the night to Spokane and Pocatello and across the Canadian border into British Columbia, Alberta, and Saskatchewan.

The Pacific Northwest was one of the bloodiest regions of the coup. Almost the entire state of Oregon fell to massive numbers of lesbian militia who had never forgotten the brutal butchering of two gentle women in southern Oregon in the 1990s. The murder had gone ultimately unpunished when the man convicted was released on a technicality. Most of his body was found in his truck three weeks later. His head was never recovered.

Now EG has decided to run in the election for County Supervisor. His platform is simple: All heterosexuals—"Breeders" as they are derisively referred to in the GLLM—must leave the county. They will be allowed to take with them only their liquid assets and one automobile. Their houses will become the property of the county and will be used to house the indigent.

First to be taken care of are homeless gay and lesbian citizens. Next, gay and lesbian couples with children who are in need of housing. Then, any homeless person who has resided in the county for more than ten years, regardless of sexual orientation. The only exception to any of these rules are the immediate allocation of 40 of the houses, which will be turned over to VOP's (Veterans of the Plague) and their families.

Anyone not leaving the county by January 1—two months after the election—will undergo incarceration and house arrest in a resort built by the Japanese in the northeastern part of the county and "appropriated" in the uprising by the GLLM. Families of childbearing age will undergo forced sterilization. Breeder children will be taken from their biological families and placed with gay and lesbian families to be raised free from prejudice.

Schools will teach children to tolerate people of any race, culture, or religious belief—everyone that is, who is not heterosexual or fundamentalist Christian. Breeders must always be considered suspect, and Christians must register with the county. Children in schools will be taught about the Revolution and what started it.

They will learn that the election of a right-wing newspaper reporter and radio talk show host to the office of President of the United States resulted in the attempted deportation of all Spanish-speaking Americans and all Asians who had not been born on American soil or who could not pass a written government-administered American language examination. Government jobs had been denied to anyone who could not prove European ancestry.

All non-Christian houses of worship, including synagogues, were declared public property, and tax-exempt status was denied to all non-Christian churches. People of the Plague were forced to report to a central registry and lists of people infected with the Plague virus were published in newspapers.

It was against the law to hire a known homosexual for any position that dealt with the public, and any employer or landlord could, for any reason, terminate or evict a known homosexual or a person not born on American soil. All trade with foreign nations was sharply restricted, and businesses fled en masse to Latin and South America, Africa, and Southeast Asia, where American megacorporations enlarged their industries with the cheap labor of Third World nations.

Women were denied equal opportunity protection under the law and tax credits were granted to families with children if the wife did not hold employment outside the home. Surtaxes were applied to families when both parents held full-time jobs.

These are the conditions that eventually led to the overthrow of the government. The Revolution ironically used as its motto a slogan employed by the reactionary president during his presidential campaign—a slogan even more ironic in so far as it was originally coined and shouted by African-American revolutionaries in the 1960s: Power to the People.

So now EG, encouraged by local political clubs and loyal readers of his many and varied books on the nature of good and evil, has thrown his hat into the political ring. He knows with certainty that he will serve as supervisor for the county because it is widespread knowledge that if he doesn't receive the majority of the vote—which is unlikely since his only opponent is a retired judge from Marin County who denied zoning permits to Plague hospices in two parts of his county prior to the Revolution—the GLLM will seize the position for EG by force if necessary. So rather than travel the county making speeches, he is writing his acceptance speech.

He has decided to add to his platform the requirement that any heterosexual who resides in the county may be used by any gay or lesbian individual or couple for sexual favors at any time. All that is required is that health exams be performed before and after the act if the Breeder is a "one-time encounter" or on a monthly basis if the Breeder is a domestic slave. Also, a gay or lesbian individual may indenture any heterosexual for a period of up to three years, providing that the individual provides accommodations for the person. No description or inspection of the accommodations is required.

EG is looking forward to serving as county supervisor. He has decided he enjoys power and is extremely gratified by watching heterosexuals demeaned in public.

10:19:59:59:05 A.M.

This morning he takes Hari to the beach, as he does every morning. He parks the truck, releases the Doberman, takes his *mala* from his pocket, and begins his ascent up the path toward the dunes, saying *japa* as he goes. The first 54 prayers he recites in Sanskrit: *Om Bhuh, Bhuvah, Svah. Om Tat Savitur varenyam bargo devasya dimahi. Di yo yo nah prachodayat Om.* The second 54 he prays in English. "Creator, Sustainer, Destroyer, O Lord of Faculties, seated in my heart, may I carry out your commands as dictated by you in my conscience."

This morning, while walking up the dunes, he encounters a man coming down the trail. He is a large man with white hair, a flushed face full of burst blood vessels, and a protruding stomach. He is wearing a food-stained, once-white T-shirt.

The man is accompanied by two small dogs, which seem to be mostly Chihuahua. One is old and moves slowly. The man is shouting at the older dog from the time they come into view. The older dog is looking back over its shoulder at the man with a mixture of disdain and fear. The dog looks like it lives in the wild, not with a human. It has burs in its coat, dirt matted on its head. Its eyes burn with a kind of wild rage. The dog turns to look up at EG as it passes, and EG looks into the dog's eyes. They are weary eyes. EG empathizes with the Chihuahua.

As the two men pass one another, EG greets the man, who greets him in return. But the man is distracted by the older dog again, who is now in the process of exchanging tail-sniffing greetings with Hari. The man begins to call the dog, shouting loudly and cursing. The dog ignores his owner.

The man lurches toward the dog several times, almost losing his balance and falling over. He kicks at the little dog, cursing violently and shouting, "Motherfucker, son of a bitch, motherfucker," over and over at the old Chihuahua, who dodges the man's foot in such a graceful, almost rehearsed way that EG realizes the dog has danced this dance before.

EG considers the man, who is now tottering and teetering in his attempts to make contact with the dog by way of his foot. EG thinks he looks like a cancan dancer, only fatter and older, and, of course, dressed all wrong. The man has a thick Irish accent that is growing more and more indistinguishable. EG thinks, *Could he be drunk so early in the morning?*

He says to the dancing man, "I wouldn't come either if you were going to kick me."

The man shouts, "You don't know this dog. This son of a bitch wants to fight. He'll tear into your dog. I don't want him to get killed, the goddamn little motherfucker."

EG points out, "Neither one of them is growling." He calls Hari away from the Chihuahua and walks away from this man, who continues down the hill cursing and kicking at his dog. The last time EG turns to look, the man has tumbled into a giant yellow lupine bush and is flailing his arms in the air, wailing something indistinguishable.

He wonders how often the dogs are beaten or kicked and why the man bothers having dogs at all. But, of course, the answer is obvious: He has them so that he can beat them. That is where the man releases the intense rage he carries within.

He is enraged for reasons no one will ever know, EG thinks. Surely his wife—if ever he had a wife—has left him by now. She had friends come one morning and help her escape while her husband was at work or out walking the dogs. Together, the flock of women swept through the rectangular mint-green house on the suburban hillside, grabbing vases and pots, dresses and books, shoes and photographs—the essentials for beginning a new life—and threw them into open suitcases and cartons that the women brought with them. Then the lot of them ran to their waiting cars and tore down the street, leaving a trail of silverware and stockings on the front lawn.

Or perhaps she was a devout Catholic and couldn't bring herself to leave him.

Instead she slowly sickened with a mysterious consumption, growing weaker and weaker, more and more pale, frail to the point of needing hospital care. Finally, with only two prospects—returning home to the raging bull or slipping out of her present life—she chose the gates of heaven and died in the hospital. Of course, this enraged him even more.

He hates his job, where he has an unfair, younger boss who accuses him of being lazy, rather than seeing that he is ill, old, and has a hard time getting started mornings, which accounts for his perpetual tardiness. He has never been treated fairly at work, never been appreciated for the little things he does for the company. Everyone is envious of him, so he is constantly reassigned from one menial task to another until he is relegated finally to keeping the gate at the main entrance, where he is isolated in a four-foot-square guardhouse.

At least here he will have privacy. Here he can control his own destiny for an hour at a time. Here he can find a place to keep his refreshments away from probing eyes, inquisitive hands. It is his lot in life to be tortured like the Christian martyrs. Now he sees it as God's plan. What kind of God is this anyway? He ponders it over a refreshing swig of whiskey. Just to keep the chill off.

His small boxy house is impossible to care for, especially with his wife gone. How will he manage? Why doesn't God send him another woman? The neighbors complain about the dogs barking during the day, about his yard overgrown with weeds, the trash that swirls in his driveway. Yes, his life is a horror. Why shouldn't he be angry? Why has God forsaken him? This is what he thinks almost every night, just before the darkness overtakes him and he drowns in fitful sleep.

EG thinks of Clete as he continues to climb through the dunes. His absent father, hiding in the garage with his bottles of beer, half-pints of whiskey, trying to dissect an incomprehensible life with his chisels and screwdrivers, sort out the puzzle of his destiny by grouping and boxing nails and screws, arranging boxes of bolts, cases of wrenches, building nothing. His father, whose rote retort to any charge of alcoholism was, "I've never missed a day's work in my life. End of story."

Continuing along the trail that winds high above the ocean, EG tells himself that this too is the space between the molecules. This is the Goddess Kali, wrathful, dirty, filled with rage and venom, wearing a necklace of skulls, drinking blood from the skull of one of her now egoless victims. *This too is It*, he thinks, and repeats a verse from the Gita that he has committed to memory:

> Creatures come, creatures vanish;
> Only I am real, Arjuna, looking out,
> Amused, from deep within the eyes of every
> creature.

In the distance a fishing boat trolls along the coast, bobbing in the gently rolling waves. *The energy that moves the water*, he thinks, *is the same energy that repeats the japa, kicks the dog, fills my heart with compassion. The same force that spits the curse also whispers the name of God into the morning air. The same energy that lifts me up the dunes higher and higher, closer and closer to the vast ocean that is the unconscious also draws another man down the path, feet sinking and slipping in the sand, lower and lower, farther and farther away from understanding and wisdom, deeper and deeper into the dark, where, like that tiny dog, he will bark at what he does not comprehend, what he is too terrified to approach.*

Both of us, EG thinks, *are driven by the same force, both are expressions of the same Self. Both are the same energy at different times, in different places, both tossed temporarily about within the sea of chaos, the sea of samsara, the ocean of time. I do not understand how this happens, but I am beginning to observe it. Like the electricity in the fan, the lightbulb, the refrigerator, and the oven all at the same time, It is in the cursing man, in me, in the dogs and also in the undulating waves all at the same time.*

As he stands on the cliff looking down at Hari frolicking in the foamy surf with another dog who has come along, he thinks these things. He tries to open his arms wide enough to embrace the paradox that all things are the same thing, all things are It. He can comprehend it in his intellect, and he has glimpses of it from time to time, as he did this morning, but he cannot quite make it his experience. He smiles at himself. He forgives himself the shortcoming as he thinks, *This shortcoming too is It.* He wonders if Prabuddhananda would understand.

He's glad no one can hear what goes on in his mind.

10:19:59:59:06 A.M.

He decides to visit his father in the Old Soldiers' Home against all advice and his own best judgment. *I must do this before it is too late*, he tells himself.

He must try one last time before either he or his father dies and he is forced to carry this cleavage into a future reality to rectify and resolve.

EG is told by a staff person to look for his father in the cafeteria. The large room, immense as a high school auditorium, is filled with diners, mostly hospital staff, but here and there at round tables sit small groups of old men. Some are neatly dressed, even wearing ties; some are decked out in uniforms resplendent with row after row of purple, red, and green ribbons, and gold, silver, and bronze metals. Some sit slumped in pajamas and bathrobe, stubbly beards and disheveled gray hair betraying their dearth of visitors.

At one far corner of the hall sits a lone man neatly dressed in khaki work pants, a plaid shirt buttoned to the neck, and leather slippers. It is, he recognizes immediately, Cletus. He sits alone, eating his meal with German deliberativeness, contemplating each bite carefully, as he laboriously chews what is in his mouth.

Slowly EG approaches, sits down next to him. His father's white hair, perfectly combed with some sort of paralyzing goo, is thick and full and neatly trimmed. His eyeglasses, made of thick black plastic, slide slowly down the bridge of his nose as he saws his steak rhythmically.

The old man finally looks up at EG, and the recognition is instantaneous. Just as EG's eyes fill with fearful anticipation like the eyes of a 7-year-old boy bringing his father a mediocre report card, the old man's eyes narrow and an almost imperceptible film creeps down over his deep green pupils.

"Go see if there's any ketchup around here, will you?" he orders EG.

"Dad," EG begins, not knowing exactly what will come out of his mouth after a 12-year hiatus in what they might euphemistically refer to as their "relationship." "Dad, it's me, EG," he says, despite knowing without doubt, having seen the iron gates of fear clang shut across his father's face, that the old man recognizes him full well.

"Have you eaten?" the old man asks. "Steak's not bad." Then without missing a beat, without ever having revealed that he was looking at anything other than his plate, he leans over and begins brushing at EG's pant leg. "You've got some kind of crap all over yourself. You ought to get that off before it stains."

EG turns slowly and walks toward the door. The old man calls half-heartedly, "Where you goin'? Bathroom's that way. Where you goin'?"

EG walks out of the cafeteria, down the interminable white linoleum corridor, through the double doors, down the 27 granite steps, and over the gray gravel path that cuts between two large expanses of lawn, where, on either side, two Mexican men—one old and shriveled and wearing a large-brimmed straw hat, one young and shirtless with a red bandanna around his head—ride twin John Deere tractor mowers beneath the scorching Napa Valley sun.

10:19:59:59:07 A.M.

He opens his eyes as the world wakes. On the other side of the large plate-glass window next to the bed, the tips of redwoods and ponderosa pines reach into the gray sky. The night fog is slipping back down the mountain, roiling over large granite rocks and fat manzanita bushes, swirling around the branches of the trees as it recedes back to the ocean to rest until dusk. Then it will slowly climb back up the hill to blanket the house, the gravel drive, the silver truck sitting beneath the carport.

Anchor Bay is domed by a gray cloud cover. The soft and silver light, diffused and gentle, emanates from no single source but seems to hover at the edges of everything.

Between his legs beneath the comforter, his brown-skinned lover, a man 16 years his junior, takes him into his mouth. EG sighs, then holds his breath as Paul takes him deeper and deeper, sucking not too hard, not too lightly, knowing exactly how to please his lover.

EG watches the covers move rhythmically up and down. He pulls back the comforter. Without breaking his erotic rhythm, Paul begins making a slight slurping noise, then reaches one hand up to EG's face and slips one finger into EG's mouth. Now the sensual palette of touch, sight, smell, taste, and sound is complete and their arousal intensifies.

Paul looks up into EG's eyes and smiles as best he can with EG filling his mouth. He pauses momentarily, stops sucking EG's cock, placing his hand around him and stroking lightly. He smiles so broadly at EG that it appears he will break into laughter any second. His eyes sparkle in the silver light of the world. They are as white and luminescent as a white room EG vaguely remembers being in once, a room where the light seemed to come out of the walls.

EG smiles back, whispers, "I love you." Paul's smile widens.

EG notices that his lover's hand can't completely encircle his erect penis. Is it because his dick is so fat? Or is it that his lover's hand is so small? It looks like the hand of a young boy, a child. *Will this thought offend The Boy?* he wonders. He turns his head to where The Boy, standing beside the bed, is studying their sex.

"Does this offend you?" he asks The Boy. "Is it all right with you that I think of him as a boy sometimes?"

"I like it," The Boy answers. "I have these same stirrings inside me. "

Perhaps he didn't use the word stirrings, EG thinks. *No, he would use* feelings *probably. Or maybe, "I want to do that too."*

"I want to do that too," The Boy says.

EG laughs. "Someday you will," he tells The Boy. "When you're a little older."

"I want to now," The Boy says.

EG turns his attention back to his lover, who is still smiling, still stroking him with his delicate hand, his eyes sparkling like brown gems. EG focuses on the space between his lover's fingers, where they do not meet. *The space between the molecules,* EG thinks. *This too is Shiva.*

Now he feels himself about to erupt, the heat of his passion rising up the length of him toward Paul's smile.

"I love you," he repeats, "and I'm going to come."

Paul whispers as he giggles slightly, "Good."

"You are Krishna," EG says.

"You are Rama," his lover responds.

A thick white blast erupts onto Paul's cheek, making him laugh out loud.

"This too is God," EG says, barely able to speak. "This too is Shakti. And this. And this. And this." He thinks, *The come, the coming, the comer. Everything is It.*

"I am making love with Rama," Paul says. He takes EG, sticky and white, into his mouth without breaking his gaze into EG's eyes.

"I am making love with Krishna," EG says in return.

Beside the bed, The Boy giggles and thinks, *This is really fun.*

10:19:59:59:08 A.M.

He knew no one would understand, especially heterosexual men. He is hot and sweaty, and the lights in the room are far too bright. Also there is no air in the room, only an oscillating fan in the corner, but its arc is not quite wide enough to include EG in its cooling sweep. He thinks about getting up to move it, but at that moment the thin man with the gray mustache comes back into the room. He is wiping the top of his head, which is completely bald, with a white handkerchief that EG supposes his wife put in his coat pocket before he left the house this morning.

He has another man with him this time, a younger man wearing Levi's, a T-shirt, and high-top tennis shoes. When the younger man turns to grab a chair, EG sees a pair of handcuffs clipped to a belt loop in the back of his jeans. The young man sits down backward in the chair, straddling it. He pulls a pack of Lucky Strikes out from where they were tucked in his shirt sleeve à la James Dean, lights one, and winks at EG. Only EG sees him wink. The young man's T-shirt is a small, but his body is an extra large. Obviously he has been working out with weights for a long time. EG thinks these two men are extremely naive.

"You don't understand," EG says. "This isn't going to tell you anything."

"What isn't?" the thin bald man asks, sitting down at the table, still wiping his head.

"This," EG says, pointing to the young man. "Him. It has nothing to do with my attraction to men. It actually has nothing to do with me much at all. And it isn't about sex. You don't understand at all."

"Why don't you try to explain it to us, then," the younger man says, flipping his cigarette ash into a red metal ashtray that is already full to overflowing. As he reaches to move the ashtray closer, EG notices the prominent blue vein that runs down the center of the man's bicep. He notices how small the man's hand is. He looks into the blue eyes of the young man, who is looking at the ashtray in disgust. "Jeez, Lou, don't you guys ever clean up around here?"

Lou shrugs. "Well, we're all ears," he says to EG.

"Yeah, tell us about it."

"I already told him," EG says, nodding toward the thin bald man.

"Yeah, but now I wanna hear it. You don't mind, do you? I want to see if I can help here. Lou doesn't understand this stuff very well, but I do. Two heads are better than one, that sort of idea, see?"

"I work nights," EG begins again. "Graveyard at the winery. I go to work at midnight, get off at 8. I come home, eat breakfast, go to bed, and sleep till about 4 or 5, sometimes 6 if it's crushing season. This morning I come home, eat the breakfast my wife has fixed me, talk with the kid a little bit before he goes off to school. Then I take a shower and get in bed."

EG looks around for a window. "Could you turn that fan a little so I can feel it? It's kind of hot in here."

Lou and the younger man look at the fan, then at one another. "Sure thing," the young one says and jumps up. He moves the fan a little, comes back, holding out his hand in front of EG's face to see if he can feel the breeze, then sits down again. "OK, where were we?" he asks EG. "Oh, yeah, you were in bed naked with the little boy."

"That's not true," EG protests. "That's not how it happened at all. Do you want to hear what happened, or do you want to make it up yourself? Maybe I should just leave, and you two can do this on your own. You seem to have it already figured out."

"You wear pajamas to bed?" the younger man asks, ignoring everything EG has just said.

"What does that have to do with anything?"

"Do you?"

"No, I don't wear pajamas."

"Underwear?"

EG looks at Lou, who is giving him a straight-on deadpan look.

"I bet you like to sleep in the raw, huh?"

"What does that have to do…"

"Don't you!" the younger man shouts, slamming his hand flat on the table. EG jumps and stares at the younger man.

"Yes, I do," EG says softly, determined not to be flustered by this obvious technique. He looks at Lou again, who is giving a very thin smile now. "You probably do too," EG says snidely. "So what?"

"Nothing," the younger man says. "Go on, tell me the rest."

"Around 5 o'clock I wake up and find my son in bed with me. It's not unusual. Sometimes, just before I'm due to get up, The Boy comes in and crawls into bed with me. We lie and talk for a while, and then I get up and take a shower and shave and eat dinner and go to work."

"Does your son shower with you?" the younger man asks.

"Yes, as a matter of fact he does sometimes take a shower with me. He also takes a shower with his mother sometimes, not that it's any of your business."

"Go on. So you wake up and The Boy is in bed with you. Then what?"

"We lie and talk for awhile, kind of doze on and off. Then we get up and go into the bathroom."

"To take your shower together?"

"No, to pee. My son said he had to pee."

"Why couldn't he do that by himself?"

"You obviously don't have any sons."

"No, I don't. Explain it to me."

"When you have a son, at some point in the child's development, you must teach him to stand up to pee into the toilet and the way you do that is to pee with him and show him how it's done. Didn't your father teach you how to pee?"

"Let's leave my father out of this, shall we? So the two of you are standing at the toilet peeing. Then what?"

"Well, I was still half-asleep and I peed and was waiting for my son to finish peeing and I stretched. You know, like you do when you first wake up. I stretched a long, slow stretch.

And suddenly, in the middle of stretching, in the middle of raising my hands to the ceiling and stretching every muscle in my body, I feel this warm, wet sensation."

"You feel it where?"

"Down there," EG says, nodding toward his lap.

"Down where?" the younger man asks.

"On my dick."

"Go on."

"I was still half-asleep, like I said, so I looked down to make sure I wasn't imagining it, and when I looked down I saw that The Boy had taken me into his mouth."

"Just like that."

"Just like that."

"You stretch and the kid blows you."

"No! It wasn't like that. It was an act of love. He simply reached out to the most available part of me. It was a natural, impetuous act."

"So now you're saying that your son's sucking your cock is a natural act."

"He was not 'sucking my cock.' And yes, in this instance it was a very natural act."

"So how long did this go on?"

"Not long, really."

"How long?"

"Not long."

"But long enough for you to come."

EG sits silently. He looks at Lou, who is deadpan again, then he looks down at the table.

"The neighbor says there was a white viscous fluid running out of the kid's mouth when she opened the door. She referred to it as 'semen,' I believe."

"It's not what you think."

"Then tell me what it really was."

"I looked down, and my son had taken me into his mouth and was looking up at me smiling."

"Smiling?"

"Yes, smiling at me. The most loving, genuine, innocent smile. His face was full of love for me."

"His face was full of love, and his mouth was full of your dick. Do I have this right?"

"You're so crude. You don't understand. It was a natural, spontaneous action."

"Right. Like you coming in the kid's mouth."

"That happened before I could do anything about it. Besides, it didn't feel wrong. It felt right. It was what he wanted. It was what…it was what I wanted at the moment."

"You wanted to violate your son."

"No, it wasn't a violation. It was an act of love. It was like saying, "Look, son, this is where you came from, here, this fluid from my body is where you came from. Taste it, rejoin yourself with it."

"Jesus. You make me sick."

"I expect I do. Someone as closed and repressed as you wouldn't understand." EG turns and looks at Lou, who is still sitting with a deadpan expression. "Do you understand? Do you have any idea at all what I'm trying to tell you?"

"Fuck you," Lou answers.

"I think he'd like that, actually," the younger man says, standing up and flinging the chair back to where he got it. Lou gathers some papers and leaves the room. "I think we're done here," the younger man says. He raises his arms above him and stretches toward the ceiling. EG stares at the young man, who is staring back. Now the man winks again at EG. "I'm stretching," the young man says to EG. "Want to show me how it happened?"

EG can see the younger man is aroused beneath his Levi's. "You sexualize everything, so you can't understand," EG says. "You simply can't understand. I love The Boy. I love him. It's not what you think. It's not like that. It was a spontaneous act of love on The Boy's part, and I responded in the most loving way I knew how. It will probably never happen again."

"You can bet your ass it won't, buddy," the younger man says, and leaves the interrogation room. Just before the door closes, EG hears him say to someone in the other room, "Book that fucking pervert."

10:19:59:59:09 A.M.

Slowly, like the winding jasmine, his awareness has changed. Nothing is what it seems to be. He sees everything as it truly is. Or is he seeing everything as what he projects it to be? This question presents itself wordlessly as he orbits the golden sun in the White Room.

10:19:59:59:10 A.M.

EG steps into the basilica. Paul is somewhere nearby, perhaps looking at a pietà. It is a Roman building with a high dome, high windows, light falling in hard-edged shapes on dark marble mosaic floors. Altars with polished oak communion rails line each side of the church. The nave is open, pewless, in the European tradition. Although he is in the crypt of the basilica, he can see through large windows out across the countryside.

Suddenly the building begins to fall like an elevator out of control. He has nothing to hold on to. *Where is Paul? Where is Andre?* He lies down on a bed nearby, a bier perhaps. The building is falling with such force that he can barely move.

Through the window he can now see other buildings falling. There are skyscrapers, office buildings, cathedrals tumbling and hurtling past the window, falling faster even than the basilica. *Where is Paul? Where is Andre?*

EG knows what is happening. It is the apocalypse. It is most assuredly the end of the world. He knows this beyond any possible doubt. He thinks, *I must cover my face.* He tries to pull the covers over his face, but he can only struggle against the intense force of the motion of falling. He can barely lift his arms. He is flooded with a spectrum of sensations all at once: fear, comprehension, knowledge of his impending death. He thinks, *I am going to die now.* There can be no doubt. This is the end of my life. I will prepare for it. A never-before-felt calmness comes over him in the midst of his fear, not replacing it but complementing it. *I will prepare to die,* he thinks. *This is the moment I've been waiting for. This is the answer to all my questions. The entire world is about to die. I am about to find out what is on the other side.*

EG opens his eyes and he is sweating, breathing hard, as though he had been running. Hari is crying from the other side of the door. Paul is sleeping with his right arm crossed over his eyes, as though he were lying in an open field at noon, stealing a few precious moments before returning to the tasks of his labor. EG leans over, opens the door, and Hari jumps onto the bed and under the covers, curling up right at EG's shoulder in order to be as close as possible. EG turns on his side and wraps his arm around the huge dog. He lies there unable to go back to sleep. He lies in the growing light of dawn, filled with comprehension, fear, and the calm that comes only with deep understanding. He knows but will never tell anyone, that this was not a dream. This really happened.

<u>10:19:59:59:11</u> A.M.

Something has changed. The Earth has shifted, perhaps less than one degree, but unmistakably all things take on a different slant of light, a subtle nuance of meaning, a slight patina of dust. EG walks as though he is carrying something heavy. Not on his person but in his person. Deep inside, perhaps in his bones. *Perhaps*, he thinks, *the marrow of my bones has turned to lead.*

The blue light of California that he loves has turned slightly rust colored. White stucco houses with green trim now look dirty, as though they have been sitting on the Eastern seaboard for a hundred years. The skyline at night—the Transamerica Pyramid, for example—does not leap into the purple sky but pulses in a brown mist, as though it were rising out of the San Bernardino haze.

People on the street whisper at him as he passes, demanding, soto voce, money. Someone calls him "faggot," looking up perplexed from where he sits cross-legged on the filthy sidewalk. Men in business suits let go of drugstore doors so that they swing back in his face. Old women in babushkas clutch their handbags, bunch their coat collars closer to their wrinkled necks, lower their heads, and scurry past.

Even the beach is gray and foggy most days. Not cold and winterlike but misty, damp, warm. Hari runs ahead and disappears into the fog, tears at the ice plant, digs deep holes with obsession.

Something has changed within him, not in the world, not out there. He wonders if it is a depression. *Yes*, he thinks, *that must be it. I am depressed.* Perhaps he has always been depressed and is just now noticing it. With so much death, with so much violence, with so little comfort, how could one not be depressed? He realizes most people he knows are on antidepressants. Maybe he should ask his doctor to prescribe an antidepressant. Or, he thinks, *perhaps I should just scoot over a little and make room for it. Maybe I am just going to be depressed for a while. Maybe I am going to be depressed from now on.*

Maybe I'm sad because I'm dying. He thinks of Paul alone. He thinks of lying on his deathbed in a white room with tubes in his nose and arms, Paul looking down at him, nervous, frightened. He imagines himself unable to speak, unable to open his eyes but still seeing Paul and the room he is dying in, white and antiseptic, still hearing everything going on around him.

He imagines the moment of his death and Paul as he walks out of the room, down the corridor to the hospital elevator. He sees him walk out of the hospital into the gaping jaws of the world. He watches him sit in a coffee shop unable to cry, unable to comprehend that this has happened to him again. He has survived another partner. But not for long. He too is sick, EG sees. Too sick to fall in love again. This comforts EG in a bizarre way, for he remembers how vulnerable Paul was when they met. It had only been three months since Rick had died and already Paul had been taken advantage of by two unscrupulous men.

I must not die first, EG thinks. *Somehow I must not leave him alone. It will be more than he can bear. I must not die first.* He realizes now that he is truly depressed and has been for a long time. He understands that it is completely understandable, but he doesn't like it. He wants not to be depressed. He wants many things. This, he knows, is one of his shortcomings: desire. He is attached to the world and to life, and there is nothing he can do about it.

Odd, he muses. *There is nothing I want to do about it. After Andre died I too was ready to die. I thought I would just wait around and my turn would come. I was grateful for having had such a marvelous love in my life. I put life away and was waiting, like a man in a train station with his hat in his lap, waiting for his train to be called over the public address system. I never expected to fall in love again. I hadn't planned on Paul. I hadn't planned on loving my life again.*

EG begins to sob now. Driving back from the beach with Hari, he must pull over to the side of the road. He sits on Sloat Boulevard in front of a white-and-terra-cotta house where a Chinese woman with white hair peers at him from behind cream-colored drapes. Hari climbs into the passenger seat and puts his paw on EG's shoulder, begins to lick his face. EG does not want to stop crying. He knows this must happen. When Hari too begins to cry, EG cries even harder. This goes on until the street grows dark. Houselights flick on in the neighborhood, one at a time; the Chinese woman opens her front door, stands in her doorway trying to see EG's car as the fog, fat and gray and wet, bellies up the street, hiding everything from view.

Outside the car, standing near the back door, Cohen thrusts her large hands deep into her apron pockets and sighs. Her brow is wrinkled. There is nothing she can do now. The time will come when she can take him in her arms. He will look up at her and shudder with recognition. She will frown, but her words will be soft and comforting. She will hold him and sing "The Isle of Capri" in his ear. This is what will happen one day, in some white room somewhere. But here, on Sloat Boulevard, in the ubiquitous gray fog of evening, with the sun gone, the street lamps cold and uninviting, the houses now all but invisible, here with EG weeping and Hari whimpering, here and now there is nothing she can do.

<u>10:19:59:59:12</u> A.M.

EG is angry, but he doesn't know precisely what to do with his anger, so he has directed it inward at himself. It is an old routine. He is familiar with it but doesn't seem able to reverse it this time.

He feels like everyone he knows—although he understands it is not everyone—refuses to do the "work." Instead they want him to do it for them. They want him to carry their discomfort, figure out the solutions to their problems, and to either give them easy solutions, or if the solutions are difficult—which they almost always are—they want him not to tell them but to carry out the solutions for them and tell them when their lives are better so that they can go on without feeling the pain. Now he has to decide what to do about it. Does he confront people about this? Does he send them away? Being put in the position of having to choose between either of those alternatives makes him bitter and depressed.

Case in point. His friend Laura was unhappy in her five-year relationship. She talked about it incessantly. He counseled her as best he could to find out what she really wanted, what the problem really was. "It's never about what it's about," he told her. "Remember that."

Eventually she decided to break up with her lover. She told her that she was so unhappy she was thinking about whether the relationship should go on. Her lover, Catherine, asked if there was any way they could fix it. Laura said she thought it had gotten too far out of hand. Catherine went out the next week, rented herself a studio apartment, and moved. Now Laura is beside herself because "Catherine walked out on me."

As a result of all this, Laura has focused all her energy into her graduate work and student teaching, but all the energy is dark. Nothing is right. Everything she touches turns sour. She has a 4.0 grade point average in graduate school, but she is convinced she is "going to flunk out." She sobs on EG's doorstep. He tries to comfort her, but she refutes every positive observation he makes. He suggests counseling; she says she has "done counseling and it doesn't work." She says she just needs rest.

She stops by every morning, picks up Hari and takes him to the park with her dog, Max. Then she leaves Max at EG's house and goes to school. She picks him up after school, which is becoming later and later, sometimes as late as midnight. When she comes to retrieve the dog, EG and Paul find themselves hiding so that she'll just open the door, call the dog, see no one around, and leave without talking to them.

She refuses to do anything for herself, but she wants EG to listen to all her tales of woe and take them away from her. EG is furious.

He thinks about these things while he runs errands. At the bank someone cuts in line in front of him. He says nothing. At the shoe repair shop the woman who runs the place first waits on someone who came in after EG. At the grocery store he stands in line while the person at the front of the line requests that the cashier go over every item again because the total doesn't seem to be right. Now she doesn't have enough money to pay for the groceries, so they are deducting items one at a time until the total is equal to what she has in her purse.

"If you'd paid closer attention, you would have seen this line was going to take forever," Clete says. He is standing in line behind EG, holding a six-pack of Burgermeister 12-ounce cans.

EG responds without turning around. "There was no way in hell anyone could tell this would happen. Ordinarily I'd feel compassion toward her for not being able to pay for her groceries. I'm just in a bad mood today."

Clete continues. "You shouldn't have come to this Safeway in the first place. It's always like this; that's why you stopped coming here years ago. Why did you come here today? This is going to take forever. It's a nightmare."

"Shut up!" EG barks. The line moves now.

In the car Clete pops open a Burgie. "How could you let that Laura person do this to you? She's driving you crazy. You should pick your friends more carefully. Anyone could have seen from the very start that she's crazy. But you just don't think. That's your problem. You're stupid. You don't use your head. You've got to learn to think. Jeez!"

"Laura's in a lot of pain," chimes in Annabel, climbing into the backseat and leaning forward, her head between the two of them. "You don't know what it's like to be a woman. She's alone and has to take care of everything on her own. People try to take advantage of her. All she has is that little dog, just like me and my rabbit. All I ever had after Corky died was Bun-Bun. Neither one of you was ever any company. You can't just abandon her, EG."

EG throws open the door and gets out, walks aimlessly around the parking lot. He has to get a handle on this. He sees no solution, feels no way out of this darkness. He sits down right in the middle of a parking space, puts his head in his hands. The sun feels warm and soothing on the top of his head, the back of his neck, his hands. He wishes he could sleep right now, right here. This isn't his fault. These aren't his problems. He knows Clete and Annabel must be dealt with before he can deal with Laura.

EG gets up, goes back to the car. As he approaches he sees the two of them shouting at one another, then his father lowering his head in defeat, shaking it slowly from side to side in exasperation. He can never win with her.

EG takes a deep breath, opens the door, and gets in. "OK," he says. "Both of you—quiet. I've heard what you've been saying; now I want you to be quiet. You're both out of control, and you're both taking out on me something between the two of you, something that has nothing to do with me. I don't want to hear any more from either one of you. I'm doing just fine. I'll figure out what to do without any further input from the two of you. Now shut up, please."

EG starts the motor. Clete is staring icily out the passenger window. "And that includes facial expressions," EG says to him. "No silent approbations, no quiet martyr's suffering. From either of you. I will work this out," he says, pulling out of the Safeway parking lot onto Church Street. *This is part of the human experience*, he tells himself. *It can't all be fun. This too is It. Even if I don't understand how.*

10:19:59:59:13 A.M.

Rain, rain, rain. Rain has been falling for weeks. Water reservoirs spill over, dams strain at full capacity, their spillways kept open 24 hours a day. Streets are flooded as storm sewers erupt, jettisoning their iron grates and giving up, unable to contain the water rushing down the sidewalks into the gutters, down the 700 hills that are San Francisco.

Parks are closed to visitors, classical music must be piped into the cages at Fleischacker Zoo in an attempt to calm the restless animals. Airports operate at 25% capacity. Schoolchildren dance in their living rooms, their mothers resorting to baby-sitters, day care, and tranquilizers. Taxis are impossible to find, and drivers are bribed, their services virtually at auction on the stormy streets. Old people die of loneliness.

When the weather is like this, EG and company huddle together in the flat above Dolores Park, looking out over the city and the bay. Water, driving others mad, drives this cast of characters into closer union. "Even out there," EG says to his assembled family, "although they aren't aware of it, people are fighting or lying down with the demons they know best and fear most. They are trapped with them on the cold leather seats of taxicabs, mesmerized by visions in their tiny cubicles at the Federal Building downtown, masturbating with them in supply closets, leaving meals untouched, and walking out of restaurants rather than dining with abusive parents. "

"They are everywhere," EG says aloud, "these spirits. They are strengthened by water, invigorated by endless days of rain. Snow too will cause this phenomenon. Any prolonged abundance of water brings to life the life within us, the life around us we cannot see, the people who speak to us in dreams and course through our synapses at will. Water. Ocean voyages, shipwrecks, floods. Heart attacks and strokes in the bathtub, tangled scuba hoses in the Caribbean, a siren's bed off Lesbos. Here is where spirits rise and converge. Here is where Truth prevails upon frail mortal flesh.

"It is why men go to the desert," EG explains to his people. "Those who are seeking and those who are fleeing rush to the full nothingness of deserts. The frightened believe they can hide from these phantoms there; the wise take them along for more direct engagement. This is why I have loved the rain since I was born. Why, on rainy days in Calistoga I would sit on the back of the sofa so I could look out the window, watch the falling rain rushing over the red tiles of the porch roof, gushing and gurgling into the red rain gutters and swirling into the drain, down the pipe into the garden."

His people move closer to him, huddling with him at the window. Annabel, The Boy, Clete, Cohen, all of them are here this morning, seeking shelter, warmth, even comfort.

"I would beg for my yellow slicker, my black galoshes and spend hours in the rain, stomping through puddles, standing in the way of rivulets and streams forming in the drive or the gully at the end of the block. I could hear you talking to me in the rushing runoff of the Napa River; I listened to your Morse code messages pounded out on the yellow rubber hood of my mac. I was alone except for you. I was alone. Perhaps that is why you are so welcome now, even with your tyranny and terror, your truth and relentless pounding. You were with me in the beginning; you drove me through years of empti-ness. We simply know one another well, I suppose, you and I. Spirits of the Water. My ensemble company. Me."

10:19:59:59:14 A.M.

"I have many feelings about it," EG says to the thin bald man with the gray mustache seated across the table from him. A tape recorder sits between them. Another man, who was with them for the first half hour, has left the room for no apparent reason. The room is small, square, colorless, and empty, except for the table and three chairs. There are no windows. "On the one hand, I feel bad about it. That sort of thing is always wrong—or at best questionable. It isn't at all like me, either."

The thin bald man with the gray mustache says nothing. Maybe he is nodding his head, not so much in agreement with EG but as a sign that he's listening. EG wonders how old the man is, what he looks like naked. He imagines him in the woods, holding a rifle, and urinating against a tree; squatting in the woods; taking a communal shower with fellow hunters. EG wonders if he plays team sports, if he has children and, if he does have children, whether he molests them sexually, and if he does molest them sexually, whether it is the boys or the girls into whose room he sneaks at night after his wife is asleep. He wonders if he carries a knife, perhaps one of those Swiss army knives with the shiny red handle and a bottle opener in-side. He wonders if he is touching himself under the table.

"On the other hand," EG continues, "I think we're all better off, everyone: her, me, the dogs. Even you, I suppose. You didn't know her, did you?"

The thin bald man with the gray mustache shakes his head, says softly, "No."

They sit quietly looking at one another. EG nods his head, understanding.

"Do you feel up to talking about it?" the man asks.

EG looks up to one corner of the ceiling as though a bird were fluttering at the wall, trying to find a way out. In a moment he turns back to the man seated across the table.

"I'm sorry, what did you say?"

The man reiterates. "Do you feel up to telling me what happened?"

"Oh, of course. Naturally. That's why we're here, isn't it? How rude of me. Please forgive me. I'm a bit distracted."

"I understand," the man consoles him. "Take your time."

"Well, it was about 4 o'clock. We were taking the dogs to Glen Park. Laura usually does that by herself. I take them in the morning to Ocean Beach or Fort Funston. It's a virtual paradise for dogs. Do you know Fort Funston?"

The man nods his head.

"Do you have a dog?"

The man shakes his head. "No, I don't."

"Oh, I see." EG wonders why the man doesn't have a dog. Perhaps he lives in an apartment. Perhaps he owns a cat: not so demanding. Perhaps a dog would bark when he steals into his children's room at night to slip beneath the covers.

"Would you like some coffee, a soda?" the man asks.

"No, thank you," EG says. "I'm fine."

"It was 4 o'clock. You were at Glen Park. Go on."

"Yes. We went together yesterday because I wanted to talk with her. I was at my wit's end with her. She had recently crossed over from a terribly neurotic state to a state of true psychosis. I felt I had to intervene. For everyone's sake."

EG stops talking, looks up at the ceiling for a few seconds, cocks his head as if listening for something. Then he resumes.

"All the way there in the car, she was going on about everything that's wrong with her life. She always does that. Most of the time I can tune her out, but yesterday she was having a real psychotic break from reality. She was telling me about her upcoming trip to Spain. She described how beautiful the area she'll be visiting is, how she intends to see all her childhood friends, and all the fabulous things that the staff of her mother's villa have planned for her to do.

"As we walked the dogs along the path through the woods, she talked of going skiing and sledding, of the art museums she would visit. She'll be there for a month. I commented that it sounded like a wonderful trip and how rejuvenating it would be, especially now on the heels of her breakup with Catherine. That's when she began raising her voice and saying 'How can you say that when you know it's going to be horrible? Gloria is dying, and it's going to be so difficult.'"

"Gloria is her stepmother and a woman she hates, a woman who allegedly committed unspeakable acts of abuse on her all during her childhood and adolescence. She has never once said a kind word about the woman; she won't even call her Mother, even though the woman has been in her life since she was 12. It seems Gloria was diagnosed with Parkinson's disease about a year ago. I don't know if you know anything about this disease, but it's a very slow-progressing nerve disorder. People live with it for years. Everyone except Gloria that is, who is supposedly dying right before everyone's eyes. I said to her, 'People live for years with Parkinson's. You don't have to go now if you don't want to.' 'No,' she said, 'not Gloria. Hers is progressing very rapidly. She could die at any time. Besides, she's paying for my plane ticket.' Aha! Now the truth comes out. She's wangling a free trip to Europe out of the woman."

"So I switched the subject. 'How did your presentation in Reno go? Was the paper well-received? Did they like the audio-visual presentation? It was awfully sweet of your department chair to help you and especially to fly to Reno with you at her own expense.'"

"'They liked it OK,' she said. 'But it was a horrible experience. On the flight back we had to circle San Francisco for 20 minutes. Now my cold is back. I'm going to get sick again and miss classes and they're going to take away my teaching scholarship.'"

"Anyway, you get the idea. This went on for the entire walk with the dogs. Until we got to the end of the canyon and turned to walk back through the woods. That was when it happened. Hari was bounding past us, Max, her black Lab, was right behind him. As Hari passed, he knocked against her leg with a stick he was carrying. It wasn't big or sharp. Just a piece of limb from a fallen oak tree. Suddenly she began shouting, 'I can't do everything. I can't do it. I'm going to get an F. Now I'm going to get an F. My tits are too small. It's not my fault. I can't wear that dress and my tits are too small and now I'm going to get an F.'

"I was behind her and stopped walking when she began this ranting. Now she's turned facing me. The dogs are standing between us. Hari has dropped his stick and is looking up at her with his head cocked, trying to interpret her strange behavior. Max is crouching on the ground, trembling, like he's seen this before or is afraid she's going to hit him, which, of course, I think she would never do. She obsesses on the dog in the most neurotic way. She's always calling me up and asking what we fed him or if he ate anything on our walk because he has explosive diarrhea. That dog has never had loose stools, let alone explosive diarrhea. It's become a joke at our house. Every time one of us gives the dog a treat, we say, 'Stand back everyone—here comes Max's explosive diarrhea.'"

The thin bald man with the gray mustache smiles in spite of himself. "Then what happened?" he asks.

"Well, this is the bad part, the psychotic part. I was standing there trying to conclude whether she was letting off an accumulation of two years' frustration with her master's degree program and her recent split with Catherine or if she was actually having a complete nervous breakdown right there on the trail at Glen Park.

"Then Max began this low-pitched crying that grew louder and louder. His chin was pressed against the ground between his outstretched paws, and he was now actually beginning to wail. It was as though he was imitating her behavior or maybe having his own nervous breakdown. When that happened she reached down and picked up a huge stick, a branch I guess would be more accurate—well, you saw it. You felt how heavy it was. It took both hands for her to lift it.

"She began shouting over and over, 'I can't have these dogs. I can't take care of these dogs.' And while she's screaming this she tries to hit Hari with the limb. She was holding it like a baseball bat and swinging it toward him. Well, Hari immediately runs, but Max just lies there and closes his eyes. Then she turns, lifts the branch, and smashes him in the head with it. His right eye popped completely out of his head, and his ear was ripped half off. He let out a low moan and went limp."

"All of this seemed to happen in about three seconds. At first, when she swung at Hari, I thought she was kidding, but then…I guess I was stunned or something because I just stood there paralyzed. When she lifted the branch again I came to my senses and lunged for her. I grabbed the limb as it was coming down toward the dog again. I took it away from her and raised it above my head. Then everything gets kind of blurry after that. I distinctly remember striking her several times on her head and face and beating her body after she fell. I do remember that. I remember Max was lying on the path with all this blood soaking into his black fur and Hari running around me in circles barking. I couldn't tell if he was barking in protest or encouragement. Maybe she tortured both of them when she had them to herself.

"Then after a while I stopped. I didn't look at her. I didn't have to. I knew she was dead. I wanted her gone. I felt this tremendous sense of relief. Like we would all be free now, happy, safe. Except for Max, of course. It was too late to do anything for him. That's the part I feel bad about. That's what I regret. If only I would have acted sooner. If only I would have lunged at her when she swung at Hari the first time. But I didn't think she was serious. I thought she was just demonstrating how angry and frustrated she felt. I had no idea she intended to make contact with anything. Certainly not the dogs. She was crazy about the dogs. Anyway, I guess she really pushed a button in me, huh? It was self-defense in a way. I mean, I was protecting Hari."

There is a silence, and EG looks up at the corner of the ceiling again. He thinks he hears wings flapping. There is a spray of light on the ceiling, a reflection of light bouncing off something.

"Is that everything?" the thin bald man with a gray mustache asks.

"Yes," EG says, looking at his own hands, folded on the table.

The man turns off the tape recorder and stands up.

"So what do you think?" EG asks.

"I think you better start praying," the man answers.

10:19:59:59:15 A.M.

EG has decided to attend a six-week course at Holy Redeemer Parish. The course is for people who were raised in the Roman Catholic Church but who have left the church and now may be considering returning. EG has been wanting to augment his Eastern spiritual practice with more ritual, particularly some community or collective ritual, and this parish, which is in his neighborhood, is very "gay-friendly." So he thinks he will give it a whirl.

The first three weeks aren't too bad. EG manages to overlook some of the New Age attitudes of the nun and priest running the group. He thinks of them as "guitar" clerics, people left over from the '70s, when the radical changes from Vatican II really took hold. Also, he reminds himself, this is California.

The group has been less than receptive to most of his ideas about the divine being within a person, rather than on the outside. The only person who has been giving him support in his perspective on things is Karl, an older man who is thinking about going back to the church after a 42-year hiatus.

This week the topic is prayer. Father Mack, as he has asked to be called by the group, is reading from a book. "Prayer can be defined as an anguished cry of the soul in distress or helplessness, to a power fuller and greater than itself, for relief and comfort."

"Can we talk about this for a minute?" EG asks.

"Sure," Father Mack says, folding his hands on the open book in front of him. "What do you want to talk about?"

"That definition of prayer," EG says, working his *mala*, which he carries with him everywhere, especially here, "It makes me mad."

"Why is that?" Father Mack asks, interested but a bit irritated. This isn't the first time EG has challenged him.

"I don't pray like that, and I think it's a really limited definition of prayer. I haven't prayed like that since I was a teenager and I was afraid my father was going to find out I drove the car into the city when I was supposed to be at the movies. It's more of that male-dominated stuff, if you ask me: 'Come groveling to Daddy, who has this big paddle and beg him not to hit you with it.' It's based on fear."

Karl is nodding his head and looking around the table at the others. Sister Terry is biting her lower lip nervously.

"It's saying all the power is 'out there,'" EG exclaims, pointing straight ahead, "rather than in here," pointing first to his heart, then to his head.

Somewhere outside a horn honks and someone shouts.

"This kind of religion is intent on placing all power outside the individual. I don't mean outside the ego; I mean outside the heart, soul, mind—the essence of each human being. So the desired effect of this kind of teaching is disempowerment of the individual—the exact opposite, I would think, of the purpose of prayer.

"When you pray," Sister Terry asks, "How do you pray?"

"Well, I don't throw myself on a dung heap and cry, 'Oh, great and powerful Oz, have pity on poor, wretched, disgusting, pile of cow shit me.' For one thing, what about prayer that simply worships? What about prayers of thanksgiving? This guy defines prayer only as petitions. So according to him, I should pray by saying something like 'I'm disgusting, make my life better; give me a new car; make me win the lottery; I can't do anything, do it for me.' This is all disempowering."

"Yeah," pipes in Karl now, leaning forward, his arms on the table. "This is why I left the church in the first place. It's just what priests and bishops and popes and televangelists want—to keep the keys of heaven stuffed deep in their own pockets, hidden in their secret bank accounts."

Father Mack is getting a bit nervous, but he's not about to be seen as closed to other views. "How would you define prayer?" he asks EG.

EG stands up now and begins pacing around the rectory dining hall, where these meetings are held each week. He paces slowly, staring at the floor, measuring his words careful-ly. "When I get up every morning at Anchor Bay, I go down-stairs, get some incense, and call Hari to walk with me up the drive to the old redwood stump where we placed a statue of Buddha. I light the incense, stick it in the tree stump, and then Hari and I take our morning walk and I say my *japa*.

"*Japa?*" someone asks.

EG looks up. "Oh, that's just a Sanskrit word for silent prayer. Kind of like the rosary. I walk and say my silent prayer, which is just repeating all the names for God over and over. I look at the trees and the sky and the birds and Hari and the gravel beneath my feet and the movement of my fingers over my *mala*, my beads, and the swaying of my arms and the passing of the minutes and the gentle dance of the pine needles in the morning breeze. I think that's a prayer, all of it, because it's all an act of unification, of bringing everything back together again, of being reunited: me, Hari, the trees, the air, all movement, even the obser-vation of it all. All of it is united back into one thing again, joined in my awareness. That's true empowerment, because it's all united through my consciousness, my being fully aware, my paying attention. Not through me—EG—but through me—Consciousness. EG is merely the vehicle for Consciousness. And Consciousness is God."

"I like the sound of that," Karl adds. "That sounds much closer to God to me than a lot of preaching about hell and abortion and how it's all right to be gay but not all right to act on it. God, I hate that duplicity. Say more about the empowerment stuff."

"It empowers in a very subtle and ironic way, actually," EG explains. "It empowers my ego to surrender itself to It or the Self or the Big Consciousness."

"The Big Consciousness?" Karl laughs.

"Yeah, isn't that silly?" EG replies. "But you see how words fail us? So anything we call It is inadequate. We may as well call it Banana Split."

"What about Transcendental Consciousness?" Sister Terry offers.

EG winces. "I know some people refer to It that way, but that implies It rises above all things. Does that mean, then, that the 'things' It rises above are left behind and aren't included? Somehow that doesn't seem accurate."

"In that case, then," Father Mack says a bit sarcastically, "what isn't a prayer? I mean, if your morning walk is a prayer, then everything must be a prayer."

"Everything is a prayer if you intend it to be and do it consciously."

"Everything?" Sister Terry gasps.

"Everything."

"Anything?" one of the others inquires.

"Anything."

"Hmm." Karl is thinking.

"When you have sex," he asks slyly, thinking he has trapped him, "is that a prayer?"

"It can be, absolutely, if I make it a prayer."

"That sounds rather blasphemous," Father Mack interjects.

"I like it," one of the men around the table says. "I never feel ashamed when I'm making love with my lover. In fact, that's usually when I feel best about everything. I feel closer to God then than I usually do."

"I have the same feeling," EG adds. He looks at Sister Terry and decides to spare no one. He's already decided not to come back to the group. "When I'm making love with my partner, I often think, I am Rama making love with Krishna, or I am Jesus making love with John."

"You do?" several people exclaim at once.

"Of course. Usually at the time I look down to watch myself entering him, because that's a visual metaphor for the tremendous energy, the tremendous power of our love for one another. It's also a metaphor for reunification—the two merging into the one. So I see myself entering him and hear him moaning in ecstasy and I think, *Even this energy is God.* That's usually about the time I say to him, 'I love you.'"

"Wow," exclaims Bob, another fellow at the table, who rarely says anything at these meetings. "I think that's beautiful. Blasphemous but beautiful."

Karl jumps right on that remark. "No, what's blasphemous is making love and not thinking you're closer to God. It's all in the heart. It's all in the intention that resides in your heart."

"If you were raping him, would that be a prayer?" Father Mack asks, openly antagonistic.

"No," EG answers calmly, "because my consciousness would not be with God. My thoughts and experience would be centered in my ego, my own self-centered pleasure and gratification. But even though that wouldn't be prayer, I think it would still be It. The Energy never changes its essence. All energy is It. How we direct it, how we use it, is defined by us, by our egos. When ego is enlightened it serves the Self, directing all energy back to It. When the ego is ignorant or corrupted, it turns all energy toward serving itself, ego, or self with a small *s*. That kind of dark inertia is what breeds chaos, harm and destruction."

"And I suppose even that destruction is God," Father Mack posits.

"Why wouldn't it be? Without destruction, creation can't occur. Something must die in order for something new to be born. So it's the same energy—it's just at the other end of the process. It's like the far side of the moon. Just because it's in darkness doesn't mean it's bad. The dark side of the moon is just the 'other side' of the light side of the moon. Like negative energy is just the 'other side' of positive energy. In fact, they must both exist for one to exist. Even the Bible says, 'Unless one dies, he cannot be reborn,'" EG says, as he sits back down at the table.

The room is silent. Everyone is waiting for one of the facilitators to say something.

"Well," Sister Terry finally says, "that certainly is a unique view of things. EG has given us all something to think about this week. And I see by my watch that we're all out of time."

10:19:59:59:16 A.M.

First Peter MacLaughlin died, unexpectedly, mysteriously, leaving his partner and their friends dazed and terribly perplexed. He experienced three weeks of unexplained bruises appearing all over his body, then intense fatigue. Hospital Friday, undertaker the following Tuesday.

Then Ray. Then Bill. Then Ben, David, Clark, Lee, Mike, John, Barry, Hans. Thirty-nine others in the next five years.

When Andre was diagnosed, Andre went to bed for three days depressed. When EG was told he too was going to die, he walked out of the Seventeenth Street Health Clinic into the July afternoon and stood in the health center's garden. A huge palm tree sheltered the courtyard, spreading its 50 green arms, like fans, above the flower beds and walkways, shading the pink and white impatiens, gold and purple lantana, scarlet primroses. So colorful, so alive, so joyous, yet so silent. The weather was hot. No birds sang.

EG walked home down Seventeenth Street, up Sanchez, left on Hancock, right on Church, watching his feet take each step, waiting for the cloud of despair to descend. He had seen it countless times with others: John's nonstop drinking until the week before he died; Barry hiding in his room for two weeks, then hitting the bars every night, losing his job, then his home, then his mind, living finally in the alcove of the Wells Fargo automated teller machine, talking on an imaginary telephone to an imaginary friend in some imaginary Elysian field far away.

He waited and waited. Days, weeks, months. But it never came. His curse was not to escape his reality. His blessing was to have already faced it head-on with others and learned how to make room for Death on the living room sofa, to set an extra place at dinner for Death's bony hands, to look up in the throes of lovemaking and find only empty sockets staring back.

Despair never came. Fear of the unknown from time to time, yes. Anxiety about leaving those he loves to carry on without his affection and protection, yes. But panic, despair, retreat, these have not visited him.

10:19:59:59:17 A.M.

*From the shore, the women come to him, minister to him with
their comforting arms, their devoted hands. They come into the
darkened room, holding the hands of the children. They lift the
shades, pull back the curtains, letting the light flood into the
scrubbed room. Now the room is white with light. Now he can see
everyone clearly. He sees how they smile, how frightened they are.
He sees the old woman in the corner, how she smiles faintly while
she crochets. Her face is so wrinkled he is not sure it is made of
human skin, but he can see that her heart is in what she is doing.
She is surrounded by a faint blue light.*

10:19:59:59:18 A.M.

EG takes the dog to the beach and finds Andre there. It
is a bright day in Anchor Bay. The blue-green sea, stretching to the horizon, undulates rhythmically, a wave breaking foamy white now and then in the distance, unable to
contain its enthusiasm. Fishing boats from Point Arena
rock on the water like toy tugboats in a child's dream. The
sunlight skips on the ocean like a skimming stone, ricocheting from crest to crest, coming to rest in EG's eyes.
The dog chases field mice or runs barking at the gulls cir-
cling overhead.

"So what did you want to tell me?" EG asks Andre as they
stroll along the path that winds jaggedly near the edge of the
bluffs.

"What did *you* want to ask me?" Andre replies. "You called
me, remember?"

"Explain *advaita* to me."

Andre laughs. "Just like that, eh?"

"Why not? If you wanted the answer to a puzzle and someone you knew had the answer, you'd come right out and ask. You know you would."

"Don't you think nonduality must be experienced, rather than explained?" Andre asks.

"Of course. That's not what I'm asking. I believe I've experienced it a few times, but I want to understand it."

"You mean you want to understand It," Andre teases. "The big picture. With your nose to the carpet, you want to see the pattern."

"I'd like to."

"You should work on giving up your desires," Andre says.

"Are you going to help here or what?" EG presses. He stops walking, places his hands on his hips dramatically, the way he knows Anna or Annabel would.

Andre laughs, throws a stick for the dog. "Sit down, Little Dad," he says gently, and eases himself into the tall sea grass. EG lowers himself next to Andre and they sit facing the rolling green ocean. "Ask questions," Andre says. "I'll try to answer."

"How is it that everything is really all the same thing? I think I understand the part about the Energy between the atoms, but how are all these seemingly different, even contradictory things, really the same?"

Andre answers EG's question with a question. "How is each wave a wave unto itself, yet all together, the ocean?"

"I don't know."

"Yes, you do."

"I don't, honest."

"Form," Andre says patiently. "Each wave rises and sinks, rises and sinks. When it rises it takes on its individuality or its form, its "waveness." When it sinks it becomes part of the whole again. And yet, because it is made up of the substance of the whole—water—it's never actually different, even when it rises. Only its appearance alters. It takes a shape that gives the illusion that it is separate from the whole, separate from all other waves, even separate from the ocean itself. But that isn't so. Each wave is made of water; they are all 'ocean.'"

Andre pauses for a moment, allowing EG to think about this, then he continues. "The Energy within the ocean drives them into their illusory individual shapes. The same Energy draws them back to the ocean. Ebb and flow. On and off. Birth and death. Kind of like a computer—zeroes and ones in infinite combinations, no two alike."

"But how does that work with people?"

"You don't want to do any work at all, do you?" Andre teases, stroking the long gold-and-white grasses rising as high as his head.

"I've worked plenty. I just want some help here."

Bobbing in the water, below where they sit, a small skiff is adrift. Its bow is scraping back and forth on the rocky sand of the beach. EG can make out only one of the faded letters on its hull. It is the letter *b*.

"You know how EG and company or your 'people,' or whatever it is you're calling them these days, are really just parts of you, of your own psyche?"

"Yes, I think so."

"All people are like that. All animals, all the motion and Energy that we perceive as the universe are like that."

"I don't follow."

"Just as each of your people are an aspect of your psyche, each human being is an aspect, a projection of It. Each one is an aspect of what others call God."

"Including the bad guys?"

"Including the people and forces humans judge to be bad."

"Even Hitler?"

"Even Hitler."

"That's not possible."

"But it is."

"How?"

"You don't want to die, do you?" Andre goes on.

"No."

"Is death necessary?"

"Yes."

"Who invented it?"

"What do you mean, 'Who invented it?'"

"Where did death come from?"

"It's part of the process—it's part of creation."

"So who invented it?"

"Well, you'd have to say God invented it, I guess."

"So It invented something bad?"

"No. I mean death isn't *bad* bad. It's just…" EG is fumbling for words.

"It's just what all human beings spend most of their life trying to overcome, avoid, or do away with. Don't you see? We decided death is bad. Death is bad here on Earth, where all we can see and know is life. Ego likes life, hates death. Like the Hitler example, it's the value we give it on Earth, not it's real value. It's all the same Energy, channeled through different conduits. The way the Energy expresses itself is affected by the conduit's complex parts. When the conduit is a human being, it's the person's personality or his shape, his consciousness or, in the case of your example, Hitler, his lack of consciousness. But the Energy itself isn't bad. The Energy itself—even in its most humanly undesirable form—is still the same Energy. And later, after time goes by, humans often find the meaning or the 'good' stuff that was an indirect result of what they at one time judged to be 'bad' stuff."

"I don't like the way this sounds. Who would ever say anything good came out of the Holocaust?"

"You might be surprised. Who would ever say anything good came out of AIDS? But here you are discovering things about yourself and It that you might never have discovered had you not become sick. That's not to say you would choose to be sick, but since you are sick you've chosen—that is, directed your individual form of the Energy—toward developing yourself in the most conscious way possible. No one would ever have wished you to be sick, but that doesn't mean that something positive hasn't developed as a result of it."

"I don't know if I can comprehend this," EG says almost dejectedly.

"Faith is the leap you make when you reach land's end."

"Huh?"

"You're just in an awkward spiritual position. It's the nose of material existence pressed against the carpet of It. Since you're in the middle of your life, you're having a difficult time seeing its pattern or its purpose. But think of this: If I hadn't gotten sick and died, you never would have met Paul."

"I don't like it," EG protests.

"You don't have to like it—just get it."

"When will I get it?"

"I've no idea. Perhaps when you start moving back from the carpet, you'll begin to distinguish the pattern."

"When will that be?"

"When the wave that is you begins to sink back into the ocean of It."

"You're being very...esoteric."

"You're being very impatient. Maybe you'll get it in the White Room."

"What White Room?"

"The White Room at the end of the corridor."

"You're talking too figuratively for me."

"Well, like I said, you'll get it when the time is right."

At that moment Hari runs between them, stops, and barks at them both. They laugh, stand, embrace one another. Then EG continues his walk. By the time EG reaches the car, Andre is gone.

Hari rests his head in EG's lap on the drive back up the mountain while EG begins to ponder these new ideas Andre has presented to him. It feels to EG like he is swimming in oatmeal.

10:19:59:59:19 A.M.

It's summer and almost The Boy's birthday, which falls on the Fourth of July. His grandmother dresses him in his over-alls and sends him out to play. He goes through the gate in the backyard fence, which connects Cohen's yard to that of her neighbor, Mrs. Morgan. Mrs. Morgan's nephews Richie and Walter are spending the summer with her and every day they play with The Boy. Richie is 13, Walter is 12.

The Boy wanders through the thick vegetable garden in Mrs. Morgan's yard. He moves slowly down long rows of corn and tall green beans tied to poles that tower far above his head and make him think of the story of Jack and the beanstalk. He had an uncle named Jack, but he is dead now, just like Cohen's son, Harry. Jack's widow, The Boy's Aunt Cecilia, isn't as sad as Cohen, so The Boy concludes there are different ways in which to be dead, some less sad than others.

He pauses at the fish pond to look for frogs on the lily pads, but they aren't there this morning. On the far side of the gar-den, he finds Richie and Walter building a fort out of old lum-ber and logs, between the garage and the toolshed. They invite him to play "Fort" with them again this morning, as they have every morning for the past two weeks. The three of them work at blocking off the area between the two buildings with blankets and canvas tarps so that no one can see in; then they lay out some old blankets.

"OK," says Richie, tall, thin, and the more assertive of the two boys, "it's your turn today."

"It was my turn yesterday," The Boy replies.

"Guess you're just lucky," says Richie. Walter, who is short and husky, stifles a giggle.

The Boy begins to unbuckle his overalls while the other two watch him. "When is it your turn?" he asks Richie.

"Maybe next week," Richie says. "Hurry up."

The Boy kicks off his shoes, slips his striped T-shirt over his head. Only his underpants remain. "Those too," says Richie. "You know that."

The Boy shyly slips his white underpants down to his ankles, then kicks them toward the heap of clothes lying near the wood pile. He lies down on his stomach on the blanket and waits. It is only seconds before Richie is on top of him, slathering something wet and sticky between his buttocks. Then he feels something going inside him. It is not unpleasant but strange nonetheless. It feels just like when his grandmother gives him his worm medicine, putting on a rubber glove, sticking her finger in the Vaseline jar, and inserting her finger up his butt as he bends over the bathtub.

Richie is rocking back and forth on top of The Boy. He begins breathing heavily, then makes a grunting sound. It only lasts a few seconds, then it's Walter's turn. Walter is heavier than Richie. When he lies on top of The Boy, his long hair falls down around The Boy's face. When Walter makes his groaning sound, it is louder than Richie's and something inside The Boy swells. It feels like the time Cohen gave him an enema, the water filling him up until he couldn't hold it any longer, except there's not nearly as much water.

Now the two boys are dressing. They hear Mrs. Morgan calling them and scurry off before she comes looking. "Come back tomorrow," says Richie as he passes though the curtain of canvas. "We'll play again."

"Wait," says The Boy. "What is this?"

"What's what?" Richie says.

"This game. What's it called."

"It's called 'Fuck,' but you can never say that word in front of anyone. You'll get in trouble. Never say it in front of anyone, hear?"

But, of course, as soon as The Boy is back home, he climbs up on the kitchen counter where his grandmother is doing dishes. He sits watching her for a while, noisily slurping at a chunk of watermelon she sliced for him when he came in. Finally, he can hold it in no longer. "Grandma," he asks, "what is fuck?"

The old woman's slap comes so quickly and lands so hard he is knocked off the counter to the floor. The slice of watermelon is sent scattering across the linoleum in pink, green, and white chunks. That is all he remembers, except her admonition never to say that word again. Ever.

That is how The Boy learns that fucking is bad. Taking off your clothes in front of other people is bad. Touching other people's bodies is bad. Being alone with people, having or even fantasizing about physical intimacy and sex instantly brings back the stinging slap that came like a lightning bolt from the hand of Zeus.

The sting on his cheek stays with him for a long time. Long after Richie and Walter return home to Lakeport. Long after his grandmother dies of old age in Chicago. Even long after his first Confession, in which he tells the priest on the other side of the dark screen what horrendous things he did that summer with his two friends.

"I put the front end in the back end and the back end in the front end," he confesses, not knowing how to say it, except that he certainly can't use the word *fuck*. He has rehearsed this Confession for over a year, as soon as he learned about Confession and that he would one day have to do this. He looked forward to it in a way, having all his sins forgiven—even though he couldn't quite think of anything that felt like it was a sin.

It takes every bit of courage he can muster to tell the priest of his horrible act, and he is sure the priest will scream and come tearing around the curtain flailing his arms and ordering The Boy to leave Saint Dominic's at once.

"Three Our Fathers and three Hail Mary's and now make a good Act of Contrition," is all Father Mueller says to him. Even while he is saying the Act of Contrition there in the dark, reciting the prayer he has learned for this very important moment in his young life, his mind is on the anticlimactic nature of the moment. Maybe it isn't as bad as he's been led to believe. Maybe his grandmother doesn't know that it isn't such a big sin. Maybe in Germany, where she was born, it's more of a sin than here in the United States. Maybe he isn't going to hell after all. In fact, perhaps Father Mueller is telling him that it's OK to put your front end in someone else's back end and vice versa.

He does notice, however, that the word *fuck* still evokes the most intense reactions from people, and that while it is never heard among adults, it is the most popular word at school—at least among the boys.

<u>10:19:59:59:20</u> A.M.

It is early June when AD arrives back in California after his freshman year of college. He has thought about Donny Macgregor off and on while he was away at school in Texas, usually when he was showering in the gym. He would remember Donny Macgregor wet with half a hard-on after football practice, smiling at him as he told Victor Lyon that everybody who went to St. Vincent's High School was a Catholic queer and the Benicia High Panthers would tromp all over the Saints at homecoming.

AD remembers Donny Macgregor's admonition at the airport to call him when he gets home, so the very evening of his arrival, he telephones Donny Macgregor, who, somewhat to AD's surprise, has been waiting for his call.

"I saw your mom in the Park & Shop last week. She told me you'd be home today. I was wondering if you'd call. I can't wait to hear all about college. Let's party."

So they buy two six-packs of beer, climb into Donny Macgregor's bitchin' cherry-red '53 Chevy two-door, and head for the lake. To catch up.

"Man, you got thin. You're almost skinny," Donny Macgregor says, pulling up to the edge of the lake and cutting the engine.

"Yeah. Eighty pounds. Big difference, huh?"

"How much did you weigh when you left?"

"Two-forty, if you can believe it."

"Wow! What brought that on? How come you lost so much weight?" Donny Macgregor is fumbling in the brown paper bag on the seat between them. He's trying to retrieve one of the six-packs.

Outside, AD can see that a family has had a picnic just a few feet from where they are parked. The remains of the day's outing are scattered all along the shore: paper plates, aluminum cans, watermelon rinds.

"Oh, it's a long story," AD says, not wanting to admit he fell in love with his roommate and quickly realized that in order to seduce this guy from South Bend, Ind., who ran track and swam on the swimming team, he was going to have to give him a more aesthetically pleasing body to look at. "Just didn't eat much, kind of lost my appetite for a while. I guess I was homesick or something. You know, scared of being on my own at college, stuff like that. I guess I do look a lot different."

"So tell me what it's like," Donny Macgregor says to AD, popping open a Budweiser and handing it to him.

"What what's like?" AD asks, then takes a swig of beer. The night is warm, so they sit with the windows down, watching the reflection of the nearly full moon shimmering on the surface of Lake Herman. Somewhere in the dark an owl calls.

"College, nitwit. What's it like? Is it tough?"

"You're in college. You know as much about it as I do," AD answers, slouching down now to see the moon through the windshield.

"Aw, I'm not in college. JC doesn't count. I go to school with a bunch of lamebrains, guys like me who couldn't get into a regular college."

"There's nothing wrong with going to junior college," AD consoles, but can't help but think that if Donny Macgregor's parents hadn't been stark-raving Protestants, he too might have had a decent education and been able to enter a four-year university like AD had. "Besides," AD adds, "there are girls at Vallejo JC; there aren't any girls in my college." AD realizes he keeps saying the word *college* when *school* would do just as nicely. AD fixes his gaze on the watermelon rinds lying along the lake's edge, their white edges fluorescent beneath the moonlight. "You probably wouldn't…find a four-year university an easy adjustment.

"Well, that's one advantage JC has, all right—girls. But I'd give up girls to go to a real school." Donny Macgregor pops open another beer and slouches down in the seat himself now. "I don't know if I could give them up completely, though."

"What about Pat?" AD asks, referring to the girlfriend Donny Macgregor has dated off and on, but mostly on, for the past three years.

"What about her?"

"Do you think you'll marry her?"

"Man, don't talk about getting married. That's all she thinks about. I'm only 19, for chrissake. We're too young to be getting fucking married." Donny Macgregor reaches over and punches AD on the arm. "Man, you look good. I can't believe how much fuckin' weight you lost. I'll bet you got chicks fallin' all over you. But, man, I don't want to get fuckin' married."

AD turns in his seat now, leaning against the door and facing Donny Macgregor. He is not beautiful the way he once was, but he has become sexy; he oozes a kind of raw sexuality that has nothing to do with beauty. AD thinks, *Donny Macgregor is neither handsome nor beautiful, but he is the most sexually desirable boy I've ever seen.* "Why not?" he asks.

"Well, not to her, anyway." Donny Macgregor finishes the beer he just opened, chugging it and letting out a long, loud belch. "A-a-ah. Just what I needed after the fuckin' week I had."

"Why don't you want to marry Pat?" AD presses. Donny Macgregor has already found his third Bud and is chugging this one now too. "Are you thirsty or what?" AD asks, but then remembers that in high school, that's how they drank. They were drinking for the effect, not the flavor.

"Yeah, I guess. Just because, that's why. I just don't. I want someone…different." Donny Macgregor gestures toward AD with his beer can. "You're lookin' real sharp. I swear if I saw you on the street I wouldn't even recognize you."

"Different how?" AD presses, taking a swig of his beer, not at all interested in either the flavor or the effect. He's here for the company, specifically for Donny Macgregor's company, but he's beginning to realize that what Donny Macgregor has to offer—visual effects—is all that Donny Macgregor has to offer, and after a semester away in a "real college," where conversation doesn't confine itself to the pelvic area, AD is beginning to wonder if he wouldn't have been better off taking up his friend Ruth's offer to go to a movie.

Still, Donny Macgregor's growing enthusiasm about AD's new body, as well as Donny Macgregor's tight Levi's and T-shirt, are not to be lightly dismissed. His really, really tight Levi's. "How different? In what way?"

"Well," Donny Macgregor hems, "you know, more…adventurous. More willing to do…other stuff."

"Other stuff?"

"Yeah, other stuff."

"Like what 'other stuff'?" AD asks.

"You know, more wild stuff," Donny Macgregor says, tossing his can out the window to join the detritus of the litterbug family's earlier picnic.

"Like jumping out of planes? Like drag-car racing? What wild stuff?" AD notices that Donny Macgregor has popped open yet another beer and chugged half of it. It's clear that he's making Donny Macgregor really uncomfortable with this line of questioning. So of course he continues. "What wild stuff?"

"Sex stuff," Donny Macgregor blurts out. He sighs as though a huge weight has been lifted right off the top of his gut.

"O-o-oh, sex stuff." So Donny Macgregor is having sex problems with his girlfriend. "Like what sex stuff?

"Jus' sex stuff, man," Donny Macgregor says, slurring a little.

"You mean, like you want her to wear crotchless panties and black leather bras and she won't do it?" AD is enjoying this more and more.

"Jeez, I wish! It's not even that complicated." Donny Macgregor is beginning to relax just a bit, or rather, AD thinks, he's beginning to feel the effects of four, make that 4½ beers. "Boy, you look neat. Wait till the other guys see you. They're not gonna fuckin' believe it. I bet you could play quarterback now if you wanted."

"Well, what is it she won't do?" AD's curiosity is piqued now.

"She won't…She won't…AD, will you suck me off?"

AD does not consider himself naive when it comes to nuance, innuendo, or even the vaguest metaphorical reference. This, if he heard Donny Macgregor correctly, is what Professor Pesoli in English 101 would refer to as a classic example of a non sequitur.

"Excuse me?" was all AD could manage.

"I know you did it to other guys in school. Everyone, well, not everyone, I mean it wasn't like everyone knew, but some of the guys said you would…you know, give 'em blow jobs when they spent the night at your house or something. I don't know. All I know is, Pat won't do it. I've never had a girl who'd do it. I almost did once. There was this girl from Vallejo. She was a colored girl I picked up at a concert and we were gettin' along real good. She wanted to go to this place for a drink and said we could go to her house afterward and she'd do anything I wanted. Anything. So we were goin' to this late-night joint and all of a sudden she goes, 'Where you goin'?' and I go, 'To the joint you wanna go to, to have a drink before we go to your place,' and she goes, 'Why you goin' this way?' and I say, "'Cause I don't wanna go down Tennessee Street past the projects. It's too dangerous." And she goes, "Pull over." So I pull over and she gets out. And while she's gettin' out she says, 'I live on Tennessee Street, next door to the projects, which is where my mama lives. So good night and happy hand job.' Man, so will you? As a friend? Just this once?"

For his entire adolescence AD lay awake night after night, fantasizing about Donny Macgregor. He imagined all kinds of scenarios in which he would force him to have sex at gunpoint or they would be stranded on a desert island and he would wear Donny Macgregor down with pleading or he would fantasize doing him while he was asleep on a camping trip, on and on, thousands of different story lines all ending in the same huge gushing orgasms. But this, he never would have been able to dream up on his own.

"I'll do you," Donny Macgregor adds, as enticement.

AD blinks several times. While AD had been deep in thought, Donny Macgregor said something that sounded like 'I'll do you', but it obviously wasn't that. AD starts to ask Donny Macgregor what he said, when suddenly Donny Macgregor is in AD's lap, fumbling at his fly. "I mean, it's only fair, right? That way you won't think I'm just trying to get you to do me so I can go tell people or something. So I'll do you too, and then we'll be even. Just don't tell anyone, OK? I've only done this…I mean I've never done this before. I'm so nervous, I don't know what I'm saying. Just don't tell."

Donny Macgregor is now holding AD's penis in his hand, looking up and pleading with a half-smile on his face. "I'll do you first, 'cause otherwise I won't be able to, 'cause after I jizz I lose interest real fast, well, actually immediately. So I'll do you first. OK, here goes. I hope you like it. I'm not very good at it, 'cause, you know, I don't, I mean, I never did it before. So when you come…" AD places his hand on top of Donny Macgregor's blue-black hair, smiles into Donny Macgregor's blue, blue eyes, and pushes Donny Macgregor's face into his lap, where Donny Macgregor remains noisily busy for not one but two ejaculations.

It turns out that not only was Donny Macgregor good at this, he was very good at this—almost, AD thought, as though he might have done it once or twice before. It also turns out that once Donny Macgregor was finished, he wasn't interested in AD reciprocating. It seems Donny Macgregor had had a little "accident down there" while he was working AD up to his second orgasm. AD assumes that even though Donny Macgregor loses interest "real fast, well, actually, immediately," Donny Macgregor kept going until AD had come a second time out of good old Protestant work ethic.

10:19:59:59:21 A.M.

AD feels lost, adrift on an ocean of Feelings. It is Saturday afternoon, and he has come to St. Dominic's for the 4:30 Confession. There are only a handful of old Portuguese women in babushkas kneeling here and there throughout the dark nave of the Romanesque church. AD goes to the statue of the pietà and kneels down. He buries his head in his hands and begs the Blessed Mother to intercede for him, to ask her son, whose broken body she holds in her arms beneath the empty cross, to forgive him for his abominable sexual urges.

"I did it again last night," he prays. "I don't mean to, but I can't help myself. We get together and drink a few beers and the next thing I know I'm…you know what I do. Please help me to overcome these urges. Please help me to be good and to love you and only do your will."

Through his tears, AD takes in the pale corpus the Virgin holds in her arms. The Christ is naked, except for the sheerest hint of fabric draped in folds across his groin. His head is thrown back, limp and lifeless. His ample, muscular arms fall to either side, the delicate fingers of his perfect right hand touching the ground. His chest, thin from being denied food in Pilate's prison, yet sharply defined by the inspired sculptor, is as white as a lily from a life of celibacy, during which, AD is certain, he never once removed his garments to feel the warmth of the sun, lest the heat on his naked skin arouse in him the same sensual urges AD falls prey to, the irresistible temptations of the flesh.

The Savior's dark nipples are prominent, his slender side torn open by the Roman soldier's lance. His thighs are solid and shapely. Beneath the sparse cloth that barely covers his groin, his virgin penis must lie hidden and flaccid. What pain this beautiful man must have suffered at the hands of the sadistic Roman soldiers. AD wishes he could hold him.

If only AD had been at Calvary, he would have climbed up on the cross for Jesus. He gladly would have given up his life to spend eternity in heaven with such a man. And had he been too late, had he arrived just when the Messiah had expired, he would have helped take him down from the cross, laid him across his own lap, and wept the bitter tears of an abandoned devotee.

AD would have wept without ceasing, covering the slain Savior's beautiful, slender body in gallons of tears. Then he would have washed the divine corpse. He would have taken the tiny cloth that covers his undoubtedly perfect penis and testicles, drenched it in his own tears, and wiped the face of Jesus. Wiped his round shoulders, his statuesque pectorals. In fact, he would have licked him clean like a faithful puppy. He would have licked his shoulders, run his tongue through the soft, downlike hair beneath his sacred arms and along the cut line of his chest, up and around his nipples, sucking gently, hoping for some divine succoring milk to issue forth as a sign of compassion, a sign of forgiveness for all the many sins AD undoubtedly would have committed with the Roman soldiers had he lived in those days.

AD would lick and lick, moving his tongue carefully and thoroughly down the Savior's stomach, working from side to side, bathing every square inch of redemptive flesh. Down and down until his tongue felt the coarseness of the pubic hairs of the Lord's abdomen, down to the base of his perfect penis, fat and circumcised according to Jewish law.

Oh, look, AD would exclaim to himself when He expired, *He drained His bladder, and now there rests a single drop of healing, golden ambrosia on the tip of his heavenly penis.* With love and purest devotion, knowing this fluid to be a sacred relic, a healing potion, AD imagines himself placing his tongue on the tip of the Savior's sex organ and gently taking the fluid onto his tongue. Then, in complete adoration, unable to restrain himself, as he is whirled into devotional ecstasy, AD takes Christ's cock into his mouth and gently sucks, hoping to elicit even more of the healing juices.

It is at this moment the miracle occurs. As if to prove the Lord's divinity beyond any possible doubt, here, in AD's mouth, the Messiah's cock is hardening even in death—slowly but definitely growing erect, proving that death has no dominion over the Savior of the people. Only too happy to serve his Lord and Master in any way he can, AD sucks, gently at first, then more vigorously, feeling the head of the Divine Savior's dick engorging with His sweet, redemptive blood.

Now He is fully erect, and AD is almost certain he detects just the slightest hint that Christ is undulating His groin, pushing Himself into AD's mouth. AD administers to Him even more fervently, applying more suction. Then, without warning, in a glorious burst of everlasting, life-giving fluid, Christ erupts into AD's mouth, filling it with the most glorious, blindingly white Semen imaginable. AD's mouth fills to overflowing with the Heavenly Healing Juices of Jesus. He swallows, swallows again, and finally, after taking a third mouthful of this Semen of Salvation, the Lord is finished.

Gently, AD lifts his head, licks the Redemptive Organ of the Christ three times—Father, Son, and Holy Ghost—and looks up. Jesus is looking down at him, smiling the most tender, loving smile AD has ever beheld. It is a smile that says "thank you," that says "I understand," that says "This day you shall be with me in Paradise." Then Jesus lays back His head and returns to His previous state of lifelessness.

Someone taps AD on the shoulder. John the Beloved? Mary Magdalen? The Blessed Mother? He turns to find Father Mueller standing behind him, smiling. "Would you like to go to Confession, son? I was just leaving and saw you kneeling here. Is there something you would like to confess, or are you just here to worship our Lord?"

10:19:59:59:22 A.M.

He is conscious now. Mostly. So he allows the women and children more freedom. He sees himself as kind. He is, in fact, a benevolent despot, propped up precariously by those he oppresses. He is still trying to comprehend the first Law of the Jungle: Women are always in charge.

10:19:59:59:23 A.M.

It rains every night now. In the morning the sky begins to clear, so EG and Hari go about their day as usual, tramping through the woods, chopping paths down to the creek then up the other side of the ravine. They sit on the deck and eat lunch, looking out over the forest to the blue, blue sea beyond. Once in a while, besides the tiny fishing boats that ease into view, a large cruise ship can be seen on the horizon. Small from this distance but very distinct with smokestacks and white promenade decks, these luxury liners slip from Vancouver to Baja, California, with a short layover in San Francisco, just long enough for their wealthy passengers to hit Chinatown, Fisherman's Wharf, Williams-Sonoma, and Gump's.

EG wonders what the tourists buy in San Francisco. He wonders what they see. *What do they say to one another, strolling down Maiden Lane and Grant Avenue, laden with shopping bags and sweatshirts? What does that man whisper to his wife? What is she turning surreptitiously to look at? They had better be careful. This is San Francisco. They could disappear without a trace. Hong Kong has nothing on this city. People disappear all the time, especially women.*

EG's dreams are filled with women these nights. Young women begging him to tell his secret, old women weeping, middle-aged women smoking filtered cigarettes and staring at him vacantly. Everywhere in his dreams, there are women— women tugging at his sleeves, women hiring him for jobs, firing him for lack of commerce. Women trying to seduce him, trying to wed him, women divorcing him. What does it mean?

EG knows that whatever it means specifically, it means the same thing generally: Anna is trying to speak to him. He must bring her to Anchor Bay. He tries all day to reach her but to no avail. He waits until 2 in the morning; surely she will answer then. Nothing. He tries to reach her later that morning, but still she does not respond. There is only one thing left to do in this situation. He has done it only once before, but now he realizes—after days of trying to contact her, nights filled with women who will not go away—that he must assume her himself.

EG goes to the general store in Gualala, for there is no clothing store in Anchor Bay. He is friendly with the woman who runs the clothing department, so he does not have to explain his purchases to her or make excuses about a fictitious sister coming to visit. He simply walks in, reads to her from his list, and she fetches, one at a time, the items he needs.

Back at the house he lays his purchases on the bed, puts *La Boheme* on the stereo, and removes his clothes. Then he begins to dress. First the black panties. Next the black brassiere, which is plain, not fancy or lacy, just simple, elegant, Italian. Then comes the black slip, the black stockings, and finally the black high heels.

He races or slinks from room to room, mouthing the words to Puccini's arias, moving stylistically, dancing, swaying, throwing his hands up to heaven, tearing his hair, falling against walls, and collapsing on the floor in despair at the scene where Mimi finally dies.

He caresses Anna's body, running his hands across her stomach, up to her ample breasts. She lowers the straps to her slip and slides her brassiere down over her shoulders. He cannot wait for her clothes to come off and begins feverishly to reach beneath the black silk cups and caress her breasts, rubbing them first lightly, then savagely, giving himself up completely to her passion and his own. She wants him, she needs him, she commands him to ravage her. She struggles to get free and rises to her feet. He clutches at her, but she manages to escape, running from room to room, laughing her deepthroated laugh, until he corners her downstairs. She presses her back to the wall and closes her eyes.

He begins at her thighs, planting tender kisses on her soft olive skin. He buries his face in her crotch, tears at her panties with his teeth, until they are shredded and free, then plunges his tongue deep inside her. She cries out, moaning softly over and over, as he works his way up to her nipples, licking, nibbling, biting hard. She feels him stiff and throbbing, pressing against her, then, moist from her passion and his attention, she feels him enter her, hard, fast, ramming deep inside her. He is mad with lust and far beyond tenderness. His lack of control fuels her own heat. She cries out and grips his shoulders. "*Caro, caro,*" she moans in his ear. He slows to a gentle, slow motion, sliding delicately in and out of her. All the way out, then back in, then out again, making love to her now with the utmost tenderness. She is out of her mind with the sensation. "*Vengo, vengo,*" she cries. "*Vengo, vengo,*" he answers, and together, as if one, they reach orgasm.

When it is over they lie in one another's arms on the floor. The sunlight, gold and warm, falls through the skylight onto their entwined limbs. "*Ti amo,*" EG whispers, gently caressing her face with the back of his hand. "*Ti amo.*" She lies silent, content, her head resting on his heart.

The women come now to pay their respects, show how they envy her. They file slowly down the stairs, pass by the two lovers sprawled on the carpet, nodding, smiling. A nun genuflects before them. Anna winks at her. "*Grazie,*" she says softly. One by one, the women walk through the sliding-glass door onto the deck, down the steps, and disappear into the woods. EG drifts gently into sleep. When he wakes, Anna is gone, and a light rain has begun to fall. He sees it through the skylight, tiny drops falling on the strong, green branches of the redwood tree that canopies the north side of the house.

He closes his eyes and drifts back into a gentle, womanless slumber. The only image in his dream now is a small elephant, decorated with festival silks and painted with vibrant rouges and indigos. It walks slowly but crushingly before him, through a dense forest, trampling all obstacles in his path.

10:19:59:59:24 A.M.

AD has just turned 12. For his birthday, as usual, his Aunt Cecilia closed the hotel bar for the day and drove to Benicia, where they have moved from Calistoga so that Annabel could accept a promotion at the telephone company. The telephone office in Calistoga was closed when the town was converted to dial telephones. Benicia is still an operator-assisted town because there is a major military installation here and the top brass don't trust the newfangled equipment yet. They want a living human being to speak to. They want Annabel.

The morning of his birthday, Cecilia pulled into the driveway, the backseat of her yellow Packard convertible with red leather interior and power windows loaded with liquor bottles of varying degrees of fullness. Aunt Cecilia "plays" the bottles like a xylophone. She has done this every year for The Boy's birthday. Since he was turning 12 she decided she would play the bottles one last time, because next year AD would undoubtedly want something more "mature." She doesn't mind. It is the way things should be.

But now, two weeks after the birthday party, here is Aunt Cecilia once again pulling into the driveway, quite unexpectedly, on a Saturday morning. AD is sitting on the front porch with Corky, his three-legged cocker spaniel. Aunt Cecilia walks across the lawn with a definite purpose. She is wearing a long, sheer, red scarf wrapped around her head like the movie stars AD sees in *Photoplay* magazine. As she marches across the

and make it seem like he's won The Big Payoff or Queen for a Day, now she's asking him if he wants to have his own room.

"My own room, I guess," he says, trying to sound as nonchalant as possible. "If you don't mind," he adds, not wanting to hurt her feelings.

"Fine. Let's go into the office," she says. They move to her small office, which is right down the hall from the bar. There's one on the third floor...and here's one on the second," she says, looking over the keyboard. "Does it matter to you?"

"No. Whichever is most convenient," AD says, sipping his cherry Coke. Cecilia hands him a key. "It's 207. Right by the stairs. Now be sure you come say good night every night so I know you're going to bed and don't have to go looking all over the hotel for you when I close up, OK?"

"OK," AD says, fingering the key and staring at it. His own room, his own key. There is a God after all.

"Now go unpack. I want to show you what you're going to have to do in the kitchen."

Cecilia has explained to AD on the drive into The City that she expects him to earn his keep by washing dishes in the hotel restaurant every night. He'll start at 4 o'clock, helping her prep the salads and set the tables. At 6 the restaurant opens—except for her friend Salvatore, who comes for dinner every night at 5. "For Sal," Aunt Cecilia explains, "the corner table by the waterfall must be set with crystal and good china and silver, not the usual hotel stuff we put out for regular customers." A glass of Montepulciano D'Abruzzo should be waiting for him, set out at least half an hour early so that it can breathe properly. AD is to wash dishes until the restaurant closes at 10, then he's to help Artie, the waitress, clean up the kitchen. After that, he's on his own until 4 o'clock the next day.

AD is nervous about all this. He's never washed dishes in a restaurant before, but he's so excited about being "on his own" that he will try anything. Wow! A summer in San Francisco on his own.

It takes no time at all for him to get the hang of setting a table. Scrubbing the pots and pans is a little more than he was prepared for. He hadn't thought of pots and pans as "dishes," especially the scallopini pans, but he soon picks up some tips from Artie on how to get them clean and back out to the kitchen pronto. Each evening, after the restaurant closes and he finishes cleaning up in the kitchen, he goes for a walk in the neighborhood. Not far, just around the block for some fresh air.

It is exciting beyond his wildest imaginings to be living in The City like an adult. Imagine being able to go for a walk at 11 o'clock at night, right out the door without even telling anyone or asking permission. By the end of the fourth week, AD feels like a young man, not a 12-year-old boy. He has a job, he has a room, he gets to do what he wants during the day.

One of the things he does is go to the corner news kiosk on Polk Street, where he buys magazines. He goes with a sheet of paper that he hopes looks like a list he has been given by an adult. He walks up to the kiosk, checks his list, and picks up the three magazines he has been sent to purchase: *Redbook*, *Life*, and *Young Physique*. This makes him extremely nervous, but the man at the kiosk doesn't say anything to him, so obviously his chicanery is working.

Back in his own private room, with the door locked, he deposits the *Life* and *Redbook* onto the dresser and lies down on the bed with Young *Physique*. He turns the pages slowly, anticipating with excitement each naked and seminaked body. All the men and boys are wearing posing straps, but nothing is left to the imagination, especially with the white straps that look like they've been wetted before the photo session.

Since finding these magazines AD's life has been one painful erection after another. His penis is so raw he has to put Vaseline on it to keep it from hurting when it rubs against his underwear. *This must be hell*, he thinks, *because it feels just like heaven*. By the end of the fifth week, he has managed to purchase four of these magazines, although they are rather expensive.

By the end of the sixth week, he has reached orgasm with every model at least once and is growing bored with it. Besides, he is sure he's going to hell for this. Oh, well, that's why God invented Confession.

It is Tuesday of his seventh week in the hotel. Business is slow, so they close the restaurant at 9. A merchant marine ship is in port and the bar is busy. He can hear his Aunt Cecilia laughing loudly as she pours drinks, flirting and rolling dice with the sailors. He is finished with the dishes by 9:30 and goes out for a walk.

It is unusually warm for The City, no fog, no ocean breeze. The air is still, and lots of people are out for a stroll. After three trips around the block, AD sits on the corner of Larkin and California to watch people go by. He assumes most of them are either on their way to the movie theaters and bars on Polk Street or doing their grocery shopping at the all-night market a block up California Street. Most of the pedestrians are elderly Chinese couples or young white men with tight pants and sleeveless T-shirts.

"Hi." A voice behind him startles him, and he spins around to find a handsome dark-haired young man squatting on the sidewalk behind him. He has a warm smile.

"You're out kind of late, aren't you?"

"I just got off work," AD replies.

"Work!" the man exclaims, moving around to join AD on the curb. "I thought there were child labor laws in this country."

AD would be insulted, being a man now and all, but the guy's smile is so sweet and he's so friendly, he can't be angry. Also there is something mysterious about him and AD is curious. "I'm not a child," AD says, lowering his voice a register.

"Sorry," the man says good-naturedly.

"How old do you think I am, anyway?" AD asks.

The young man studies AD up and down. "Oh, I'd say you're all of 14."

This is going to be easier than AD thought. "Well, I'm 16," he announces most convincingly."

"You don't say," the man laughs, tousling AD's hair with his left hand. The man is shaking his head in amazement, real or patronizing, AD can't quite tell. AD's new acquaintance lets his hand linger at the back of AD's neck for a moment.

"In another month I'll be 17," AD lies, pressing his luck.

The dark-haired man smiles, his eyes twinkling in the lamplight, and AD sees something he vaguely recognizes. The two of them sit like this, reading each other's souls, then the young man removes his hand and asks, "Do you live around here?"

"I have a room in that hotel up there." AD points in the direction of his aunt's hotel.

"You really are on your own, aren't you?"

"I told you, I'm 16. I'm an adult now. At least I feel like an adult."

The man laughs again and rubs the back of AD's neck. This time he leaves his hand there. AD flushes, and his new friend can see his cheeks turn red, even in the faint light from the street lamp.

"My name's Richard," the man says, holding out his hand.

"My name's…Jack," AD says, thinking quickly, taking his uncle's name, losing, in this split second, his innocence.

"Are you familiar with gay life?" the man asks pointedly.

AD doesn't know what he means. He's never heard the word *gay* used in this context before, but even so, he somehow knows what the man is asking.

"Yes," he answers simply.

"Would you like to spend some time together?"

"Yes," AD replies.

"We can't go to my place—too many people there. Can we go up to your room?"

"Sure," AD says hesitantly. What reason might he possibly offer for saying no? This is all happening so quickly, so strangely, as though he isn't in control of his body or his words. He must do this—whatever this is.

Once in AD's room, the man takes AD by the shoulders, draws him close, and kisses him on the lips. AD has never been kissed on the lips by a man before. The first kiss catches him off-guard and he stiffens like stone. By the second kiss he is responding the way he's seen Jane Russell and Susan Hayward kiss. The man must like it because now he's removing AD's shirt. "Let's get in bed," the man says, reaching to flick the overhead light off.

AD undresses and pulls his pajamas out from beneath the pillow. His handsome companion reaches out and takes them from him, tosses them on the other side of the bed. "You won't need these," he says seductively.

AD smiles nervously and climbs under the covers. In the neon glow coming through the window, AD watches the man remove his clothes. "So you've really done this before, huh?" the man asks. AD can tell from his voice that he knows it is AD's first time.

"Yeah, lots of times."

The man climbs in and lies on top of AD. His body is solid, like the models in *Young Physique*. AD is suddenly ashamed of his own body, loose and flabby. But the man, planting kisses on his chest, tummy, groin, doesn't seem to mind. Beneath the covers, the dark-haired, lean-bodied stranger is licking AD's thighs. His is the first tongue ever to touch AD in these places, the first tongue to lick his virgin testicles, now the first mouth ever to take into it AD's 12-year-old penis.

AD's incubus slowly and tenderly sucks at what he knows has never been sucked before, and he can tell from the amount of pubic hair that this boy is much younger than 16. This excites the man and now he turns, positioning himself so that AD can take him into his mouth while he continues to suck on AD.

AD fumbles but manages to imitate his lover. "Ouch!" the man says. "Watch your teeth."

AD feels stupid. *Of course, no teeth,* he thinks. *Pay attention. Do what he does.*

They explore one another's bodies with their hands while they continue to give each other pleasure with their mouths. The man runs his hand up and down the crack of AD's butt. AD does the same to the man. The man licks the area beneath AD's scrotum. AD does the same, except AD has to stop once in a while to remove a hair, a problem his sex partner isn't having.

They are deep in the throes of sexual adventure when AD becomes aware of a familiar sound, a voice, faintly calling his name. At first he thinks it is his conscience, his guardian angel reprimanding him for such grievously sinful actions. Perhaps it is the Blessed Mother wailing at his defilement. No, it's more familiar than that. And it's getting louder, more accurately, it's getting closer.

"AD…AD…where are you?"

It's Aunt Cecilia. He forgot to tell her he was going to his room. Now she's looking for him, making sure he's all right, tucked safely in for the night. What can he do?

"AD…AD…" Cecilia calls, her voice climbing the stairs, her keys jingling in her hand.

Oh, my God, AD thinks. *What can I do? Why doesn't this guy hear her? Why doesn't he realize what's going on and jump up and put on his clothes? Why doesn't he hear her calling my name and see that he's in danger? Shit! He thinks my name is Jack!*

Now the keys are in the door. The man hears them, freezes beneath the covers. Now the door is opening, the light going on, and now there is shrieking. The man is hopping out of the bed, rushing to dress.

AD is lying with the sheet over his head, pretending to be asleep. Surely this is the end of the world. Or else it is a dream. He will lie here with his eyes closed and wait for the dream to end. He will wake up and brush his teeth and go down to Aunt Cecilia's room. The two of them will have coffee and Danish like they do every morning. Except why doesn't the shrieking stop?

"You goddamn queer. What the hell is going on here?" Aunt Cecilia screams. "You goddamn pervert. I ought to call the cops." She is striking the man on the back with her fist as he stoops to pull up his pants. "You goddamn queer bastard! I could have you put in prison for the rest of your life! You son of a bitch!"

A crowd has gathered in the hallway, merchant marines and their dates, Midwestern tourists daring to make their first visit to Babylon by the Bay.

"Get out of here and don't ever let me see you around here again or I'll call the cops." She is shouting after the man, who is hopping down the stairs two at a time, one shoe on, the other in his hand. "No, I won't call the cops, I'll call my brother Ernesto and some of his friends and that'll be the end of your child molesting days. *Strónz!*"

Aunt Cecilia slams the door, goes to the bed, and pulls the covers back from AD's face. He keeps his eyes closed. "What the hell happened?" she asks.

AD pretends like he's just waking up. "What's going on? What's all the noise about?"

Cecilia ignores his act. "How did he get in here?"

"Who?" AD asks.

"That man. How did he get in your room? Did he follow you? Did he tell you he needed a place to stay?"

AD is too traumatized to realize she is handing him excuses one after another. "I don't know how he got in," is all AD can think to say.

"Did you meet him on the street today?"

"I don't know how he got in."

"Did he give you money? Did he follow you when you were out for a walk? Did he tell you he needed someplace to sleep tonight? Were you just feeling sorry for him? What happened?"

"I don't know."

"Well, get your clothes. You're sleeping in my room from now on. We'll make up a bed on the sofa. Jesus Christ! God-damn queers. They're like rats. They're everywhere. You can't turn around for one goddamn minute."

AD slips his pajamas on while Cecilia pulls clothes out of the dresser drawer. He lifts his suitcase from under the bed, but Cecilia throws the clothes on top of the dresser and says, "Come on—let's go. We'll get the rest of this stuff tomorrow."

AD lies on his aunt's sofa staring at the street lamp outside the window until it blinks off with the rising of the sun. He will survive this—somehow.

Two anxiety-ridden days later, after calling his mother and asking if he can come home, he tells Aunt Cecilia that his mother is missing him and would like him to come home now. Also, a friend of his is having a 13th birthday party that he really wants to attend. Would it be all right for him to leave? Would she drive him home in a day or so?

Of course, she does drive him home, and while she is sitting at the kitchen table with Annabel, AD is in the next room with his ear to the wall. But Aunt Cecilia doesn't tell his mother what happened. As far as he knows, she never told. He later concludes that she was just as embarrassed by it as he was. But he never forgets his rite of passage into adulthood, and after this, nothing about men ever seems quite the same.

<u>10:19:59:59:25</u> A.M.

EG is going to Nordstrom's to buy himself something extravagant. He has no idea what it will be. It isn't about the object; it's about the experience. He wants to indulge himself. Annabel is with him. She is busying herself in the vanity mirror attached to the visor, refreshing her lipstick. She loves Nordstrom's.

"Tell me about your father," EG says as they turn onto Market Street.

Annabel's lipstick hand freezes for just one detectable moment. "I don't know anything about him and you know it."

"Tell me anyway," EG says, easing the car to a stop at a red light. A bedraggled man with long hair, wearing an army jacket stands on the median strip holding a sign that says WILL WORK FOR FOOD. GOD BLESS. Scrawled at the bottom in barely legible letters of a different color than the rest of the sign, al-most as an afterthought, is the word VETERAN.

"Why do you torture me like this?" Annabel asks, closing her lipstick.

"Because you love it so."

"He left when I was 6, for chrissake. He went on a train trip and never came back. Wes took over as head of the family and never allowed anyone to mention his name again. There. That's all I know." The light's green. Annabel snaps her purse closed.

As EG moves the car slowly into the intersection past the veteran with his hand-scribbled sign, their eyes meet. The veteran doesn't turn his head, but shifts his eyes in case EG might break down at the last moment and thrust a $5 bill out the window. In the few seconds that they encounter one an-other, EG sees two things. First, the man's face is delicately and exquisitely chiseled beneath the stubble and grime of liv-ing on the streets. It is the face of an Italian Renaissance painting, high cheekbones, aristocratically jutting jawbone, full, expressive lips. The second thing he sees is something in the man's eyes. He knows this man, has seen him before, will see him again. Then the moment is over and the car is past the concrete median strip and across the intersection. When EG looks into his rearview mirror, the man is turning, look-ing after the car, his long, grimy, honey-colored hair falling to the middle of his back, his torso twisted, revealing his thin waist, a waist that EG associates with that of a hungry man, an ascetic or a middle-class homosexual, who spends four nights a week at the gym.

"Well, then, make something up," EG says, turning his at-tention once more to his passenger and the traffic around him. "You must remember something."

Annabel fumbles for a Pall Mall, lights it, stares out the side window. EG knows she will break down now. He's seen that look before. He has been inside that look before.

"I remember how he smelled," she begins.

"Women always remember smells," EG says, shaking his head. "They can't tell left from right, but they always remember smells."

"Do you want to hear this or not?"

"Sorry, I'm a sexist. Go ahead."

"He smelled like trains."

"Trains?"

"Trains. Like the inside of trains. When you first get on or just start climbing aboard, there's this smell of grease, like axle grease mixed with the smell of leather and gravel and weathered wood and metal and...I don't know. Like trains."

"Did he work on a train?"

"He worked near them. He was a Morse code operator for Western Union, and all the Western Union offices in those days were in the railroad stations. If you wanted to send or pick up a telegram, you went down to the railroad station." Annabel takes a deep drag from her cigarette, blows it out the window. "And he was always tired. He would come home and take off his khaki jacket and tan cap, hang them up on the hook near the front door, then collapse into the big overstuffed chair in the parlor. He'd call out, 'Where's my little girl? Where's my Annie?'"

"Annie? He called you Annie?"

"Yes. He was the only one who ever called me that. I'd come running and jump up on his lap and he'd give me the biggest hug. God he was strong. I thought he'd break my bones he hugged me so hard." She flicks her cigarette ash out the window, then takes another deep drag from it. "Funny, huh, when you think about it? He was either giving me crushing hugs or not there at all. I don't remember anything in-between. He'd come and go, come and go. Sometimes he'd be gone for weeks. Our mother would tell us he was traveling for his job, but we didn't believe her. I hated it when he'd leave. I'd get up in the morning and he'd already be gone and Mom would be sitting at the kitchen table crying. A few weeks would go by and then he'd show up again, come strolling in like he was just getting home from work and we should take no notice, just go on as usual, as though he had never been gone."

"Do you think he was really working or do you think he was drinking or they had fights or what?"

"I think he couldn't help himself—he just had to wander. "

"Maybe he was running from something. Maybe he was a criminal."

"You're so dramatic. He was a man. Men do that, in case you haven't noticed. They follow their hormones. Men like to wander, to explore, to have adventures. You're just like him."

"I am?"

"Yes, but then I suppose all men are like that. There's always some other place to see, another person to screw, another adventure just around the corner."

"God, I'm not like that! I don't wander."

"In your mind you do."

"That's a lot different than disappearing for six months when you go for the evening newspaper. You're wrong about this. I'm not like that."

"You are."

"I'm not."

"Well, you used to be…before you met Paul."

"Well, maybe a little…when I was younger."

"My father was a young man when I knew him. He was probably in his early 30s, maybe even late 20s. People married young in those days you know."

"What happened after he left?"

"We'd all pretend he was on a business trip and wait for him to return, and then one evening while we were listening to Jack Benny on the radio, or one morning while I was eating oatmeal at the breakfast table, he would saunter in the door with whatever it was he had gone after that evening tucked under his arm, like he hadn't been gone but for a few minutes. I think he could actually even make himself believe it. He was so casual about it all. It was actually part of his charm, I think. Again, kind of like you."

"And no one ever said anything to him about it?" EG says, ignoring the last comparison.

"No one but Wes. When Wes got into high school, he started confronting him about lots of things. They fought constantly."

"What happened after he left for good?" They are now pulling into the garage behind Nordstrom's. EG is reaching to take the parking ticket out of the automatic dispensing machine. A computerized female voice is saying, with extremely studied enthusiasm and vivacity, "Welcome to the Fifth and Mission Street Garage. Please keep your ticket with you."

"Shut up!" EG yells at the machine. He smiles at Annabel. "I hate that woman's voice." He hands the ticket to her and heads the car for the up ramp. "So go on, after he left and you realized it was for good…"

"Well, of course, I never would admit it was for good. I kept telling myself he was coming back. Then after about a year, Wes came to each of us, including my mother, and said we were forbidden ever to speak of him again, in or out of Wes's presence."

"Did you?"

"No. I loved my brothers as much as I loved my father. Maybe more. We stopped talking about him altogether. "

"But surely you had thoughts about him."

"Of course. I missed him. Even when he was away for short periods I missed him. I loved him a great deal. I used to think I saw him on the street. Every once in a while I'd run up behind some man wearing a khaki waistcoat and a tan cotton cap and I would be so sure that when he turned around it would be my father. But of course it never was."

"That must have been a horrible way to live. Missing him so much, waiting, watching."

"I suppose it was," she says, opening her purse and depositing the parking garage ticket. "It made me afraid to get very close to men. I would try of course, but then I'd always pull away or do something to sabotage things before they walked out and never came back."

"But you haven't done that with Clete."

"Haven't I?"

EG saw that she believed she had. That while she had not caused the breakup of the marriage, she had indeed undermined the bond of the relationship. She was smiling at him most sardonically as he looked deep into her eyes. Annabel clicks her purse shut to break the spell. "Clete smelled like guns, which smell a lot like trains. Maybe that's what it was."

"So you do remember your father after all," EG says as though he is winning an argument. He pulls the car into a parking space on the fourth floor.

"Let's say I have memories. And I have you. You're a lot like him."

"I don't see how," EG says, his hand on the door handle.

"You smell like trains too."

"But I'm not going anywhere."

"I know. That's why I'm here. Now let's go buy you the most expensive jacket Nordstrom's has to offer. And let's have fun doing it."

10:19:59:59:26 A.M.

There is no happy ending to this story, he thinks, as he climbs out of bed to take another pain pill. He thinks of the illness as a bad father or a corrupt political leader: benign to public perception but once the doors are closed, menacing and abusive—making promises that will never be kept.

A month ago his physician began giving him testosterone injections. The result was increased energy, building of lean muscle mass. He began exercising more, walking, running, lifting weights. Sex between him and Paul has grown in both frequency and quality, but now the exercise has resulted in a damaged nerve in his left arm, which causes him excruciating pain that runs from his shoulder to the tips of his fingers.

The pain wakes him at night and makes it impossible for him to lie on his left side; yet, because of sinus infections, he cannot lie on his right side either. If he lies flat on his back, the peripheral neuropathy in his feet and left leg cause his limbs to go numb. He must sleep with a pillow under his knees. It feels unnatural to him after a lifetime of sleeping on his left side.

He lies in bed and looks at the alarm. It is five after 5 in the morning. He rubs his arm. He knows it is no use staying in bed, so he rises. The dog stirs, the cat races down the hall toward her food bowl, and he stumbles toward the kitchen in the dark, his arms outstretched in anticipation of the opiate that will make his morning bearable. He thinks, *Don't complain; there are people in worse pain who can' t get drugs. At least you have drugs.*

<u>10:19:59:59:27</u> A.M.

EG has had a restful sleep—8½ hours—waking only once to go to the bathroom. He rises and goes downstairs and puts up a pot of coffee. He stands at the sink, washing cups left over from last night's dessert. Outside it is raining lightly, a warm spring rain that will nourish the newly planted purple hebe and pink leptospermum.

Across the lawn near the Shinto gate, billowing clouds of yellow Scotch broom glow like golden lanterns. Brilliant raindrops fall onto the carpet of tan-and rust-colored redwood needles that carpet the earth beneath the trees.

Suddenly, without warning, EG begins to weep, overwhelmed with loss and grief. As he cries he is aware of himself crying, almost as though part of him is observing himself from outside himself. He is crying for the dead, not for Andre or Pete, not for Rick or any of the dozens of friends who have died before him, but for all the many dead in general and for himself, in particular. It is as though he is someone else, someone who has survived him in the future, who is standing at the sink of the house in Anchor Bay, looking out the window onto the gray, drizzly morning, missing EG, who has died.

Perhaps he is experiencing what Paul will experience. Perhaps he has flashed forward in time and is living inside Paul, who is grieving the loss of his soul mate. Is he now Paul in the future, thinking of EG, who will never stand at this sink again, who will never rise softly, kiss his lover—who smiles without opening his eyes—pad gently down the stairs to make coffee, fill the thermos, return upstairs, and slip back into bed beside him? Has EG flashed forward into Paul's consciousness, which has flashed back to this moment?

EG observes himself weeping for his own death, missing himself, longing for himself not to die but to live and go on living and caring for the ones he loves. Then EG's awareness returns slowly to the body at the sink, returns to participating in the sobbing, the heartache, the deep, aching loss. Now EG stands looking out at the rain. He is sadder than he has ever been before. EG is also aware that this experience, in one form or another, happens to him more and more.

One time, EG thinks, *I will go and not come back. I will rise up, look down on myself, my aching heart, my life splayed about me like a spilled box of photos, and I will be gone. I will be dead. And somehow it will be all right to leave. Somehow. It's just that here and now, in the company of Paul and Hari, with my heart so full, the forest so green, the rain so delicate in the branches of the trees, I can't imagine leaving. I can't imagine it being all right at all.*

10:19:59:59:28 A.M.

The room pulses with his rage.

10:19:59:59:29 A.M.

EG lies very still, out of pain for the first time in his life. He takes this opportunity to think back on his life of pain and sorrow. He has no memory of a time when he wasn't in pain. One day, when he was 2 years old, Annabel found him on the floor of his room, screaming in agony. He had no wounds, no bleeding, no particular place on his body that he was clutching, so she sat on the floor, trying to comfort him, thinking perhaps it was indigestion and it would pass with the comfort of a mother's love. But three hours later she gave in and telephoned Doctor MacGrain. He told her to bring the baby in immediately.

Days of testing at the hospital in Santa Rosa reveal nothing. Finally they resort to admitting him to Children's Hospital in San Francisco. Three more days of tests reveal the problem: rheumatoid arthritis. There is little that can be done:
buffered aspirin in massive doses, small amounts of pain
killers, sometimes heat, sometimes ice packs. The doctors
send them home with no hope, telling his parents, reluctantly, that the child will probably not live into adolescence.
Annabel is disconsolate, but she never gives up hope. Clete
resigns himself to yet another failure in his life.

Around the time The Boy turns 6, a new drug is discovered that is so powerful, so revolutionary, it is assigned a
classification all its own. The drug is called cortisone, and
it is prescribed for The Boy with great joy. For two years
The Boy returns to normal. He is able to attend school with
the other children in Calistoga; he runs to his mother when
she calls him for lunch, climbs the jungle gym in the grammar school playground, explores the lower branches of fat-
limbed walnut trees along Fourth Street. Annabel's prayers
have been answered.

One day, a year later in the school cafeteria, laughing at the
silly faces Irene Carenzolli is making with her mouth full of
mashed potatoes, The Boy grips his stomach, grimaces, and
vomits his lunch onto Irene Carenzolli's new plaid jumper.
The vomit is filled with blood. A week later, after batteries of
tests back at Children's Hospital, The Boy is released to go
home. The cortisone in its early, raw form has given The Boy
a bleeding ulcer; worse than that, it has sensitized him to the
drug. He can never take the medication again without risking
anaphylactic shock.

So begins a life of physical disability, ghoulish pain in every
joint of his body, and nearly total helplessness.

Every two to three years for the next 15 years he undergoes an operation to break certain bones in his body, sever certain joints, reattach others so that he can change positions in the specially built bed in which he lives. He lies within a jungle of levers and wires and extenders rigged up to pulleys so that he can comb his hair, wash his face, pull the swing-away tray closer, tap on the electric typewriter. Three large mirrors are strategically placed, enabling him to see the entire room by moving his head the two inches in either direction that is the extent of his range of motion.

Eventually, with great difficulty and patience, he is able to force his legs and back into positions that enable him to be lifted out of the bed and into a wheelchair. And although he receives most of his education at home, The Boy is strong-willed. He fights hard and attends high school for his senior year, graduating summa cum laude with the rest of his class. When his name is called to receive his diploma, AD pushes the button on his palette wheelchair, maneuvers up the specially built ramp, and crosses the stage to the entire auditorium's standing ovation.

He goes on to attend college on his own, enrolling in a program for independent living in San Francisco and relying on attendants sent by the Visiting Nurses Association. After graduation he finds employment with a magazine, editing copy and writing book reviews at home. His attendants continue to be provided by the VNA, and Annabel visits him every chance she gets, which is not easy since Clete will not drive into The City and bus travel between Benicia and San Francisco is limited and requires three transfers. Nevertheless, she remains faithful to her only child and makes it to his apartment at least once a month, until her sudden death the year EG turns 25.

Once Annabel is gone, Clete virtually disappears from EG's life. Refusing to drive into The City, and hating to talk on the telephone, EG is isolated from Clete unless EG initiates some kind of contact. After three years of making telephone calls that never last more than three minutes, writing letters that go unanswered, and being unable to travel to Benicia without a special vehicle and driver, which he has to reserve two weeks in advance, EG gives up trying to forge some sort of relationship with his father. Now, at the age of 28, he is completely on his own.

Besides the understandable grief and frustration at his physical condition, EG has also had to learn to cope with the fact that he is gay. Gay, trapped in a body that not only is unpleasant to look at but also doesn't even move unless it is moved for him, EG long ago gave up all hope of ever having a romantic relationship of any kind, let alone one of substance.

One of EG's attendants, who was also gay, bought him a prostitute for his 25th birthday. But even the callboy was uneasy, quickly bringing EG to orgasm with his hand, then rushing out the door, saying he had another client way out in the Avenues and he had to hurry or he'd be late. That was EG's first and only sexual encounter. He told himself he was lucky to have had that one.

But then someone new is assigned to be his attendant. Leo is from Oregon, new to The City, and a country boy at heart. He tells EG he grew up on a farm just across the Oregon border with six brothers and four sisters, one of whom was crippled as a result of polio. It was his family "chore" to take care of her while they were growing up. He seemed to like it rather than to resent it. "Making someone in pain smile is the biggest high I can imagine," he tells EG. It was inevitable, EG supposes later, on reflection, that he would eventually fall in love with one of his attendants.

Against all odds, and flying in the face of tradition and medical ethics, Leo also professes his love for EG. That is the happiest day of EG's life.

After three months Leo moves in. He has to leave his position with VNA, since it is strictly forbidden that attendants and nurses be romantically involved with patients. EG doesn't mind. He is living on a trust fund that Cohen set up for him, and he would rather pay Leo directly and cut out the middle man. This way, the entire amount is Leo's, rather than the $7.50 he was paid out of the $15 an hour EG paid the VNA.

Leo goes out of his way to help EG get out more. They travel, renting a specially equipped recreational vehicle and driving to the desert, the mountains, Yosemite, and now Oregon. In Oregon they are visiting Leo's family. They are simple people, quiet, uneducated, obviously very poor. They seem suspicious of EG and not overly friendly; neither are they warm toward their son. Leo says they have never fully accepted his being gay.

Leo and EG sleep in the RV, where EG has a specially designed bed that can be cranked and shifted, allowing him to change the position of his arms and legs. The contraption allows him to sit up, lie down, even rotate left and right. But in the RV he is more dependent on Leo, since all the levers and pulleys he has at home, which enable him to have nearly full use of his hands, had to be left behind.

The RV is parked behind a dilapidated barn at the edge of a pine forest about 200 yards from Leo's family's house. Lying there in the Oregon night, his lover sleeping close by, EG is grateful for all his blessings. "Thank you," he whispers into the dark. "Thank you."

The next day Leo has errands to run in town. He is gone all day, but no one comes out to the RV to check on EG. He is starving by the time Leo returns. Leo apologizes, goes into the house to get EG some dinner, returns about an hour later with a bowl of stew and two slices of white bread and margarine.

"Leo," EG says, "I think I want to go home tomorrow if that's all right with you. I'm tired and not feeling too good. As odd as this probably sounds, I miss my own bed." EG laughs at his little joke of missing such an uncomfortable bed. Leo is frowning.

"I have a couple more aunts I'd like to see before we leave, EG. It seems such a shame to come all this way and not get to see them. They'd be so hurt. Just a couple more days, OK?"

EG gives in. They've come this far, and Leo has been so kind, taking care of him devotedly for so many months now. They decide to leave in two days. But two days later, when EG mentions it, Leo resists. "It's Friday," he says. "Traffic will be terrible. Let's wait until Monday. We'll leave bright and early Monday morning."

The weekend drags by for EG, who is left alone in the RV every day while Leo visits his "relations." Although promises are made that someone will look in on him and at least bring him lunch, no one comes. Friday night EG is alone until almost 10 o'clock. When Leo returns, his breath is heavy with whiskey and he fumbles around, dropping food and spilling milk while he is trying to feed EG.

"Sorry, honey," he says. "My Aunt Loretta made me sit and drink with her while she told me the sad story of her life this past year. She's so lonely, I just couldn't leave her. You'd love her. Maybe tomorrow we can go over there together."

But the next day Leo has another urgent errand to run for yet another aunt who lives on the other side of the county. It's best if EG stays here. Leo doesn't come home at all Saturday night. He stumbles in Sunday morning, disheveled, his T-shirt on backward. EG hasn't eaten, has soiled and peed the bed. He tells Leo no one answered his cries for help.

"We're leaving, Leo. Tomorrow. That's it. I can't be left like this every day. I'm miserable. You have to take me home. You can come back if you have to, but I need to be at home."

"You know," Leo says, sitting on the bed next to EG, "I don't ask for much around here." He is slurring his words, and it appears he's already been drinking this morning. "All I ask is to visit my relatives once in a while, and now that we're here, all you can think about is going home. It's not fair. My Aunt Jessie told me if I come see her before we leave, she'll give me some money. We can always use money, babe. You think I like taking money from you? I hate myself when I have to mooch off you."

EG is beginning to feel guilty. Leo has taken excellent care of him up to this point, and this is the first thing he has actually asked for. Except for the watch, so he wouldn't be late for work. There was the car, but Leo didn't ask for that. That was EG's idea, because Leo was missing the last bus from his apartment in the Haight and would sometimes be away all night or else have to take a cab, which he really couldn't afford. And the clothes were also EG's idea. He felt sorry for Leo, having to shop at the St. Vincent De Paul Society for his clothes.

The cash EG doles out to Leo is for incidentals that are really as much for EG as for Leo. And everyone deserves a night off once a week to go out and get away from the difficulty of being tied to an invalid. Maybe two nights. During really trying weeks three nights aren't out of the question. Naturally, by the end of the week, all of Leo's money has been spent running errands to the corner bodega, the drugstore, the coffee shop. So it seems only fair to EG that he should slip Leo an extra $20 or $30 so that he can go to a movie on Friday night or out with some of his friends on Saturday night. They're always getting together at the Midnight Sun for drinks or celebrating someone's birthday, anniversary, marriage, or divorce. A little more time here in Oregon to visit some poor aunt isn't too much to ask.

The thought also crosses EG's mind at this point that should he insist on leaving, Leo might create an ugly scene, and the truth is, EG could do nothing about it.

"But you've got to tell someone in the house to feed me. Just bring me lunch is all I ask. I can hold my bowels until you come home, but I have to eat. And you have to come home. I can't go all night."

"I'm sorry, honey. My family is just like that. They're shy and a little backward, but they're good people, and they haven't seen me in so long. I'm all they have."

Leo brings his 10-year-old sister, Opal, out to the RV and tells EG that she will be the one responsible for seeing to EG's needs while he's out the next day getting money from this aunt, who also happens to live on the other side of the county.

Opal is a pasty-faced girl who is so obese she can't button the back of her navy-blue jumper. She wears shoes without laces, her hair is in braids, and her black plastic-framed glasses are as thick as magnifying glasses. She has red jam down the front of her blouse, something brown and crusty on her forearm.

"All right, but please be back by dinnertime," EG pleads.

Leo swears he will be.

At noon, as Leo promised, Opal opens the door of the RV, steps in, and stands looking at EG.

"Hello," EG says.

Opal just stares at him.

"Are you going to bring me lunch?"

Opal says nothing.

"I'm pretty hungry," EG says. "What are we going to have for lunch today?"

Opal looks around the RV, then back at EG. She shrugs her shoulders.

"Well, anything will do. Will you go get me something to eat?" EG asks as cheerfully as possible.

Opal continues to stare, her eyes seemingly as large around as the thick lenses of her glasses.

"Please?" EG pleads.

Opal turns and leaves the RV. A few minutes later she returns. This time she has one of her older brothers with her. His name, EG remembers, is Del. He is about 15 and is as skinny as any child EG has ever seen. He is wearing overalls and orange galoshes; his hair is long and matted. Opal stays by the door of the RV, but Del steps right up to the bed. He looks at EG and says, "Leo says you're rich."

EG tries to ignore this. "Did you bring me some food?" he asks.

"How much money do you have?" Del asks.

"Could you get me some water?" EG asks, ignoring the boy's impertinence. *This is a strange family*, EG thinks. *I'll be glad when we're out of here.* "A glass of water? Please?" he presses.

"How much will you give me if I bring you a glass of water?" Del asks.

EG is desperate at this point. "I'll give you a dollar for a glass of water."

Del disappears out of the RV before EG can tell him there's a sink in the rear of the vehicle. He returns a few minutes later with a Mason jar half-filled with water.

"Thank you," EG says. "Can you hold it up for me?"

Del asks, "Where's the dollar?"

EG has no choice. "Over there in that coffee can," EG says, nodding toward a built-in shelf near the front of the RV behind the driver's seat.

Del retrieves the can, rifles through it, and takes all the money he finds, including the change, and stuffs it into his overalls. Then he hands the water to Opal and opens the door to leave. "You hold it for him. He gives me the creeps," Del says, and disappears.

Opal steps forward with the jar of water, unsure of what is expected of her.

"Just hold it up and tip it so I can drink it," EG says.

Opal stares at him.

"Just hold it up to my lips," EG says as patiently as he can. He is feeling not only weak physically, but mentally he is at the end of his rope. It is clear that he is trapped here. Unless Leo will take him home tomorrow, as promised, he's a prisoner.

Opal tips the jar toward EG's lips. He sips, but she is tipping the jar too far. The water pours into EG's mouth and he begins to choke, coughing and sputtering, spitting the water into the air. Opal drops the jar and runs from the RV.

For the next several hours EG lies in his wet bed watching through the open door, hoping that Leo will return or one of his parents will happen by. EG, weak from lack of food and fluids, is beginning to feel slight panic attacks. He must get out of here. His blood sugar is low and he dozes on and off, waking now and then to a barking dog or a slamming door. Once he thinks he hears a gunshot in the woods.

At dusk he hears whispering outside, then footsteps. Two heads peer through the open door. Del has returned with a friend. They stare in, whispering back and forth to one another, then climb into the RV.

"Please get me some water," EG says hoarsely. His dry and chapped lips stick together when he tries to speak.

"That's Opal's job," Del says. "I gave her a dollar to watch out for you. Didn't she bring you some food?"

"No," EG says. "Just some water, please."

"I can't," Del says. "I'm busy."

"Shit, look at this," the other boy says, standing in front of the portable stereo system. "This is what I want." The boy tries to lift it up, but it is bolted to the table to keep it from sliding off when the RV is in motion. "What the fuck?" The boy turns to EG. "How the fuck do you get this thing off the table?"

EG can't believe this is happening. He stares at Del's friend, who is about 16 and has small, mean eyes. The rage inside the teenager is etched in the lines of his face, which seems much older than his apparent age.

"What are you lookin' at, freak?" the boy shouts. "You fuckin' freak queer motherfucker. I said how do I get this out of here? You better answer me or you'll be sorry." The boy raises his hand in a menacing gesture.

"Keep it down," Del says. "You want my pa to hear you?" Del turns to EG. "Just tell him how to unlock that thing, OK?" Del says to EG. "He's real mean when he gets mad. Just let him take it. You can buy another one."

"Please don't do this. Please. I need help," EG pleads.

Del's friend moves to the side of EG's bed, pushing Del out of the way. "You're a fucking queer, aren't you? Look at this fuckin' queer, man. He's more queer than your brother. Look how fucked up he is. He can't even move, man. You can't even move, you know that, queer? I could do anything I fuckin' want in here and you couldn't do a fuckin' thing about it. I could fuckin' kill you and you couldn't do shit." The boy laughs.

"Settle down, man," Del says, moving to the door and closing it. "You're gonna get us in trouble."

"Lemme see something," the boy says pulling back EG's bedclothes. "O-o-oh, he's wearing a nightgown, just like a lady. Fuckin' queer. I wanna see something.

"Seth, what the hell are you doin'?" Del says, moving to the bedside and standing next to his friend. "Ferd says guys are queer 'cause their dicks are so small. I want to see. I never seen a queer's dick." Seth throws the nightshirt up over EG's stomach.

"Shit, his dick's not little," Del says. "It's bigger'n yours." Del laughs and slaps Seth on the back. "A lot bigger'n yours."

"Shut the fuck up," Seth says. "You're probably queer, too, just like your fuckin' faggot brother." Seth leans over, jutting his menacing face close to EG's, staring him straight in the eyes and squinting. "I'm gonna ask you one last time, fuck-face. How do I get that fuckin' stereo off the table?"

EG says, "I don't know, Einstein. Do I look like I'm the one who fastened it there?"

"That's it," Seth says. "You're in big fuckin' trouble now." With that, the boy begins knocking things over, pulling books off shelves, yanking pots and pans out of their cupboards, throwing bedclothes on the floor. He even takes a butcher knife and slashes EG's mattress. Del tries to stop him, but the boy is stronger and on a rampage. Del runs from the RV.

EG thinks maybe he is dreaming this. It's too bizarre, too macabre to actually be happening. If only Leo would come back. But Leo doesn't come back. By the time Seth leaps out of the RV, cursing EG and all "fuckin', corn-holin', cocksucking fag-gots," the inside of the vehicle is nearly destroyed. When his at-tempts to free the stereo from its bolted down frame failed, the boy took the largest skillet in the RV and smashed it to pieces.

EG lies naked in the rubble, grateful that the boy didn't stab him. Then he feels the vehicle sinking—first the front left, then the right, then the rear, as Seth slashes all the tires.

EG lies there all night. Now he has diarrhea and the bed is reeking with the smell. Even though he hasn't had water in almost 24 hours, he has urinated in the bed twice. EG doesn't know how much time has passed, but it is dark again before Leo finally appears. He is extremely high on alcohol and drugs, but he is freshly shaved and showered. And he is not alone. The man with him is about Leo's age, a little taller, with dark hair and a beard. They are both stunned at the condition of the place.

"What the hell happened?" Leo asks, pulling down EG's nightshirt to cover him and picking up the bedclothes. "Who did this?"

"My name's Vic," the other man says, extending his hand to EG. EG just looks at him blankly. "Well, fuck you too," the guy says. "Unfriendly motherfucker," he says to Leo.

"He's a crip, man. I told you that," Leo whispers. "Hey, baby, I need a favor," Leo says. "I need a little money."

EG can't believe what he's hearing. "Please, Leo, please," he murmurs. "Take me home. Please."

"OK, sure, but first I need some money. Just a little. Just $100." He rummages in the debris for the coffee can, but it's empty. "What happened to the money?"

"Leo, please take me home."

"We been robbed! Who robbed us? Was it Del? That little cocksucker. I'll kill him." Leo bolts out of the RV.

"Please help me," EG says to Leo's friend. "I'm sick. I need a doctor. Please. I'll pay you."

This gets Vic's attention. "But what can I do? I can't do anything to help."

"Take me to a hospital. Please."

"I can't do that. Leo'll get pissed. He's got a temper, man." Vic lifts his shirt, revealing a long red welt on his stomach. "Look what he..." He stops himself, tucks his shirt back in. "Anyway, the hospital's a long way off. And the tire's are all flat. How the fuck did they all get flat at once?"

"I'll give you $1,000 to take me out of here."

The man stares at EG in disbelief. "You got that much money? Really? Shit, I'd suck your gimpy-assed dick for $1,000. How do I get you out to my car, though? You're pretty fucked up."

EG rallies his strength enough to tell Vic how to lift him, how to carry him, how to position pillows under him in the front seat. By the time Leo gets back to the RV from beating his brother, EG and Vic are two miles down the road.

EG is nearly completely dehydrated and lapsing in and out of consciousness in the front seat of Vic's 1989 Olds Cutlass. Vic is trying to ascertain how he will get his $1,000. "We could stop at the bank on the way to the hospital. There's one right on the way."

"First I have to get to a doctor. Something's really wrong inside. I feel like I'm going to die. I'll write you a check at the hospital."

"You can't. I don't have a bank account. It'll just take a minute. You can withdraw the cash, and then we'll head straight to the emergency room. It's only five minutes away from the bank."

Everything is spinning for EG. The trees outside are moving in circles—the dashboard of the car is on the ceiling, then on the floor, then on the ceiling. He feels like he's going to lose consciousness.

"You can make it into the bank, can't you? I know, we'll use the drive-through window. It won't take long."

"Jesus Christ!" EG musters, unable to hold back his anger any longer. "I'm dying here, and all you can think about is money. I shouldn't have to pay you anything to save my life. You could be charged as an accomplice. I was kidnapped. I was tortured."

"Kidnapped? You're going to tell them you were kidnapped?"
EG begins to nod out.

"Hey! No kidnapping, OK? Don't say anything about kidnapping. I just found you there and took you to the hospital.
OK?" Vic slaps EG awake. "You're not going to get me mixed
up in this are you? I'm doing you a favor here."

"Right," EG mumbles. "A $1,000 favor."

EG falls unconscious again. The next thing he is aware of is
that he is being moved, then warm water on his face, now sticks
or needles, wet and scratchy. He hears a muffled bang, the sound
of a car engine growing more and more faint. EG struggles to
open his eyes. There is nothing but a blinding light above him,
a warm, golden light. He closes his eyes and passes out.

When EG wakes he looks up to find Andre staring down at
him. He's wearing a red baseball cap. Another man is with
him, also wearing a baseball cap. They are in a huddle over
him. EG closes his eyes again. Then he hears a woman's
voice. He opens his eyes. A beautiful blond woman in a white
dress is holding out a large red pill toward him.

"It will help," she says. "It will make things easier."

"It's too difficult," he says.

"Please," she says.

"I can't. It seems easy to you to take one pill. But for me it's
very hard. It hurts. Something's not working right. Here," he
says, placing a hand in the center of his chest. "In here."

EG closes his eyes, feels himself fading from the inside out. It is
as though his organs are disappearing, evaporating. His liver,
heart, kidneys. He can't feel his feet. He can't feel any of his limbs.

This isn't so bad, he thinks. *I don't feel any pain. For the first time
in as long as I can remember, maybe the first time ever, I feel absolutely
no pain. And my mind is growing clearer. I'll just lie here and wait to
see what comes next. I will lie here and listen…lie here and wait.*

<u>10:19:59:59:30</u> A.M.

And now for the afternoon pills:

2 blue-and-white antiretrovirals
1 white oval antiretroviral
6 brown oval gel cap protease inhibitors
1 sexagonal antiretroviral catalyst
1 white oblong antihistamine-decongestant
1 white skinny oblong psychotropic to counteract the side effects of the three antiretrovirals
4 round red pills to ease the inflammation of the muscles irritated by the antiretrovirals
2 yellow capsules to antioxidize the blood toxins from the antiretrovirals
2 round pink tablets to assist the nerves damaged by the antiretrovirals
1 round beige capsule to assist the nerves damaged by the antiretrovirals
1 amber gel cap to antioxidize the blood from all the other medications
3 small round red gel caps to replenish essential skin supplements depleted by the other medications
1 white large oval tablet to prophylax against lung infections
1 round white tablet, also to antioxidize the blood against all the toxins from other medications.

<u>10:19:59:59:31</u> A.M.

While EG's physician is caring for him, he is caring for her. They travel one weekend to Anchor Bay, where they discuss her feelings of dissatisfaction and emptiness. She has been depressed for several months. "Why?" she asks EG. "Why should I feel so empty inside? I have everything I've ever wanted."

They are sitting by the fireplace in front of the wide windows that overlook the redwood forest and the ocean in the distance. But today, with a heavy rain falling, everything is hidden in a misty blur, and it is like looking at the world through fogged glass. Theresa sits on the raised hearth of the fireplace, building and tending a fire. EG crochets a violet prayer shawl by the window.

"What better explanation could there be?" EG asks.

"You mean I'm bored because I have everything? I thought of that." She pokes the kindling, which is resisting her attempts to ignite it.

"You love everything you do. You're *the* HIV doctor on the West Coast, soon to be *the* HIV doctor anywhere. You run the first integrated-care practice in the country; you have a de-signer-built home on the water; you can't possibly keep up with all the requests for speaking engagements or invitations to sit on boards of directors; you're married to one of the pret-tiest and smartest women in the city. I'd say that was damned good reason for boredom in your case."

"But that makes no sense."

"For you it does. Tell me this—what kind of a spiritual life do you have?"

Theresa turns back to tend the fire and is quiet for a few moments. "I guess that's it. I don't have a spiritual life. I guess that's what I'm looking for. Someone asked me the other day how many times I've experienced pure bliss in my life, and I could only think of two. Two! Can you believe it?"

"What were they?"

"Once in Jamaica, where a woman I was seeing and I spent the entire day on a deserted beach. God, it was beautiful. Just the two of us all day alone in that deserted place. Paradise."

"And the other experience?"

"It's not just one incident really, but it's all wrapped up in one image. My grandmother used to sit in her rocking chair and I would sit with my head in her lap. I loved my granny so much, and those moments were pure bliss for me. Those are the only two I can think of. Isn't that pathetic?"

"It's two more than a lot of people have. Answer me one more question," EG continues, as he sits in the red leather chair by the window working on the shawl. "Of all the people you have ever known, dead or alive, who is it you have loved the most, more than anyone else?"

Without even having to think, she answers, "My granny. No question."

"Why?"

"She loved me so much and was so good to me. My granny was the only person in my life who gave me unconditional love. Simply unconditional, no strings attached." Theresa reaches for a madrone log from the wood pile on the hearth next to her and places it on the fire, which is now catching nicely, the flames shooting up, through and around the dry pine kindling.

They are both quiet for a while, EG working his violet yarn, Theresa poking and prodding the logs, which are hissing, popping, and shooting sparks upward into the dark tunnel of the chimney. She is momentarily swimming in reveries of white sand beaches, palm trees, the touch of sun-browned skin; she is lost in memories of porches with rocking chairs and aproned laps, a soft hand stroking her hair, a quiet voice telling her how perfect and lovely she is.

Theresa stands up from the fieldstone hearth and sits in a chair across from EG. "So how do I get a spiritual life? I gave all that up years ago. It's all bullshit as far as I'm concerned. Priests and Confession and all that money and hypocrisy!" she says.

EG cannot help but smile. "I don't know about all that stuff, but I do know about your spiritual life. You already have one. Just the way you already have bliss."

She looks at him quizzically.

EG laughs out loud. "The look on your face expresses exactly the way I feel when you start reading off the results of my blood work." They both laugh now. "Do you want to know what I see as the real problem here?"

"Yes, of course, why am I going through this otherwise?"

"It certainly isn't that you've never experienced bliss; the problem is you have the wrong definition of what bliss is. Like most people, you think it's a feeling."

"Well, it was my therapist who asked me and she said, 'How many times in your life have you felt pure bliss?'"

"That simply proves my point. Even the professionals are confused."

"But everyone is looking for that feeling; everyone is looking for bliss. If it's not a feeling, what is it?"

"A very wise woman once said, 'If you understand something with your mind, you do not have right understanding. You must experience it. Then you will have true understanding.' I've contemplated that for a long time. And I've concluded that it is absolutely correct."

"What does that have to do with this?" Theresa reaches down into EG's yarn bag and picks up a skein of violet yarn. "God, this is soft. And it's so beautiful. Not my color, usually, but I haven't been able to stop looking at it, it's so lovely."

EG smiles at Theresa's digression, but he isn't about to let go of the conversation. "I think the same thing this wise woman said about reason can also be said about feelings," he continues. "If you understand something with your emotions, you don't have right understanding."

"I'm not sure I'm following this."

"Look, bliss is no more feeling titillated or high all the time than loving someone is having constant orgasm. It's not one thing or another; it's all things. It's full consciousness. When you're aware that your relationship, for example, is both wonderfully joyful and horribly painful, that's bliss."

Theresa sits squeezing the soft merino wool, trying to comprehend what EG is saying.

"Think of how sad you are that I'm dying, that Paul is dying; yet, there's nothing you can do about it. All you can do is love us and give us the best medical care you know how. But through this experience you also come away with wonderful things, like this weekend, the intimacy of our love for one another, new insights into who you are, the satisfaction of giving me new insights into who I am and what lies before me. Think of how you come to a clearer understanding of the human dilemma; remember the incomparable richness of standing next to someone as you help him cross out of this life into whatever lies on the other side. That is a great, great joy. But it wouldn't be happening—we wouldn't be sitting here this weekend in this marvelous house in front of this magnificent fire above that beautiful and powerful ocean having this intense conversation, which is sad, but nevertheless enriching—if it weren't for the dreadfully painful fact that I'm dying and you're my doctor and there's nothing we can do about it. No epidemic: none of this. We wouldn't even have met."

EG looks up just as Andre walks by outside the window. He is smoking an extra-long cigarette. He turns his head as he passes and smiles at EG. EG pauses for just a moment with the pain of missing him, then goes on with what he is saying.

"If we can hold the joy and the sorrow, the knowledge and the feelings of all this, that's the full experience and that is bliss. That's consciousness. That's what I believe God is: nothing more than total consciousness. "

Theresa gets up, pokes at the fire for a few minutes, then returns to the chair. "Well, OK, that's all nice and theoretical, and I may even agree in principle, but the question I want answered is, 'Why aren't I happy?'"

"Because you aren't aware of what you have. There's a film over the eyes of your awareness. It's like being in a white room that has a layer of grime over it. It's white, but you can't see it until you scrub it off. You've experienced true bliss more than twice. You have a spiritual life, but you just haven't recognized your spiritual life because you've had the wrong definition for it, just like you've had the wrong definition for bliss."

"Hah! What is my spiritual life?" she asks, picking up the yarn again.

"When you close the examining room door with one of your patients and the world is kept outside and you don't have to be the ball-busting woman doctor fighting in a male-dominated, sexist environment, you become your grandmother. The men and women you see in those examining rooms are you as a child placing your head in your grandmother's lap. Your granny is your image of God, and in those moments you worship her best by becoming her. You might say you merge with the 'granny' part of yourself to have a spiritual experience with other human beings who need the same unconditional love that you yourself seek.

"You reach out to them in their most dire circumstances, at the point in their lives when they need unconditional love the most, more than medicines in fact. You reach out and

heal their hearts. That little room is your sanctuary; the examining table is your altar. You touch your patients, you kiss
them, you hug them. I know no other doctors who do that.
When your patients die, you mourn, sometimes for a long,
long time. You recount to me not the patients you are close
to but the patients you can't get close to. Those are your co-
nundrums, the ones who remain distant. The patient-doctor
dilemma in your mind is not that you get too close to patients
but that you can't get close enough. That's exactly the opposite of the dilemmas of every other doctor I know.

"That, my love, is your spiritual life, and it is as rich as any
I've ever heard or read about. It's certainly richer than mine.
You just haven't had the correct definition for it. You were
looking for something else, when it was right in your own
backyard all along—Dorothy. And call it whatever you want,
or don't call it anything at all. The important thing is that
you stay conscious of it, not what you call it."

"So why aren't I happy?" There is a plaintive, exasperated
expression on her face now. She is a practical Yang-type. She
wants action, results, the momentary problem solved.

"I guess because you've been trying to find happiness in
the wrong places. You're not going to like what I'm about to
say, mostly because it's such a cliché these days; nevertheless, it is true: What you're looking for doesn't exist outside
yourself. It isn't summer in Provence, the leather interior of
a BMW, the cover of *Time* magazine. It exists in your heart.
Perhaps you find it when you look into the eyes of another
person, perhaps you find it when you close your eyes and see
your granny. But it's always within you. Look there, physician, and heal thyself."

At first Theresa looks up as though she has been insulted.
She sees in EG's face a look of utter compassion, and they

smile at one another tenderly. He holds up the work he has done so far on his prayer shawl. "It is a beautiful color, isn't it? I'll make you one just like it when I'm finished."

Outside the rain has stopped falling, the clouds have rolled by, and the ocean glistens silver beneath the light filtering through the clouds. The redwoods and pines are dripping with crystalline raindrops. The fire roars, the weather warms, the two sit silent. Healer, healed, healing, all the same.

10:19:59:59:32 A.M.

The evening breeze rushes among the redwoods high above where EG sits on the porch watching the sun set into the ocean. An osprey cries as she circles her nest, weary from the day's food-gathering for her hungry chicks. Yet she will stand sentry throughout the night, watching for the owls who congregate in the heavy limbs below her nest.

The gathering wind rings the bronze bell hanging in the deep green branches of the redwood at the corner of the house. EG thinks:

> *The bell.*
> *The ringing of the bell.*
> *The ringer of the bell.*
> *These are the same.*

And:

> *This thought.*
> *This thinker.*
> *This mind.*
> *These are the same.*

He ponders:

Then who is saying this?
Who is making the observation?

Finally:

What I know, I know, regardless of how I
know It.
Now the task is to expand It from thought to
experience.

As EG gets up to go inside, he thinks to himself, *Thinking*
this much could give someone a really bad headache.

10:19:59:59:33 A.M.

The boat has stopped rocking; the tubes have backed up; the
White Room has ceased moving.

10:19:59:59:34 A.M.

Today is the day Andre will die.

It is June. The weather is warm, the atmosphere is clear,
and the California sky is brilliantly blue. EG wakes at dawn
after a fitful night lying next to Andre, who, despite having
one eye open, has been in a coma for three days.

Their Doberman, Axel, sleeps with them, sometimes at the
foot of the huge bed, sometimes forcing himself between
them. He is restless. The entire household is restless. Andre's
sister Monique has been with them for a week. Ron, their best
friend, has been standing vigil with them around the clock.

As the sun rises over Mount Diablo across the bay, EG dresses. He slips quietly from the house and drives to the flower market, where he purchases dozens of flowers: peach, white, and scarlet gladiolas; red and yellow roses; white and gold daisies; purple, magenta, and blood-red tulips; amber, white, and crimson asters; speckled Peruvian lilies; magenta, gold, and pale yellow nasturtiums with red centers; cerulean dahlias. EG and Monique place them around the room in vases, pitchers, cans—anything they can find. Ron fills each with water.

Last night, as Monique and EG gathered around the bed to say good night to Andre, EG quietly told him that it was probably time to let go and make the leap. He told Andre how much he loved him and how happy his life had been with him for the past nine years. Then Monique told her brother she would be there until this was over and that she would love him and keep him with her forever.

Monique squeezed her brother's hand and said good night, her heart sinking at his inability to respond. Then EG kissed Andre good night and, as their lips touched, Andre kissed him back. Monique let out a little gasp. "I saw that," she exclaimed in a whisper. "He kissed you back."

"Yes," was all EG could say.

Now EG is lying next to Andre. He places some saline drops in his open eye and replaces the black patch he has tied around Andre's head to keep out the light.

Ron sits on the back porch steps smoking a cigarette and petting Axel, who is lying in a patch of sun next to him. Monique slumps in the stuffed chair next to the bed, the chair that has practically been home for EG for the past eight months.

Now at almost 1 P.M. on this startlingly beautiful June day, Andre begins to gasp and sputter like a drowning man breaking the surface of deep water. He takes deep breaths and moans softly. First he breathes deeply and quickly, then not at all, then deeply and spasmodically again. His breathing starts and stops, starts and stops. Monique jumps to attention; EG slides into a kneeling position on the bed, taking his lover into his arms, raising Andre's head and chest so that he might breathe more easily. EG and Monique look at one another, confused and fearful.

As they wait for some change in this pattern, Axel, who is trained not to get on the bed without permission, leaves Ron's side on the back porch, bolts down the hall, through the bedroom door, and leaps onto the bed. He circles twice and curls up next to Andre, placing his head squarely across Andre's legs, his brown eyes wide and mournful. This is the sign EG was looking for. What was begun 18 months ago with Andre's diagnosis is coming to completion.

EG whispers into Andre's ear the Hindu prayer Andre taught him many years ago: *Om Namah Shivaya, Om Namah Shivaya.* Over and over he repeats this ancient prayer, helping Andre to keep It in mind as the end nears. "I bow to God within."

As suddenly as the spasmodic breathing began, the breathing ends. All breathing. It is over.

10:19:59:59:35 A.M.

O son of noble family, listen without distraction. Although the Bardo of the Peaceful Deities has already appeared, you did not recognize, so you have wandered farther on to here. Now the blood-drinking wrathful deities will appear. Recognize them without being distracted.

O son of noble family, he who is called Glorious Great Buddha-Heruka will emerge from within your own brain and appear before you actually and clearly: His body is wine-colored, with three heads, six arms, and four legs spread wide apart; the right face is white, the left one red, and the center one wine-colored; his body blazes like a mass of light, his nine eyes gaze into yours with a wrathful expression, his eyebrows are like flashes of lightning, his teeth gleam like copper; he laughs aloud with shouts of "a-la-la!" and "ha-ha!" and sends out loud whistling noises of "sh-o-o-o!" His red-gold hair flies upward blazing; his heads are crowned with dried skulls and the sun and moon; his body is garlanded with black serpents and fresh skulls; his six hands hold a wheel in the first hand on the right, an axe in the middle, and a sword in the last, a bell in the first on the left, a scythe in the middle, and a skull-cup in the last; his consort Buddha-Annasvari embraces his body, with her right hand clasped around his neck and her left hand holding a skull full of blood to his mouth; he sends out loud palatal sounds and roaring sounds like thunder; flames of wisdom shoot out from between the blazing vajra hairs on his body; he stands on a throne supported by garudas, with one pair of legs bent and the other stretched out.

Do not be afraid of him, do not be terrified, do not be bewildered. Recognize him as the form of your own mind. Recognition and liberation are simultaneous."

10:19:59:59:36 A.M.

EG is taking Hari to the beach but decides to stop at the coffee shop in the Castro and get a cappuccino to take with him. As he is about to make a left-hand turn into the driveway next to where he will get his coffee, he hears honking and shouting. Hari, meanwhile has begun inexplicably to bark out the back window. He looks into the rearview mirror and sees a strange figure behind him on a low-rider motorcycle. The man looks crazed. EG, doesn't complete his turn now; instead, he puts down the window and shouts, "I'm sorry, I can't hear you. What did you say?"

The man shouts, "Move your fucking truck, you fucking faggot, you goddamn fucking faggot."

This is all EG needs to hear to know he must torture this person. "What? I can't hear you."

The man sidles his motorcycle up to the driver's window. EG sees him fully now. He is wearing a leather motorcycle jacket, leather pants, and has many heavy, complicated chains tied to his body. He has a scraggly red beard and orange hair that hasn't been brushed in weeks. Instead of a motorcycle helmet, he wears a Nazi war helmet. And most noticeable of all, he is wearing thick yellow glasses. EG can't help but stare at the glasses. He thinks, *These glasses are yellow. Not amber, not rose, not any color I've ever seen before. The lenses are actually bright yellow. That must hurt his eyes.*

Now the man is shouting in an almost inhuman voice at incredible volume while Hari, from behind EG's seat, is barking ferociously through the slit of back window EG has left open. The man is lunging his body toward EG but trying to hold up his bike. He screams, "Move your fucking truck, you fucking faggot, you goddamn, cocksucking, fucking faggot, you fucking faggot."

EG thinks the man will burst the blood vessels now straining beneath the skin of his neck. EG thinks the following things all at once: *This man is insane and is going to hit me; this voice is beyond human ability, so where is this voice really coming from?; this is Kali, presenting Itself to me for some reason I must try to understand; what this man is doing has nothing to do with me; this man is going to hit me; this man could hurt Hari.*

Now a huge crowd has gathered on the sidewalk. Customers and shop owners have come out from stores all up and down the street to witness the disturbance. The man continues to scream and be clearly understood above the roar of his motorcycle, the engine of which he is revving as he shouts.

EG can only sit silently staring at this apparition. Then suddenly, for no apparent reason, the man scoots his cycle back behind the truck where he originally started, shouting his epithets the whole time. Now he is sitting there screaming again, as if the scene had just been run in reverse.

EG, believing that the man's actions have nothing to do with him and that this is actually God presenting Itself to EG and that he must now go off and contemplate all of this, pulls into the driveway. He gets out of the truck and steps to the curb, but the man on the motorcycle has vanished.

People on the sidewalk gather around, commenting on the insane scene they have just witnessed, reassuring and comforting EG. Hari has stopped barking but has jumped into the front seat and is now standing guard.

While he is getting his cappuccino, EG thinks, *Too bad he didn't hit me. It would have been an automatic three years in prison for a hate crime since he was screaming "faggot" at me.* Then EG puts the thought away, realizing that he really didn't want to be hit and that the man might also somehow have managed to hurt Hari.

A few minutes later, walking through the dunes at Fort Funston, EG ponders his experience. He recalls the two old men on the Bell Path, hears Prabuddhananda's exhortation to experience It. EG sits atop a dune as Hari runs barking after a low-flying flock of pelicans. Hari has already forgotten the motorcycle maniac; now there is only this, only the pelicans, the sand, the salty air and running. Running and barking and being fully alive right now.

10:19:59:59:37 A.M.

EG has won his bid for supervisor. In fact, he is not only supervisor, but he has also been elected president of the board of supervisors. In that capacity he also serves as commander in chief of the Mendocino Militia, the new name for what was once the Gay and Lesbian Liberation Militia.

He has taken to wearing camouflage army fatigues, a camouflage cap and a gun belt with ammunition. His pants are tucked into high-top black army boots. He has been exercising with the militia almost every day and working out at the militia base gymnasium, where, after exercising, the male troops take group showers and engage in an hourlong ritual of sex, where there are no prohibitions, save that no one is allowed to reach orgasm except on Mondays. This exercise increases self-discipline and maintains a high level of testosterone-induced assertiveness among the male troops.

EG's first test in his new position is a serious political and military problem. A small group of Breeders from the Sea Ranch compound armed themselves and went into the hills on New Year's Eve, the day before the ordinance went into effect that allowed the county government to confiscate all their property and to indenture Breeders and their children. Children of Breeders are being taken from their parents and placed in gay and lesbian homes; heterosexuals who have not left the county are to be interred in camps.

This guerrilla group, calling itself the Sea Ranch Liberation Front (SRLF), intends to attempt an overthrow of the newly elected government. It is up to EG as commander in chief of the militia to foil this plan. He has learned that the leader is a 44-year-old securities broker who once served in the Marines. EG has also learned that organizing the SRLF was a last-minute idea and literally put together overnight. As a result, there was no time to protect certain valuables, such as family.

EG pulls up to the broker's Sea Ranch home with a convoy of militia. They surround the house, and EG and eight highly trained soldiers—called the Hanuman Brigade—kick down the front door. The house is ostentatiously mammoth and sits directly on a cliff overlooking the ocean. The entire front of the house is made up of glass doors and windows opening onto multilevel decks. Green waves crash on the rocks below.

Once inside, EG sits in the living room and waits for his troops to find the man's wife. They bring her downstairs and throw her on the floor at EG's feet. A black Labrador retriever barks and circles the soldiers, who are all carrying automatic weapons.

EG rests his muddy boots on the ottoman in front of him. The woman, a former model, is kneeling now on the other side of the ottoman. Her long, strawberry-blond hair is disheveled and hangs all around her. She is wearing a white cotton blouse and beige gabardine slacks. She looks too dressed up for just sitting around the house.

"Were you going somewhere? Did we interrupt your travel plans?" EG asks, flicking his cigarette ashes onto the plush tan carpet. She gives him a menacing look. EG laughs. "Forget it, bitch," he says. "You should have left when you had the chance. Did you really think we were going to take our time grabbing your beautiful house? Did you actually think we wouldn't carry out our plan?"

"You won't get away with this," the woman says, gathering her hair now and tossing it over her shoulder. "Tom will get you in the end. All of you."

"In the meantime," EG says, sniggering derisively, "where is Tom? Where did little Tommy and his band of pathetic over-the-hill Sea Ranch Breeders run away to?"

"I'd die before I'd tell you," the woman says.

"Oh, nothing so fortunate for you, I'm afraid, my buxom blond," EG taunts.

One of the soldiers comes downstairs with papers in her hand. "Moira, that's her name."

"Moira, is it? Are you a little Irish lassie then?" EG says sarcastically.

"What's it to you?" the woman spits.

EG leans forward in his chair, resting his hands on the ottoman, his face just inches from hers. "Because Moira, I hate the Irish. They're mean, drunkard sons of bitches. And they can't fuck worth a damn."

The soldiers all laugh.

"I've never had a good Irish lay. Never. Not once. Pathetic bastards. That's probably why they drink themselves to death."

"Fuck you!" she shouts, and begins to stand. A woman soldier behind her kicks her in the back, sending her sprawling across the ottoman.

EG reaches out and grabs her by the hair. "Actually, we thought we might fuck you. All of us."

EG stands. "Hold her there," he orders, and two men grab her arms and pin her down over the ottoman. EG walks around behind her, grabs her slacks at the waist with both hands, yanks once, and they fall down around her knees on the floor, her panties sliding with them. "Nice ass, eh, Courtney?" EG asks the woman soldier next to him.

"Very nice," Courtney responds, and prods the woman with the tip of her rifle. Moira jerks, but the men hold her tight.

"I'll flip you for who goes first," EG says. "No, on second thought, you go first. I feel like watching her grimace and twist."

Courtney pulls off her backpack and retrieves an 18-inch black dildo as big around as her forearm. It is attached to a belt, which she straps onto her waist without even taking off her fatigues. She kneels behind the woman and rams it into her. The woman shrieks in agony. "Oh, baby, you've got such a nice cunt," she says as she rams the dildo deeper and harder into her victim. The woman is screaming at the top of her lungs and crying now. Blood is pouring from between her legs.

The retriever is barking wildly but keeping a safe distance, near the front door.

EG gets down on the floor next to the woman, puts his face near hers. "I'm sorry, we didn't quite understand you. Where did you say Tommy is?"

"Fuck you!" the woman shouts.

EG looks up at Courtney. "She says she wants to fuck you," EG says.

"Next time," Courtney says, and slaps the woman's ass so hard she leaves a red hand print on Moira's white buttock. Courtney continues to ram the woman, and the woman screams over and over, "He'll kill you. He'll kill all of you."

"Leave her alone. Stop it!" A teenage boy is running into the room now from where he has been hiding somewhere in the house. Two of the soldiers grab the boy.

"Everything comes to he who waits," EG says, eyeing the boy. "See Courtney? I'm being rewarded by the Goddess for being so polite and letting you go first. This one's mine. Strip him," EG commands.

The soldiers strip the boy naked. He is slender, with large, muscular thighs and a round bubble-like butt. His skin is pale, but he has a distinct bikini line from days on the Sea Ranch beach.

"Let her watch," EG says to the men holding down the boy's mother as he unbuckles his fatigues and lets them drop down to his ankles. "Put him on his hands and knees," EG orders.

The men push the boy to the floor, one of them holding his head down to the carpet, forcing him into a position that leaves his butt sticking up in the air, his head and shoulders pressed against the carpet. The retriever begins to bark louder.

"Fifteen," the boy screams. "Fifteen. I'll be 15 next week."

"I've never had sex with a 14-year-old before. Not that I know of anyway. What's your name?" EG asks, interrupting his thrusts and leaning over the boy's back to be nearer his face.

The boy gasps, his body slumping with the easing of the pain. "Steven," he says breathing heavily. "Please stop. You're hurting me."

"Yes, I know. But it hurts kind of good, doesn't it, Steven?"

"Please, you're ripping me apart."

"You're right, I am. In fact you're bleeding down here," EG says, wiping the boy's thigh with his hand. "I guess I'd better finish up fast, huh?" With that EG begins pumping again, rising up on his feet so that he is squatting behind the boy. He pulls all the way out. The boy sighs. Then he rams into him again and begins to thrust in and out of the boy faster and faster, the boy shrieking louder with each thrust inward.

"No, no, please stop. Please," the boy cries.

"Very well, Steven. Whatever you say," EG says hoarsely. "I'm going to stop right...right...now."

The boy screams and tries to wriggle free as he feels the contractions of EG ejaculating into him.

"There," EG says, withdrawing and standing up. He reaches down, takes the boy's T-shirt, wipes himself off, then throws the shirt on the boy's naked body and pulls up his pants. The soldiers who were holding the boy down him let him go and the boy slumps to the floor in a fetal position. "You two can have him now," EG says. "But take him upstairs. I can't stand the sight of blood."

The men drag the naked boy to an upstairs bedroom where the screaming begins all over again. The woman, still being held by the two soldiers, is in a state of shock. She is sitting on the blood-soaked carpet staring at the floor. Courtney has put away the dildo. From the kitchen, a gray-haired soldier, holding the receiver of a wall phone, shouts to EG, "They've found them. They are at the lighthouse after all. They're surrounded, but they won't come out."

"Who cares?" EG snarls. "We'll wait them out. Just don't kill them. I want Tom alive. You know, Moira," EG says, squatting down in front of the woman, "you've been really helpful, but you're a first-class bitch. A rich bitch my mother would have called you. I don't think you can be reprogrammed. You Irish cunts are too stubborn. What are we going to do with you? You want her?" EG asks Courtney. "She's got a great body."

"Fuck, no," Courtney says.

"Courtney doesn't want you. I don't want you. No one wants you now, Moira. I'll bet Tommy won't even want you. You're used goods. Besides, you've got a bad attitude. But that boy of yours, well, now, he's a different story. That red-haired lad has a real tight hole. He's going to be very popular back at the barracks. Yes, ma'am, very popular. I think we might have to shave him, though. I can't stand red asshole hair. I don't know why, it just bothers me when I'm sticking my tongue in there."

The woman begins to sob harder now.

"You're a mess, honey," EG says. "But I promise to take real good care of your son. I'll see to him personally. OK?"

Moira looks at him with contempt. "May you burn in hell," she says, and spits in EG's face.

EG flinches, quickly wipes the spittle off. "Definitely not reprogrammable," he says and stands up. "Shoot her," he orders. "Then bring the boy to the barracks. Fucking Breeders," EG says, stepping over the dead dog lying near the splintered door. As he walks across the yard, a gunshot from inside the house makes him jump. Realizing what it was, he smiles, reaches for his cigarettes, and climbs into the jeep. If he hurries, he can reach Point Arena before sunset.

10:19:59:59:38 A.M.

Yet another sleepless night. EG rises, goes downstairs to the kitchen, stands in the light of the open refrigerator. He can find nothing to soothe or satisfy him. He moves first to the dining room window, looking out into the dark, knowing he is observed by the creatures of the night who forage in darkness for their sustenance, who by day would fall prey to hawks and osprey and wild dogs.

He thinks, *It is just you and me, my nocturnal friends, both of us unable to sleep—you out of necessity, me out of…out of what? Can it really be the drugs keeping me awake? It's more like I'm being called, like I wake hearing my name being whispered from some dark part of the house. Who could it be? What could it be?*

EG looks around the room. A few embers from the evening's fire shimmer and glow in the stone fireplace. The two sofas, positioned at right angles, sit before the hearth; EG's crocheting lies in a heap where he left it on the green love seat.

He moves away from the window to the darker part of the room, sits and watches the embers glow and pulsate before him like a heart hidden in ashes. On the far end of the larger sofa he sees, as his eyes adjust to the darkness, Cohen in her plain white cotton nightgown and her clumsy brown slippers. Her hair is braided into a long, gray whip that hangs over her shoulder. It falls to the sofa and coils around three times, its tip resting in the circle's center like the head of a vigilant cobra.

She is peeling an apple with a paring knife, letting the long, unbroken coil of skin ease gently into her lap, a serpent dancing its hypnotic descent to the white field of Cohen's nightgown.

She tosses the apple peel into the fire, cores the fruit, and offers a slice to EG. The room is fragrant with the apple peel baking in the embers and Cohen begins to sing softly to EG. "On the beautiful isle of Capri, just my baby and me…"

EG moves closer to her. As he scoots over, his bare feet hit something hard and cold on the floor. He peers over the edge of the sofa and there at Cohen's feet lies a long, hooked scythe. The curved blade is shiny and slick from use, and the wooden handle is dry and split. He stares up at Cohen for an explanation, but she does not look at him; rather, she slices and hands him, one at a time, thin sections of fruit, until the entire apple is gone. Then she looks deep into his eyes, a serious look, the kind she used to give him when he strayed too far down the block or said something unkind about one of her friends.

He doesn't know if he should say anything. He wants to touch her, but her look is so confusing, so mysterious and icy. He takes a chance and reaches out his hand. At the same moment, the tip of her coiled hair rises like a serpent and hovers in the air between them. His hand freezes where it is. He looks at Cohen pleadingly, frightened, then back to the serpentine braid of hair. He looks at Cohen again, but now her eyes are gone and there are worms crawling out of the sockets. She reaches down, picks up the scythe, and with one clean slice cuts halfway through EG's neck.

EG places his hand over the deep gash trying to stop the bleeding, but it won't stop. He places both hands to his neck and wails at Cohen's betrayal.

The bleeding only begins to subside when Hari, having finally come downstairs to find where his master disappeared to, begins to lick at the wound. He licks and licks until EG opens his eyes to Hari's ministrations, the morning sun bright through the plate-glass window, the sound of a bird's wings beating somewhere beyond the screen door.

10:19:59:59:39 A.M.

Like every Sunday, EG calls his mother from Houston, where it is hot but raining. Summer is coming early to the Gulf Coast. His mother wheezes a pathetic hello in California, where the sun is shining, the sky is blue, and the terra-cotta tiles on the Spanish style houses bake warmly in the golden sun. Calla lilies ring the small two-bedroom house on the Carquinez Straits, where EG's mother lives her desperate life with EG's father, who, this morning, is already at Wink's Bar and Grill on Main Street watching the 49ers game with his buddies.

"I'm going to die," Annabel wheezes into the receiver. She sucks on her atomizer.

EG sighs. "Mother, you're not going to die; you just have to do something about all this."

"No, I can tell. This is it, really. I can't breathe. My asthma is getting worse all the time."

"Mother, you can't breathe in that marriage. That's what's getting worse all the time. You just have to find the courage to do something about it," EG says again. This is the same conversation the two of them have had between Texas and California every Sunday for the past three months.

"Come home," his mother pleads. "I need you here."

"Mother, I'm not coming home. I have a job. I'm going to marry Beth. I'm not coming home."

"I'm dying."

"You're not dying. It just feels like it because you're so un-happy. You're suffocating in that marriage." EG feels his rage and sorrow having its weekly tug-of-war in his heart. "You have to find a way to get out of there. You can do it. Emily will help you. Jean will help you. It's not like you don't have any friends. Tess would help you. You have to start thinking of divorce. At least separation."

His mother coughs and wheezes. It sounds bad on EG's end of the phone, but then she is the consummate actress as well as the ultimate hypochondriac. "Come home, honey. Come home if you ever want to see me again."

"I have to hang up now. I'm not at my place. This isn't my phone. I'll call you next Sunday and we'll talk about this more. We'll figure out a way for you to do this."

"Come home, honey. I'm going to die soon."

"Mother, I'm not coming home. I'm staying here. I have to live my life and you have to live yours. I'll help you as much as I can, but I'm not coming home. That won't solve anything. You have to do this yourself."

"I'm dying, EG."

"I love you, Mom. I'll call you next week. Say good-bye."

"Good-bye, honey."

"Bye, Mom."

"Good-bye."

EG goes through the week sporadically tormented as usual. Between this new public relations job, where he feels he's in way over his head, and his mother's hysteria, there is little relief. His fiancée lives in the dorm on campus on the other side of the city. EG has a tiny one-bedroom apartment on top of an old Victorian in the Montrose area. At night, Houston's closeted homosexual community uses the street he lives on to meet one another, engage in sex in automobiles or in the bushes of the neighborhood's stately homes. EG has moved here by sheer coincidence. At least that's what he believes now, fresh out of school, barely an adult.

Driving to work at the end of the week, he sees the new billboards his firm has thrown up all over town. They all feature his friend Carol Haney bending over and peeking into an oven. A blue flame is prominent in the upper right-hand corner of the billboard and the caption beneath Carol's high-heeled shoes reads, GAS GETS THE JOB DONE BETTER. It is a new campaign to get people to switch from electricity to natural gas.

The billboard is practically everywhere, as though workmen went out and tore down everyone else's advertising during the night and threw up Carol Haney in her powder-blue suit and cloche hat, looking into a Harvest Gold oven.

It is only EG's first week at this new job, and today, Friday, the entire office is attending a going away party for one of the firm's vice presidents. Since EG is low man on the seniority totem pole, he must stay and answer the phones. He finds himself by 10:30 that morning awash in a sea of lights on the two telephone consoles at the front desk. He is trying to get his mouth to tumble through the verbal tongue twister that is the name of the advertising firm that employs him: "Goodwin, Dannenbaum, Littman, and Wingfield, can you hold for just a moment? Goodwin, Dannenbaum, Littman, and Wingfield, can you hold for just a moment?" He is gaining respect for the switchboard operator moment by moment.

EG is glad it is Friday. Tonight, he and Beth will drive to Austin to visit college chums for the weekend. He is halfway through the lights on the phone when a woman's voice asks to speak with him. "This is EG," he says. "Can I help you?"

"EG, this is Emily. Emily Alameda. EG, I have some bad news. Your mom passed away this morning."

EG stands in the entryway of Passalaqua's Funeral Home as though all time between that phone call and this moment never took place. He is trying to figure out which hallway to walk down, which room his mother's body might be in, who all these people are who touch him, hug him, whisper in his ear.

Then, from down a long corridor to his left, walks Cletus. He is wearing the only suit he owns, a light gray two-button suit that is two sizes too big for him. And now—is this really happening, can this be true?—his father, is holding out his arms as he comes toward him, holding out his arms to embrace his son, wrapping his arms around him stiff, cold, as though he were the corpse, climbed out of the coffin to welcome EG to his own wake. And though in later years EG will remember this exactly the opposite—his father being the stiff and sanguine one—EG's arms go completely rigid and he is unable to embrace his father, unable after all these years, with no practice at such physical intimacy, with no experience that he can recollect of ever having even touched his father's body with his own hands, he is unable to fold his arms around his father, unable to place the flat of his palms against this man's back, to feel the warmth of his body, the solid muscles of the back that has toiled for 50 years to earn the money that kept a roof over his head and the head of his dear, dead mother.

EG is unable to touch him, unable to hold him, unable to feel him, as though his father's embrace were like the emperor's new clothes and only EG were able to see the sham of it. Only EG is able to feel there is nothing to feel. Only EG knows the emptiness of his father's arms, which are now filled with his only son, a son lost to him long, long ago. EG is simply unable and, even if he were able, unwilling to feel his father's presence.

"Where is she?" is all EG says to him.

"Down there," his father says, pointing to the hallway down which he has just walked.

"I'll take you," Emily says, and she takes his arm and leads him to his mother's casket in a small room filled with flowers.

The casket is simple gray metal, probably the cheapest one Phil Passalaqua had, maybe even a "close-out." Maybe Clete was able to get it on sale like he did the pink-and-purple Dodge.

"This was the most appropriate thing I could find in her closet," Emily says, referring to the powder-blue cotton suit Annabel is wearing.

It is a suit he knows his mother hated. It was cheap and not well-made and was completely unflattering to the figure she was so proud of. "It had to be slit it up the back, so I didn't want to put her in anything really expensive. I did her hair just the way she liked it," Emily says, sniffling.

"And who put this here?" EG asks, touching a white rosary in his mother's cold white hands, which are folded over her waist.

"I did. Those are the only rosary beads I could find in her dresser. You gave her those when she was baptized, didn't you?"

"Take them off of her."

"But aren't those hers? Aren't those the ones you gave her?"

"My mother didn't even know how to say the rosary. She did all that for me. I was 10. I thought she'd go to hell otherwise. She didn't even know how to say the goddamn rosary. I want them gone by tomorrow." And EG turns and walks out, walks home in the warm June evening.

EG spends the next day locked in his mother's bedroom, going through her personal items. He finds a diary he didn't know she kept. The last thing she wrote the evening before she died was this: *He won't let me call the doctor. He won't let me call the fire department for oxygen. I can't breathe. He slammed the door and shouted, "Sweat it out!"*

He has just finished reading this final entry when the telephone on the night stand rings. "EG?" the voice inquires. It is his friend McCann from Austin.

"McCann. Thanks for calling."

"How are you holding up?" McCann inquires. His voice resonates with concern, but there is nothing patronizing in his tone.

"All right, I suppose. It's not at all what I expected."

"Better or worse?"

"Worse. Much worse, actually."

"But you're all right?"

"I have no regrets about my actions, but I certainly have lots of feelings about everyone else's."

"EG, I have something to tell you. Something strange and ironic. Carol Haney is dead."

"What? How?"

"She killed herself two days ago. The same day your mother died. And get this. She did it by blowing out the pilot light, turning the gas on, and sticking her head in her oven."

There is a long, silent pause as both EG and McCann now picture Carol Haney as she appeared on thousands of billboards for natural gas, in her powder-blue suit, high-heeled shoes, and cloche hat, her perky little face looking out at the thousands of potential consumers whizzing by beneath her feet. Little did they know that she was about to stick her head in that oven and breathe in that clean, natural odor until she stopped breathing altogether. Little did anyone suspect that Carol Haney was about to find out for herself if GAS GETS THE JOB DONE BETTER.

Suddenly, at the same moment, as if on cue, EG and McCann burst into uncontrollable laughter. They laugh until they cry, EG rolling back and forth on his mother's bed, the phone in one hand, her death diary in the other. Laughing and rocking to the ironic rhythm of the Waltz of Death. For EG, Death will never mean quite the same thing again. For EG, although he doesn't realize it here and now, it will, from this moment on, be difficult, almost impossible, for Death ever now to have dominion over the deepest, clearest part of his psyche.

EG wakes to find himself slouched in a terribly uncomfortable vinyl armchair. The room is nearly dark, a hazy light coming from nowhere in particular. The walls are slightly luminescent, the bed a shimmering metal-and-white mound on the far side of the room. He cannot remember what day it is or where he is. Has he returned to Houston? Has he buried his mother?

He rises and walks to the bed. The woman in the bed follows him with her hazel eyes until he stands over her. She smiles thinly.

"Mother! I'm confused," he says to her. "Is this a dream? Was the other a dream? What's going on?"

"None of that is important," she says weakly. "Only this matters. Say the things you want to say. Now."

"I'm not sure I know what you mean."

"Yes, you know. You know precisely. Say them quickly."

"I love you. I'm sorry I didn't come when you asked me to. It's not because I don't love you. You must know that. You must know how deeply I love you."

"Yes," his mother says softly, smiling more broadly now. "I do know that. Despite how completely mad I am, despite all that I did that hurt you, all that I didn't do to protect and cultivate you, yes, I know you love me, my darling."

"But I couldn't come home. If I had chosen you over myself, it would have been the end for both of us. No, that's not true. It would have been the end for me. I would have lost my integrity, my self-respect. I would have gone against everything I believe in. This was your problem, your situation. I had nothing to do with its creation, nothing to do with your relationship with him. It wasn't mine to fix nor my responsibility to rescue you from your own life."

"I know. I forgive you."

"I didn't know any of this then," EG says, taking her hand. "I couldn't know it. Please forgive me, Mother. I love you as much as I've ever loved anyone."

"I do forgive you, EG. I forgive you completely, as you must forgive me. You did exactly the best thing. For us both. You freed me from this mortal wound. You gave me flight. It was your refusal to step into my chaos that empowered me with the gift of breathlessness. I simply closed my eyes and let go. Once you had let go of me, I could let go of all this, even you. I knew then that you truly no longer needed me. I was free. Thank you for that. Thank you for not allowing me to cling and suffer and become more attached to flesh and breath. Thank you."

"Mother, I don't understand. Where am I? What's going on here?"

"Don't you recognize this room?"

"I don't. I recognize the feeling in this room, but I don't recognize the room. Where are we?"

"I must go now. This time it's forever. Well, what will seem to you like forever."

"Mother, what's going on? Please. Will I wake now?"

Annabel laughs with a strength that alarms EG. She laughs and laughs and rocks back and forth. He sees now her diary in one hand, a telephone receiver in the other. She laughs until she weeps, and then she is gone. She disappears, but not suddenly like magic, nor does she slowly evaporate before EG's eyes. No, in fact EG isn't sure she disappears at all—rather the room grows brighter.

The walls begin to radiate as though a white-hot light is coming from the other side of them. The sheets on the bed glow and vibrate, whiter and more blinding than sunlight on snow. Above him, the ceiling seems to disappear, being replaced by a white radiance, until EG finds himself standing in the center of the white room with nothing visible, no familiar smell in the air, nothing within reach to place his hand upon, no saliva in his parched mouth.

But somewhere above, in a far corner of the room, near the ceiling he cannot see, he hears the distinct song of a small bird and the fluttering of its wings. It is more a moan than a song, like the cry of a mourning dove. A mourning dove. That is what it is. He knows this with utter certainty although he cannot see it, cannot turn, cannot open his eyes. There is only the whiteness burning through his closed eyelids and the low, mournful moan of the dove and the fluttering of wings above him.

10:19:59:59:40 A.M.

EG sits up in bed. The room is dark. No light comes from the window. No one is there. He tries looking about the room, but it is useless. There simply is no light in the room. There has never been such darkness, such blackness, such a vacuum of lightlessness.

The absence of light makes him think he can't breathe. *This must be it*, he thinks. *This must be the moment. Of course*, he thinks, the panic giving way to ironic humor. *I would go now, when the room is dark and everyone is gone. Of course*, he thinks, *the very thing I have always dreaded most comes to pass: being alone at this moment. I must remember this is all a projection of my own mind. There is nothing wrong with being alone. This is fine.*

This is perfectly all right. It simply doesn't matter. I have to do this alone, anyway, no matter how many people are in the room.

EG lies back. The pillow is stiff and the mattress too firm. This is not his bed. This is a hospital bed. *It doesn't matter,* EG says to himself. *I will not be afraid. There is nothing to fear. Everyone is here somewhere. I don't see them, but I believe that they are here somewhere.*

Then EG hears a quiet laughter coming from the side of the bed. He turns his head to hear it better and suddenly, although no light has entered the room, he can see Cohen sitting beside him, crocheting something white. "You are here after all," EG says to her.

It was just a little flash, Cohen says, without speaking. *Like a time blip into the future. You might think of it as a preview.*

"What does it mean?" EG asks.

Nothing, Cohen replies. *It means nothing. That happens sometimes when you're getting close. You handled that very well, by the way. We're all quite impressed.*

"Who is?"

All of us. Just lie back and rest. It's almost over. We'll be right here.

"So I'm not alone?"

Cohen laughs again, this time louder. *Oh, my child, you've never been alone. If you only knew the crowds you move among day in and day out. You'll see. You'll see. She laughs again. You're only alone when you think you are. It's all illusion, my boy. It always has been.*

"I don't understand."

Now don't lose confidence here at the end. Will yourself to it. You're doing fine. Rest, child. Rest. The most difficult part is ahead.

"But you'll be here, right?"

We'll be here. It's up to you to remember that. Everything now is up to you.

<u>10:19:59:59:41</u> A.M.

Christmas has arrived, and EG sends everyone he knows the following poem.

The Last Christmas

What will we do if the manger is empty,
the ox and the ass gone, the place dark?
What shall we think?
How will we feel?
Do this: walk 'round and 'round
the stable, saying over and over,

> I know you are here somewhere,
> I know you are here.
> I do not feel it.
> But I believe it.

What will we do the year the Christmas
poem doesn't arrive?
What shall we think?
How will we feel?
Do this: shut the door, sit down,
close your eyes, fold your hands
in your lap, say over and over,

> I know you are here somewhere,
> I know you are here.
> I do not feel it.
> But I believe it.

What will we do stretched out on the cross
of the white room, alone in the dark
with only the tubes

and the thin shaft of light glaring
through the open door?
What shall we think?
How will we feel?
Do this: think only of the one
you love, say over and over,
I adore you, I adore you, I adore you.

Death, too, is a Goddess, warm, soft,
smelling of powder.
She sings a song sweet as a June breeze.
Sit at her feet. Say it; say
     I adore you, I adore you.
     I do not feel it.
     But I believe it.

Say it now, as practice,
for one Christmas it is sure to happen:
the poem will not arrive. Or
—who could believe it—
it will arrive and you
will be stretched out on the cross of the
White Room,
alone in the dark with only the tubes
and the thin shaft of light glaring
through the open door.
What shall you think?
How will you feel?
     when it is just you
     and the glaring
     light
     through the open

door
and the tubes
and the empty
manger?

What will you think?
How will you feel?
What will you say then?

10:19:59:59:42 A.M.

EG decides to visit his father in the Old Soldiers' Home. He turns to The Boy, who is playing tug-of-war with Hari. The Boy bolts upright, staring fearfully at EG, his left arm wrapped tightly now around the Doberman's neck.

"Don't worry," EG says aloud to The Boy. "We're not going anywhere. I would never put you through that again. I love you far too much."

The Boy sighs, smiles, lies down on the living room floor, placing his head on the soft warm haunches of the big dog, as though this Hari, this Remover of Sorrows, were a giant pillow.

10:19:59:59:43 A.M.

They have decided to interview The Boy immediately, without waiting for the social worker to arrive from Napa. The younger man, Curtis, will be the lead on this. In fact, he will be the only one in the room besides The Boy and will tape-record the interview.

Curtis is immediately struck by three things when he meets The Boy. First, the child is beautiful. He has a presence about him, not just a physical beauty. When he looks at you, his eyes appear to be pools of liquid emerald. He is wearing blue shorts, and his legs are like the legs of a marble statue, perfectly formed, white, almost translucent. The Boy's cheeks are rosy the way choirboys are portrayed in British travel brochures or Hallmark Christmas cards. His hair is the color of caramel and a shock of it sticks straight up at the back of his head. It reminds Curtis of Alfalfa in the *Our Gang* short subjects they show at the movie house along with the main feature. He smiles just being in The Boy's presence.

Also, The Boy is extremely precocious. He possesses a wealth of knowledge, and his vocabulary is better than that of anyone in the police station. He is quiet and observant, walking around the station house picking up objects for closer scrutiny, flipping through magazines, pausing now and then to read something. He points out to Curtis on the way into the interrogation room that "there are two r's in interrogation. The sign on the door has only one.

Finally, Curtis is struck by the anomaly between The Boy's maturity and his chronological age. He acts much older than he looks. He can't be more than 6 or 7, yet he carries himself like an adult, seems to be thinking like an adult. Curtis thinks The Boy is kind of spooky. He is determined to know him better, to uncover the mystery.

"Have a seat," Curtis says to The Boy, closing the door to the interrogation room.

The Boy struggles to pull one of the Bentwood chairs out from the wooden table, then climbs up onto it. Curtis sits to his right and begins to fool with one of the reels of the tape recorder, which has been placed in the center of the table.

"You have big arms," The Boy says, looking at Curtis's biceps.

"Well, policemen sometimes have to arrest bad guys, and once in a while they don't want to be arrested and I have to get into a fight with them. It helps to have big arms when that happens."

"Like my dad," The Boy says.

"I didn't fight with your dad."

"I meant his arms. My dad has big arms. Not as big as yours, though."

"Tell me a little about your dad," Curtis says, finally getting the tape recorder working.

"Well, he has big arms."

"Yes, you already told me that," Curtis says, amused by the boy's naïveté.

"Do you always wear T-shirts and jeans to work? I thought policemen wore blue uniforms and hats."

Curtis laughs. "Well, sometimes we have to disguise ourselves so the bad guys don't recognize us and we can sneak up on them."

"Oh." The Boy squirms around in his chair, taking in the rest of the room, then turns back to Curtis and says, "I love him."

"Excuse me?"

"My dad. You asked me to tell you something about my dad. I love him," The Boy says, watching the tape recorder reels go round and round. "And he has big arms."

"What do you and your dad like to do together?" Curtis begins fishing.

"My dad works at night and has to sleep during the day. Graveyard they call it. But he doesn't really work in a graveyard. They just call it graveyard. 'Working graveyard' is what they say when you go to work at midnight. So I have to be quiet when he's sleeping. Most of the time I just play outside or downstairs at Cohney's. She's the lady who takes care of me. I love Cohney too."

"Don't you play with your friends?" Curtis asks.

"Walter and Richie, but they're not around this week. I play with them.

"So you didn't play with your friends today?"

"Uhn-uhn."

"And you didn't go to Mrs. Cohen's?"

"Uhn-uhn"

"And you didn't play outside, did you?"

"I did for a while, but then it started to rain, so I came in the house."

"When you came in, what did you do?"

"Mom went shopping with Auntie Ceecee, so I didn't have anything to do."

"So what did you do? Who did you play with?"

"No one."

"Did you listen to records?"

"No."

"Did you read comic books?"

"No."

"Well, what did you do, then?" Curtis asks, growing a little exasperated and wanting to get to the point.

"I took a nap."

"Alone?"

"No."

"With your dad?"

"Uh-huh."

"Do you always take naps with your dad?"

"No. Hardly ever. I'm not supposed to go in there during the day. I get in trouble if I wake him up."

"Does he ask you to take naps with him?"

"No. I always have to wait until he's asleep and then sneak in and get in bed with him."

"Is that what you did today?"

"Yes," The Boy says sheepishly. He fidgets with his Mickey Mouse watch. "Am I going to get in trouble? Are you going to put me in jail 'cause I woke my dad up?"

"No, son. You're not in any trouble at all. Tell me what happened when you woke up from your nap."

"We got up."

"What did you do when you got up?"

"We were going to eat watermelon, but Mrs. Morgan came in and started screaming at us, so we didn't get to. Do you have any watermelon here?"

"No, I don't think so. Why did Mrs. Morgan start screaming at you and your dad?"

"I don't know. I think because she never saw a naked man before. It's July, you know. Everybody has watermelon in July. Are you sure you don't have any watermelon?"

"I'll tell you what. When we're finished here I'll go look in the refrigerator downstairs and see if we have any watermelon. But first, let's finish this up," Curtis says. The Boy is staring at him with the big emerald eyes, which are now taking on flecks of deep brown. His small alabaster arms are folded across his blue- brown- and green-striped T-shirt, and he is swinging his bare legs back and forth, sometimes banging his Buster Brown shoes on the wooden crossbars of the Bentwood chair.

"Were you and your dad both naked?" Curtis continues.

"Uh-huh."

"How come?"

"We were taking a nap."

"Do you always take a nap with your dad naked?"

"No. My dad sleeps naked. I always sleep with my underpants on. He taught me that. He says when I get older I can sleep naked, but now I should wear underpants or pajamas to bed. I don't know why."

"But when Mrs. Morgan came in you were both naked. Why is that?"

"We were peeing."

"So you took off your underpants to pee?"

"No, I pulled them down to pee. Why are you always asking questions about being naked?"

"Why do you think I'm asking these questions?"

"Probably because you have big arms and you like to see naked bodies."

Curtis feels himself flush and is glad no one else is in the room. He looks at the reels of tape going round and hopes the transcriber won't take down every single comment. "No, I'm asking them so I can find out exactly what happened today, because Mrs. Morgan says she saw one thing and your dad says it was something else and we're trying to find out exactly what happened."

"Why don't you just ask me what happened? I'll tell you."

Curtis is beginning to feel a bit uncomfortable in The Boy's presence, as though it might be The Boy who is conducting the interview. "OK. Fair enough," Curtis says, adjusting himself in the chair so that he is sitting straighter. He folds his hands on the table in front of him. The Boy does likewise. They are both getting down to business now.

"So," Curtis begins again. "Did your dad touch you today?"

"Yes, of course," The Boy answers.

"Where did he touch you?"

"Under my arms."

"Under your arms?" Curtis asks, bewildered. "Does he like to touch you under your arms?"

"I don't know. He only does it when he's tickling me or picking me up to swing me around. He was swinging me around. It's a game we play. I like it a lot. It's like being in an airplane."

"Oh. Did he touch you any place else?"

"Yes."

"Where?" Curtis asks in a hushed voice, leaning toward The Boy slightly, as though to assure the confidentiality of their conversation. The Boy leans toward Curtis in a similar fashion.

"On my head. He mussed up my hair."

Curtis considers whether The Boy might be toying with him but decides that's not really possible, given The Boy's age. "Did he ask you to touch him anywhere else?"

"No."

"Did he place your hand on his body?"

"No."

"Did he touch your body with any part of his body?"

"No."

"Did you touch his body with any part of your body?"

The Boy thinks for a moment. "Yes, I guess. If you think my mouth is part of my body."

"You touched your dad with your mouth?"

"Uh-huh."

"What part of your dad's body did you touch with your mouth?"

"His penis."

Curtis swallows, sits back, takes a breath, then continues. "Did he ask you to?"

"No."

"Then why did you do it?"

"Because."

"Because why?"

"Just because. I just did. There was this drop of water there and I just licked it off."

"You just licked it off. That's all?"

"Uh-huh."

"You didn't do anything else?"

"Like what?" The Boy is restless now and gets up and begins wandering about the room, walking 'round and 'round the table.

"Well, did you put your dad's penis in your mouth, or did you just lick off that one drop of water?"

"It tasted good," The Boy says. Now he is standing beside Curtis, leaning against him. The Boy places his small hand on Curtis's bicep. " Make a muscle."

Curtis obliges, making his bicep contract into a large-bellied muscle that strains at his T-shirt sleeve.

"Neat," the Boy says.

"It tasted good? Is that what you said?" Curtis asks, trying to keep The Boy on the subject.

"Yeah, it tasted salty. I liked it." The Boy is still feeling Curtis's muscle, and Curtis is still posing for him.

"So then what happened after you licked it off?"

"Do you have waves?" The Boy asks, tugging at Curtis's T-shirt where it tucks into his Levi's.

"Waves?"

"Yeah, waves on your tummy. My dad has waves on his tummy. Muscles." The Boy has now pulled Curtis's shirt completely out of his Levi's and lifted it up to his neck. "You do have waves."

"Yes, I guess I have waves." Curtis laughs at all this. This is the most curious kid he has ever met.

"Will I have waves some day?" The Boy asks, running his hand back and forth over Curtis's stomach.

"If you work out. If you do sit-ups, you will."

Now The Boy has laid his head against Curtis's abdomen and is softly brushing his cheek back and forth across the downy hair that runs from Curtis's navel to somewhere beneath his Levi's.

"What are sit-ups?" The Boy asks.

"It's an exercise," Curtis says, uncomfortable with this physical contact with the child. "Don't you know what sit-ups are?"

"Uhn-uhn," The Boy says, bolting upright. "Show me. I want to have waves too. Show me."

The Boy tugs at Curtis's arm and coaxes him out of his chair. Curtis lies down on the floor but jumps up into a sitting position immediately. "Ouch!" he yells.

"Is that a sit-up?" The Boy asks. "Do sit-ups hurt?"

Curtis laughs despite the pain. "No. I just lay down on my handcuffs. Shit, I don't have the key. I can't show you now," Curtis says.

"Please, please show me now. I won't talk anymore unless you show me how to make waves. Pl-e-e-ease. Purty pl-e-e-ease with apricot jam on it?" The Boy is now bent over, hands on knees, his emerald-green eyes with flecks of brown right in Curtis's face. Their noses are almost touching. This is probably the cutest kid he has ever seen. And he would love to break this case before the know-it-all college grad social worker arrives.

"OK, OK," Curtis says. He stands up and unbuttons his Levi's, slips them down over his boxer shorts to his knees, so that his handcuffs are out of the way, and lays back down on the floor.

"You have ducks on your underpants," The Boy observes, pointing at Curtis's boxer shorts, which are peppered with green-and-brown mallards floating in reeds.

"Yeah, I like ducks. This is a sit-up," he says and executes one sit-up, his hands folded behind his neck. "See?"

"That's all there is to it? That's how to get waves?"

"Well, you have to do more than one to get waves."

"How many?"

"Lots. Every day. As many as you can do," Curtis says. He is continuing to do sit-ups for The Boy's amusement.

"How many can you do?" The Boy asks, apparently enthralled by the secret to obtaining waves on one's stomach.

"I do 100 every morning and 100 every evening."

"Wow! Do 100 now."

Curtis laughs. He knows he's going to have to do 100 sit-ups before The Boy cooperates, so he just keeps going. He counts out loud while The Boy watches, walking 'round and 'round Curtis's body, first squatting down near his feet so that he can look into Curtis's eyes as he comes up to touch elbows to knees, now squatting down beside him, his face just inches from the waves he so admires.

"One hundred," Curtis pants at last and collapses onto his back out of breath. "So," Curtis says, between breaths, "are you…going to tell me…what happened next?"

Curtis closes his eyes against the glaring fluorescent lights on the ceiling. He is sweating hard, and it feels good to lie still for a minute. His stomach muscles ache with the burn of the sit-ups. Suddenly he feels something wet and warm on him. He raises his head to see what it is and finds that The Boy has taken Curtis's penis, which has flopped out of his boxer shorts during the sit-up exhibition, into his mouth. Stunned by this, Curtis can do nothing but stare at the child in shocked amazement. The only other thing Curtis seems able to manage is an immediate erection.

The Boy places his small hand on Curtis's penis, and Curtis sees that it doesn't even wrap all the way around it. The Boy is now smiling at Curtis and sucking with an amazing amount of pressure. The image of Curtis's 13-year-old niece, whom he accidentally walked in on while she was taking a bath at the family cabin last summer, flashes into his mind.

Suddenly it isn't The Boy at all but his niece's small pink mouth, her sand-colored hair, her intense eyes looking up at him. Instantly, before he can protest or do anything about what is happening, Curtis erupts in orgasm and just at that moment, just as he sees the first dribble of semen run from The Boy's lips, the door opens and in steps Roberta Marchioni, MSSW, Napa County Child Protection Services.

The Boy turns and looks up at her, the viscous white fluid running down his chin and says, "Officer Curtis is showing me how to make waves."

10:19:59:59:44 A.M.

EG is discovering that even in Anchor Bay he is not immune to, nor hidden from, fear. He wakes sometimes at night in the dark room, eyes flashing open, gripped in the massive bear-hugging arms of Terror. All air has been sucked from the room; his lungs are a vacuum. He sits up, gripping the sheet. Outside, the stars twinkle beyond the pines, constant and dispassionate, safe from the explosion or implosion of emotions. Beside him, Paul sleeps quietly, or is it Andre, motionless, deep in a morphine dream?

EG lies back against his pillow, telling himself that this will pass. The night will pass, fear will pass, life will pass, and he will be free from this fear, free from the soft fetters that bind him to his idea of himself. He prays himself back to sleep, bowing to himself, to the Self within, to the space between the molecules that form his body.

But in the morning he wakes in nearly the same state. Paul sleeps beside him, naked, happy, more content, he told EG yesterday, than he has ever been in his life. The white room shimmers, cornerless in the early morning light. The bed, a white cloud splattered with colors refracted through the prism that hangs at the window, floats above the floor, a cumulus nest on which EG and Paul recline.

Hari sits beside the bed, staring pleadingly at EG, whining softly. EG knows it is no use: the Doberman has begun to wake at sunrise every morning and demand the ritual walk up the drive to the mailbox. EG dresses slowly, fear and anxiety rising and falling in him like the tides of Anchor Bay at the foot of the mountain. The sun isn't above the tree line yet, and the drive will lie cold in shadow, so he delays the *puja* walk, makes coffee, tries to work. It is no use. He cannot push one key of the keyboard, cannot concentrate on anything.

Hari is still whining. EG attempts to distract him with bones and biscuits. Hari buries each one somewhere in the house, then comes back and sits at EG's feet, staring, waiting. EG gives in. He puts on his jacket, lights incense and candles, and does his *pujas*.

First, Ganesha and Parvati in the living room. Then out to the Quan Yin garden, where he asks the Mother of Compassion to calm him, to have mercy on his fear, to whisper it away with inaudible consolations. He then continues up the drive, where he asks the Buddha-Amogasiddhi to "kindle my mind with the fire of your mind; kindle my heart with the fire of your heart; kindle my soul with the fire of your soul." He leaves a candle burning before the statue of the meditating Buddha, along with incense stuck into the redwood stump upon which the Buddha sits.

The entire forest is still. Unlike yesterday, when there was a crisp breeze in the air, this morning is completely quiet. Nothing moves; no sound is heard, except for Hari, tramping through the underbrush somewhere off in the woods. *It is like the white room upstairs*, EG thinks. *It is like a vacuum. Perhaps*

I have died already and this is my death dream. Perhaps I died in my sleep and this is the bardo state, the island between death and rebirth. Maybe I am walking in the space between lives. The path I choose this morning may determine everything. I must remember what I have learned. I must stay conscious that everything is a projection of my own mind. Everything is up to me.

EG finishes his prayers, goes to the storeroom to get a pair of clippers, and walks back up the drive. He cuts purple ceanothus, yellow Scotch broom, pink leptospermum. Back on the porch he fastidiously clips, prunes, arranges them in a tall rough-hewn vase that Paul found at a secondhand shop in Fort Bragg. He places the arrangement on the Parvati *puja*, lays his *mala* at the feet of Ganesha, and prays once again.

"Lord Ganesha," EG whispers, "manipulate the obstacles as you see fit. Mother Divine, soul of my soul, heart of my heart, Good Mother, hold me in your compassionate arms. Hold us all in your compassionate arms and ease our fears. Teach us to sit with our fears and not to be devoured by them."

Once again EG sits down to work. Now he can open his heart to himself. He feels as though his mind has been kindled with a new fire and, while his fear is still present, it is he holding it, rather than it holding him. He begins: "EG is discovering that even in Anchor Bay he is not immune to, nor hidden from, fear."

He looks up. The candle is burning on the Parvati *puja*. Ganesha is floating in a cloud of incense. *I must remember always to keep first things first*, EG tells himself. *Eat when it is time to eat; sleep when it is time to sleep; pray when it is time to pray. Puja first, then writing. Soul before body, heart before mind, prayer before ego.*

EG writes the next line: "He wakes sometimes at night in the dark room, eyes flashing open, gripped in the massive, bear-hugging arms of Terror."

The rest comes easily.

<u>10:19:59:59:45</u> A.M.

It is early June when AD arrives back in California after his freshman year of college. He has thought about Donny Macgregor off and on while he was away at school in Texas, usually when he was showering in the gym. He would remember Donny Macgregor wet with half a hard-on after football practice, smiling at him as he told Victor Lyon that everybody who went to St. Vincent's High School was a Catholic queer and the Benicia High Panthers would tromp all over the Saints at homecoming.

AD remembers Donny Macgregor's admonition at the airport to call him when he gets home, and so the very evening of his arrival, he telephones Donny Macgregor, who, somewhat to AD's surprise, has been waiting for his call.

"I saw your mom in the Park & Shop last week. She told me you'd be home today. I was wondering if you'd call. I can't wait to hear all about college. Let's party."

So they buy two six-packs of beer, climb into Donny Macgregor's bitchin' cherry-red '53 Chevy two-door, and head for the lake. To catch up.

"Man, you got thin. You're almost skinny," Donny Macgregor says, pulling up to the edge of the lake and cutting the engine.

"Yeah. Eighty pounds. Big difference, huh?"

"How much did you weigh when you left?"

"Two-forty, if you can believe it."

"Wow! What brought that on? How come you lost so much weight?" Donny Macgregor is fumbling in the brown paper bag on the seat between them. He's trying to retrieve one of the six-packs.

Outside, AD can see that a family has had a picnic just a few feet from where they are parked. The remains of the day's outing are scattered all along the shore: paper plates, aluminum cans, watermelon rinds.

"Oh, it's a long story," AD says, not wanting to admit he fell in love with his roommate and quickly realized that in order to seduce this guy from South Bend, Ind., who ran track and swam on the swimming team, he was going to have to give him a more aesthetically pleasing body to look at. "Just didn't eat much; kind of lost my appetite for a while. I guess I was homesick or something. You know, scared of being on my own at college, stuff like that."

"Huh? What's to be scared of?" Donny Macgregor asks. He has retrieved two Budweisers, handed one to AD, and is now drinking his in one long gulp.

AD watches, astounded, listens to Donny Macgregor belch for about 30 seconds, then answers the question. "I don't know, just being in a strange place and all. I'd never been to Texas before." Donny Macgregor is now chugging Beer Number Two. AD is somewhere between amused and grossed out. He forgot about high school beer drinking: effect over flavor.

"So what's it like? College, I mean."

"You're going to college; you know what it's like."

"Sh-i-i-it!" Donny Macgregor slurs, "JC ain't college. It's glorified high school." He thinks for a moment, then adds, "but it's not a pushover. They make you work your ass off. I don't even have time to play baseball this year."

"But I thought you had a baseball scholarship," AD says, swigging his own beer now, thinking perhaps he'd better catch up with Donny Macgregor so that they're sort of on the same wavelength.

"I did till they took it away from me midsemester and gave it to that queer Catholic asshole Jimmy MacInerney from St. Vincent's," Donny Macgregor says, pitching his beer can out the window and rummaging for another one.

"They gave you a scholarship and then took it away? How can they do that?"

"I don't know. They said it was because I got an incomplete in my midsemester report, but I know that's not true because lots of guys get 'em. But the coach used to go to St. Vincent's, so they give most of their scholarships to those fuckin' pope-lovers. I don't know how I ever got one in the first place. Must have been a mistake. They probably read my name wrong on my application. Instead of Macgregor, they probably thought it said Butt-fucker."

AD watches now as Donny Macgregor finishes Beer Number Three and opens Beer Number Four. "You really hate Catholics, huh?" AD asks, figuring this may be his last opportunity to get to the bottom of all this.

"They're all queers," Donny Macgregor says, tipping his Bud. AD wonders if he had a funnel, would it be possible to simply empty both six-packs down Donny Macgregor's gullet without him even stopping for air?

"What do you mean by that? Obviously, all Catholics aren't homosexuals, if you mean it literally. If you mean it figuratively, then what do you mean by 'queer'?"

"You sound like my English professor," Donny Macgregor says, looking at AD with just a slight touch of contempt. "Is that how they teach you to talk at a four-year college?"

AD is getting a little fed up with the antagonism, which he doesn't think is warranted. After all, this get-together was Donny Macgregor's idea in the first place. "No, actually, I learned to talk like this before I went away to college. But answer my question. I'm really interested. Why do you hate Catholics so much?"

"'Cause they're fucked up. I mean, really, doing everything the pope says. Some dago clown who walks around in a white dress all the time, carrying that little purse on fire, and corn-holing altar boys? That's queer, man."

AD thinks Donny Macgregor isn't making much sense any-more and thinks he probably never will on this subject. Ob-viously, Catholics are just a convenient scapegoat for all his rage. AD decides to let the subject drop. Donny Macgregor, however, now wants to pursue it.

"I mean, you're Catholic, aren't you?" Donny Macgregor presses on.

"Yes, as a matter of fact I am."

"And you suck cock, right?"

"Is this why you invited me out tonight, so you could insult me? I thought we were friends," AD says, raising his voice just a little, finding his irritation outweighing his feelings for Donny Macgregor by more than just a little.

"We are, man. I'm not saying anything against you person-ally. I'm just trying to make a point. You do suck cock, right?" Donny Macgregor is being very nonchalant about all this, rummaging around in the bag again, tugging at yet another can of beer, his speech beginning to slur just a little.

"Well, if I did, I certainly wouldn't tell you. It's none of your business." AD now chugs the rest of his beer and dips into the bag himself.

"Don't get all pissed off. I don't care. I mean I know you do. Everyone knows it."

"Everyone knows it?" AD asks, figuring that everyone does know it by now, but not about to give an inch in this argument.

"Well, not everyone, but all the guys do. You sucked off Richie King, right?"

"What?"

"And Ray Holland, right?"

"Who told you that?"

"And you gave blow jobs to Jimmy Orr and Phil Reynolds, didn't you?"

"Phil Reynolds?"

"Yeah, Phil told me that himself. And Patrick Houlihan, but he's a Catholic, so he probably blew you too. He's such a queer."

"Wait a minute. This is absurd," AD says, beginning to feel backed into a corner.

"I don't care, man. I'm just trying to make a point. Catholics are queers. They like to suck dick. You want to suck my dick? You can. I don't mind. I let some guy at JC go down on me once. His St. Christopher medal kept getting caught on my dick. It was hilarious. I almost laughed, but I didn't want to spoil the mood."

"So let me get this straight. You got your scholarship taken away and given to somebody else because that guy is a Catholic and you're not. It had nothing to do with your grades or anything. Is that right?"

"Yeah, that's right. So now I got to get a job six hours a day and go to school at night, which I'm not crazy about the commute 'cause I gotta go down Tennessee Street in Vallejo."

"What's wrong with Tennessee Street?" AD asks.

"Well, nothing, if you don't mind havin' about ten jungle bunnies trying to jump you at every red light." Donny Macgregor tosses Beer Can Number Five out the window and, predictably, forages in the moonlight for Number Six.

"I never knew you felt this way. I mean, I thought we were friends, but I guess I was wrong about that. I should have known nothing's different from when we were in the fifth grade."

"I didn't even know you in the fifth grade," Donny Macgregor says.

"That didn't stop you from pelting me with garbage every day after school," AD responds with a sharp snap.

Donny Macgregor laughs. "Was that you? Man, I used to wait for you every day. I couldn't believe you didn't walk home some other way. Every day I told myself, 'Today, he'll go around the hill,' but sure enough, 3:45 would roll around, and there you'd be, coming up the hill, lugging that big fuck-er of a school bag. You were somethin' else. I never knew that was you."

"Well, it was me. And things don't seem to have changed much, do they?"

"Sure they have. We're friends now, aren't we? Why shouldn't we be friends?" Donny Macgregor asks, genuinely perplexed. He turns now, facing AD, his right leg leaning up against the back of the tan leather seat, his left leg stretched out with his foot touching AD's calf. Donny Macgregor takes a swig of his Bud and waits for AD's answer.

"Why? Well, for one thing you hate Catholics and I'm a Catholic."

"Well, that's true, but you're an exception. You're my friend."

"But you just got through telling me I'm not an exception. You just got through telling me I—like all Catholics—am queer and suck dick."

"Hmm. I see your point. OK, so you're Catholic and you're queer and you suck dick. But I can still make an exception. C'mon, we're buddies."

AD is somewhere between furious and totally confused. Can this person really be this ignorant? Has AD overlooked this for the past two years just because he wanted to be close to all this beauty? "Look, why don't you just give me a ride home and we'll pretend like we never met."

"No, man, that's not right. I like you. Besides, I broke up with my girlfriend. You know how it is." Donny Macgregor moves his left hand to his crotch and gives a little squeeze.

"I'm not following," AD says, following perfectly.

"Look, why don't you just suck me off and get it over with. I'm practically the only guy left in Benicia you haven't gone down on. It's OK, I don't mind. I thought maybe we'd get to do it before you left for college, but your mom was always goin' everywhere with us. I wanted to do it on the way to the airport that night, but she came with us then too. So do it now, why dontcha?"

"Have you always felt this way about me?" AD asks.

"I don't feel any way about you. We're friends. You can't help it if you're Catholic. C'mon, man. You'll like it; I'll like it. C'mon." Donny Macgregor is practically begging now. "I'll bet you never had one this fat," Donny Macgregor teases, unbuttoning his Levi's and pulling out his claim to fame.

It was at this point that AD had a Catholic brainstorm, a kind of beatific vision, which he would later refer to as the Miracle of Lake Herman. "OK," he says, "but there's not enough room in the front seat. We have to get in back."

"Good idea," Donny Macgregor says. He chugs the last of Beer Number Six and scrambles over the front seat.

"And you have to take your pants off. It's no fun if you don't take your pants off. It's too confining. You have to be able to wrap your legs around my head."

"Man, you're a pro, aren't you?" Donny Macgregor exclaims, slurring his words even more now. He unbuttons his Levi's and slips out of them, kicking off his tennis shoes in the process. Now he's sitting spread-eagle in the backseat of his bitchin' cherry-red '53 Chevy two-door, rubbing his "chick choker."

"Shirt too," AD says. "I want you completely naked. I've always had the hots for your body, and I want to see you naked while I suck you off."

"Whoa, this is gonna be good," Donny Macgregor says, struggling with his T-shirt. "C'mon, man, get back here and get on it."

"OK, but I have to move this bag first," AD says, shoving the beer bag onto the floor and sliding behind the wheel. "We have to play a kind of game. We have to pretend like I just found you here sleeping in your car. I'm going to crawl back there and you pretend to be asleep while I blow you."

"Huh? What for?"

"It's the only way I can do it. See, Catholics believe this is a mortal sin if both people consent to it. But if one of us doesn't really know what's happening, like if he's kind of sleeping, then it's not a sin."

"Jeez, Catholics believe that shit?"

"Yeah, it's just how we're taught. The pope made up that rule."

"Weird, man. OK, I'll pretend I'm asleep," Donny Macgregor says, lying down on the seat, one foot stuck up in the back window, one on the floor.

AD takes a last look at what he's about to pass up, allows himself a fleeting moment of vacillation, and then in one swift motion, opens the door, releases the emergency brake, steps out, gives a hardy shove, and stands back as Donny Macgregor, buck naked in the back of his bitchin' cherry-red '53 Chevy two-door goes rolling into Lake Herman.

AD stands there long enough to both enjoy the spectacle and make sure Donny Macgregor gets out of the car alive. As soon as he hears him shouting and sees him flailing his arms in the water, AD high-tails it to the highway and thumbs a ride with the next passing car.

As he stands on the side of the road in the moonlight, AD begins to sing.

> This earth is but a vale of tears, O Maria.
> A place of banishment, of fears, O Maria.
>
> Triumph all ye cherubim,
> Sing with us, ye Seraphim,
> Heav'n and earth resound the hymn:
> Salve, salve, salve, Regina!

10:19:59:59:46 A.M.

"It's hell to get old," Annabel used to tell him. EG believes it is one of the reasons she died at such an early age. She just couldn't bear to watch her beauty fade.

EG knows how she felt. He is turning 50. His body has been fighting off the virus for 14 years, trying to overcome the poisonous drugs he takes, as well as giving in to use and gravity as he grows older.

He stands naked before the mirror and takes painful inventory.

His arms reveal only a hint of their once shapely, muscular form. Gone are the veins in his biceps, the bulging triceps. His shoulders are no longer round but slope, the bones visible through the skin. His chest, which he coveted as one of his two greatest physical assets, now covered with gray hair, has surrendered its battle with gravity.

When he was a young boy, fat and self-conscious about his weight, the boys in school used to grab at his sagging chest and shout, "You've got titties like a girl. Let us feel your tits." The sweater that was part of his parochial school uniform clung to him and accentuated his chest. He was mortified by it and used to pull at his sweater constantly, trying to get it not to cling. All his sweaters were misshapen, stretched out in the middle where he was perpetually tugging at them. *I've come full circle*, he thinks, looking at himself in the mirror. *I might as well be back in St. Catherine's school yard.*

His waist is straight, not shapely at the hips. He thinks he is built like a refrigerator, and now he even has a "spare tire" that hangs over his belt when he dresses.

His dick looks bigger to him. In fact he is sure it is growing. He has heard wives' tales that a man's penis gets larger as he grows older, but he thought it was just wishful thinking. Now he knows it is true. Proof positive that Nature does have a sense of humor—a cruel one.

His legs, his second best attribute in his youth, also sag, the skin loose and dry at the thighs. His quadriceps are no longer prominent as they were when he played tennis and rode a bicycle.

"And yet," he says aloud, looking up and down in the mirror, "I love my body. It has served me well, and I have never fully appreciated it."

Most of the time EG is content just to be alive, happy that his body works as well as it does and looks as good as it does. But once in a while, when Clete is in the room or some beautiful young man walks by, he holds in his stomach, sticks out his chest, looks at his reflection in a shop window, and thinks, *Who would ever look twice at me?*

He remembers the days when men pursued him, asked him to dance at the clubs, bought him drinks. He thinks of how he met one such man on Fire Island on a Sunday afternoon at

Tea Dance in The Pines. The man had been smiling at him. EG smiled back. The man, about 25, lean and handsome, came over, put his lips to EG's ear, and said, "Can I run my hand through the hair on your chest?"

Another time, he was riding his bicycle along Wisconsin Avenue in Georgetown when traffic snarled and he decided it would be quicker to walk his bike on the sidewalk. He passed a clothing shop near Twenty-eighth Street and a young clerk was standing outside. The fellow smiled as EG passed. "Good morning," EG said.

"Great legs," the man said.

EG stopped. "Thanks. I always think they're kind of fat."

"Not at all. They're beautiful. I shouldn't admit this, but I stand out here every morning and wait for you to ride by, just so I can look at your legs."

EG blushed and was at a loss for words.

The man smiled. "I don't have to open the shop for another 15 minutes. Why don't you come in and let me lick the sweat off your thighs."

Those days are gone, EG muses, *gone forever. But now I have Paul, and I don't miss those days. I only miss the beauty of the body I once had. Now I have to find my beauty elsewhere.* EG dresses, looks at himself one last time in the mirror, and smiles wistfully. "This happens to everyone," he tells his reflection. "Do it with grace and dignity. If you lived in China, you'd be revered for your age. Thank you, Body, for serving me so well for so long."

10:19:59:59:47 A.M.

An overwhelming comprehension has pervaded EG: He is going to die soon. He has begun a new clinical trial for a new

formulation of a drug that is quite promising. It requires, however taking an additional 18 pills per day along with another
antiretroviral for an even greater synergistic effect. This
brings his daily pill consumption to a total of 63 pills.

18 Saquinavir gel caps (the new drug)
6 Ritonavir (the other new drug)
1 Bactrim
2 Zovirax
4 AZT
3 Beta Caratene
3 Coenzyme Q
1 Vitamin C
1 Vitamin E
1 DHEA
3 Ultram
9 Ibuprofen
1 Claritin D
1 B 12
3 Blue-Green algae
1 Multivitamin gel cap
1 B6
1 Zinc
1 Selenium
2 Vicodin

The side effects of the new drug are primarily fatigue and indigestion. The fatigue, while random and unpredictable, is relentless when it occurs, and sometimes it lasts for days. One day
he feels energized; the next four days he wants to remain in bed.

This awareness of his impending death is more experience
than understanding. It is something he knows and feels, and it

transcends logic or reason. These drugs are the state-of-the art treatment for his illness, and he is at a point in his disease progression at which he is on the verge of contracting opportunistic infections. So this new drug is the next and last hope of staying relatively healthy. If it doesn't work, or if he must stop taking it for any reason, his death will be hastened considerably.

He feels closer to death than he has ever felt before. It is permeating his day, coloring his experiences, sharpening his actions and reactions. Above all, it brings with it a new anxiety. Who will care for Paul? Who will care for Hari? What lies on the other side?

The newest symptoms that have crept up on him are intensified and heightened senses of hearing and smell. The slightest odor—a cigarette being smoked by a passerby on the street, an egg frying, even window cleaner hours after it has been used—is detectable even if he is in bed with the door closed. Sounds no one else can hear—a car turning the corner at the foot of Church Street, a coin falling in the apartment below, tennis balls being hit in the courts in Dolores Park a block and a half away—all sound to him as though they are occurring right next to him.

And then there is the bird. He has looked everywhere for it, poking up the chimney, climbing onto the roof to inspect the eaves, even walking the roofs of the neighboring houses. He knows it is there somewhere, this bird whose wings he can hear flapping softly in the dark, whose low mourning wakes him in the night.

10:19:59:59:48 A.M.

By the time EG arrives at Point Arena Lighthouse, three of the eight men inside have been killed, two wounded, and two have surrendered. Only Tom, the organizer of the Sea Ranch Liberation Front, is still barricaded inside. EG takes a bullhorn from one of the militia captains and aims it at the lighthouse.

"Tom, this is EG. Let me come inside. I'm alone and unarmed. Let's end this thing before there's any more bloodshed."

EG's plea is met with gunfire.

"Tom, be reasonable. There's no way you can escape here. If you'll talk this out with me, maybe we can let you go. We'll give you safe passage across the border, but you have to talk with me. We have to reason together."

More gunfire. Tom shouts, "You're a fucking liar, faggot." Another shot rings out, just missing one of the militia standing near a green van. The window of the van shatters.

"Tom, we have Steven."

Several minutes go by.

"Tom, I'm coming in. I'm unarmed. Kill me if you feel you must, but remember, we have your son."

EG turns to one of the women holding an automatic rifle near him. "Go get the boy," he says. The woman says something to the soldier beside her and the two of them climb into a Jeep and drive off. EG unstraps his holster and walks to the lighthouse. He pushes open the door and begins the long climb up the circular stairs. At the top, Tom is waiting with a revolver aimed at EG's head.

"Whew! I thought I was in shape, but these stairs say something different." EG takes the last three steps as Tom steps back, holding the gun steady with both hands. His eyes are filled with an intense hatred unlike any EG has ever seen up close.

"May I sit?" EG asks, gesturing toward a wooden captain's chair near the desk. The desk is actually a circular counter attached to the lighthouse wall. It wraps around the entire 360 degrees of the lighthouse. It is littered with papers, sandwiches, empty beer bottles, and a half-filled bottle of Jack Daniels. "Tom, we're in a conundrum. You can't get out and we want to go home. Now you've got me at gunpoint, but we have your son. It's really a nasty bind we're in here. What do you propose?"

"I propose you suck my dick and then I shoot you in the head. That's what I propose," Tom says venomously.

Despite the situation, or maybe because of it, EG looks Tom over. His years in the Marines are obvious by the shape he's in. Like EG, he's wearing camouflage fatigues. In the heat of the closed-up lighthouse, he has stripped down to his T-shirt. EG takes in Tom's sweaty, round, tanned shoulders and biceps, the veins bulging at his neck and in his forearms. *This is almost a cliché porn story*, EG thinks. "Well, Tom," EG answers, "the first part of that doesn't sound like a bad idea to me, actually."

"Stand up," Tom orders. EG stands. "Turn around," he says, and when EG turns Tom frisks him. Finding no weapons, Tom spins EG back around to face him and slaps him hard across the face, knocking him to the floor. "You perverted cocksucker," Tom says. "I ought to kill you."

"Before you pull the trigger," EG says calmly, "let me just paint a picture for you. Right now your son, Steven, is at the militia compound. He's safe and probably enjoying a warm meal. Now what happens after dinner is up to you. You probably think this is going to be like the movies. EG starts to sit up, but Tom kicks him back to a lying position, resting his boot on EG's chest. See what I mean, Tom? You're acting like Rambo. And you think this is about living or dying, about giving up your life for what you believe in. For us queers, you're right. We're willing to die for this. But for you, it's a little more complicated."

"You're sick," Tom sneers.

"Be that as it may, you see, Tom, we know what it is you fear most. You fear dicks the most. So if you make this complicated…no, let me be more frank. If you shoot me, we're not going to shoot you. We're going to fuck you. We're going to fuck you day in and day out. And if you shoot me and then shoot yourself, we're going to fuck your boy. Back in the barracks, we're going to strap him into a bunk and one by one, all 347 militiamen are going to be ordered to rape your son."

Tom kicks EG in the ribs. "Faggot!"

EG grimaces and grabs his side where Tom's boot landed, but he doesn't lose his concentration. "And they will, Tom, because one of the stereotypes you Breeders have of queers—faggots, as you like to call us—is true. And that is, that, just like you, Tom, we've got lots of hormones raging around inside us. We're always ready for a piece of ass. Especially a nice piece of tender 14-year-old ass like your son."

Tom kicks EG in the ribs, then in the head. EG is now bleeding from a cut near his right eye.

"This isn't exactly the best negotiating strategy you've got going here, Tom," EG says. "If this goes on much longer, you're going to have to shoot me because I'm going to be so angry, I'll want revenge. Right now, all I want is to end this and go home. I'm tired and hungry. You must be too. If you just end this now, you and your boy can leave tonight. You can't take anything with you, but the two of you will be given safe passage into Sonoma County. But first you've got to give me that gun and end this, Tom. Please, for everyone's sake."

"Where's Moira? Where's my wife?"

"You can take her too, of course," EG says, not bothering to mention that he would have to pack her in a body bag.

Tom is beginning to wear down. "You wouldn't dare hurt my boy. You'd go to prison for life. They'd gas you."

"Yes, that's right. On the other side of the Mendocino County line they would, but I'm never going to cross that line, Tom. Never. There's nothing out there I want. And they can't get in here. And even if they could, it's our rules on this side. So since we make the rules, I can pretty damned well do what I want, can't I? How about it, Tom? Can we go home now? There's a car out there with your son in it. You could walk out of here, get in that car, and be driven down to the bridge. After that you're on your own."

"Do you know how much I hate you?" Tom asks.

"I have a pretty good idea," EG responds, wiping more blood from his face. "But I have to tell you, I don't know why. Until today, I'd never done anything to you personally. In fact, until the Revolution, none of us had ever done anything to you personally. All we wanted was to be left alone and to be treated like anyone else in this country is treated. Well, any white Christian."

"You don't even deserve to live, let alone have rights," Tom says. He removes his foot from EG's chest and goes to the desk. He sits on the desktop, pulls out a pack of Camels and lights one, but he doesn't set down the revolver.

"Why?" EG asks. "Why do you hate us so much?"

"Because you're fucking perverts. I don't suppose you've ever read the Bible."

"Oh, that. OK. Sorry, I thought you had a real reason. You know, like being molested by a gym coach or an older boy...or maybe your father. Common wisdom, not to mention the best psychological theory, says that anyone who has an obsessive hatred of homosexuality is actually afraid of his own feelings of homosexuality. Often that starts with some unnatural relationship with a family member like a brother...or a father."

Tom glares at EG, picks up a beer bottle on the desk, and throws it at him. "Shut your fuckin' mouth about my father. You don't know anything about him. He was a good man."

"OK, OK. So he didn't rape you. He didn't sneak into your room at night or take you on 'special' camping trips, just the two of you, and bring only one sleeping bag."

The veins on the side of Tom's head look like they're ready to burst. "Shut the fuck up, I said!" Tom jumps up and kicks EG in the head again several times. "Shut up about my father," Tom says, but now he's crying. "Get up!"

EG struggles to get to his feet. He is bleeding from his mouth, his left ear, and three or four cuts on his cheek. His head is throbbing, and it feels like his left jawbone is the size of a baseball. He touches it, but it's numb. He hopes he can find a doctor when he gets back to the compound—if he gets back.

"Tom, this is getting out of hand," EG says. His tongue is cut and he is having trouble speaking. "Please, one more time, let's get out of here."

"You're a nasty fucker. You say things to provoke people, just to make them angry and irrational. You get off on it. I've heard you speak at rallies; I've seen what you do to people, working them up into a frenzy, filling them with rage. You know exactly what to say."

"It would seem that's true tonight, anyway, eh?" EG mutters, wiping his bloody hand on his pants.

Tom punches EG in the stomach. "Cocksucker. Get on your knees."

EG looks at Tom, trying to read his eyes.

"I said get on your knees, cocksucker. Now!" Tom screams at the top of his lungs as he pushes on EG's shoulder with his free hand, forcing him to the floor.

EG kneels on the floor in front of Tom. "Guess what, butt-fuck? You did make me mad. You've made me irrational. So now I'm going to shoot you. I'm going to watch your brains go flying all over the room and I'm going to get off on it, the way you get off on sucking dicks. Ready? Ready to feel this .358 go flying through your skull?" Tom pulls back the hammer, and EG hears the familiar click. The same click he would have heard had he stayed in Tom's house this afternoon after giving the order to shoot Moira. The same click he heard when Courtney shot Tom's Labrador retriever. Now the click was for him. The last click he will ever hear if some miracle doesn't occur.

"Dad?" Steven's voice is being amplified over the bullhorn outside. "Dad, are you OK? It's Steve. Please come out."

Tom is completely taken aback by this development. He looks out the lighthouse window, but it's too dark to see anything. He can feel the pounding of his own heart. EG is looking up at him, hoping Tom will give in to his natural instinct to save his son.

"Dad, they're going to hurt me if you don't come down. They're going...to...make me...make me...do bad things."

Tom begins to weep. "I hate you so much," he says to EG, holding the gun up to EG's forehead. "I hate you so much. God, please give me the strength to pull this trigger."

"Then you'd better also ask him to give your boy strength. He's going to need it more than you are", EG whispers. "I gave you a chance to get out of this, Tom. I came in here with an offer to let you walk out and leave the county. Why are you doing this? What is driving you so obsessively? Why do you hate me so much? What happened to you?"

"Shut up!" Tom screams. He takes a step backward and fires. EG closes his eyes, waiting for the bullet to rip into his skull. But the shot is fired into the floor. Then another one, and another, as Tom screams over and over, "I hate you! I hate you! I hate you!" He keeps firing until the chamber is empty. When EG hears the clicking of the empty gun, he slumps to the floor.

Within minutes militia soldiers are storming up the stairs. When they get to the top, they find the two of them sitting on the floor, Tom sobbing, EG holding the side of his head.

"Thank God you're all right," Courtney says, as she reaches to help EG to his feet. "We didn't know what the hell happened up here. We were afraid that…"

"No, no. I'm fine. Tom just got a little emotional is all. Take him and the boy to the compound. Feed them and let them clean up, then hold them in the barracks bathhouse. I have to think about what comes next." EG turns to Tom, who looks like he's in shock. EG places his hand under Tom's chin and turns his face up toward his own. "Now, my friend, it's my turn."

EG goes home, takes a shower, eats a sandwich, and drinks two beers. He swallows two Vicodins left over from some dental work he had a couple months ago. Then he puts on a fresh camouflage suit and climbs into his 4Runner. He sits in the dark of the driveway smoking a cigarette and taking in the pine and redwood forest that slopes down to the ocean. A half moon is working its way across the sky; the stars are brilliant. EG sighs, starts the motor, and heads toward the compound.

By the time EG arrives at the compound, Tom and his son are sleeping in separate holding cells. "I want Tom kept here in one of the glory hole rooms in the Central Training Building. Keep the boy at the barracks. I'll explain the details later, but for now I want Tom fed and kept comfortable. Just don't let him out of the room. Keep the place open so people can come in here for sex. In fact, put the word out that there should always be at least two people in the room next to him having sex, preferably women. Tell Thao to meet me in his room right away."

EG goes to Tom's room, sits down on the edge of the bed. Tom wakes with a start and sits up, fists clenched.

"Feeling better?" EG asks.

Tom is groggy, stiff and sore from being on the run and a little rough stuff from some of the soldiers. Most of the fight is gone out of him. "Yeah, I guess."

"You should have taken me up on my offer while it was still good. Now the terms have changed."

Tom stares at EG expressionless. Angry as he is, he's too tired to argue. "What are they?"

"You and the boy can still leave, but now there are conditions."

"Where's my wife? I want to see her," Tom says.

"We'll talk about that later. For now, we have to work out the arrangements here."

"I want to see my wife," Tom says, mustering some venom despite his fatigue.

"I promise you, you'll be together soon. But first we have something to settle between the two of us."

"What do you want now?"

The door opens and Thao walks in. He's a young Vietnamese man of 22, lean, soft-spoken, and extremely beautiful. Before the Revolution he was studying to be a tax attorney, working part-time at the Securities Exchange Commission in San Francisco, going to law school at night. He is gentle but determined, single-minded. He is one of the most loyal and dedicated soldiers EG has. Thao stands just inside the door.

"Come in, Thao. I want you to meet Tom Twomey. Tom, this is Thao." Thao goes over to the bed and extends his hand. Tom shakes hands reluctantly. "The two of you have lots in common, actually. Thao knows a lot about investments, stocks and bonds, that sort of thing. His family also went through a war and escaped. Barely. Lots of things the two of you can discuss. He'll be your companion here until our terms are met. He's going to keep you company and tend to your needs."

"You mean he's going to be my guard," Tom says sarcastically.

"Not at all. There are guards outside. The building is completely secured. Your escape is the last thing on my mind, I assure you. After all, Steven is in another building under even heavier guard than you. Besides, I think we're going to reach an agreement before long and you'll be free to go."

"And what are these terms you keep referring to?" Tom asks. He is scrunched up against the wall, hugging his knees.

"Well, just as soon as you and Thao become friends, you're free to leave," EG says, smiling.

"Friends? As soon as we become friends?"

"Special friends. Very special friends, if you get my meaning," EG says, his smile broadening just slightly.

"What the fuck are you saying? I don't even know this…" Tom's voice trails off as he catches on. "You're a sick fuck."

"Well, that may be, but that's not your concern, is it? Your only mission, Mr. Twomey, whether or not you choose to accept to it, is to get inside this beautiful smooth-skinned young man." EG reaches out and takes Thao by the waist, turning his back toward Tom. "See this?" EG says, patting Thao's butt. This is your mission. And let me tell you, it's a fabulous assignment. Take it from me—I know. In fact, once 'inside enemy lines,' as it were, you'll probably ask Thao to desert and go with you when you leave."

Tom jerks as though he might lunge at EG. Thao whips around, raises his hands in a posture of self-defense. Tom freezes, then slumps back to the wall. "That'll never happen."

"Of course, it's completely up to you, Tom. You may like it here and want to stay indefinitely. And who knows, by the time you decide, Steven may have come to enjoy himself so much in the other barracks he may choose not to go with you." EG stands and goes to the door. "Well, you two have a nice time getting to know one another."

For the next four days Tom ignores Thao, except for some occasional small talk. By the end of the week they are discussing securities issues on the stock market, at least the stock market as it existed before the Revolution. Within two weeks, they are actually chummy.

The constant sex going on in the other rooms, the groaning and moaning of the women, the loud dirty talk of the men, has become a constant drone that Tom can tune out most of the time. It is most difficult at night when the bathhouse is busiest and Tom is bored.

A small table with a lamp sits next to the bed. At bedtime Thao undresses before turning the lamp off. Tom, while of course not being attracted to Thao's body, cannot help but look at it. His skin is smooth, soft, almost translucent in the warm lamplight. Thao's long hair, which he wears tied in a ponytail during the day, falls far below his shoulders when he lets it down at bedtime. Tom watches every night, just before lights-out, as the boy unwraps the rubber band that holds his hair and lets it fall around his smooth, round shoulders. In the lamplight it shines like strands of fine black silk.

"Look," Tom says one night, as Thao strips down to his briefs, the white elastic band bright against his dark skin, "I'm never going to have sex with you, but it's ridiculous for you to sleep on the floor. Why don't you sleep up here?"

"I don't want to make you uncomfortable," Thao says. "I'm fine here on the rug. Honest. This isn't my idea you understand. I'm following orders. This really is an army. It really is a war. I'm obeying my commander in chief. I wouldn't be doing this if I didn't have to. I'm a prisoner too, in a sense."

Tom scoots over against the wall. "I won't be any more uncomfortable than I already am. You'll see, this isn't the Ritz, but it's softer than the floor. And it's warm." He pats the bed next to him, turns to face the wall. Thao slips beneath the rough army blanket and the mattress and the two of them fall to sleep.

For the next week and a half, they sleep together but have no physical contact, other than an occasional inadvertent flopping of arms on top of one another during the night. For the first week, EG comes in each day to see how things are progressing, but then he decides to leave them alone, not wanting to enrage Tom and constantly renew his resolve to stay distant from Thao. EG arranges for Thao to report to him every afternoon in his office.

"He's not going to give in, but he wants to. I can tell," Thao says to EG one afternoon, while Tom is showering.

"So he's weakening?"

"I'd say so, but you have to remember, now it's a contest. Under other circumstances he would have jumped my ass by now. I'm sure of it. But he's in a pissing contest with you."

"Very well, we'll change it for him a little, see if we can't lure his hormones to the surface."

That evening, Thao announces to Tom that there are going to be different arrangements. Since it's obvious Tom isn't going to give in, Thao has requested that he be allowed to occupy the room next door, at least at bedtime, just to give each of them more comfort and a little privacy. There is a door between the two rooms, which up to this point has been kept locked. Now it is opened and the two move freely back and forth.

Thao has decorated his room a bit with a second lamp, a chair, and a few candles. They live like this for almost two weeks before there is any sign of Tom's attitude changing toward Thao. One evening, while Thao is undressing in the candlelight, he sees in the mirror that Tom is watching him through the glory hole, which is about four inches wide and six inches up and down. Thao doesn't let on that he sees him but takes his time undressing, rubbing lotion over his entire body. When he gets to his pubic area he strokes himself into an erection, but Tom turns away.

This ritual goes on every night for a week and a half before Tom doesn't turn away. He watches Thao until, throwing his head back, his long hair cascading behind him, he ejaculates. The next night Thao repeats the performance, but now he has moved the bed so that it is against the wall directly opposite Tom's vantage point through the hole in the wall. He lies on the bed stroking himself and whispering over and over, "Tom, oh, Tom, fuck me, fuck me."

At first Tom jumps back, thinking Thao has seen him, but when Thao keeps up the talking after Tom has moved out of his range of vision, he decides that Thao is simply fantasizing. This goes on in one form or another for over three weeks.

One evening, before bedtime, as Thao and Tom are saying good night, Thao goes to Tom, puts his hand on his shoulder and says, "I think I've grown very fond of you. I wish we were in a different situation."

"Yeah, me too," Tom says, and pats Thao on the shoulder. "You're the first Oriental friend I've ever had. I knew there were some good ones out there, but I'd never met any. You're OK."

"We have another thing in common I've discovered," Thao says. "I'm also very lonely. If for any reason, something should happen between us, just to relieve the tension, I mean, I wouldn't say anything unless you wanted me too." Thao looks at the floor. "I guess I've grown to like this arrangement. I had no friends out there. You're a good man." Thao then goes into his room and closes the door.

That night he looks directly at Tom as he masturbates. Tom does not turn away.

Three nights later, during their nightly ritual of exhibitionism and voyeurism, Thao gets up, walks to the hole in the wall, and backs up to it. He waits for several minutes, but nothing happens from the other side; he goes back to his bed and turns out the light. The next night he does the same thing. And the third night, also the same. Each time, he returns to his bed untouched and, just before he turns out the light, he looks in Tom's direction, finding that he is not watching, that he has obviously moved away when Thao has offered himself for Tom's pleasure.

The fourth night, as Thao presses himself against the hole in the wall, he feels Tom's hand lightly running across his butt, lingering just a second or two when his fingertips dip slightly into the soft, warm separation. Just one touch.

The next day, as they are playing poker, Tom says, "I hope you don't mind my saying so, but you have skin just like a woman."

"I don't mind. As long as you don't mind," Thao says, looking up at Tom with a shy smile.

Tom doesn't look away. "I don't mind," he says.

"Maybe—if you decide to get out of here, that is—maybe it would be one way for you to go through with it. If you thought of me as a woman, I mean."

Tom looks at his cards, moves them around in his hand.

"Sorry," Thao says, "I was just trying to be helpful."

"No, it's not that," Tom confesses. "I've thought the same thing myself."

That night, against the wall, Thao feels Tom entering him but makes not a sound; he doesn't even breathe heavily. He knows that anything at all that breaks Tom's fantasy, whatever it is, would mean his withdrawal. The act takes less than two minutes. The next day, while Tom is in the shower, Thao leaves a small note on his bedside table. It says simply, "Thank you."

The next time, two nights later, it takes a little longer. The next time longer still, as though Tom might be trying to make the sensation last a while. "I think he's battling with his guilt each time," Thao says to EG. "He fucks me through the hole so he can pretend I'm a woman, but he won't touch me when we're in the room together. Then, after he fucks me, he's distant the next day. He stays away from the hole for the next night or two and then by the third day he has to have it again."

"The strange thing is," EG says, "he's not telling us. He doesn't want us to know. What's that about? I thought he wanted out of here so badly."

"I think he does," Thao says, "but even more than that, he either doesn't want to have given in to you, or he doesn't want anyone to know he's done this. Particularly his son, I would imagine."

"Hmm. OK Then here's what we'll do…"

That night, as usual, Thao does his little striptease by candlelight, backs up to the wall, and Tom moves closer, drops his underwear, lubricates himself and slowly slides into the soft, tight ass pressed up against the hole in the wall. He moves very slowly tonight, noticing how Thao is contracting his muscles more than usual, giving him added pleasure. The fucking goes on for more than five minutes before Tom ejaculates, pulls out, wipes himself off and goes back to his bed. By the time he lies down, the candle in Thao's room is out.

The next day, as they are exercising in the yard, Tom says to Thao, "That was incredible."

Thao looks at him perplexed. "What was incredible?"

"You know."

"No, I don't. What?"

"Last night. Whatever you did, it was really fantastic."

"Oh, that. I'm glad you liked it." Thao smiles and nudges Tom with his shoulder.

That night, again, Tom feels Thao's butt contracting, making himself tighter and tighter. Tom is moaning despite himself; this is too exciting for him to keep quiet. From the other side of the wall he hears Thao whisper, "Fuck me harder, Tom. You're such a man. Your dick is so big. Fuck me, Tom. Fuck me deep." This talk makes Tom come almost immediately. As he ejaculates he thrusts even deeper and says in a loud voice, "Oh, baby, take it, take my big dick. Oh, man, oh, fuck." He is almost shouting.

The door between the two rooms opens and EG flicks on the light. Tom quickly pulls himself out of his consort and turns away to face the far wall as he pulls up his underwear.

"Tom," EG says, "sometimes I think you keep things from me. How long has this been going on?"

Tom says nothing, remains facing the wall.

"Now why didn't you tell me you were fucking Thao? That's not playing fair. I thought you wanted to leave here? I thought you wanted to be with your son?"

"I do," Tom says.

"It sounds like you were really enjoying that, Tom. I think it would be polite of you to thank Thao in person. Thao, come in here." Thao joins EG in Tom's room.

Tom doesn't turn around.

"Don't you want to thank Thao?" EG asks in a mocking voice. "No? Well then you should at least thank your new sex partner." At this Tom turns around, a puzzled look on his face. Standing on EG's left is Thao, fully clothed in his military garb. Standing on EG's other side, being held up by two soldiers, is Steven, his hands tied together, his mouth bound with tape. The boy's eyes are wide and red.

EG pushes on the shoulder of one of the soldiers until they have turned the boy around so his backside is facing Tom. The boy's buttocks glisten with lubricant; there is a thick, white fluid dribbling from between his cheeks. Tom knows what it is. EG slaps the boy's butt, then spreads his cheeks wide. "This is the 'incredible' ass, Tom. This is the one that you thought was 'really fantastic.' And we all agree with you, don't we guys?" EG laughs and Tom lunges at him but not before Thao and two soldiers standing at the ready just inside Thao's room intercept him.

"Tom, this is war. It's a war you and your kind waged thousands of years ago. We didn't ask for it. At first all we wanted was to be left alone. Then, as our numbers increased, despite your fag-bashing and witch-burning, we got uppity. We started thinking, 'No it's not enough just to be left alone. We want to be treated like human beings. We want our rights.' And this is where it's ended, Tom. With people like you thinking you can deny us housing, beat our brains out, let us die without medical care, and keep us out of the workplace. But of course you know all about that don't you, Tom? You're one of them. You're one of the Breeders who've killed us by smashing our skulls open and spilling our brains out on the sidewalks of the cities we work in, the sidewalks built with our own tax money. So see, Tom, how gentle this really is? This is nothing. We haven't laid a hand on you. In fact, we gave you 'really fantastic' sex. And this is how you pay us back, by trying to bash me. Put him down," EG says to the soldiers holding Steven.

The two men take him to the bed and throw him down.

"Him too," EG says to the men restraining Tom. "I'm going to leave you two alone together now. I'm sure you'll want some quiet time together, quality time after that great fuck. It could be just like the movies; you can lie in each other's arms and share a cigarette, even have that talk with your son now, the one you've probably been putting off for so long. You know, about the birds and the bees."

As EG is closing the door, he turns back toward Tom. "And forget about leaving. Think of all this as a gift from me to you. Food, shelter, clothing for the rest of your life. And, of course, 'really fantastic' sex." EG closes the door and locks it. Tom can hear him laughing all the way down the hall and out the door.

10:19:59:59:49 A.M.

Suddenly, almost overnight it seems, everything changes yet again. New drugs are discovered to combat the virus. In a few short months research labs throughout Europe and the United States come up with a variety of ways to attack the virus. Clinical trials are initiated, approval processes are expedited, and suddenly, miraculously, it seems as though EG might live. The hope of living a long life now becomes an actual optimism.

Although he thought this was what he wanted, oddly enough, EG is not comforted. He believed he wanted to live into old age, creak about in the garden on Church Street, huff and puff through the woods at Anchor Bay long into senility. He used to fantasize about sitting in his rocking chair on the porch, listening to Paul play Mozart on the recorder, but now he finds himself irritated, even enraged.

EG has gone to great lengths over the past several years to accept his inevitable death. He has, in his words, "retooled my mind, heart, and soul to live with one foot in life and one foot in death." He has striven to think always of God and remember his own death, as the Scriptures say, to walk on the right side of Death, to be present in each moment, not to sacrifice the present for the future, to live each day as if it were the last day, to ask each morning, "If this were my last day alive, would I do what I am doing?" EG has found the truth in the Truisms, the kernel of genuineness in each cliché. He has worked hard to accept that he must comfort those around him, as he begins to deteriorate right in front of their eyes. And now this. It is too much.

EG has worked hardest at learning to let go of things. He has practiced for years by giving away the possessions he loves most, stopping himself in the heat of argument and saying, "OK, you win. We'll do it your way." He has walked away from friends in distress rather than try to help them. He has even stood back and let Paul writhe with his own demons at times, rather than trying to take them away from him. He is prepared to lie on his deathbed and let the world remain, while he moves away from it. He hopes he is ready even to let go of Paul. And now this. It is too much.

He is reminded of the character in Dostoevsky's work who is led each day from his dank dungeon to the prison courtyard to stand in front of the firing squad. The prisoner watches the line of soldiers march out, raise their rifles, take aim, and then, at the last minute, hears the order to "hold your fire." Then the prisoner is marched back into the prison and thrown back into his cell. This happens every day for years until the prisoner begs his captors to shoot him. It is too much.

EG goes to the San Francisco Gun Exchange and purchases a .358 handgun. He enrolls at the San Francisco Gun Club and takes lessons at the shooting range on Lake Meritt every Wednesday. Then he takes his gun and goes to the San Francisco campus of the University of California and finds the

AIDS research laboratory. He walks in one Sunday morning when there are very few security guards on campus and shoots everyone in the lab, including the research animals.

EG walks down the hill and waits for the N Judah, takes it to Nineteenth Avenue, then transfers to another bus, which he takes to the Golden Gate Bridge. He makes his way through crowds of Sunday tourists and cyclists to the mid-point of the span and, without a moment's hesitation, he zips up his green cotton jacket, climbs over the railing, holds out his arms, and leans forward.

The soft, clear summer air caresses his smiling face as he floats forward, the puffy white clouds and sharp blue sky sliding by above his head. Now the dark green roil of the Pacific comes into view, a red sailboat, a white sailboat, a larger boat with passengers. He is descending like a gull, flat, even, his arms held out like wings. The air is cool, but not cold, the green water is rushing toward him at tremendous speed, the golden abutment of the bridge's north tower, larger than he has ever seen it before, speeds past him.

At the back of the passenger boat, two men are staring up at him. He can see their faces, their dark eyes wide in disbelief. They are holding onto the railing against the will of the turbulent sea. One of them is pointing at him. EG smiles at the man. EG thinks, *It is this easy. Just this easy.*

EG also makes, as he falls, two intriguing observations. First, his life is not flashing before him like everyone says it does when one jumps to one's death, and second, he is not passing out as he has often heard people do when they fall from great heights. He finds this immensely interesting but turns his attention back to the matter at hand and says, one last time, *This too is It.*

He feels the cold of the water even before he hits it, then the water on his chest and face, but it doesn't feel like water;

it feels like concrete. All breath is knocked out of him, and he feels one single moment of intense pain in every cell of his body. The green of the ocean turns to black.

10:19:59:59:50 A.M.

The room is empty.

10:19:59:59:51 A.M.

O son of noble family, listen well and understand. Hell-beings, gods, and the bardo body are born instantaneously and spontaneously. When the peaceful and wrathful deities appeared in the Bardo of Dharmata, you did not recognize them, so you collapsed with fear. Now you have your consciousness returned to you. Recognize this now as the Bardo of Becoming and stay vigilant, for this is your last opportunity to avoid rebirth.

Enter now the Bardo of Becoming and say this prayer as you tread this dangerous path:

> *Now when the Bardo of Becoming dawns upon me,*
> *I will concentrate my mind singly,*
> *and strive to prolong the results of all good actions,*
> *close the womb entrance and think much of resistance;*
> *this is the time when perseverance and pure thought are needed most,*
> *I must abandon jealousy and meditate on the beloved as It.*

<u>10:19:59:59:52 A.M.</u>

EG feels lost, adrift on an ocean of Feelings. It is Saturday afternoon, and he has come to St. Dominic's for the 4:30 Confession. There are only a handful of old Portuguese women in babushkas kneeling here and there throughout the Romanesque church. EG goes to the statue of the pietà and kneels down. He buries his head in his hands and begs the Blessed Mother to intercede for him, to ask her son, whose broken body she holds in her arms beneath the empty cross, to be his friend.

Through his tears EG takes in the pale corpus the Virgin holds in her arms. The Christ is naked except for the sheerest hint of fabric draped in folds across his groin. His head is thrown back, hanging limp and lifeless.

"Please, Lord, be with me always. Teach me to walk through my life as virtuous as you, as kind, as loving, as compassionate. Show me the way, Lord."

If only EG had been at Calvary, he would have climbed up on the cross for Jesus. He gladly would have given up his life to spend eternity in heaven with such a man. And had he been too late, had he arrived just when the Messiah had expired, he would have helped take him down from the cross, laid him across his own lap, and wept the bitter tears of an abandoned devotee.

As he holds his Beloved in his arms weeping in desolation, planting tender kisses on the Savior's cheek, adrift in an ocean of abandonment, he feels the corpus stirring. Could it be? Is this the true sign? EG looks into the face of Christ, whose eyes are open now. "It's me, Lord. It's EG come to comfort you. Please don't die. Please don't leave me."

"I shall never leave you, my son. I am always with you and you with me. This is illusion, my boy, all illusion. I abandon no one, least of all you."

EG pulls Christ closer and rocks him gently back and forth, singing softly through his tears, "On the beautiful isle of Capri, just my baby and me…"

10:19:59:59:53 A.M.

At the invisible window of the White Room, women gather. The old women among them, heads wrapped in babushkas, eyes dark and sad, rock in the rhythm of Time Lost. Their lives, like heavy tumors, have concentrated in their withered breasts, their parched wombs, monuments to The Past, Hope, and Despair.

The young women, bright-faced with skin like alabaster, hair as dark as a raven's wings, crowd at the window. These younger women are waiting to see whether the older women's predictions come true. Will he indeed rise up, recognize they are there at the invisible window? Will he call out to them? Will he beckon them to come inside? Will he recant all neglect and abuse? And will they, if he does not, simply turn and walk away, shaking their heads, their skepticism and distrust affirmed once again? Can they remain that unattached and still be women? Can they restrain themselves from entering the White Room through the invisible window, singing the song the bird is singing now in the uppermost corner of the White Room?

10:19:59:59:54 A.M.

The sky above Anchor Bay is mottled with clouds as the storm passes. Spring has officially come to Mendocino County. The deciduous azaleas are blooming neon yellow; Scotch broom washes the entire roadside and the hills beyond with wide streaks of gold. Purple-and-white lupines huddle in clumps along the highways and country roads. The osprey has returned to her huge nest atop the tallest dead tree on the hilltop. She is screeching daily, making her presence known.

This morning, as EG takes his *japa* walk around the property, the osprey is mating with her husband, whose wings flap wildly against the blue sky above their round heap of grass and sticks and rags. When it is over, the male strides out of the nest onto the broad limb at the top of the redwood snag and watches EG carefully as he walks along the gravel road below. *Is he boasting,* EG wonders, *or is he making sure I mean no harm?*

Soon there will be chicks again, like last spring and the spring before that. Mrs. Osprey will be busy night and day finding food, carrying it back to the nest, feeding her demanding, squealing babies.

As EG rounds a turn in the road, he comes face-to-face with a doe and two fawns. They freeze and the doe stares hard into his eyes. EG stops, stands still. The fawns look him over, then meander across the road into the small meadow, as their mother keeps watch on EG. She is not as trusting as her offspring. EG speaks softly to her, "Good morning. I'm sorry if I startled you." The doe blinks, then turns and bounces into the meadow. She catches up with the fawns, gives some invisible command, and the three of them bound into the trees, not running but not tarrying either. The doe knows the people on this land mean her and her fawns no harm, but she has encountered poachers before and will take no chances with the lives of her babies.

As EG steps onto the porch of the house, the sun breaks through the clouds again. He sits in the rocker and looks out over the ocean in the distance. There are no sounds, no moisture in the air to cloud the view from Anchor Bay. From here, he can see as far toward Asia as any human eye can see from North America. If he were to die right now, right here in the green wooden rocking chair, he wonders if he would, when he awoke, be able to tell the difference between this and Paradise.

<u>10:19:59:59:55</u> A.M.

Another sleepless night. EG rises, goes downstairs to the kitchen, stands in the light of the open refrigerator. He can find nothing to soothe or satisfy him. He moves first to the dining room window, looking out into the dark, knowing he is observed by the creatures of the night who forage in darkness for their sustenance, who by day would fall prey to hawks and osprey and wild dogs.

He thinks, *It is just you and me, my nocturnal friends, both of us unable to sleep—you out of necessity, me out of…out of what? Can it really be the drugs keeping me awake? It's more like I'm being called, like I wake hearing my name being whispered from some dark part of the house. Who could it be? What could it be?*

EG looks around the room. A few embers from the evening's fire shimmer and glow in the stone fireplace. The two sofas, positioned at right angles, sit before the hearth; EG's crocheting lies in a heap where he left it on the green love seat.

He moves away from the window to the darker part of the room and sits and watches the embers glow and pulsate before him like a heart hidden in ashes. On the far end of the larger sofa he sees, as his eyes adjust to the darkness, Cohen in her plain white cotton nightgown and her clumsy brown slippers. Her hair is braided into a long, gray whip that hangs over her shoulder. It falls to the sofa and coils around three times, its tip resting in the circle's center like the head of a vigilant cobra.

She is peeling an apple with a paring knife, letting the long, unbroken coil of skin ease gently into her lap, a serpent dancing its hypnotic descent to the white field of Cohen's nightgown.

She tosses the apple peel into the fire, cores the fruit, and offers a slice to EG. The room is fragrant with the apple peel baking in the embers, and Cohen begins to sing softly to EG. "On the beautiful isle of Capri, just my baby and me…"

EG moves closer to her. As he scoots over, his bare feet hit something hard and cold on the floor. He peers over the edge of the sofa and there at Cohen's feet lies a long, hooked scythe. The curved blade is shiny and slick from use and the wooden handle is dry and split. He stares up at Cohen for an explanation, but she does not look at him; rather, she slices and hands him, one at a time, thin sections of fruit until the entire apple is gone. Then she looks deep into his eyes, a cold, serious look, the kind she used to give him when he strayed too far down the block or said something unkind about one of her friends.

He doesn't know if he should say anything. He wants to touch her, but her look is so confusing, so mysterious, so icy. He takes a chance and reaches out his hand. At the same moment the tip of her coiled hair rises like a serpent and hovers in the air between them. His hand freezes where it is. He looks at Cohen pleadingly, frightened, then back to the serpentine braid of hair. He looks back to Cohen again for some encouragement, but her expression has not changed. EG cannot be separate from her any longer, yet he is afraid.

"You have never lied to me," he says to her, almost as a question.

"I have never lied to you," she repeats.

"You have always done what is best for me," he laments.

"I have always done what is best for you," she answers.

"I trust you," he says.

"You trust me," she says back.

"This must be safe or you wouldn't be here," EG states with conviction.

"This must be safe or I wouldn't be here," Cohen says.

"You're scaring me," EG cries.

"I'm scaring you," Cohen says.

"I don't want you to hurt me," EG exclaims.

"You don't want me to hurt you," Cohen says, but now she is reaching for the scythe.

"Cohney!" EG screams and throws himself past the menacing coil of snake. He wraps his arms around her, winces his eyes closed, and holds her tight. EG holds on to her for a long time before he realizes she has wrapped her large talcum powdered arms around him and is rocking him back and forth in the light of the fireplace. The room is pungent with the fragrance of apples. EG looks up. Cohen's emotionless expression is gone now; she is smiling.

"Cohney," EG says softly, beginning to cry.

"There, there, child. Did you have a bad dream?" Cohen asks gently.

"Was it a dream?" EG asks.

"Everything is all right now," she says.

EG pulls himself away from her and peers over the sofa. The scythe is still there. He looks back at her, confused. "It's still there," he says.

"Do you know what a scythe is used for?" she asks him.

"For chopping things down?"

"For clearing a path."

"Oh," EG answers. He returns his cheek to her bosom and watches the red coals in the fireplace. *Like a heart glowing in ashes,* he thinks. "A path," he says aloud. But Cohen just continues to rock back and forth with him in her arms. And as she rocks, she softly sings, "On the beautiful isle of Capri, just my baby and me…"

10:19:59:59:56 A.M.

EG and his longtime friend Gloria are standing on the deck of her Malibu beach house. They have just finished an intense conversation about EG's turning 60 and not wanting to face it. Gloria has told him he must start getting his act together. "You can't go on buying boyfriends, running from plastic surgeon to plastic surgeon, producing all the movies you want to star in because no one will cast you in the romantic lead any more. There really is more to life than movies, New York restaurants, the Italian Riviera, and sex."

EG has been deeply depressed for several weeks and has come to Gloria for comfort. This isn't exactly the kind of comfort he had in mind.

"Excuse me," a voice interrupts from the sand below them. They both look down over the deck railing. A long-haired boy, whom EG has been watching play volley ball all morning, is standing in the sand smiling up at them. His white teeth sparkle in the California sunlight, his broad shoulders are freckled from countless days on the beach. "Aren't you…?"

"He certainly is," Gloria says, as EG smiles at the youth.

"Wow! Like you're like my favorite. I've seen like every movie you ever made. Well, most of them, anyway."

EG is beaming now, holding in his stomach, reaching for the sunglasses in his pocket. "Why thank you. That's very kind of you."

"No, man, I mean it. I watch *Last Encounter* like about once a month, at least. You were totally awesome in that."

"Thanks," EG says again.

"I know you must get really tired of this kind of thing, and I don't want to like intrude or anything, but if I went back to my car and got something to write on, would you like maybe give me an autograph?" The young man is visibly excited at meeting EG in person. He is dancing back and forth on the hot sand now.

"Tell you what, why don't you come around to the gate and step inside for a minute and I'll sign a copy of my autobiography for you. I have an extra one upstairs."

"Wow! Really? You mean it?"

EG laughs out loud, completely transformed from the dark mood he's been in for several weeks. "Of course I mean it. Here, come to the gate," EG says, following the railing around the deck, showing the boy the way.

Gloria watches as EG goes down the half-dozen steps to unlock the gate. Then the beautiful young man with the long, flowing hair and what EG estimates to be no more than 8% body fat, at most, follows EG back up the steps, across the deck and through the sliding glass doors.

As the two of them step inside, EG says, "Actually, I think it's up in my room. Follow me. Have you ever thought about auditioning for a film yourself? You certainly have the face for it. And that smile. You wouldn't even have to have your teeth capped."

The young fellow, obviously flattered at such attention from a celebrity, giggles audibly. Upstairs, they have barely stepped inside the bedroom, when EG shuts the door, turns, and says, "I think you are possibly the most exquisite creature I have ever seen. You must allow me to arrange a screen test. I insist."

"Wow!" the lad exclaims.

"I'm producing a film in the fall that features a surfer. It's not the lead, but it's a very important part. There are nude scenes, however. That won't be a problem, I trust?"

"No, man. I love to go naked."

"Well, just to be sure, I mean, so I won't be wasting your time or anything, could you slip out of your shorts now and walk around the room a bit? Just to make certain." EG sits at the foot of the bed now, a bit light-headed, taking in the physical perfection standing before him in Gloria's guest room. He is considering that what he told the boy about being the most exquisite creature he's ever seen may not be a lie after all.

"Oh, I get it," the young man says. He smiles slyly, thinks about it for a moment, then says, "Sure. Why not? When will I ever get this chance again?" He unties his colorful baggy volley ball shorts slowly, provocatively, having seen actresses do such things in movies since he was a child growing up in the Valley. Then he lets them fall by their own weight down to his ankles.

His dick, as EG had guessed from the boy's protruding lower lip, long toes, and large hands, is a fantasy come true. Yet it is not as erotic as the rest of his body, lean, brown, covered with sun-bleached blond hair.

The boy now steps slowly out of the multicolored shorts, walks around in a small circle, then strides to the foot of the bed, letting his dick come to rest just inches from EG's flushed face. "So what do you think? Will this work for your movie?" the boy asks.

EG looks up into his blue eyes and swallows hard, gulping audibly. The boy laughs, throwing back his head, his long, sand-colored hair dipping below his waist. He runs the fingertips of his right hand across EG's cheek, stroking him tenderly. "Kiss it," he whispers.

EG obeys, kissing the boy's penis lightly. It is warm and musky. He closes his eyes and smells his father sleeping naked beneath the sheet, his deep strong scent filling his lungs.

"Again," the boy says, not like an order but kindly, gently. Then he adds, "please."

EG places his lips at the tip of the boy's penis, and then without a word of either explanation or adoration, turns his head and plants a tender kiss on the boy's hand. As he does this he feels a sharp pain in his left arm. At first it is just a stabbing pain that strikes and vanishes. But it returns in a second, intensifying beyond forbearance. He clutches the boy's thighs with both hands and tries to speak, but nothing comes out.

The pain is now shooting up his arm, past his shoulder, and into his chest. His vision is beginning to blur. EG groans and grips the boy's legs tighter.

The boy pries EG's hands from the backs of his thighs and takes them into his own as he kneels down before EG.

"I'm here to help," the boy says. "No one wants you to be alone."

EG blinks and tries to focus on the boy's face. The young man's eyes have turned from blue to sparkling white as if there were diamonds where his pupils should be. "Help me," EG gasps as the pain grows even stronger, his breath shorter.

"That's why I'm here," the boy says. "I'm here to help you."

"That sound," EG mutters and lifts his eyes toward the ceiling. "That sound..."

EG falls forward into the boy's arms, through the boy's arms, through his chest, his waist, his buttocks, his thighs, his feet, to the floor beneath. He lies on the floor of Gloria's guest room as the walls grows brighter. The room shimmers with light. It is so white the furniture dissolves, the corners disappear, the edges vanish. The boy too is gone now, and all that is left in the White Room is EG, lying on the floor, listening to the soft rustling of wings in a far corner of the room near the ceiling.

10:19:59:59:57 A.M.

EG stands in the kitchen and counts out, bottle by bottle, his 20 morning pills, watching the gentle rain falling outside. *Somewhere, someone is dying,* he thinks. *Right now, somewhere in the world, a person is letting go of everything he knows, everything he loves, all that comforts and eases him in his life.*

"Yeah, Einstein. You."

He doesn't turn, doesn't have to. He knows it is Clete. He is sitting at the kitchen table reading the morning paper.

"I don't mean dying like 'I'm-dying-of-this-disease' dying. I mean dying as in 'one-minute-alive-next-minute-dead' dying. Besides, nobody asked you."

EG swallows his pills and turns toward the living room. Cohen is in the red chair darning a pair of The Boy's socks. She smiles up at him over her glasses, which are halfway down her nose. *Pay no attention to him,* she says without speaking, then goes back to her darning.

EG comes and stands next to her, looking out the front window. The ocean is gray in the distance, the pines and redwoods dark green on the slope in front of the house. "I want to die when it's raining, Cohen," he says. "I don't want to die when the sun is bright and the sky blue, with Hari running about in the woods chasing rabbits, foraging in the underbrush, unaware that I'm going. I don't want to have to leave the Earth I love so much when it's at its most alluring, most inviting, most vibrant. I want to slip away in the rain, when it won't be so difficult to go."

"Then that's how it shall be," Cohen assures him.

"Are you certain?"

"No, but I will tell you so. For when it's time to leave, you won't care what the weather is, how dark or bright the sky is that hovers over you or whether or not Hari is chasing rabbits or lying by your side."

"Oh, but I will care about Hari. Axel was there with Andre. He knew somehow what was about to happen, and I'm sure Andre knew Axel was there with him. I know he helped Andre let go. I know this for sure."

"Then that's how it will be."

"Are you certain?"

"No, but I will tell you so."

"But you know everything about it. You are it."

"I am only Cohen. I am not it."

"But don't you know how it will be? Can't you see it now, even sitting here?"

"Neither am I Cassandra, little one."

"But that's how I want it. That's how it must be or I will not die peacefully," EG states emphatically, slipping into his boyhood manner, here with the woman who literally raised him for the first eight years of his life.

"You will die how you will die. Right now, you are in an Ocean of Samsara, and the waves you are riding are simply swells of Fear. You will die exactly as you are living."

"And how is that?"

"You tell me."

"How I'm living?" EG laughs. "God, I wish I knew the answer to that one."

"But you do, my child. Say it now."

"Well, I live trying to be conscious every moment of the fact that everything is It. I guess that's the best way I could sum it up."

"Everything?"

EG wonders if this is a test. Is Cohen baiting him, or is she asking a real question?

"Everything," he says with conviction.

"Even this moment?"

"Even this moment."

"Even this conversation?"

"Yes, even this conversation."

"Even this fear?"

EG pauses, looks at Cohen bent over his blue-and-red argyles, pulling the needle through the fabric, her glasses almost at the tip of her nose. He laughs as he kneels before her, placing his hand on her large aproned knee. Through the window, EG sees Andre walk down the steps of the deck, smoking a cigarette, not looking back. Cohen does not look up from The Boy's socks. "Yes," EG says, in a whisper. "Yes, even this fear."

"And him?" Cohen asks, nodding beyond EG.

EG looks behind him. Clete is sitting now on the sofa in his dirty work clothes, grinning, balancing a beer on his thigh, his face unshaved from three straight days of crushing grapes at the winery. He is waiting for EG's answer. EG turns back to Cohen, who hasn't looked up once from her loving service. "Yes, Cohney," EG answers. "Yes, even him."

Cohen smiles as she makes a knot in her darning thread and raises it to her mouth to bite it off with her false teeth. From behind him, EG hears Clete say, "Atta boy, way to go. Right answer."

EG turns toward his father and finds him now young, radiant, in tan gabardine slacks, white shirt open at the collar, his black hair brilliantined and shiny, a wide smile on his smooth, young, alarmingly handsome face. His brown shoes are polished almost to a spit shine. And there is nothing but admiration in his eyes. "I love you, son. You're so damned smart. I'm so proud of you."

EG can't believe his ears.

He turns back to Cohen for an explanation, but she is just staring at him, smiling her best old lady smile, the darned socks held up for EG to take from her.

"But…but…I don't understand."

"Sure you do, child. If you didn't, this wouldn't be happening."

"What is happening, Coney?"

"It. This. This is It."

10:19:59:59:58 A.M.

The Moment has arrived.

10:19:59:59:59 A.M.

EG lies in a white bed in a White Room moving through his life, moving closer to the open door.

The bed stands firm on the floor of the White Room, which is turning, turning around the sun.

The bed stands firm and still, while EG moves slowly, motionlessly through the beginning of the end: a tiny white skiff in the immense blue Ocean of Time.

The tip of the bow of his fragile bark scrapes gently on the beach of the tiny Isle of Space.

He lies motionless, moving, rocking like a babe in a cradle.

His eyes are crusted shut, his lips too. A young woman comes periodically to dip cotton swabs in water and gently roll them over his lips to moisten them. She places a hand on his head, her lips on his cheek. She whispers to him softly. Words we cannot hear.

The White Room moves imperceptibly around the sun. And so EG moves on, and this is what he sees through his crusted eyes as he lies motionless in the firm white bed that sits on the polished white linoleum floor in the empty White Room.

Slowly, like the winding jasmine, his awareness has changed. Nothing is what it seems to be. He sees everything as it truly is—or is he seeing everything as what he projects it to be? This question presents itself wordlessly as he orbits the golden sun.

He doesn't always live in his intellect but mostly. There are other venues for his being, but in saying that even, just that way—"there are other venues for his being"—he realizes he is in his intellect even now.

But his awareness is changing slowly, like the winding jasmine. And here at the edge of the Isle of Space, he is now aware of even this.

He is conscious now. Mostly. So he allows the women and children more freedom. He sees himself as kind. He is, in fact, a benevolent despot, propped up precariously by those he oppresses. He is still trying to comprehend the first Law of the Jungle: Women are always in charge.

From the shore the women come to him, minister to him with their comforting arms, their devoted hands. They come into the darkened room, holding the hands of the children. They lift the shades, pull back the curtains, letting the light flood in. Now the room is white with light. Now he can see everyone clearly. He sees how they smile, how frightened they are. He sees the old woman in the corner, how she laughs and rocks while she crochets. Her face is so wrinkled, he is not sure it is made of human skin, but he can see that her heart is in what she is doing. She is surrounded by a faint blue light.

The boat has stopped rocking; the tubes have backed up; the White Room has ceased moving. EG now knows he is dying.

The Boy is confused and frightened. AD is self-conscious and anxious. He is bored in self-defense. *This is not where I belong,* he thinks to himself. EG raises his head from the white pillow and rages, "You think I belong here?" The old crone looks up reproachfully from her crocheting. EG lowers his head back to the stiff white pillow.

> The room is silent with his fear.
> The room pulses with his rage.
> The room is empty.
> The Moment has arrived.
> The Moment is Now.

July 2

Cohen gathers her crochet work into her burlap bag, folds her glasses, and tucks them into their case. Then she slips them into the bag with the lace work. She retrieves a white handkerchief from somewhere in the bosom of her housedress, wipes her nose gently, and replaces it, tucking it carefully between her breasts. She rises from the rocking chair and waits for EG to climb slowly out of the bed. The room is so white now that none of the corners can be seen. It is like a white fire but neither hot nor cold. There is, in fact, no temperature at all.

Cohen gestures for EG to fall in behind her as she begins to walk. They are moving without really walking, just moving outward from the White Room, away from the white bed. As they move, Cohen speaks to EG. "I will tell you something new, my sweet," she says. "I will sing you the true lyrics to 'The Isle of Capri,' the deeper meaning of 'After the Ball Is Over'. Listen now, child, to what I say to you, as we leave the White Room forever."

And Cohen, in as soft a voice as EG has ever heard, begins to sing:

> Eye cannot see It, tongue cannot speak It,
> mind cannot grasp It.

That which makes the tongue speak but which cannot be spoken by the tongue—that alone is God, not what humans worship.

That which causes the mind to think but which cannot be thought by the mind—that alone is God, not what humans worship.

That which makes the eye see but which cannot be seen by the eye—that alone is God, not what humans worship.

That which makes the ear hear but which cannot be heard by the ear—that alone is God, not what humans worship.

If you think you know God, you live in delusion; all that you can know are images of God. All you can hold onto are ideas of God.

Those who realize that God cannot be known, truly know;

those who claim that they know God, know absolutely nothing.

The ignorant think that God can be grasped by the mind; the wise know It in a different way.

When you finally understand that God acts through you, as you, in every action you take, only then do you attain true freedom.

When you realize this truth and cling to nothing in the world, that is the moment you` enter eternal life.